STATE OF TERROR

STATE OF TERROR

JOHN BROWN

THOSE WHO WOULD GIVE UP ESSENTIAL LIBERTY
TO PURCHASE A LITTLE TEMPORARY SAFETY,
DESERVE NEITHER LIBERTY NOR SAFETY.

Benjamin Franklin,
Historical Review of Pennsylvania, 1759

THE CAUSE OF AMERICA IS IN A GREAT MEASURE
THE CAUSE OF ALL MANKIND.

Thomas Paine,
Common Sense, 1776

WAR IS THE HEALTH OF THE STATE.

Randolph Bourne,
The State, 1918

10 9 8 7 6 5 4 3 2 1

ISBN: 978-0-9913059-2-6 (print)
ISBN: 978-0-9913059-0-2 (ebook)

Dedicated to all those who still believe
that liberty is something worth fighting for.

Contents

1

The Bigger Issues

T OM BENSON DROVE TO THE METRO STATION, trying to make his meeting on time, for a change. Traffic crawled in the over-crowded lanes reserved for ordinary commuters. The sign overhead read "Trains Next Exit," but at the rate things were moving he wouldn't be exiting the highway for quite some time. He gazed at the virtually empty lane to his left, marked "Express Lane for Official Use Only—$5,000 Fine," but dared not try it. Cameras at either end of the sign were trained on the highway. "Today's Threat Level Is Orange," scrolled a message. "Report Suspicious Items or Activities to the Authorities." While he sat idling in traffic, police vehicles and dark lim-ousines with blacked-out windows sped by occasionally to his left. He wished, just once, that he could drive in the official lane in rush hour at full speed. No such luck for him today. Sighing, he resigned himself to being late for his train yet again.

Once inside the station, he lined up at the security check-point. *"Attention,"* boomed the loudspeakers. *"Please report suspicious items and socially dangerous persons. The Washing-ton Metropolitan Area Transit Authority and your Transportation Security Administration appreciate your compliance."* Upon pre-senting his ID for inspection, he dumped his keys, shoes, jacket, watch, belt, wallet, phone, computer, and briefcase into a gray plastic bin and pushed it onto the conveyor belt. Entering the scanning booth, he held his hands over his head, facing one direction and then the other. He collected his things and got dressed, made his way to the platform, and bounded up the stairs just as his train began pulling away. The impassive conductor watched him sprinting for it as the alarm sounded and the doors shut.

The next train arrived 13 minutes later. Two Transit Authority cops with drug and bomb-sniffing dogs stood by the train doors as the passengers scurried in and out. The cops chatted among themselves, talking of this and that, while their dogs eyed the passengers with fanatical intensity, emitting low, resonant growls whenever something caught their interest. One of the dogs sniffed Benson's crotch, leaving a wet mark on his pants.

Benson gave the cops a long, dirty look.

"What's your problem?" one of the cops sniffed. "He's just doin' his job, ya know?"

"At least someone is."

He found a seat on the train between a group of Middle Eastern men wearing expensive suits and stern expressions. The air was rank with their pungent cologne. It was the only available seat in the car and he didn't feel like standing for the whole ride. They must be associates traveling together, he guessed, yet they didn't speak to, or even glance at, one another. He looked around awkwardly, avoiding their eyes. With all that was in the news lately, distrust and fear ruled. If there were that many of them, why wouldn't they just take a taxi or a limousine? Wouldn't it be quicker? By the look of things, they certainly had the money for it.

Despite his better instincts, he'd begun to suspect anyone looking even vaguely Middle Eastern. He couldn't help it. He was sure that others held their suspicions, too, if privately, for fear of being labeled narrow-minded or racist, yet it didn't seem all that unreasonable. All the terrorists were Arabs, weren't they? And what was the big difference between Shiites and Sunnis, anyway? They all looked the same to him.

The interminable ride ended after some 20 minutes. Benson hurried up the stairs to the street, breathing in the fresh air. He strolled into the lobby of the historic Chase Bank of America building. The floors and walls were Italian marble, the vaulted ceilings covered with reliefs depicting the founding of the Republic. He liked the history and the magnificence of the place. It made everything done here somehow seem more important.

Benson rode up in an elevator packed with grim-faced office workers, all of whom stared straight ahead, looking at nothing. Amid the uncomfortable silence, they each finally arrived at their floors, hurriedly stepping off. For Benson, an office on the top floor meant the journey could take several awkward minutes. He could have run the stairs in far less time, but despite the morale-boosting posters in the lunchrooms exhorting the employees to get some exercise, the security department wouldn't allow it anymore, the bastards.

Benson stepped off the elevator. A young woman was waiting for him. She smiled warmly at his approach.

"Good morning, Tina."

"Good morning, Mr. Benson. Everything is ready, sir."

Fifteen minutes late, Benson took his seat at the head of a large conference table and prepared to open the meeting. He was distracted from the task at hand by the overhead lights. They gave off a low buzzing sound that he found irritating. The new eco-lights may have saved a few pennies, but they were harsh and unnatural. He turned them off and rolled up the window blinds instead, letting the sunlight stream into the room. Moving back to his seat, he prepared to greet everyone but was cut off before he could begin.

"Okay, so I'd like to offer the 'thought for the day' before we get started?" said Kay, a pale, middle-aged woman with a boyish haircut.

Someone in the room groaned at her announcement, but she paid not the slightest heed. Her story went on at length.

Some people sat upright, respectfully paying attention; others slumped in their chairs. A young man was preoccupied with his laptop, a constant frown on his face. The keyboard tapping annoyed Benson even more than Kay's reflection. With a circular motion of his hand he implored Kay to wrap it up. The meeting had begun late and it was getting ever later.

"So I'm, like, pissed about my muddy shoes, right? So then I see a man walking around *with no feet*." And with that, Kay sat back with a smug expression.

Benson stared at her with a mix of pity and amusement.

"What?" Benson said, shaking his head. "What?"

"See—well, you go around kinda sorry for yourself, you know, and it's like, hey! There's someone—"

"Yes, I get it. There will be no more of these 'thoughts for the day,' thank you very much."

He looked at his watch and gave Kay a withering glance, the meaning of which seemed entirely lost on her. Getting down to business, he presented a series of schematics for a more efficient underwriting process. It had taken many months of work from many departments to pull it together.

"So that's the plan," Benson said, summing up his presentation. "This will eliminate useless busywork, unnecessary approvals and delays, and we'll pass the savings on to our customers. I know everyone here is too busy, so I'll direct the requirements engineering myself. I'd like to thank everyone for their contribution in putting this together. We can all be proud of what we've accomplished. Comments?"

There was silence. Someone coughed.

Kay looked down at the table, deep concern on her face.

"Well, I, um, I think, you know, maybe we should just dialogue with people and hear them out first? You need permits from the bank czar, right? And the regulatory czar would need to issue special waivers? There are strict controls on this sort of thing, you can't just offer what you *feel* might be a good deal to customers, you can't change the official process that's filed on record just like *that*," she said, snapping her fingers for emphasis. "There are guidelines that must be followed, you know? There're a whole mess of permits, and then there's all the forms and the approvals and the lawyers and the administrative hearings. This all takes a whole bunch of time."

Kay shook her head doubtfully. She turned to her colleagues for a glimmer of support but no one would return her gaze. She faced Benson with an earnest expression.

"Of course, I support you 100 percent—no, 110 percent. I mean, what do you think?"

"Thanks for sharing."

A painfully thin woman at the table twisted her face in thought, looking down at her notes as she spoke up.

"It's like … " She paused, attempting to choose her words carefully. "Look, I'm not sure you're really hearing what we're saying. Some people have been saying some things—"

"*Some* people? *Some* things?" Benson shot back, perhaps a little too aggressively, but his patience was wearing thin. "What the hell are you talking about?"

Maybe it would be too much to expect unrestrained enthusiasm, but he had at least hoped for simple cooperation. He was making it easy for them; all they had to do was go along with what they had already agreed upon. He would even let them take all the credit. Instead, he was meeting unaccountable resistance and ambiguous insinuations. He felt himself getting hot and took a deep breath to calm down.

"I feel what Stacy's saying is, 'Okay, look, maybe we should just listen to each other?' " Kay said. "You know?"

Benson gazed out the large window framing the room. Sparrows and pigeons swooped and bobbed, darting and flitting in the sunshine, happy and free. How he wished he could join them. One of the birds in particular caught his attention, a hummingbird of some extra large variety unlike any he'd seen before. It had a ruby-colored throat like those buzzing around now and then in his backyard, only much bigger. It was surprising to see a hummingbird in the city, especially at the eighth floor. Hovering by the window, it seemed to be staring inside, looking right at him.

Benson forced his attention back to his wretched meeting and gazed, absentmindedly, at Kay, who immediately turned away. He wondered how anything got done around here. If it weren't for the Office of Human Capital Management, he'd have fired their lazy asses in a heartbeat.

Benson sat bored at his desk, looking out the window and daydreaming. This was becoming a disturbingly common event. He was trying to fight it and not succeeding. He had everything he'd ever wanted—a wonderful wife, a great son, and excellent health. Career, money, cars, house; he had it all. He had successfully climbed the corporate ladder. Although they were now financially secure, each subsequent promotion and raise wasn't nearly as gratifying as he'd expected. He certainly didn't feel anywhere near rich. He had come to realize that past a certain point, chasing more of the same was futile. Having more things may have added some extra measure of fun in their lives, yet, deep down, he wasn't really any more content today than when he and Jane had started out as broke newlyweds so many years ago. In truth, those were good years, exciting years.

Interrupting his reverie, Fred, a junior colleague in the Department of Government and Regulatory Affairs, suddenly appeared in front of his desk, clutching an oversized mug bearing the corporate logo and a picture of his face. These had been distributed at the company picnic as a morale booster, along with surplus promotional merchandise normally given away to customers at the holidays—pens, notepads, calendars, mouse pads, and other such swag. The custom picture mugs were a big hit at the last picnic. Everyone had eagerly lined up in front of a wall for their shots.

Benson remembered these picnics mainly for the disturbingly casual garb in which some of his male colleagues appeared, dressed in tank tops, basketball shorts, and beach sandals, their hairy shoulders and knobby knees on display. The women could be just as bad, sporting revealing tops and short skirts or tight shorts, bulging in all the wrong places. They'd bend over for the barrel race or potato sack jump or something and he'd have to look away out of a decent respect for decorum, especially if Jane was there with him.

"Tom? Earth to Tom."

Fred laughed at his little joke.

"Hey Tom, you're gonna be late for the meeting, dude. We're gonna talk Rule 140-D, Accounting for Transfers of Financial Assets and Repurchase Financing Transactions."

"Sounds like fun, Fred. I'll be there in five minutes—and don't call me 'dude,' dog."

Just beyond his window, the birds swooped and soared gracefully in the warm breeze, barely flapping their wings, riding the wind. No cage and no rules. No meetings. Some men try to stoke their flagging enthusiasm by gambling, drinking, or womanizing. One-dimensional and self-destructive; not for him. He wasn't achieving anything here anymore; he needed new challenges. He was beginning to feel as if he were shackled to his desk, caged in his little office. The moment he left the building every night was the best part of his day. He would rejoin Jane and Daniel, his son.

It was shortly after the last company picnic that Benson had decided that it was time to get more involved in the bigger issues. He would devote his energies to something more than just a job. Unlike all the other presidential elections he could remember, each of them proclaiming to be the most critical contest in a generation, or that, if the other candidate won, the country would be overrun by rampaging hordes looting grocery stores and stealing cars and other such nonsense, this one truly seemed important. The country was facing serious threats from inside and out. He would not sit and watch while his beloved country went into decline.

He became captivated with the idea of changing the world and personally making a difference, jumping at an unexpected offer to be a campaign "bundler," hosting fundraisers and coaxing friends, relatives, and business contacts to donate to the cause. The very idea charged him up, invigorating him with new passion and purpose. The people with whom he would work would be intellectual, freewheeling, high-energy types. He knew that it would take up most of his weeknights and weekends while he struggled to devote enough hours to his job at the bank, and he wouldn't have much time for family. Still, it would be temporary and he was getting into it rather late anyway, as political campaigns go. He would make this small sacrifice for his country. No doubt, he would make great contacts, too. It would almost certainly further his career. Jane would understand.

It took an enormous amount of money to mount a competitive campaign. So much was at stake and up for grabs, so many laws and regulations, so much money and power, that the competition between the parties to raise funds dominated the energies of everyone down the line. When not making speeches and shaking hands, even the candidate himself would spend entire days at a stretch holed up in hotel rooms, constantly on the phone soliciting and making ever more promises to donors. The entire campaign was maniacally obsessed with raising and spending money, relentless promotion, and expensive media buys.

"Joseph King For President" posters swathed the campaign headquarter's walls, featuring the candidate in various poses, many of them vaguely heroic or uplifting—King staring off into the horizon, King pointing off-camera to the future, King with a confident and wise smile. These portraits were typically rendered in simple primary colors, below which appeared inspirational slogans, including "He Gets the Big

Picture," and "The Right Man, The Right Time," and "Looking Out For You, America." Gazing at these posters evoked a certain emotional response that Benson found difficult to describe. Not pride and not pleasure, but an upbeat, warm kind of feeling. He couldn't put his finger on it exactly. Perhaps it was something about the artwork.

He pushed himself to shake hands and solicit donations at numerous fundraising parties, making sure to contact everyone and hit them up for money. It was an activity he came to loathe soon enough, all this hustling, but it had to be done and he was already committed to seeing it through. At any rate, the revelers expected to be hit upon; it was why they were there.

"Can you spare some change?" he would say. "Right—thanks anyway."

At one such campaign cocktail party, typical of many to come, Benson approached a wealthy-looking woman and shook her hand. It was getting late and many of the party-goers were becoming drunk. This proved to be the best time to secure pledges.

She held on to his hand, not letting go.

"We really need King," Benson said. "We really need a strong leader. He's looking out for us. Can we count on your support?"

"What's that?" The woman seemed confused, needing to collect her thoughts. She moved in uncomfortably close, touching his chest with her other hand, her face barely an inch from his, giving off a scent of cigarettes and strawberry cosmopolitans. "Yes, well, I guess he's better than the other guy, what's his name? I always get them mixed up."

"Carp. The other guy's name is John Carp."

2

Identification, Please

C ITIZENS WERE NOW COMPELLED to carry a new kind of identification—kids over 15, too. Benson's son, Daniel, received his REAL ID in the mail one day. He opened the official envelope and peered inside before scooping out a short form letter and a thick plastic card. He had been expecting to receive his permanent driver's license after successfully passing the exam many weeks before, but this seemed to be something entirely different.

His picture appeared on the card's right side next to a holographic pyramid, a glowing human eye at its apex. A beam of light from the eye illuminated a globe of the world. "CITIZEN," in large block letters, was overlaid on the pyramid's base. "USID" appeared on the left side of the card. Just below this was printed "Department of Homeland Security" and Daniel's identification number, name, and home address. At the base of the card, an optical memory strip with symbols embedded into its mirrored surface held his fingerprints, digital photographs, retinal images, facial geometry, voice prints, medical records, and DNA sequencing.

Daniel turned his strange new identity card over to examine the reverse. The seal of the Department of Homeland Security covered the entire right side in soft green hues. Overlaid on top of the DHS mark was "ID 009-99-D121," Daniel's number. On the lower left was a microprocessor;

a gold square with raised lines running through it. Along the card's base was a long sequence of bar codes.

"Dad, what the hell is this? No way I'm carrying this creepy card. This is bullshit."

"It's like the old driver's license—and watch your language. You'll be needing this to attend school and travel anywhere. At least you got yours in the mail—I have to appear in person."

Some years before, new passports had been introduced with embedded radio frequency identification and digital biometrics. No one had put up a fight. The State Department quietly explained that these enhanced passports had kept radicals, agitators, and dangerous fanatics from entering the Homeland. For reasons of national security, further details could not, of course, be revealed. In much the same way, REAL ID internal passports could help identify criminals, extremists, and insurgents already in the Homeland. Microchips inside the cards transferred data to readers placed throughout all the major cities, linked through the Internet into a globally networked system tracking terrorist movements. REAL ID would also be used to establish employment eligibility, replacing the popular "E-Verify" program.

Citizens were required to produce identification upon demand. It became a routine matter of law and order, and everyone got used to it soon enough. As a series of public service announcements warned, you couldn't tell just by looking if someone was in the Homeland working on the job legally. He or she could even be a terrorist. One of these announcements, broadcast during children's programs, featured a collage of average-looking adults represented by a mix of ethnicities, genders, and attire. Some were professionals in suits toting briefcases; others wore denim overalls with hammers and saws in hand.

"Hey kids!" said the announcer. "Can you spot the terrorist?"

Another group of adults carefully drawn from the same socioeconomic strata flashed on the screen.

"Can you spot the terrorist in *this* group?" asked the announcer. "Well, neither can we. You can't tell just by looking. If you see something, say something. Call 1-800-TIPS. And now, back to the show."

"No shoving, please!" police on horseback called out every few minutes through bullhorns.

Citizens lined up around the block in the early morning, waiting for their turn to enter their local Department of Motor Vehicles for processing.

"You over there, move along quietly!"

Police in their smart new black uniforms and helmets patrolled up and down the lines, watching carefully, occasionally taking notes. The long lines of people, impatient as they were, dutifully submitted, already having been alerted by mail that it might take all day to be photographed, fingerprinted, scanned, indexed, interviewed, and stamped for their REAL IDs.

Benson and Jane advanced agonizingly slowly, often coming to a complete halt for several minutes before moving again. They came to stand in front of a giant green and yellow poster promoting greater threat awareness. Divided into eight panels, each of them asked in turn: Are terrorist groups in the area? Are they violent? Do they attack Americans? How active are they? How sophisticated are they? Are they predictable? Will local citizens warn Americans? What tactics and weapons are used? The panels were illustrated with cartoon drawings, including one of a hooded terrorist holding a handsaw to a child's neck, one of a color-coded threat meter like those used at the airports, and some depicting hate-message graffiti, car bombs exploding, and other violent images.

"I don't get the point of these," Benson said, waving his hand dismissively at the poster. "Unless you work for some kind of State intelligence bureau, there's no way you could answer those questions. Even then, you probably wouldn't have a clue. It just ends up leaving you more afraid, but then, maybe that's—"

"Say a terrorist has no criminal record, okay?" Jane said. "Let's say he's brand new at the terror biz—he isn't on a silly watch list. He could get a REAL ID like anyone else, right? And wouldn't having a REAL ID make it even *easier* for him to go and do his terror thing?"

"Hmm.... You can't be the first to have thought of that. Homeland Security has all these highly paid experts to think about this stuff. It's their job, so they must have already—"

"And if he's not already in the U.S., a new terror guy could just come in with a visitor's visa like anyone else, right? Visitors don't have to get REAL ID, it's only for citizens, but if foreign terrorists really want one they'll just buy fakes and conceal them with tinfoil, or maybe they'll forge a visitor's visa and a passport if that's easier. There's always a way."

"Jane, keep it down, will you?"

Step by plodding step, they made their way into the applicant holding area. They passed another poster, this one depicting a long line of faceless people all wearing the same nondescript, gray clothes. Its mood was dreary and dark. "Are Your Documents in Order?" it asked. "Citizens Without Valid ID can be Detained. Annual Renewals with Satisfactory Drug Tests now Accepted at this Location."

They advanced a few more steps until, at last, they stood in front of the applications processing clerk.

"Hello, my name is Felicia, employee 02B-2331," said the clerk.

Behind Felicia was an old Norman Rockwell poster tacked up on the wall between filing cabinets. The scene depicted a mother and father who had just tucked their idyllic moppets into bed. The children had already fallen asleep as the doting parents looked on. On the bedroom floor was an old-fashioned rag doll. "Ours to Fight For," the poster caption read. "Freedom from Fear."

"How you doin' today," Felicia said in a flat tone, looking over the documents Benson handed to her.

"Fine, just fine."

Frowning at the papers, Felicia suddenly left her station to check a notice posted on a bulletin board. She came back and turned Benson's application around on the counter, pointing at the offending section with ultra-long, sparkling purple fingernails. Bracelets on both her wrists rattled on the counter when she leaned over. She shook her head, looking at the documents.

"Sorry, we got a problem, hon," she said, looking out over the crowded waiting room. "Form 4562-3C has your first name as Thomas but this one here, it says, Tom. See that? Shoot, I must've seen a thousand Tommy's with a 'y,' Tommie's with a 'ie,' Thomas' with and without a 'h,' if I seen one. We need the *same* legal name on all your docs, hon, you understand? Also, your address over here, it says Elm *Avenue*, but it's Elm *Street* on this one, you see that?"

Glancing at the wall clock, Felicia waited a moment for Benson to take in all the transgressions. Scooping up the papers without warning, she shuffled them until they lined up precisely at the corners and stapled them together.

"You fix these source docs and come back, okay? And because you're filing 'married,' Jane here will need to come back, too. And don't forget your urine samples. You have a nice day," she said, looking out at the crush of waiting people. "Next!"

"Whoa there, Felicia, just wait a second," Benson said. "I can't take another day off work for this. I won't stand in line again, that's just not going to happen. I'll mail it."

"Sorry, mail's not allowed, but you can appeal if you want."

Felicia pointed at a cluttered table strewn with piles of forms.

"You go complete the forms that apply to your particular situation, then you go join the appeals line so we can process you. You'll be notified within 120 days of our decision. The application fee is still the same $240; no extra charge for appeals."

"That's $240 for both of us?"

"No, $240 *each*, and next time, please have your check ready and attached to the application. That'll speed up processing, you understand? Next!"

It felt good to be out in the sunshine with Jane. The birds were singing in the trees. A gentle breeze rustled the leaves. Their dog, Petey, hadn't been walked in a while, and he trotted happily next to them.

Standing in their path ahead was a policeman wearing one of those new black uniforms, all decked out in matching helmet, flak vest, and mirrored, aviator-style sunglasses. A curly cord ran from inside his shirt collar up his neck to an earphone inside the helmet.

Benson was in an expansive mood.

"Good day, officer. How goes the War on Terror?"

He regretted his quip the moment he said it. He had supposed it would be lighthearted, even witty, but the cop's severe expression indicated otherwise.

"Tom, don't joke around with these people!" Jane whispered between clenched teeth. "You can get in serious trouble, like at the airport."

The officer stared at Benson. Petey let out a low growl.

"Petey," Benson said, "it's okay, boy. Some people have no sense of humor, but not you, Officer...." He struggled to read the name tag.

"Officer Fresher, it looks like."

"The name's Officer *Friscker*."

"All in good fun, you know."

"War on Terror..." Friscker said, not taking his eyes from

the dog. "That supposed to be some kinda joke? You a jokester, is that it?"

Benson said nothing.

"Identification, please."

Benson hesitated. He'd done nothing wrong; this low-ranking beat cop had absolutely no right to demand any documents. Pedestrians on the sidewalk slowed down to gawk, glancing behind as they strolled past. The cop waited silently behind his sunglasses. There seemed no point in a hopeless showdown. Benson opened his wallet and showed his ID to the cop.

"Take it outta the wallet."

Petey growled, but Benson did nothing to restrain him this time. He would have liked to growl himself. He removed the card from his wallet, as ordered. He felt an intense disdain for this hoodlum in a uniform, but he hoped it didn't show. Nothing good could come from showing the least hint of disrespect to a law enforcement officer. Petey, however, wore his heart on his sleeve, as it were. He curled his upper lips and snarled, baring his teeth.

Keeping a wary eye on the dog, the officer examined Benson's REAL ID with a miniature flashlight, casting a purple glow on the card. He waved the card under the light, waiting for the RFID chip to register on the wireless reader he wore on his utility belt. Nothing happened, so he swiped the card through the reader slot and waited. The Automated Targeting System remained silent. He entered Benson's ID number on the keypad, but still nothing came of it. Clearly disappointed, he thrust the card rudely back at Benson.

His fangs bared, Petey lunged for Officer Friscker with a ferocious growl. Benson pulled him back just in time with a quick tug of the leash.

Friscker fell over backwards in fright.

"Restrain that goddamn thing!" he yelled from the ground, his helmet skewed. "You shouldn't have no dog like that, I could shoot him right here on the street, goddamn mutt."

He collected his flashlight and Benson's REAL ID from the ground. Benson offered him a hand, but he proudly refused, fixing his helmet and pushing himself to his feet. Curious pedestrians stopped at a respectful distance and stared.

Friscker handed the card to Benson, rather more gently this time. Attached to it was a green paper slip.

"I'm not scared a' no mutt," Officer Friscker said quietly, glaring defiantly at Petey.

Petey reared on his hind legs, barking furiously. Benson restrained him just out of reach of the officer.

"Oh, this is no mutt." Benson looked at his dog with undisguised pride. "He's an excellent guard dog—for our own protection, you know. What's this green thing?"

"That there is an Anti-Social Behavior Order, sir. That ASBO requires you to be off the streets by 2200 hours."

He smirked and walked away.

"You have a nice day, sir."

"Hey, what the f—" Benson began, but Jane yanked on his arm and mumbled into his jacket.

"Do—not—say—anything."

3

Just Say No

A PRISONER IN A BLACK SHROUD covering his head and torso balanced precariously on a stool. He lost his footing and struck the concrete floor with his elbow.

On all fours, a male prisoner wearing a dog collar and leash was led around, naked, by a female soldier. She even rode on his back and swatted his bare butt.

A German shepherd barked ferociously at a cringing prisoner trying to protect his face, the lunging, snarling dog barely held back at the end of a long chain by his master. The piercing, explosive barks ricocheted off the bare concrete walls.

The news reports portrayed all these scenes and more from the overseas detention centers as if they were somehow monstrous and criminal. Perhaps for the average person, far removed from the reality of fighting a hard war, they were indeed upsetting or offensive to contemplate. The public wanted its wars to be cleansed of any visible brutality. They preferred not to see innocent terror victims blown up by the side of some remote road. They didn't want to witness their soldiers torn apart in battle and suffering in unspeakable pain, or dead, stacked like firewood in body bags. That would be too personal, too upsetting. Too real.

Benson wasn't much impressed with these deliberately provocative reports from the war front. If certain techniques yielded valuable intelligence that saved even one soldier from

18

harm, it would be worth it, wouldn't it? It isn't torture; it's humiliation, he reasoned. It helps break them down. There's no lasting harm.

Benson recalled a truly grisly incident that had also made the news. Hooded terrorists had sawed off a captured soldier's leg as he shrieked away in agony. They held up the severed leg for the camera as if they were showing off a prize fish they'd caught, singing praises to their God. Benson had felt infuriated and sickened.

Amputation, burning, electrocution—now that's real torture. Our enemies have no qualms about inflicting the worst torture imaginable. Not since the Dark Ages have we seen anything like this.

Benson knew the trauma of war. He'd seen men's limbs blown off, their insides spilling out onto the dirt, choking on their own blood. He'd seen screaming villagers fleeing the searing flames, chemical sprays and napalm explosions chasing after them, their flowing white robes and scarves flapping in the wind as they scattered wildly. He'd heard a soldier screaming in unbearable agony for his best friend to kill him quickly and end it.

Special Ops, Task Force 88.

In two tours of duty he'd been in the middle of hell. He had stood firing into the void, unable to see through the fog and smoke, his brothers cut down by machine gun fire; yelling and crying in pure panic, shells screeching overhead, a pandemonium and terror that couldn't be conquered by any amount of bravery or sheer force of will. Real war wasn't anything like those movies in which the hero would walk off into the sunset and everything would be set right. He saw things no human being should ever see. When he returned, he was not the same man who left. No soldier was. They all returned physically or mentally scarred, some more than others.

Despite the losses, the battles he'd fought back then had at least ended decisively. When going head-to-head with the enemy, superior training, technology, and numbers always won out. His company would march their prisoners down the road, the prisoner's hands clasped on top of their heads as ordered, bowed in defeat, slogging onward.

Our former enemies knew when they were beat, but these jihad types keep coming back for more punishment.

They don't fight head-to-head.

They don't give up.

When we kill them they just send in more to the slaughter, like ants.

We don't understand how they think.

We don't know what they want.

They have no rules.

Quick and strong, Benson had excelled in hand-to-hand combat, even entering competitions. Years later, he still trained in the martial arts. He had acquired a fondness for the ideas of balance between opposing forces, of action and reaction, of the continual quest to harmonize mind and body through mental and physical discipline, but his taste for actual combat had evaporated. He moved into the officer ranks and went into software engineering, rising to lead some of the most advanced COMSEC research, publishing classified papers on cryptosecurity, transmission, emission, and traffic-flow network security. He discharged a full colonel—a rare feat for an enlisted man—earned an MBA, and tackled the corporate world. He had wanted to give something back to his country for molding him into the man he became—disciplined, skilled, and focused—but had never found quite the right outlet.

Growing up, he was taught that the world is gray, that everything depends on circumstances and feelings, that there are no absolutes. Yet, he often found the world to be more black and white. There *is* good and evil; there *is* right and wrong. There *are* universal truths. There had to be, or the world would make no sense. There would be nothing to believe in.

• • •

Demonstrators marched around in a circle, carrying signs and chanting. "Make Love, Not War," read their signs in professional lettering, and "Give Peace a Chance." They were protesting in support of a domestic terrorist, a "suspected associate of a presumed sleeper cell," as the media had put it, arriving for arraignment at the courthouse. Watching it all on the news, Benson was incensed at their flagrant idiocy, their self-hating death wish.

There are people out there who sympathize with these rats— the enemy within. If we're going to survive as a country, these collaborators must be destroyed.

Surrounded by a hostile crowd, the bearded prisoner struggled furiously to escape the police holding him down, restraining him only by piling on top. He screamed in exasperation, looking around, wild-eyed.

"I—I am—innocent!"

He could hardly breathe from the weight of all the cops crushing him.

"I am please—to have—"

He struggled to fight his way out from under the pile of cops.

"United State U.S. right!"

"Shut up, you freakin' terrorist!" shouted someone in the crowd. "You'll get what's comin' to you!"

Benson couldn't believe the audacity.

These murderers are sure quick to scream about their rights. Terrorists have no rights.

The prisoner managed to wrestle his way upright. Someone hurled a rock at him. It found its mark; blood streamed from the nasty gash that opened up his cheek. The police hustled him inside the courthouse to avoid a wild mob scene.

"What do they think this is, some lawyer show?" someone shouted.

"This is no TV show—we're at war!"

• • •

It had the spirit of a revival-tent meeting. Everyone believing, everyone excited to be a part of something uplifting, almost magical; a feeling that they, the loyal supporters, were making a real difference, that they would change the course of history. Benson cheered at the big rally, applauding right along with everyone else. Feeling just a bit foolish, he nevertheless went along for the ride with the exuberant throng. It's like a sporting event, he told himself; you cheer on your team. It was intoxicating to let loose and absorb the crowd's energy, and harmless, besides.

The sound system reverberated through the stadium, making it difficult to hear what the candidate was saying, though it hardly mattered. Being here was the important thing.

"Hey, it's great to be in, um, New Hampshire," Joseph King opened. "Live free or die, right? Gotta love that."

A huge movie screen above the stage projected King's image. Draped across the stage were red, white, and blue banners proclaiming the "Restoring National Honor Tour™" and its website, RestoreNationalHonor.us. The cameras followed King, picking up his every movement as he addressed the rally of screaming supporters.

There were nothing *but* supporters at these big bashes. Attendees were prescreened to probe their backgrounds and gauge their support before they could be issued tickets to these officially designated National Special Security Events. Everyone else who wished to attend was forced behind police barricades a half-mile away to special "free speech zones," out of sight and out of mind, their infantile protests, chants, and placards practically invisible.

Joseph King mentally rehearsed his last line, a memorable phrase he had come up with all by himself. His speeches were filled with zingers sure to be picked up on the news.

Reading from hidden teleprompters, he went through his usual routine, peppering his speech with words like "duty" and "obligation," "struggle" and "sacrifice," "service" and "loyalty," "unity" and "strength." Good words. Solid words. Patriotic words.

"Thank you. Thank you, my friends," he said to fervent clapping.

He bowed his head humbly while waiting for the raging applause to subside.

"Of course, the real credit goes to the American people. And I'll tell you something else—"

He had arrived at the big finish, ready for the moment with his dramatic signature line. It was part of a theme he had developed over the last few months. He struck a decisive pose and waited a beat.

"When it comes to questioning terrorists, what's the *other* party's answer?"

The audience responded right on cue. Like the lyrics of a popular song, they knew their line by heart.

"Just—say—no!" they thundered in unison.

The candidate smiled and clapped and the audience happily laughed and clapped with him.

"Hey, thanks New Hampshire, you've been great. Thank you!"

4

Multi-Stakeholder Solutions

"Senator! Senator, over here! hey, Senator!" the reporters shouted, desperately trying to attract attention over the noise. Aides yelled into their cell phones. Well-dressed crowds swarmed into the Capitol rotunda, their clamor amplified under the imposing cast-iron domed ceiling. On a magnificent fresco far overhead, George Washington rose to the heavens in glory, flanked by Liberty and Victory, but no one paid any attention.

A senate hearing had just opened its doors. Reporters jostled to get interviews as their camera operators illuminated the impromptu gatherings forming in the lobby. Beefy security agents in black uniforms and tall boots manned surveillance posts just outside the building on this dreary day, machine guns on their hips. From outside, the throng in the rotunda looked like a festive, raucous party.

"I think we have, you know, achieved something important today for the American people," Senator Dixon said. A little breathless, with a rosy blush spreading across her face, she was visibly excited to be announcing this latest breakthrough on live television. This couldn't but help her reelection prospects.

The reporter took his microphone away, tapped it, and then held it to her mouth. She leaned into it.

"It's like—"

"Hang on," interrupted the reporter. "Sorry, Senator."

He turned to the woman behind him fiddling with the sound boom.

"C'mon, get the sound feed working!"

After a short delay it was fixed.

"Okay, we're back; go ahead, Senator."

"We had to do something, you know, real quick, and today we've done just that."

Dixon smoothed her skirt and cleared her throat.

"We've done *something*. The people have spoken and we're paying attention. Since day one we've worked tirelessly—"

She was cut off by a man who came up from behind. He pressed a blade against her throat.

"Shut up!" he screamed. "Shut the hell up!"

The crowd fell silent. Dark and scrawny, of medium height, with short black hair and a closely cropped beard, the young man wore a cheap dark suit and dirty white running shoes. He breathed in spurts, hyperventilating, his body tense with fright, his knife hand trembling badly. The blade's sharp ceramic edge bit into the senator's neck. A thin line of blood trickled down her throat. His free hand stroked her neck, scratching the soft skin, and then crept down to grasp the cord tied to the hidden belt of explosives ringing his waist.

Senator Dixon twisted her head sideways, trying to escape the knife's edge.

"Please . . ." she cried softly. She shivered uncontrollably. "Just let me go, I'm begging you ... *please*."

He turned his angular face away from her. With wide eyes, he stared at the cringing people all around him slowly backing away, their hands raised in surrender. His attention became riveted on the commotion from the rear as men and women alike fought each other trying to bolt the lobby. His face flushed hotly; his breathing became labored.

Senator Dixon weighed whether she should stomp the spike of her heel down hard on his foot, giving him blinding pain for a few seconds and then run for it, but panic kept her paralyzed.

His hands were damp and cold. The knife cut deeper.

"Please, someone, help! Help me!"

The crowd stared back in dumb amazement.

Someone yelled, pointing at the explosives peeking from beneath the man's jacket.

"He's got a bomb!"

Screams filled the air as the throng made a renewed mad dash for the only available exit, but it was nearly blocked by body scanners and x-ray machines, the other exits having been sealed off for security reasons.

Fighting their way in against the tide of people, police rushed into the rotunda. Their guns drawn, they surrounded victim and assailant, now isolated in the middle of the lobby. Those who couldn't get out or who fell in the initial stampede cowered and hugged the walls, setting off alarms as they got too close to the paintings and statues.

One of the policemen motioned to the others to lower their guns. They did so exceedingly slowly, their eyes never leaving the attacker.

"C'mon, buddy, just tell us what you want, we can work it out, you know?" the policeman said, shouting over the alarms. "We all been in tough spots before, it can't be *that* bad. I was your age once, I know what it's like, you know? Let's just talk it out and calm down, okay? Hey, kid, I'm Rick. Rick Fisher. What's your name?"

"My name—my name—B-Babur. Babur."

Babur looked as if he were about to cry, his voice barely audible over the alarms. With his body shuddering in waves, his hands clenched the knife and cord tighter. Senator Dixon twisted sideways even more, trying to escape the sharp edge pressing into her throat. The pain seared. She felt herself growing nauseous and faint.

"Good, that's real nice, Baba, real nice. Hey, Baba, where you from?"

"Bah-*boor*. Bah-*boor*, acehole!"

Babur's body stiffened with rage. Breathing rapidly, he hugged his captive closer.

"Hey, Barber, you know what? I gotta son your age, you know that?"

Babur glared at Fisher.

"Turn the fuckin' alarms off!" Fisher yelled in a flash of anger. "I can't fuckin' hear myself *think*!"

Fisher turned back to Babur, apologetic.

"Sorry, son, it's just that you remind me so much a' him; I got a picture right here, you wanna see?"

"Shut the hell up! You—you will stay back! I kill this slut and everybody I also kill unless you—"

The explosives erupted in a staccato series of deafening blasts around Babur's waist, blowing out the windows and scorching the sandstone walls, taking with them centuries of art treasures. Twisted bodies and human fragments littered the bloody lobby. A woman's arm lay on the floor, still clutching a remnant of her purse. A man and woman lay in a death embrace, their bodies ripped with the nails and glass Babur had used for shrapnel. An elderly man lay contorted behind the pedestal base of the Thomas Jefferson statue, his dead green eyes open, his face drained of all color.

"My fellow Americans, intelligence sources suggest this was a cowardly attempt to disrupt your federal government and send the Homeland into anarchy."

Disheveled and weary, President Curtis "Brushfire" Cox read the prepared statement into the cameras in a somber tone. He had wanted to ride out the last few months of his term in office without any more crises. He'd had enough of national emergencies and international incidents and natural disasters the previous eight years. There was always some calamity underway. He wondered why he had ever run for this impossible, thankless job. After the first year or two, it wasn't fun or rewarding anymore; that was certain. He'd gladly hand the whole mess over to King or Carp right now; it wouldn't matter to him which one. He didn't give a rat's ass for either of them. He would retire, write his memoirs, and get paid handsomely for delivering short speeches to chambers of commerce and trade associations. Maybe he could serve on a few corporate boards or head up a charity or something. Life would be good again.

Donning reading glasses and getting down to business, he peered down at the statement placed on the desk before him.

"The terrorist threat that led to the declaration on September 14, 2001, of a national emergency, continues. For this reason, I have determined that it is necessary to continue in effect the national emergency with respect to the terrorist threat."

He looked up with tired eyes. The backdrop was not the usual plush office setting staged for such events. It more resembled a bunker or a command post.

"You can rest assured that essential government services will go forward. They tell me we're at COGCON 1. All mission-critical functionality is now deploying from the Mount Weather Emergency Operations Center. That includes senior officials from every federal department as well as all your congressional leaders. Your federal government will continue to deliver exceptional service."

He went on to say that this was an isolated incident, not part of any real pattern, and that he expected normal operations would resume in a week or so once everything had been cleaned up.

In contrast to the bleak mood at Mount Weather, people in parts of the Middle East celebrated in the streets. Masked men shot AK-47 rifles into the air with one hand, to the delight of the revelers. Boys looking barely 10 years old, sporting green bandanas and track suits, flourished play rifles and toy rocket-propelled grenade launchers. A grizzled man flashing a gap-toothed smile waved a small sign up and down and back and forth, trying to attract the attention of the foreign television cameras. Scribbled in English, it read "helo form yor partanor in peas." These and similar events quickly vanished from the major newscasts.

Professional commentators deliberated the deeper meaning of these spontaneous festivities. Were they demonstrating against postcolonial social injustice? Or could it be the emotional outpouring of peoples born of a common heritage spanning more than a thousand years? Maybe, they suggested, we couldn't make sense of it through the myopic lens of Western culture. It could even be that there were no simple answers readily at hand. But Benson knew the meaning of their exuberance. It was clear enough for anyone with half a brain; Joseph King had already spelled it out in plain language, had he not? They hate our freedom of religion, he had said compellingly, our freedom of speech, our freedom to vote and assemble and disagree with each other. New enemies call for new tactics, he'd added. Surely it couldn't be that hard to grasp.

The ambassador for Babur's country appeared in a televised ceremony at St. Anthony's Cathedral in New York. He called out for understanding and acceptance; collaboration, not isolation. In perfect, very lightly accented English, he called upon Americans to "join hands and reach out in terms of embracing a sustainable platform of multi-stakeholder solutions." He appealed for an international committee of "equal partners building a shared vision by which a roadmap to peace can be leveraged."

The American dignitaries seated in the front row and the ambassadors and their entourages trucked in from the nearby United Nations nodded their heads in solemn concurrence.

Benson found it difficult to listen to such sanctimonious drivel. The polite speeches, the hushed ceremony, and the respectful memorial service were whitewashing the enormity of the evil this terrorist had committed. He recalled a very different newscast he'd seen some time before, one vastly more relevant to the problem confronting the world than this idiotic remembrance would ever acknowledge. A video had been released to the media—who had actually broadcast it—with lurid warnings of "disturbing graphic images." The video featured hooded terrorists sawing off their hapless prisoner's head. The terrorist's joyous singing could barely be heard over the ghastly suffering of their wretched victim, who wailed in terror while they held her down. It was some sort of chant to their God.

Much as he had wanted to, Benson couldn't take his eyes from the screen. One of the terrorists triumphantly held the bloody head aloft when the video abruptly cut out, never to be broadcast again. It left Benson revolted. He couldn't imagine a crueler and more horrible death. He would have greatly enjoyed strangling these monsters himself as a fitting punishment. Join hands? No. Multi-stakeholder solutions? He thought not. Lining them up in front of a wall to face a firing squad would be more like it.

5

Time for a Change

" T IME FOR A CHANGE," the bobbing signs read.

"Believe in America."

"Forward."

"Hope and Change."

"Win the Future."

"Hope is on the Way."

"Something to Believe In."

"Everything for Everyone."

"It's our Turn."

"We Deserve It."

Tricked out in garish clothing in the official red and blue party colors, flourishing hats bearing trademarked catch-phrases, the crowds waved their signs back and forth and up and down, trying to get the attention of the cameras and of each other.

The band played timeworn standards everyone knew by heart, except that campaign buzzwords, among them "align-ment," "empowerment," "leverage," and "stakeholder," were cleverly inserted into the original lyrics. The party delegates to the convention laughed and shouted uproariously, dancing off their excitement, many of them already drunk. After several hours of such fun, the older conventioneers plopped into their seats, gulping oversized, party-branded soft-drinks and munching on bags of donated snack foods, fervently awaiting the kickoff of festivities by the acclaimed keynote speaker.

With the selection of the party nominee long a certainty, the crowds would roar their approval of the Anointed One, and the ratings would pop, at least for a time. "Momentum" was the word the campaign strategists were using. "We gotta get some momentum going, Benson," they kept telling him. "Let's step it up. We're expecting strong voter turnout this time, it's neck-and-neck."

Beyond the convention, the party elites would have little further use for the rank and file. When the stage lights went down the convention delegates would drift away and go back to wherever they had come from.

As a campaign fundraiser, Benson was obliged to go to the party convention in the late summer. He asked Jane to go with him. It would be like a romantic vacation, he said, but she had declined—wisely, as it turned out. They wouldn't have had any time together.

A very tall man stood next to the candidate on the podium, topped with a brightly colored hat bigger than his head, festooned with campaign buttons. The band stopped playing. Cheering and clapping erupted from the audience, rising to a dull roar. The lights in the audience dimmed, focusing all attention on the brightly lit center stage. Senator Mel Ziller beamed and put his arm around the candidate's shoulder, who looked more like a youngster standing beside him than someone who just might become the most powerful man in the world, the hope of a generation.

Smiling broadly, Ziller waited for the noise to subside.

"Like some of you, I keep asking myself which leader running today has the vision, the willpower, and yes, the backbone to protect my family. Without too much doubt, there is but one man to whom I am willing to entrust their future, and that man's name is Joseph King."

The crowd went wild. The speaker raised his hand and the commotion died down.

"Now, the terrorists would kill us if they could. To quash that threat, Joseph King has told Americans that their private plans and private lives must be repealed by an overriding public danger."

The audience leapt to their feet.

"King! King! King! King!"

The candidate waved to the delegates with a sheepish smile. With the mammoth senator looming over him, whose arm still hugged him close, King appeared somewhat uneasy. The speaker shook King's shoulder back and forth in a comradely manner, apparently enraptured with King. King pretended to enjoy being roughly jostled, playing along like a good sport, even though his already creaky shoulder ached even more.

Stooping over, Senator Ziller spoke into the double microphones.

"Where is the bipartisanship in this country when we need it most? I remember when the *other* party believed it was the duty of Americans to fight for freedom over tyranny—but not today!"

The crowd frantically waved their signs up and down and back and forth.

"The world cannot afford an indecisive America. Fainthearted self-indulgence will put at risk all we care about in this world. In this hour of danger, Joseph King seems to have the courage to stand up, and I'm proud to stand up with him."

Mel Ziller released his painful grip from King's shoulder and stood up straight to his full, towering height.

"So may I introduce to you!" he shouted over the rising noise. "The man you've known for all these years! Joseph F. King—"

The audience spontaneously rose to their feet, exuberant with their applause, their shouts of joy thundering through the great hall and overwhelming the rest of his introduction. With a shrug, Senator Ziller walked off the podium, holding his giant hat with one hand to keep it from tipping over.

King saluted the audience in the formal military style, although he had never done any real service outside of a desk job, nor had any of his family going back several generations.

"Reporting for duty!" he said to tumultuous applause, snapping his hand back smartly to his side. "Hope is on the way!"

He wore his serious warrior's face until the applause and cheers died down.

"It's wonderful to be here, it's certainly a thrill. You're such a lovely audience, we'd like to take you home with us, we'd love—"

He was interrupted by applause and laughter, and he laughed good-naturedly himself.

"In all seriousness, our campaign is about more than replacing a president, it's about saving the soul of America."

He waved to the congregation, receiving their hoots and whistles.

"What brings us here tonight is love of country. We'll find out just how great a nation we can be. My administration will create tremendous new opportunities for national service. We'll fight growing challenges on all the issues, like jobs and education. I will ask for your service and your active citizenship when I'm president—and don't tell me America is *out* of service. We've gotta rise about that. People of all ages, stations, and skills must serve a cause greater than just themselves and their families. The social welfare requires individuals to put away their narrow, selfish interests for the good of society. We're all in this together. A world in which we're only thinking about ourselves and not thinking about everybody else, in which we're considering the entire project of developing ourselves as more important than our relationships to other people—that's a pretty narrow vision. So everybody's gotta sacrifice for the greater good. Everybody's gotta give. Everybody's gotta—"

He was interrupted by a standing ovation; a tumultuous clapping of hands and waving of flags ensued.

"Everybody's gotta have some skin in the game."

King became pensive.

"We can't just drive our SUVs and eat as much as we want and keep our homes at 72 degrees and then just expect that other countries are gonna go, 'Okay, whatever.' That's not leadership. That's not influence. That's not gonna happen."

The applause rose and fell in a great wave.

"As citizens of the freest country on Earth, you should have the right to a good job, the right to a decent home, the right to adequate medical care, the opportunity to enjoy good health. You should have the right to a secure retirement, the right to a good education. You deserve it. *We* deserve it. So let's give this to ourselves."

The audience clapped away in delight, nodding in complete agreement.

"So what does it mean to be an American today? It means workin' hard, prayin' hard, and pledging allegiance. Sacrifice, duty, and loyalty. Paying your fair share, and service to country. We're gonna energize the American spirit, restore our sense of pride and our national purpose—but that's not all!"

Benson sat in the VIP booth next to Burton Chesterfield, a high campaign official. Dozens of party workers milled around wearing colorful campaign hats and buttons. Floor-to-ceiling one-way windows gave them a commanding view of the show. The crowd was cheering and whistling. Benson was glad he did not have to sit with the rabble in the bleachers. They'd cheer anything.

"Magnificent!" Chesterfield said. "People need something to believe in."

He wore a proud smile.

"Tom, you helped make all this possible."

Benson was thinking about what King had just said. He put it down to political hyperbole. King needed to say things, even if a bit sensational at times, that would rouse the audience and generate a few headlines. Once the election was over he could put some of the more over-the-top campaign rhetoric aside and become a true leader, more reasonable and more thoughtful. More presidential.

"Tom?"

"Yes, well, I like to think that I might've helped."

"C'mon, you did more than just *help*," Chesterfield said, giving Benson a slow, exaggerated jab in the shoulder. "You're just about one of the best bundlers we have. You know, we were thinking about a place for you later on. We need someone with your dedication and talent; we like your initiative. Think about it, okay? Here, you need a 'Win the Future' button. Put this on."

He handed Benson a WTF button and wandered off to the bar. Benson slipped it into his pocket.

"We also care about healthcare," King went on. "We care about children and seniors. Good jobs at good wages. Clean air and water. Immigration. The economy. Social Security. National security. Illegal drugs. Prescription drugs. Affordable housing. Fair taxation. Family values. Crime. Inflation. Education. Energy. Trade. And even warm weather!"

That brought down the house. A woman in the front row turned around to face the galleries, and, with exaggerated arm gestures, started up a chant that rolled through the hall.

"Time for a change!" she yelled, repeatedly whipping up her hands for everyone to follow her lead. "Time for a change! Win the future! Time for a change! Win the future!"

King jauntily doffed his jacket, loosened his tie, and rolled up his shirtsleeves. Grabbing a wireless microphone, he went out into the audience, shaking hands as he spoke. Yelling and cursing into their headsets, his security detail scrambled to keep track of him.

"And we'll create a new kinda politics that'll transform this country, change the world, and free this nation from the tyranny of oil," King said. "The rise of the oceans will slow and our planet will begin to heal."

King clasped the microphone under his arm and used both hands to shake those of his delighted and stunned audience, moving nonstop with the vigor of a much younger man.

"Details to follow!"

♪♪ *"Mine eyes have seen the glory of the coming of the Lord,"* ♪♫

♪♪ *"He is trampling out the vintage where the grapes of wrath are stored."* ♪♫

♪♪ *"He hath loosed the fateful lightning of His terrible swift sword,"* ♪♫

♪♪ *"His truth is marching on-n-n-n."* ♪♫

With considerable gusto, the band played the "Battle Hymn of the Republic" a few times. The conventioneers got to their feet and sang along. Even King marched in place to the beat, saluting the audience as he stepped. When it was finally over, cheers and clapping filled the convention center.

Just outside, a spirited protest was in full swing, held at bay by squads of battle-clad police holding their riot shields in an impenetrable ring around the building's entrance. Demonstrators with signs marched around in a circle, while others paraded a crude, evil caricature of King; a giant, grotesque paper mache puppet on a stick that they twirled over their heads. They were calling King bad for working families, captured by the special interests, and a warmonger. At intervals, they would tire from their labors and stop for a break. Benson watched it on the monitors. The show outside seemed much more interesting to him than the one inside.

Benson laughed to himself. These soft pansies had been indulged all their lives, filled with a phony self-esteem that had left them mentally and physically unfit. They looked like they hadn't worked hard a day in their lives. Wars are messy; there's no such thing as a clean, quick War on Terror. Combatants are captured and tried, sometimes in secret. The worst ones are even executed. There's collateral damage.

King clasped his hands together in front of his chest, a devout expression on his face. Thousands of euphoric people before him giddily jumped up and down.

"My friends, we're gonna come together and restore the great American experiment."

He looked skyward, as though he were about to pray.

"National unity! We're gonna strive for national greatness, now how 'bout that?"

The crowd went wild. Another chant began rolling through the convention center in waves. "It's our turn!" they yelled. As the wave hit each section, the conventioneers stood, raising their hands in the air, and then sat down. The effect was of an undulating ribbon going round and round.

"It's our turn! We deserve it! It's our turn! We deserve it!"

A blast shook the building. Billowing smoke blew out from the end of the convention center. Most of the partygoers ran madly for the exits, abandoning their plastic souvenir bags and convention kits, scrambling over each other in their desperation to escape. The security guards couldn't resist the onslaught, giving up and getting carried along outside the hall with the streaming crowd.

King dropped where he stood, peering about while his security detail ran everywhere. One of the agents spoke into his shoulder radio. He got down on the floor and whispered in King's ear. King got to his feet, looking around warily, brushing the dust off his shirt. He took his place behind the microphones again, watching the fleeing delegates.

He set his face in a fearless, squinty-eyed expression and tapped the microphone to check that it was still working.

"My friends, nothin' to be scared of, don't panic. Keep calm and carry on. A stove blew up in the kitchen is all. C'mon back, everything's all right."

• • •

Downtown, a band of protestors gathered at a busy intersection. Loudspeakers on their minivan played an old recording at a shrieking pitch.

♪♪ *"I'm proud to be an American ... "*♪♫
♪♪ *"'Cuz at least I know I'm free-eee."*♪♫
♪♪ *"And I won't forget the men who died ... "*♪♫
♪♪ *"Who gave that right to me-eee ... "*♪♫

They waved their signs back and forth for passersby and film crews. The selections included "Support Our Troops," "Freedom Isn't Free," "These Colors Don't Run," "No War, No Peace—Know War, Know Peace," and "No Peace for Oil."

Another band of demonstrators set up a counter-protest on the opposite corner, yelling nasty epithets, even hurling bottles and cans at their opposition across the street. Not to be outdone, their signs included "War is not the answer," "Who Would Jesus Bomb?", "Resistance is Fertile—Pick Fruit, Not Fights," "Go Solar, Not Ballistic," and "How Many Lives per Gallon?" They cranked up the loudspeakers mounted on top of a decaying old bus emblazoned with their witticisms. There was a loud, electrical hum, and then buzzing and static. At last it was fixed and the battle was joined.

♪♪ *"All we are saying ... "*♪♫
♪♪ *"Is give peace a chance."*♪♫

The simple chant repeated in an endless, hypnotic loop, enhanced by shrill tambourines rattled by the demonstrators trying to drown out the other side.

♪♪ *"All we are saying ... "*♪♫
♪♪ *"Is give peace a chance."*♪♫

Drivers brought to a standstill angrily honked their horns in a torrent of noise. Pedestrians held their ears to stifle the clamor. The demonstrators donned sandwich boards plastered with their slogans and moved out onto the sidewalks, banging their tambourines aggressively in people's faces.

"C'mon, everyone, sing it loud, sing it proud! All we are saying ... yes, that's it! Is give peace a chance ... again! Let's do it! All we are saying—"

From out of nowhere, riot police in Bulldog X SWAT trucks careened onto the sidewalks. Protesters and spectators alike fled for their lives before the blaring sirens and brilliant red, white, and blue strobe lights. The police within jumped out awkwardly, their riot shields, helmets, tall boots, visors, armored vests, and weapons slowing them down. They immediately unloaded smoke rounds and flashbang grenades from their M4A1 carbines into both groups of protesters.

Temporarily blinded, dazed and deafened, the protesters stumbled in confusion. Their riot shields held before them, the police descended on the hapless protestors, surrounding them in a tightening circle until all the groping demonstrators were roughly corralled. Herded onto a fleet of unmarked school buses painted flat gray with steel mesh windows, they were handcuffed to the seats and promptly driven away, the engines rumbling and whining. It was all perfectly executed and over in minutes.

6

Let's Make the Right Choice

JOHN CARP AND JOSEPH KING SMILED BROADLY and waved to the audience. Striding confidently from left and right stage, they warmly shook hands, clasped each other's shoulders, and whispered something apparently amusing. They mounted the podium, each taking their assigned lecterns.

"Welcome to the presidential election debates," the lovely moderator began.

She thanked the numerous corporate, union, farm, foundation, environmental, education, public relations, healthcare, special interest, and State sponsors profusely. She expressed her own deep gratitude to the candidates, seemingly awestruck to be in their presence.

"I would ask you to speak from the heart," she said to the candidates, "about how you would navigate this country through the challenges America faces. Tell Americans what you would say personally, sitting in their living rooms."

Upon directing her first question to King, she leaned forward in her seat, smiling provocatively.

King looked at the moderator for a long moment. Her blue eyes were fixed on his. She pushed back her long blond hair and played with her earring. Breaking her intent gaze, King peeked at his notes on the lectern. He peered at the audience, and then stared again at the moderator. She smiled invitingly back at him. He was suddenly lost for words, befuddled, his mind racing.

He took a sip of water, and then set the glass down carefully. He picked up a pencil and then put it down, lining it up exactly even with the lectern's edge. He took another sip of water. He had vanquished all opponents for his party's nomination, outmaneuvering and crushing every challenger. Now it was Carp's turn to fall. Bolstered by this thought, his confidence returned as swiftly as it had vanished.

"You know," he said, clearing his throat, "I'm glad you— see, we need, we need to lower those taxes. Americans in the bottom 25 percent, they need relief. Stimulate the economy so we can fund more programs. We'll go line by line through the federal budget to reduce wasteful and ineffective programs. We'll get tough on waste, fraud, and abuse. We need a president who is ready on day one to be commander-in-chief of our economy. I will be that president."

Taking another sip of water, he glanced down surreptitiously, the glass having been placed next to his notes.

"We've journeyed into the heartland of America. I'm from the heartland myself and I know these people. We've met with real Americans and they're telling us to get our financial house in order. Cut, you know, the deficit with all the money saved. Lower interest rates for working families so they can buy more washing machines and refrigerators and cars, and that's good for jobs and it's good for the treasury. Simplify the tax system, and we—that's a priority. You can take that to the bank."

He put both hands decisively on the lectern and stood tall. It was now his opponent's turn.

"We have a plan for that," Carp said.

He glanced down at his notes for a split second.

"This country has a proud heritage."

He pointed at the audience.

"I know the middle class, I was one of them. We've spoken to middle-class people all over this great, proud country— and the middle class deserves a tax cut."

A woman clapped.

"Please hold your applause to the end," the moderator said, "if you can; I certainly understand your enthusiasm. Mr. Carp, will you please continue?"

"Yes," Carp said. "Lower taxes for all but those in the top 75 percent. Comprehensive tax reform, keep it simple, keep it fair. We've got, what, like 73,000 pages of tax code, rules and regulations, something like that? That's ridiculous, it's unacceptable."

Someone applauded in the audience, and soon others joined in.

"Key programs to help the less privileged and the under-privileged, the disenfranchised and the disadvantaged. Jobs programs—and a special blue-ribbon, bipartisan commission to cut waste and use the savings, all the savings to invest in the—in the future. Cut these crazy interest rates and this inflation for more infrastructure investment, financed by a new kind of national infrastructure bank. Get America moving again, building for America's future."

"Thank you for sharing your affirmative vision for our country, Governor Carp. And now, Governor King: Where do you stand on border security?"

She flashed him a brief but unmistakably coquettish glance. King wasn't sure anyone else caught it; the way her eyes smiled, the way the corners of her mouth turned up slightly.

"Hey, uh, I'm uh—I'm glad you asked, Sierra. That's, you know, that's an important issue. Control our borders so, uh, terrorists and illegal aliens can't get in, make no mistake, anyone could just walk in here and—well, you know, terrorism will be *the* priority when I'm president. Another, you know, it's education. Education is so important—that's a big issue. I mean, it's all about our young people, isn't it?"

He bit his lower lip, overflowing with sudden emotion.

"No dream is beyond our reach. Our children must come first, the young people of America, our future. Together, we're strong." He clasped his hands together in the air. "It's a new morning in America."

In the VIP booth high over the stage, party workers spoke on their phones and typed on their laptops. Burton Chesterfield, the high campaign official, spotted Benson and ambled over. His tie skewed, somewhat drunk and greatly animated, he couldn't contain his elation.

"This guy's great! Tom, isn't he great? He really connects with the voters. I'd do *anything* for him. He's just killing that poor old Carp. Got that whole charisma thing going on, you know? He's so ... what's the word? So *inspiring*."

Benson stood and stretched. He was weary from sitting around. The long flight from home, the time zone change, the noisy hotel and the nonstop meetings, which proved to be a complete waste of his time, had all taken their toll. The show had been a long time setting up, and it wasn't even nearly over. He thought of all his work piling up at the bank and Jane being alone for the long weekend.

"Tom?"

"Yes." Benson massaged his tired neck. "Yes, I suppose you could say that. He's got *something*, all right."

"We have a plan for that, for tightening our borders," John Carp said, jabbing his finger at the audience as he spoke. "Details of our, ah, our plan will be worked out by a team of experts as soon as, you know, when we take office, like on the first day of our new administration—the Administration of Hope, we're calling it. But basically, you know, no one will be able to get in without permission."

"Hey Tom, you hear this guy? He's got a 'plan for that!' "

Chesterfield laughed so hard that he sloshed most of his drink on the floor.

"He's got a plan for everything, this guy. He just cracks me up."

"And we'll educate the young people on their obligations to their country," Carp said with a stern expression, looking at one side of the audience and then the other. "Freedom isn't free you know; you should do something to pay your country back. Being a citizen comes not only with rights but with fundamental responsibilities."

He hooked a thumb toward his chest.

"Now that's how it works where I'm from, and speaking of where I'm from, in my home state we've done a tremendous job educating all the youngsters—"

Carp squinted, pointing out a woman somewhere in the small gallery of spectators. Everyone turned to see who he was pointing at.

"And Emanuela Lopez in the audience with her *abuela* over there proves what we can accomplish if we *work together*. Now that's the right business model for America—working together."

"Working Together!" was a big slogan in his campaign, and he let the words resonate.

"She's *under*-disadvantaged, but she's going to Harvard anyway to study Women's and Transgender Equity Studies on a full State grant made possible by *working together* and investing in our young people, the future of America."

Sporadic applause broke out. The moderator let it go on.

"Excellent, Mr. Carp, most uplifting. Working together is so important, I'm sure everyone here would agree. Thank you *so* much."

She paused for a moment, as if reflecting on the profound wisdom of Carp's words, and then turned to her notes.

"And now, Joseph F. King, I have a question for *you*."

She looked up at him from her position below the podium, running her eyes from his face all down his body, where she lingered, and back again.

"What's your position on preemptive war? Is it good? And please stay within the time limit."

There followed some scattered laughter.

She licked her lips.

"Can you, um, Sierra, can you please repeat the question?"

"Certainly. What is your position on the doctrine of pre-emptive war?"

She looked straight into his eyes without blinking, and put a finger lightly to her bottom lip, pulling it down just slightly.

"Okay, Sierra, look, that's—that's a good question, an important question. With all due respect for my, for my, um—my opponent, Governor Carp over there, why wait for them, you know, to come over here and murder us in our sleep? My honorable opponent, you know, he doesn't seem to understand that. Out of touch with the mainstream."

King looked at the moderator. She leaned forward in her chair, the slightest smile playing across her full mouth. Her lips parted slightly.

"You—you, ah, you, you find out—you find out, you see, you find out what they're planning, okay, and you stop them *first.*"

King looked at the audience with a deadly serious expression. He directed a withering glance at Carp. Carp shifted on his feet and looked away.

"So let's be clear," he said, speaking again with sudden conviction, avoiding Sierra. "Look, we have to make, you know, keep folks safe and sound, that's what government's all about, that's the number-one job. Better safe than sorry, right? As your president, the people will be real safe and you can take that to the bank."

He removed his microphone from the stand, stepping to the podium's edge, and reached out his hand to a small boy in the second row, waving to the child and his parents.

"Sir," the moderator objected, rising from her seat. "You can't—"

"Little Benito Rosetti, that's him over there with his folks in the audience, they're good people from the heartland, he wrote us and said he's scared and will the president keep him and his mom and pop safe and get the bad guys?"

King nodded his head in a knowing, wise way.

"And I wanna tell, um, Benny here, he can rest easy when I'm president. I was actually in a war, and it's hard, but we gotta make the tough choices."

King descended the small flight of stairs and went out into the audience, shaking hands as he spoke.

"We're no longer in a position to keep minding our own business, just wait it out and see what happens, as Governor Carp might say. What *happens* is a big, smoking mushroom cloud, that's where they're headed with this. Obviously, we can't continue to rely only on our military to achieve all the national security objectives that we've set. We've gotta have a civilian national security force that's just as powerful, just as strong, just as well-funded. And they're gonna need diplomatic-style immunity to do what they gotta do. That's what America expects from the leader of the free world, the president of the United States of America!"

King walked backwards to the stage, shaking hands as he went, taking his place again on the podium.

"At the end of the day, you got a stark choice in front of you." King paused thoughtfully. "Couldn't be starker. We're focusing on the issues, facing the challenges, staying on message. Fighting hard for working families, standing up to the special interests. So you got a real stark choice after all. Now, if we make the *wrong* choice as a nation, then the terrorists have won—and no one wants that. God bless us, every one. Goodnight, America."

"Governor Carp," Sierra the moderator quickly responded, cutting off the budding applause, "you've written and lectured extensively on this topic in the most prestigious journals and distinguished universities, where you are considered an expert. Please, enlighten America tonight."

Carp grinned, waving at the audience, ever upbeat.

"The fact of the matter is, is we have a plan to keep the war over there, not over here. My top military advisors have worked out what they call the Flypaper Strategy. How it basically works is you wipe them out on *their* turf, not on yours. If they want to start a fight by threatening American interests or whatever, well, we'll finish it for them. We've never backed down from a fight and we're not about to start now. Speaking of fights, our challenger over here was only a desk jockey in the Chair Force. There's a difference between commanding a platoon and commanding a desk."

Half the audience laughed and applauded heartily. When the clapping finally died down, Carp continued.

"I, uh, I fought in a war, you know, so I know all about it, I know what it's like, our brave fighting men and women. We're proud to have served our country and I—that is, America—can't stay on the sidelines. We have to move the ball into the end zone."

He took a gulp of water.

"You only get so many downs, so let's score a touchdown!"

Carp solemnly stared into the cameras to address the viewers directly, as it were.

"We gotta play offense against the terrorists living among us, you put them on the defense. You root them all out, you root 'em out from their hiding places and you deal with it. It's time for a new beginning. It's time for real leadership. Look, if we make the wrong choice, there's gonna be riots and looting, there's gonna be tanks in the streets. I'm not kidding this time—so let's make the *right* choice. Let's *work together*. Thank you! Thank you very much!"

The debate was now over. The candidates clasped each other's hands and shoulders, and whispered what appeared to be something intimate and amusing to each other before walking off the stage together.

7

Hail to the Chief

KING WALKED WITH A JAUNTY AIR. Even though a frigid wind blew on this threatening January day, he was without an overcoat, hat or gloves. He was freezing, literally in pain, his feet and hands turning numb, and yet he strode relaxed and at his ease, as if it were a midsummer's day at the beach. Although the streets were windswept and dry, it was well cold enough to snow. He was accompanied by his wife, Priscilla, who wore a bulky overcoat, matching hat and mittens, and high boots. Barely restrained by the barricades and riot police lining every inch of the route, throngs of captivated onlookers shouted and waved as the Kings made their way to the Capitol in this first-ever pre-inaugural parade. The handsome couple mechanically waved their hands back and forth, a frozen smile fixed on their frozen faces.

Surrounding the Kings was a phalanx of security agents on foot, dressed in heavy black overcoats. Dark SUVs with blacked-out windows drove slowly in the rear. The lightbars mounted on their roofs flashed rotating red and blue lights, their headlights blinking in a blinding sequence. Revving their engines, dozens of police motorcycles with sidecars led the procession along Pennsylvania Avenue in a double V formation. Sniper teams positioned themselves on top of the buildings along the route, sighting their Remington Modular Sniper Rifles equipped with sound suppressors on various spots in the crowds.

Benson and his wife naturally expected to be invited to the inauguration, or at the very least to some of the celebration galas held throughout D.C. the week afterward, but he heard nothing from the organizers. Emails and telephone calls went unanswered. Jane returned the special dress and shoes she'd bought.

The Kings ascended the steps to the Capitol's West Front. Dignitaries seated in the reviewing stands, wearing the official Presidential Medal bearing his likeness around their necks, complained incessantly of the biting cold. Indeed, the event should have been moved indoors, but King had insisted that it be held outside so long as it didn't snow. The pageantry would be so much better and the impact far greater, he insisted, especially for a live broadcast.

With Priscilla and his adult children standing behind him, King raised his right hand in the air, his left hand on a Bible, repeating the oath of office recited by the chief justice.

"I do solemnly swear . . . "

"I do solemnly swear," King said, suddenly anxious, despite having rehearsed this exact moment thousands of times over the last two years. Deeply tired, he was unable to sleep the night before, refusing any medication for fear of lingering side effects that might interfere with delivering his inaugural address. He did, however, take the liberty of tossing back a stiff drink or two to steady his nerves.

"That I will faithfully execute the office of president of the United States . . . "

"That I will faithfully execute the president of the United States."

"And will, to the best of my ability, preserve, protect, and defend the Constitution of the United States."

"And will, to the best of my ability, preserve and protect the Constitution of the United States."

The audience clapped politely. King shook the chief justice's hand, accepting his congratulations, and then clasped his own hands together and raised them overhead, facing one direction and then the other. At long last, it was finally over.

The last two years had been spent constantly giving speeches or traveling to speeches. Speech hell. He had traveled back and forth across the country in the immense campaign bus, the quaint and creaky "Love Train," the lavish party jet, and even a faux stagecoach, delivering speeches at every little burg across the country until he was hoarse. Inevitably, there would be hecklers and protesters interrupting until security hustled them away for interrogation. Then there were the unceasing interviews, campaign briefings, fundraising dinners, and the calls to potential donors from his hotel, dawn to midnight, seven days a week.

Everybody had wanted something. Business donors demanded special tax breaks, powerful State jobs, subsidies, guaranteed low-interest loans, grants, and other such aid in return for their unreserved support. Union leaders extracted promises to raise minimum wages to uncompetitive levels and erect taller trade barriers as the price for delivering their member's votes. The healthcare lobby sought higher tax payments, farm organizations stood firm on a boost in minimum prices and export subsidies, numerous pressure groups received pledges to ban products and activities they opposed, and on and on. He began to feel more like a mere conduit for other people's designs than the most powerful man on Earth that destiny had dictated he become.

He hardly ever saw his dear Priscilla or his devoted family except for brief photo opportunities arranged at campaign stops. He was desperately sick and tired of it all, and now it was finally at an end. What sort of person would do anything, say anything, and sacrifice everything to get this job? The kind of person who could repair the nation, he told himself many times, and now he could get to it.

The U.S. Marine Band played the traditional ruffles and flourishes on the drums and bugles four times, followed

by a rousing "Hail to the Chief" and 21-gun salute. The
proud new president turned to face the spectators on the
West Front, standing in front of a white railing and a cluster
of microphones. The dignitaries were seated. The crowd
respectfully quieted.

History had been made here; legendary inaugurals that
were still revered. "The only thing we have to fear is fear
itself," and "Ask not what your country can do for you, ask
what you can do for your country," and "With malice toward
none, with charity for all," had been uttered here. Words
that had spurred a nation. Words that inspired the country
to greatness.

King raised his hands high and looked back and forth at the
vast audience before him. The wind gusts messed his hair; he
smoothed it with one hand while keeping the other in the air.

"My friends, fellow dignitaries, distinguished guests, this
century must be an American century," he read from the
concealed teleprompters. "In an American century, America
has the strongest economy and the strongest military in the
world. God did not create the Homeland to be a nation of
followers. America is not destined to be one of several equally
balanced global powers. America must lead the world, or
someone else will. And Americans," he said with a dramatic
pause, "will *not* be led. Americans will *not* be ruled."

That was a pretty strong opener, King thought. That last
bit might become the most memorable part of the entire
speech, his signature "legacy" line. It could even appear on
a presidential statue honoring his public service someday.
He saw wide agreement in some of the nodding heads and
reserved applause.

"My fellow citizens, we might be bound by a common set
of ideals, but let's celebrate our diversity, too. Let us reach
out to improve the welfare of all our citizens. Looking out
for you, working together, getting the big picture. Let us
summon the political will to actively advance our democracy

and remoralize our nation. New programs will be designed
to help our children. Opportunities will be aligned and our
families will be empowered. Our policies will leverage the
economy, create millions of new high-paying jobs, make life
easier for countless people, *and* clean up the environment—
all at the same time. We'll have affordable, high-speed light
rail going everywhere. We'll legislate generous living wages
and bring down the cost of housing, and then folks will need
to buy more washing machines and refrigerators and cars to
go with their new houses. That's good for the economy and
it's good for jobs."

This was met with spirited applause.

He had spent hours with his speechwriters getting the
next part just right, taking most of it directly from his new
executive departments' existing mission statements.

"Your federal Department of Energy will ensure America's
security and prosperity by addressing its energy, environmental, and nuclear challenges through transformative science and
technology solutions. They'll prohibit energy exports to help
keep prices low and supplies plentiful. We'll be self-sufficient
and help support American jobs.

"Your federal Department of Education will promote
student achievement and preparation for global competitive-
ness by fostering educational excellence and ensuring equal
access regardless of ability. They'll develop new comprehensive student testing programs, new teacher certifications,
new benchmarks, and new mandatory, uniform curriculums
across this great and diverse land.

"Your federal Department of Health and Human Services
will improve the health, safety, and well-being of America.
Their goal is for all Americans to live longer, healthier, more
prosperous, and more productive lives so they can get back
to work and contribute their fair share.

"Your federal Department of Labor will foster, promote,
and develop the welfare of wage earners, job seekers, and

retirees; improve working conditions, advance opportunities for profitable employment, and assure government benefits and special rights. They'll advocate for rewarding, lucrative careers and mandate full employment—and when everyone's working and contributing, the treasury will be full.

"Your federal Department of Commerce will make American businesses more innovative at home and more competitive abroad. That'll make the USA number one again and help broaden the tax base, too."

He looked out at the audience, clenching the microphone, disappointed. Their reaction seemed a bit tepid.

"There are those who don't understand that the economy must be managed. For the greater good. For fairness. For equality."

The wind whipped right through his thin suit jacket, chilling him to the bone.

"Stimulus."

He barely fought off the nearly irresistible urge to shiver.

"Economic stimulus, social stimulus, national stimulus. Progress can't just happen on its own. Society must be organized and directed to promote the general welfare, to stimulate innovation, and encourage the arts and sciences. The greatest happiness of the greatest number will be our guiding principle. We'll demand increased social investment, tighter regulations, and stricter standards. We'll seek a much greater and more equitable contribution from those who are able to pay more. Corporations—"

His speech was interrupted by thunderous clapping and cheering. King respectfully acknowledged the acclaim.

"Our corporations and unions must be reorganized into public-private stakeholder cooperatives partnering with the State to serve the national interest in the New America. The State itself must be boldly reimagined with a daring new vision statement. This is the basis of our New Economic Policy, which will repurpose all aspects of economic development, particularly with regard to sustainable economic infrastructure and information technology.

"And we're still committed as ever to winning the War on Drugs, the War on Illegal Workers, the War on Poverty, the War on Crime, and the War on Terror. A nation that can send a man to the moon can certainly rise to the challenge of winning these wars. Now, it may be that none of these wars have ever been *won*, in a purely technical, narrow sense. But we can't just give up. I don't believe in giving up. Washington didn't give up. Roosevelt didn't give up. Kennedy didn't give up. We didn't become a great nation by giving up.

"Now, some may ask, 'How are we going to stop drugs on our streets when we can't stop it in our schools and prisons? How are we going to stop all these illegal aliens from working American jobs? How are we going to eliminate visible poverty? How are we going to make our streets safe from terrorists?' Well, maybe if we tried harder, that's how!"

A gust of bitter-cold wind sent some debris flying up the steps. Apart from a strange tingling sensation, he no longer had any feeling in his hands.

"Drugs are bad. They impoverish the soul of this mighty nation. The big cartels are from Mexico and Panama and other countries. They send illegal aliens into the Homeland to sell these dangerous drugs to our children—numerous studies prove exactly that. And weren't those 911 terrorists illegal aliens? The War on Drugs and the War on Terror must be a single enterprise devoted to national security."

King sensed that he had the people thinking. He knew it by instinct; the audience was with him. He decided right then to depart from the prepared text.

"And speakin' a national security, make no mistake, my friends, without national security, there's no other kinda security. Our grave nation faces a grave foreign threat. We can't meet a grave foreign threat with internal chaos. The terrorists use our freedoms against us. So it follows that we need a more intelligent, a more *nuanced*—if you will—understanding of the Constitution to bring it up to date.

"Our nation's at war against a far-reaching network of violence and hatred. We destroy them, my friends, or they destroy us. All right, so you're with us or you're with the terrorists! Time to choose sides, time to take a stand. We've been fighting them with one hand tied behind our backs, but today—today, we ask for your trust. Today, you know, we're reaching out to all citizens, young and old, black and white, rich or poor, men, women, doesn't matter. My administration—"

He was interrupted again by resounding applause.

"My administration will double-down on previous well-intentioned efforts and restore your faith in government. We must go on the offense against radicals—and offense is the best defense. I'm talkin' preemptive intelligence, you get 'em *before* they cause trouble, but you still respect the rule of law—and you can take that to the bank."

"King! King! King! King!"

"Now, some of the events of the last couple years, in terms of our national narrative, have damaged the American brand."

He banged his fist on the lectern.

"That's gotta stop and it *will* stop."

King bowed his head while waiting for the raging applause to die down.

"We've become a nation of crises. We got a moral crisis, an economic crisis, an energy crisis. We got a spending crisis, an immigrant crisis, a foreign crisis. We got a leadership crisis. A failure to act, and act now, will turn these crises into catastrophes."

King solemnly held up his hand to quiet the boisterous crowd. Without warning, he grabbed a microphone and went over to the dignitaries' section, shaking their hands as he spoke, his voice ringing throughout Capitol Hill and beyond.

"National renewal, national unity. Shared sacrifice, transparency. Accountability, restoring your faith in government. Now *that*'s what I'm talkin' about!"

The VIPs were flabbergasted.

"This administration will reflect America. Inventive, intelligent, informed, motivated to succeed. We'll modernize programs and streamline the bureaucracy—but now's not the time for big philosophical debates, all right? This country needs a leader, not a reader."

"King! King! King! King!"

He pumped his fist in time with the crowd's chanting, his suit jacket flying open.

"King! King! King! King!"

"Thank you, D.C., you've been great! Thank you, America!"

The sidewalks were filled with people eager to witness the post-inaugural parade from the Capitol to the White House. Kids bundled up against the cold sat up high on their father's shoulders to get a better view. Old folks draped in heavy blankets sat up front in folding lawn chairs.

LAV-300 armored personnel carriers lumbered down the street, their six huge tires rolling slowly. Equipped with thermal sensors, computerized tracking devices, night vision, tear gas launchers, and other sophisticated riot apparatus, the all-black, amphibious vehicles were marvels of tactical urban warfare. "POLICE" in white reflective letters adorned the fronts and backs; machine gun turrets rotated around. Up on top, helmeted officers in flak vests and mirrored sunglasses waved to the spectators on both sides of the street, occasionally throwing Hershey's Kisses® and M&M's® to the frozen sidewalks. The kids scrambled to scoop up their treats.

Next up were contingents from the Army, Navy, Air Force, and Marines, along with brand new members of the fledgling Civilian National Security Force, all of them resplendent in their dress uniforms. They were joined by units of the Army

National Guard and Air National Guard from all 50 states, Puerto Rico, and the District of Columbia. Led by drummers and trumpeters, each branch marched in its own column. In unison, they played "The Battle Hymn of the Republic" set to a modern jazz arrangement, and "The Star-Spangled Banner."

♪♪ *"O say can you see, by the dawn's early light,"* ♪♫
♪♪ *"What so proudly we hailed, at the twilight's last gleaming ... "* ♪♫

Many of those seated in the crowd rose as the marchers went by, covering their hearts with their right hands in reverence, silently mouthing the lyrics.

♪♪ *"O say does that star-spangled banner yet wave ... "* ♪♫
♪♪ *"O'er the land of the free, and the home of the brave."* ♪♫

"Thank you for serving our country!" people yelled out to the steely faced service members marching past.

Bulldog X SWAT trucks glided along the route, flashing their brilliant red, white, and blue lights and blipping their powerful sirens. These imposing armored trucks, 10 feet high and 26 feet long, sported ballistic glass and multiple gun ports. With all their windows blacked out, they seemed driverless, as if by piloted by remote control.

The grand motorcade made its way in the middle of this impressive procession. The president's limousine, nicknamed "The Beast," was a gigantic, bombproof Cadillac with eight-inch thick military-grade armor plating on the doors and five-inch thick reinforced steel plate under the chassis to repel bomb blasts. The bodywork, a combination of hardened steel, aluminum, titanium, and ceramic, was designed to break up projectiles. The cabin featured a sealed-air recirculation system to protect against chemical attacks. Five-inch thick ballistic glass, night vision cameras, pump-action shotguns, and tear gas cannon gave it a bunker-like level of protection.

Heavily armed Secret Service agents walked alongside all 18 feet and eight tons of The Beast, accompanied by black SUVs and dozens of police motorcycles at either end. Two specially trained Secret Service agents chauffeured The Beast. In the back seat was the president and First Lady Priscilla, in a monotone brown outfit that matched her hair, elaborately made up with powder and paint. The thick glass and armor plating kept the interior hushed and isolated, cocooned from the outside. The spectators couldn't see much through those heavy windows. Still, the First Couple could wave at the crowds and speechify from within.

In a booming voice projected through loudspeakers mounted on The Beast, President King addressed the celebrants, many of whom were dancing on the sidewalks behind the barricades.

"My friends, we have come to change the tone in Washington. It's time for a new beginning. It's time for real leadership. We'll reach across party lines and break the gridlock. Together, we'll build our future and make America great again. Together, we'll become a better, stronger country. It's time for a change."

8

You Will Please Come with Us

Benson looked at all the papers piling up on his office desk. The campaign season and its laborious aftermath was finally over and it was time to get back to work. Somewhat dispirited, lacking his usual tenacity, for the last few weeks he had done just the minimum necessary to get through the workday. He stared at all his emails, not wanting to open any of them. It would probably take several hours to get through them all. His phone rang. He let it ring through into voicemail. He was suddenly overtaken by a panicky feeling of being confined, chained down in his office by all this work in front of him. He felt anxious, in need of escape.

Grabbing his suit jacket, he headed for the elevator and took a brisk walk outside. He stopped at a sandwich counter and went to a nearby park, enjoying the mild, early spring weather while he ate.

Before returning to his office, he entered the bank branch downstairs. Making his way to the front of the line, he handed a deposit slip and checks to the teller. She spent an inordinate amount of time tapping the keys on her terminal while he waited.

The teller held the checks up to the light and examined each one carefully.

"Sorry Mr. Benson, we can't deposit these checks. There doesn't seem to be anything wrong with the checks themselves;

there's some problem with your REAL ID. We can't access your account."

"There must be a mistake. Who do I talk to?"

"Not sure ... " She drummed her fingers on the counter. "Try the ATS call center."

"ATS?"

"Automated Targeting System. It's probably just a simple error, yes, I'm sure that's it. We've had *mucho* problems with their new system. Sorry, there's nothing we can do, but I'm sure they can resolve this. Have a nice day." She locked eyes with the next customer in line. "I can help whoever's next?" she called out.

Benson closed his office door and got on the phone.

"Welcome to your Department of Homeland Security," said a deep, professional announcer-style voice. "Prensa ocho para el español. Your call is important to us. Please stay on the line and a representative will be with you shortly."

The phone went dead silent.

Kay came by, peering at Benson through the glass walls of his office and pointing at her watch. He shook his head and motioned her to go away with repeated flicks of his hand. He would have to cover that glass with blinds or something. She continued looking in for a moment, watching him pace, and finally left.

Benson wasn't sure that his call was still active. Looking out his window, he held on for several minutes more until a pleasant singsong voice came on the line.

"Hello, you've reached ATS, a service of your Department of Homeland Security in collaboration with your FBI Terrorist Screening Center. My name is Rhonda, badge number 6377B. This call will be monitored for quality control purposes. Who am I speaking with today?"

"I'm sure you already know that on your screen."

"Naw, we don't have nothin' like that here, sir, you'd be surprised." She giggled. "Who am I speaking with, please?"

Rhonda wore a headset and a friendly smile. The warehouse space in which she worked was filled with hundreds of headset-clad clerks like herself sitting inside tiny low-rise cubicles as far as the eye could see. High above, suspended from the open metal beams of the roof structure, was the FBI-TSC logo with its blue and red stars superimposed on a globe of the world.

Benson had to give Rhonda his ID number and go through all the particulars before she would offer any help.

"Okay, so what the hell's going on? Why am I on a watch list?"

"I'm sorry, we are not allowed to confirm or deny the existence of a *watch list*, as you call it. Why do you feel you would you be in our TSDB?"

"TSDB? What the hell—"

"The Terrorist Screening Database, sir."

"Listen, Rhonda, how do I clear my name?"

"I'm sorry, we're not allowed to articulate further on that specific issue. Thank you for calling DHS. If there's anything further we can assist you with, please don't hesitate—"

"Rhonda, put your supervisor on the phone. Now."

The line went dead again, then music played; an old hit set to the accordion. A string of commercial advertisements ran uninterrupted. After yet another musical interlude a click came on the line and then a moment of silence.

"Excuse me, sir?" It was Rhonda. "Are you still on the line? I'm sorry, but my supervisor's either away from her desk or on the phone. I can take your name and number, Mr. —"

"You already have everything, Rhonda 6377B, so let's not go through this again. How can I see my file?"

"I'm sorry, sir, we don't disseminate those deliverables, but even if we did, it'd be classified. I never even seen them myself. You think after six years here, not including my family medical leave of absence, they'd at least—"

"What the hell am I supposed to do?"

"Well, you could leverage substantiation that might impact your innocence," Rhonda said, stumbling over the words, as though reading from a script.

"How do I prove I'm innocent when I don't know what I've done?" Benson struggled to control himself. He didn't want this Rhonda person hanging up on him or transferring him to telephone limbo.

"Well, if we open a conversation after this point in time, you'll be notified when we initialize your Preliminary Pre-Investigation."

"And that will be," Benson said, "when, exactly?"

"I'm sorry, it's impermissible to articulate further in reference to controlled data."

"What the hell am I supposed to do in the meantime?"

"Okay, look, sir, there's a backlog of 8.1 million names in the register. This might take a while, okay? In the meantime, just carry on like normal pending final disposition. You don't have to do anything right now. Please be patient until we initialize your PPI *if* the department decides—"

"My what?"

"Preliminary Pre-Investigation, like I already said. If you wanna check on your status, we're open from 0930 to 1100 hours and from 1400 to 1500 weekdays except for State holidays and inservice days and—"

"But if there's a problem with my ID I could lose my employment authorization. I wouldn't have permission to drive, take a train, or fly. Already, I can't access my bank account. How am I supposed to live?"

"Hey, I'm just doin' my job, you know?"

There was a moment's awkward silence, and then, as pleasant as ever, she said, "Now you have a nice day."

Sirens wailing, a squad car and armored SWAT vans raced down a quiet suburban street, screeching to a halt at a stately house in an affluent Virginia neighborhood. Paramilitary

police clad in camouflage assault uniforms, reinforced body
armor, and combat helmets streamed out of the vans, their
snub-nosed M4A1 carbines at the ready. They took up their
positions on the front lawn and covered the entrance. The film
crew from the reality television show "*COPS*" scrambled to
set up their equipment. Once the cameras starting rolling and
the sound check was completed, the lead camerawoman gave
the thumbs-up.

Two officers in long black coats exited the squad car.
Strolling up the front walk, looking back to ensure that all was
ready, one of them banged hard on the door with a meaty fist,
rattling the sidelight windows. The police hunkered down on
the lawn, training their weapons on the door.

Benson opened his front door a crack. He peered out at the
curious scene before him. Petey howled furiously, launching
into a series of piercing barks echoing through the house.

"You are Thomas Benson?" one of the officers shouted
above the din, his question barely intelligible.

Benson took a long moment to observe these officers
and their contingent spread out before him. Judging from
their uniforms, gear, and general demeanor, it appeared that
they anticipated some resistance. This veritable strike force
couldn't have been assembled just to apprehend jaywalkers
or public littering scofflaws.

One of the officers, whom Benson took to be the man in
charge, held up an official-looking shiny badge, but put it
away hastily, an annoying formality with which he plainly
did not care to be bothered.

"You are Thomas Benson?"

Having to shout over Petey angered the officer, but Benson
did nothing to hush Petey's powerful barking. The officer
repeated his question a third time, yelling at the top of his
voice, looking back at the television cameras.

Benson gazed impassively at the officer and then commanded the dog to sit. Petey growled, deep and rumbling,

reluctantly sitting back on his haunches, against his better judgement, as it were.

"Your identification, please," Benson said. He motioned the officer to hold up the badge again so that he could properly inspect it. Looking behind him first, the officer begrudgingly produced his identification in its black leather case.

"Take it out of the wallet," Benson said.

The department and its division were unfamiliar to Benson. These cops were not from the local Alexandria police department. He looked at the officer in his black coat in silence. He directed a cold gaze at the other officer; judging from his white shirt, probably a lieutenant eager to prove his mettle in the presence of his superior. The young men spread out on his lawn squinted through their rifle's sights.

"I was just on my way to work."

"We need to ask a few questions first."

"Where's your warrant?"

Reaching into his coat, the officer shoved a paper into Benson's hand. It looked just like any standard business letter, ending with "Your cooperation in this sensitive matter is greatly appreciated," signed by one Duke Johnson II, Deputy Vice Director, Special Investigations Directorate, Department of Homeland Security.

"What the hell's this?" Benson crumpled it and threw it to the floor. "That isn't a proper warrant."

"It's a National Security Letter—kind of like a warrant. Lieutenant Millstone, you will record that we were granted permission to search the premises."

"Yes, Commander."

"I do not grant permission to search," Benson said, flatly, to no one.

The lieutenant signaled the men behind him. Charging into the house, they brushed Benson aside. Some headed upstairs and some made for the basement; others rushed through the ground-floor rooms.

Petey growled, low and menacing. Petey had been Benson's loyal companion for many years. Benson often took him to visit the children's hospital and the nursing home, wearing his special, little blue service dog vest. The patients and residents would kiss and hug him, and he would bring them some joy in the way only a dog can.

Working industriously inside the house, the police yelled to each other, carting items up and down the stairs, taking them outside. Benson's electronics gear, a sophisticated collection of audio and communications equipment he had assembled with pride over the years, was ripped from the walls and carried right past him, the electrical cords and wires dangling free.

"Mr. Benson," said the commander, "you have any hidden safes here? Any weapons or cash?"

Benson gazed at the commander with a stony face.

"Raise your arms for me, please."

The commander felt under Benson's arms, then patted down along his torso.

A harsh, guttural growl emerged from Petey, low and steady and rumbling deeply. His body stiffened and his hair stood on end.

The commander ran a hand down Benson's chest and felt the inside pockets of his jacket, pulling out a wallet and phone, which he dropped onto the floor. He squeezed the jacket's front pockets and removed keys and some coins, tossing them on the floor, too. Coming in closer, he reached around to Benson's shoulder blades and felt down his back. He grabbed Benson's buttocks, feeling the back pockets, and then patted and squeezed the front pants pockets, one at a time. He cupped Benson's groin, making him wince.

Petey gave a bloodcurdling snarl. The commander backed up a step, his attention riveted on the dog. Petey bared his fangs and leaped, knocking the man hard onto his back. Jumping on top of the commander, he tugged at his black coat, ripping it to pieces, as if possessed.

"Petey, stop," Benson said, but only halfheartedly.

Nevertheless, Petey stopped to look at Benson. The commander seized the brief respite, swiftly unholstering his gun and bringing the muzzle to Petey's belly. A deafening explosion ricocheted through the house. Petey's guts were sprayed over the floor and walls. The police came running madly down the stairs and up from the basement.

"You killed my dog." Benson balled his hands into clenched fists. "You shot my dog, you son of a bitch!"

The commander got to his feet clumsily, training his gun all the while at Benson, who looked as if he might himself leap and attack. At length, apparently satisfied that Benson wasn't going to tackle him, he looked down at his tattered coat, examining the multiple rips with great concern.

"Mr. Benson—"

The commander took a deep breath. He held up his shredded belt with dismay.

"You can collect your things on the floor and then you will please come with us. We'll explain on the way."

Hustling him to the squad car and roughly pushing his head down to fit inside, they shoved him in and slammed the door shut. The sides of the car displayed the new police motto, "For Your Own Protection." The rear and side windows were blacked out. The flat vinyl rear seat was torn in places, stained, and reeked of disinfectant. A metal grid in front of a thick plate window partitioned the front seat from the back. Up front were Lieutenant Millstone and the commander, whose name Benson had forgotten. An armored SWAT van drove in front, another following exceedingly closely, its powerful headlights shining directly into the rear seat.

The lieutenant occasionally removed the car's police radio handset and said something into it, but Benson couldn't make out any of the words.

"Hey! Aren't you going to tell my wife where I am?" Benson yelled, banging on the partition. "Where're we going? Do you hear me? Hello?"

The cops paid him no attention. Benson turned around to look behind but could see nothing, the looming headlights of the rear van dominating his sight with its blinding glare.

The procession of vehicles continued along the highway, traveling in the empty special express lane reserved for official use. The commuter lane to their right was snarled with traffic. Over the roadway there appeared a colorful threat-level meter. "Today's Threat Level Is Orange," said a sign below the meter in glowing letters. "Report Suspicious Items or Activities to the Authorities." Cameras on either end of the sign were trained on the highway.

The procession arrived in front of three bleak, imposing concrete buildings. The street was strangely deserted. Watchtowers were set high on the corners of each building. Snipers patrolled the labyrinth of catwalks connecting the complex. The vehicles pulled up to the entrance, blocked with a heavy sliding gate on which was written "No Photography/Prohibido Fotografiar."

The van driver in front swiped a card and the creaky gears pulled the gate open. The squad car and the two vans drove past a glass booth holding a listless guard. He watched them pass into the courtyard. Etched into the walls of the building in front was "Honor Bound to Defend Freedom." A prominent symbol some 50 feet overhead depicted a pyramid with an open eye at the top. Light shone from the eye onto a globe of the world. "Scientia est Potentia" was inscribed at the base of the pyramid.

Everyone got out but Benson. The police moved to the rear of the car and opened his door. The two officers in their long black coats walked in front, a few of the paramilitary police following closely behind. Entering one of the buildings, they headed swiftly down a long corridor, passing an official portrait of President King mounted on the wall. He wore a faint, lopsided smile, a flag hanging limply behind him. Descending a flight of winding steel stairs to the basement, the clack of their heels echoed off the concrete block walls. The place smelled of fresh cement and new paint.

Benson emptied his pockets of his wallet, keys, phone, coins, watch, and pen, depositing them into a gray plastic bin. He removed his belt and put it into the bin. A bored police sergeant placed the bin on a shelf holding other such containers. Benson stood in front of a painted cement wall with heights marked in one-inch increments for a series of mugshots, facing in one direction and then the other.

The sergeant led Benson to a room for fingerprinting and body scanning. When they were done, he pushed some forms across a counter for Benson's signature.

Benson started to read the fine print but quickly gave up.

"What's all this?"

"Jus' sign 'em," the sergeant said, grumbling under his breath, "asshole."

9

Providing the Appropriate Tools

I<small>T WAS JUST AFTER</small> K<small>ING TOOK OFFICE</small> that a skinny young man wearing a backpack opened the heavy glass door to a shopping mall near D.C. His backpack was so large that he was having difficulty negotiating the entrance. Seeing him struggling, a woman ran out in front and opened the door wide for him. He said nothing and entered the mall.

Spinning around, he took in the multitude of shops with their brightly colored signs advertising deep discounts and special offers. It was the President's Day weekend holiday in February, one of the biggest sales events of the year. People strolled past the stores weighed down with shopping bags. Festive music drifting from the second floor caught the young man's attention. A nonstop stream of shoppers went up and down the escalators.

He lumbered past a kiosk and paused again to have a look around. The place was absolutely bustling. A personable young salesgirl in a checked apron suddenly appeared, startling him.

"Hi, I'm Jasmine, would you like to try one of our truffles? They make great gifts; we can even spell the name of the recipient, one letter on each chocolate. Everyone loves chocolate, don't you?"

"I am not. I am not feel my hungry at this time."

The heavy pack dug painfully into his spindly shoulders. With a jump, he hiked up his load and moved a short distance away to a play area in a central concourse jammed with parents and toddlers. He removed his pack and sat on a bench, watching the youngsters play on the climbing structures, their mothers and fathers hovering over them. He stared out into space. A few of the mothers shot him a sharp glance before returning to their tykes.

Jasmine had watched him leave her kiosk and followed him to the play area, careful to stay just out of sight. Was she being stupid? The mall was always full of strange people, and it wasn't right to discriminate. She'd seen plenty of other foreigners acting oddly, but so what? They just weren't acclimated to their new country, that was all. They had different customs, different mannerisms. This one looked like he was from Afghanistan or Iraq or someplace far away like that. That shouldn't make any difference, should it? After all, many of her American customers had bizarre piercings and rings and tattoos all over their bodies and they were perfectly normal. It wasn't right to judge by appearance. Maybe this poor guy was confused or upset. Maybe he was just plain tired.

Even so, the look in his eyes wasn't right. It gave her an uneasy feeling. She watched him sitting on the bench, gaping at the children playing. After deliberating awhile, she finally pulled out her phone and dialed 1-800-TIPS.

A voice came on the line.

"Hello, I wanna report a suspicious item and a socially dangerous person. So this guy, he's got a big backpack and he seems sort of crazy, so I just thought maybe it's, like, I don't know, a bomb or something? It sounds crazy, right? Hello? Anyone there?"

The phone went silent, long enough for Jasmine to seriously consider hanging up and trying again. Then a recording came on.

"Thank you for calling 1-800-TIPS, a public service of your Department of Homeland Security. All operators are currently busy serving other customers. Your call is important to us and will be answered in the order received."

Jasmine kept watching the man. He was gawking at the young mothers, a bewildered look on his face. He wiped his nose on his sleeve. She became convinced that he was clearly not normal and had no business here, becoming increasingly anxious while waiting for her call to be taken.

"We are presently experiencing an unusually high call volume. For faster service, please visit us on the World Wide Web, at www.dhs.gov. Otherwise, please stay on the line, and your call will be answered in the order received."

The young man rummaged through his pack. He got down on the floor on his knees. He silently mouthed something and gazed upward.

"Hello, this is 1-800-TIPS, a public service of your Department of Homeland Security, my name is Lateshia, ID 878-61-B264, this call is being recorded, what is your name and ID number, please?"

"What's the difference? We got an emergency here!"

Again, the phone went silent, and then clicked.

"I'm sorry," Lateshia said. "We are presently experiencing technical difficulties. Your call is very important to us. Can I put you on hold for a minute?"

The explosion ripped through the concourse several hundred feet in every direction. People were knocked violently to the hard tile floors and smacked against the walls, coming to lie amid the glass shards and wreckage. Razor blades and nails slashed through their flesh.

Farther out in the mall, panicked shoppers fled for their lives, scrambling to get outside, vainly screaming above the pandemonium to reach their families and friends. A few brave souls bucked the fleeing crowds, running back inside to help the survivors writhing on the floor. Sirens blared in the distance.

The reporters took their seats in the press briefing room. The flags off to the side hung half-mast. On the lectern, below the DHS logo, appeared its new signature slogan: "Only YOU

Can Prevent Terrorism." Brawny agents in dark suits stood on either side of the podium.

Secretary Cherkov made his entrance, plopping down some papers. Gaunt, with slumping shoulders and a small paunch, he had an unhealthy, cadaverous look about him, with sunken eyes, bony cheeks and strands of hair plastered in an unconvincing sheet over his head. A longtime running enthusiast, he was often photographed jogging with the president, a pack of Secret Service agents trailing just behind.

He fussed with his half-eye reading glasses before removing them from his nose entirely, letting them dangle from their cord around his neck. A few reporters stood, waving their hands in the air, hoping to be the first to be granted permission to ask questions.

He looked up at the reporters, cleared his throat, and put his glasses back on as he read in wooden tones from his prepared statement.

"The department has issued a preliminary finding." He cleared his throat again, intermittently looking at the reporters over the top of his glasses as he spoke. "Our fact-finding determination is still ongoing, however, we are prepared to say at this time that this mall tragedy is a cowardly act. We believe this may not have been a 'lone-wolf' terrorist incident, but may have been part of a vast network of sleeper cells hidden somewhere in the Homeland. We plan to hunt these vermin down and bring them to justice. There is no hole these animals can crawl into that we can't also crawl into."

Secretary Cherkov looked up from his papers and peered at the gathering over his reading glasses. The cameras recorded every tic of his face, everything he uttered, and it made him jumpy. He wasn't normally like this. He had temporarily left a high-paying job as the CEO of a prominent aviation security company with lucrative State contracts to head DHS. Normally relaxed and forthright at department meetings and even cabinet sessions, the intense scrutiny here put him on edge. Highly self-critical, he had stopped watching his own performances on the news.

"We can't confirm anything of a specific nature at this particular timeframe, but it looks like it—it may have involved a, um, a robust effort targeting killer deliverables."

He instantly regretted uttering such gibberish. He never used to speak like this, but everyone around him spoke in jargon and acronyms, and it was rubbing off. Mrs. Cherkov had told him many times that he should stop trying to impress people with big, fancy words. It only made him look more foolish, she had said.

He shuffled through his papers, during which there was a long, strained silence in the briefing room, until, at last, he found what he was looking for.

"Oh, and in order to, uh, maximize interactive capabilities, the president has issued Executive Order 16058 to facilitate synergies re security optimization. This order is designed to help roadblock similar, unfortunate episodes moving forward."

"Mr. Secretary! Mr. Secretary!"

"Yes, you over there."

The secretary pointed to a woman standing in a field of reporters. Her face was somehow familiar although he couldn't quite recall the name. Denise, Desiree, Denisha, something like that. The White House chief of staff had told him to avoid calling upon a reporter by name unless he was quite sure. It would avoid an embarrassing gaffe that would be played endlessly over the Internet. The secretary made a mental note to make all these reporters wear name tags next time.

"Mr. Secretary, what should ordinary people do in another attack, and like, what if it's bioterrorism?"

Secretary Cherkov blinked and fidgeted. He removed his reading glasses and then put them on again. He scanned his notes but there was nothing there of any help. This wasn't really his area. He wished to God that they would ask something about aviation security for a change. For the next briefing, maybe the questions could be submitted in advance, too.

"Stock up on plastic sheet and duct tape. Next question? Yes, you over there."

President King took the ceremonial seat before two thick documents, labeled *Volume One* and *Volume Two*, both impressively bound in black leather, the paper edges covered in gold leaf, the official seals of the Office of the President and the Central Intelligence Agency embossed in their padded covers. The desk at which he sat was decorated with a "Protecting The Homeland™" banner and the presidential seal. A giant flag hung in the background. With ceremonial signing pen in hand, he looked to his left and right, politely acknowledging the senators and representatives behind him. They stood stiffly with fixed smiles while the photographers clicked away.

King held the pen aloft for all to admire.

"My friends, today I'm proudly signing into law The USA PATRIOT Enabling Act."

He wore a triumphant smile.

"This will be sort of a roadmap going forward."

With the mall attack still painfully fresh, the legislation had met with only halfhearted opposition. By pitching it as just a technical update of existing law, he was able to push it through rather swiftly. It demonstrated real leadership and working together, just as he'd promised in the campaign.

"This new law will help unite and strengthen America by providing the appropriate tools required for intercepting and obstructing terrorism," King read from a statement before him. "In other words," he said, looking up, "our police, intelligence and military communities are gonna be tracking the terrorists. We're gonna watch what they say, where they go, who they meet. We're gonna intercept their communications and obstruct their plans. We're gonna come down hard on them before they cause trouble."

King scrawled his hallmark illegible signature on the inside covers of *Volume One* and *Volume Two*, stamped "SECRET."

"This terrible mall bombing holocaust, where hundreds of decent, law-abiding Americans suffered a cruel death in a blazing inferno, cut down by razor blades and nails, among them innocent young mothers and their little girls and boys playing in the courtyard, people out buying things and supporting the economy, paying their taxes, minding their own business—we dedicate USA-PEA to their sacred memory. Our hearts go out in prayer to them. Let's now take a couple seconds to reflect in silence."

He bowed his head for a moment.

"Having these new tools could help thwart terrorists before they even get started, and just because we're providing these special tools to our protection communities doesn't mean we're gonna just use them indiscriminately. There will be strong oversight within the executive branch. The proceedings of the secret court authorized by the Act will be periodically reviewed by select members of Congress in private committee. 'Judicious' is the word we're using—there'll be judicious oversight and review."

He set his pen down and gazed at his signature on the landmark statute, his first major achievement in office.

Breaking the uncomfortable silence, a white-haired senior statesman unclenched his transfixed smile. Sporting flag pins on both lapels of a navy suit hanging limply from his bony frame, he launched into an unsolicited commentary.

"Americans, why, they oughta feel proud of us for the remarkable speed we showed by, ah-h, passing all this classified legislation." He beamed, baring a mouthful of unnaturally perfect, starkly white teeth. "This 2,409-page bill—it hasn't even all come back from the printer, but it's already law."

The president congratulated each of the dignitaries by warmly shaking their hands and even hugging some of the more attractive ones.

Make eye contact; keep it moving. It could make an audience of thousands feel as if they were personally connected to the speaker. President King stood on the podium looking out upon the multitude of cheering admirers, acknowledging them with waves and smiles, fixing his attention on particular people in the middle distance and then directing his gaze at those in the foreground. A gigantic movie screen above the stage followed his movements, capturing everything, framing his face in close-up. Now and then he pointed at someone and grinned while nodding, as if they were sharing between themselves something lighthearted and private. He silently clapped as he moved around the stage, as though he was congratulating the audience for something wonderful they had done.

Red, white, and blue banners were draped around the stage, emblazoned with "Celebrate America National Tour™" and a promotional website, CelebrateAmerica.biz, where fans could buy merchandise and hand-signed souvenirs.

Secret Service agents positioned themselves at the corners of the stage, clasping their hands in front of them, their eyes constantly moving from behind dark sunglasses. Exceptionally large men unaccustomed to the confining fit of their dark suits, they shifted on their feet and squirmed.

King held up his hand and the crowd quieted. He graciously thanked the local dignitaries present, astonishing them with detailed praise for particular accomplishments each had pulled off over the last year. Adopting a thoughtful expression, he paused, and then read his speech as it scrolled slowly down the hidden teleprompters. His amplified voice boomed throughout the coliseum.

The speech was a rousing history of the Republic, from its revolutionary founding to the persistent threat of insurrection even today. The movie screen filled with gorgeous panoramas of sacred, legendary battlegrounds; of doting, model-like parents preparing their adorable, cooperative children for school in the morning; of weary soldiers marching against lush sunset backdrops. The accompanying soundtrack provoked awe and lumps in the throat.

"Freedom is never more than one generation from extinction," King said, coming to the end of his speech.

He looked out upon the audience with grim resolve.

"With the distance of history, the questions will be narrowed and few."

He pointed to the audience.

"Did this generation of Americans take the threat seriously," he said, his voice breaking with emotion, "and did we do what it takes to defeat that threat?"

He put his hands on his hips, a fleeting but intent gaze fixed on random individuals as his eyes swept across the crowd. Their passions powerfully stirred, the multitude leapt to their feet in jubilation.

"King! King! King! King!"

With the wild crowd chanting and dancing, King raised his arms in triumph.

"Celebrate America! A stronger America begins at home!"

He repeatedly punched his fist into the air for emphasis.

"It's morning again in America! A thousand points a' light! Putting people first! Workin' together! Freedom's on the march! Win the future! Reporting for duty! Hope's on the way! Yes, we can! Country first!"

"King! King! King!" roared the audience.

"Thank you, New Mexico! You are indeed the Land of Enchantment."

• • •

Hundreds of analysts wearing clip-on badges and head-sets sat before banks of monitors located in a massive office complex. A former warehouse, the newly converted command center's open-beamed ceiling soared dramatically. The second and third floor catwalks led to offices framed in floor-to-ceiling windows, out of which the supervisors and assistant supervisors, managers and assistant managers, and directors and assistant directors could observe the worker bees in the dimly lit work gallery below.

Video walls surrounding the work gallery were grouped by type. One group featured local and national newscasts, another focused on talk-show podcasts; still others monitored morning television programs and local police reports. The largest video wall was for the Incident Map, a satellite view of geographic sectors that could be zoomed in and out, filled with blinking icons in different colors representing the locations of "Terrorism Events and Other Suspicious Activity," according to the map's legend.

Dominating the central wall was a circular logo of white lightning bolts radiating from the center of a dark pyramid set on a blue background, framed by a circle of white stars. "Scientia est Potentia" was inscribed on the bottom of the dark blue ring surrounding the logo. "Driftnet Fusion Center 86" curved around the upper half. These centers had sprung into operation almost overnight. Here, magazine subscriptions, travel and telephone records, print and electronic book purchases, social networking site transcripts, emails, judicial records, website browsing histories, and procedures from the National Medical Databank were linked to a central database for threat analysis.

Despite the initial excitement, monitoring the routine activities of the local population had turned out to be exceedingly monotonous. Listening in on random telephone conversations could take hours each day and was generally boring work. Reading all the texts and emails proved far too tedious for the analysts to wade through over a work shift of seven long hours, including union-mandated breaks and lunch. With few exceptions, the entries on Facebook, Twitter, and the other social networking sites were deathly dull, filled with blurry pictures and cryptic accounts of people revealing what they had for breakfast and the movies and TV shows they had seen recently, along with inane comments from their friends and followers. Who cared? Even the people for whom they were ostensibly posted weren't much interested. To the analysts' profound disappointment, the titillation factor was just about zero.

These intelligence analysts, most of whom were quite new on the job, were told only to watch for "suspicious things." The *Analyst's Desktop Binder* helpfully supplied 377 keywords in 14 categories ranging from Domestic Infrastructure Security to Weather Emergency. Among the keywords to be on the lookout for were "assassination," "attack," "Taliban," "nuke," "anthrax," "bomb," "narcotics," "enriched," "IED," "jihad," and even the seemingly innocuous "Iran," "exercise," and "DHS." It further specified that analysts should catalog media reports "reflecting adversely" on DHS or the federal government, as broadly defined. Such suspicious things, they were told in training, might indicate a terrorist plot in the works.

After the first few months of operations in Driftnet Fusion Center 86, no one had stumbled across any such plots, eager though they were to find them. Sadly, it seemed that they probably never would.

To help while away the time, the analysts set up a betting pool on the most lewd conversations they came across, whether originating by voice, text, or online, voting for the winners in the staff lounge where they took their lunch every day at 11:30 a.m., sharp. The supervisors, managers, and directors stayed in their offices most of the time doing email and reading, trying to keep up with the latest issues of *Intelligence Today*, *CIA World Intelligence Review*, *Daily Intelligence Summary*, *Weekly Warning Forecast*, *NCTC Terrorism Dispatch*, *IC Terrorist Threat Assessment*, and a vast catalog of publications from hundreds of agencies.

One day, two analysts peered at a monitor, thrilled by what they saw. It was exceptional to turn up something that looked even remotely suspicious.

"Dude, check out the entry on this blog," Carlos said to his colleague, Rusty. "Says here, 'I'd nuke those terrorist assholes myself, mass assassination or like poison their narcotics with anthrax.' Is that messed or what? There's also stuff here mentioning jihad, terrorist attack, and Taliban. Those are the magic words, my man. Let's run it through the dictionary, link their identities in GUARDIAN with something on the voice-traffic analyzer, and we'll forward it to NSA and our FBI terrorism unit. Maybe we'll get a bonus for this one."

"Yeah, I think I saw it yesterday, but I wasn't sure what to do. I got these transcripts with words like "narcotics" and "nukes" and "prepping," plus emails and a tip that was called in, but I dunno, Carlos, the whole thing looks sketch, for sure, but Guardian's a lotta trouble, you know that. It takes, like, days, to go through it, you gotta get special FBI clearance, you gotta download all the service packs ... "

Rusty shook his head doubtfully.

"I don't know if it's worth the trouble. How about we just send them everything we have and let *them* figure it out? And anyways, that's their job, not ours."

10

Show Him His Room

Upon booking, Benson was escorted to a basement interrogation room by a gloomy policeman. The small room of unfinished concrete block walls was furnished with a scarred, bare-metal desk and a few folding metal chairs. On one of the chairs sat Lieutenant Millstone. His boss, the commander, stood near the desk, his shredded coat draped over the back of a chair.

"Please, have a seat, Mr. Benson."

After all that had happened, Lieutenant Millstone was astonishingly friendly, as though they had never met.

"Can I get you some coffee?"

Benson stared into his eyes. It unnerved the lieutenant and he looked away. He rose and left the room without a word.

"Mr. Benson," said the commander, "do you know why you're here?"

Benson sighed.

"I thought you would tell *me*."

"Please, have a seat. I'm sure we can get this all straightened out before too long—with a little cooperation."

Lieutenant Millstone returned, setting down a white foam cup of coffee on the desk before Benson. Next to it he placed a pink packet of artificial sugar and a white plastic container of imitation cream.

"I'm Commander Kip Clancy. You can just call me Kip, and this is Lieutenant Michael Millstone. Tom, do you know why you're here?"

"Yes, we've already been formally introduced—back at my house, wasn't it? Kip—that short for Kipling, I take it? You can just call me *Mr. Benson*. How are you, Kipling? Things are well with you? Another routine day of armed robbery and felony animal cruelty?"

"I go by the nickname—if you don't mind," said Clancy, slightly ruffled. "Mr. Benson, you do realize the Homeland is at war, don't you? The old rules don't apply. There is a time for war and a time for peace, with different laws for each. And this is a time of war."

"That's absurd, ridiculous. I won't say anything without proper counsel. I'm an American—I have my rights."

He looked around at the tiny room with its harsh, softly buzzing lights.

"What is this place?" Benson shouted. "Why am I here?"

"You hear that?" Lieutenant Millstone sniggered. "He has rights!" Millstone shook his head and slapped his hand on the desk, heartily amused. "Terrorists have no freakin' rights."

Commander Clancy barely suppressed a snicker himself. He folded his hands on the desk and leaned forward.

"'Unlawful Enemy Combatants,' Mr. Benson, come under different legal jurisdiction."

"Enemy combatant? What the hell are you talking about? No, you've got the wrong man."

"It's all duly reviewed and official," Lieutenant Millstone said, opening a thick folder filled with loose papers. He went to the first document and spread it out on the desk. Locating the relevant paragraph with his index finger, Millstone read haltingly.

"'An Unlawful Enemy Combatant is a person who has engaged in hostilities or who has purposefully and materially supported hostilities against the United States who is not a Lawful Enemy Combatant.' You see?"

"I do not see."

"Read the rest," Clancy said.

"Okay ... yeah. Here it is ... 'Be it known that Mr. Thomas David Benson has been determined to be an Unlawful Enemy Combatant, as defined in section 3930-2, §948(a) of the Military Commissions Act of 2006, as amended, by the Combatant Status Review Tribunal established under the authority of the Secretary of Defense.'"

Commander Clancy studied Benson's face during Millstone's little recital. He had taken a class in human "affect" at the academy, a one-day course in the interpretation of emotional states observed under duress. The instructor had said that one could learn to read facial expressions and look for "tells" during interrogations. With this knowledge, the instructor claimed, one could also learn to be a pretty fair poker player, too.

Clancy eyed Benson with a faint smirk.

"Would you like to tell us *now* why you're here?"

Benson sat in his chair, speechless.

"Mr. Benson," Commander Clancy said in a low voice, "we got us evidence of a conspiracy."

He gazed directly into Benson's eyes, apparently looking for his *tell*.

"You have business and financial transactions with Saudi Arabia, and possibly Iran," added Lieutenant Millstone, "and maybe Syria or Iraq. There could be a violation here of the Espionage Act, criminalizing distribution of confidential national security information."

"My bank has clients in the Mideast—"

"Looks like you subscribe to some *nasty* weapons periodicals. We got a tip from our informant, let's see here ... " Millstone said, rummaging through a pile of documents. "*Guns and Ammo* magazine."

He looked at Benson with a damning expression.

"I hunt and fish. So what?"

"And what exactly do you hunt with assault-style rifles?" Clancy said, pointing his finger at Benson. "C'mon now, let's get real. Your mail carrier reported you get strange things, fringe magazines, letters from suspect organizations—"

"It's junk mail!"

"Junk mail, you say."

Clancy held up a letter contained within an opened envelope, gripping it by the corner with tweezers. He looked at Benson with a snide expression. The envelope bore a red crescent.

"Here's one the Residential Waste Compliance Engineer fished out of your recycling bins. It appears to be a solicitation addressed personally to you from some kind of Muslim charity, it looks like. How do *you* just happen to be on their mailing list? Those things are fronts."

"Fronts, you say. Maybe that's why it was in the recycling bin."

"The Utilities Inspector in your neighborhood reported unusual lines and hookups to your cable and utilities," Clancy said, rummaging through the documents. "We found a bunch of electronics and communications gear in your house, way more than average. So who were you communicating with, Mr. Benson?"

"No one! I mean, a lot of people. I like electronics."

Lieutenant Millstone pored through reports stamped with the DHS blue eagle seal and surveillance photographs stamped with the National Geospatial Intelligence Agency logo strewn all over the desk. Benson glanced at some of them from upside down. There were pictures of him on his boat, fishing on the lakes, and a few of the family relaxing in the backyard. Jane was somehow photographed taking a bath from outside their second floor window, stirring his anger. There was a picture of his late dog, the sight of which aroused fresh pangs of grief. There were satellite views of his house and roadside surveillance cam shots of his car with the date, time, and location in yellow type printed in the corner. He thought he recognized his likeness from a grainy picture of a man in a coffee shop that he often frequented on his way to work. There was one of him and Jane dining at La Grande Maison, a romantic restaurant they'd enjoyed a month or two before. There were even some photographs of Daniel coming and going on the school bus.

"Neighbors report seeing lights on late every night," said Commander Clancy, examining a report.

"It's the Mideast time zone, I already told you."

"Talking to shady friends overseas?" Lieutenant Millstone said. "Your Internet, chat group, and email transcripts reveal an abnormal interest in jihad, terrorist attack, Taliban, you know, those kinds of things. We also recorded conversations containing words like "narcotics" and "nukes" and "anthrax" and even "prepping." Federal law outlaws 'cyber bullying' —any electronic communication with the intent to coerce, intimidate, harass, or cause emotional distress—and this sure as hell looks like something that could distress someone."

Clancy again examined Benson closely for some kind of response, perhaps the revealing *tell* for which he was still waiting.

Benson merely shrugged.

"I discuss current events with friends all over the world— not 'shady' friends."

"Friends!" Clancy said. "Interesting that you should mention that. It so happens that one of your Friends on Facebook is a Friend of an alleged domestic insurgent, and he, by the way—this domestic insurgent—is Friends with other alleged sleeper-cell terrorists."

Millstone skimmed through a pamphlet called *FBI Communities Against Terrorism: Potential Indicators of Terrorist Activities Related to Internet Cafes*. "Be part of the solution," it said. "Preventing terrorism is a community effort. If something seems wrong, notify law enforcement authorities. Call 888-705-JRIC and mention 'Tripwire.'" The pamphlet had hand-scribbled notes on the margins.

"Watch for people who 'Are overly concerned about privacy, attempts to shield the screen from view of others,'" Millstone read aloud from the pamphlet. "'Acts nervous or suspicious.' 'Always pays cash.' 'Travels illogical distance to use Internet café.'"

"It's on my way to work."

"You were observed doing all those things, Mr. Benson," Clancy said, "not just once, but many times. You always pay cash at this coffee shop, too. You go on the Internet there, I'll bet to avoid tracking, am I right? That's certainly suspicious. Your behavior-pattern threat analysis is anomalous."

Clancy circled a small graph on his report with a red pencil, and put a check mark next to another chart.

"No, sure doesn't look good."

"You're in deep trouble, Mr. Benson," Millstone said, "but we're here to help."

Millstone opened a document stamped with the official seal of the Office of the Secretary of Defense.

"We also got us a probable violation of Section 810 of the PATRIOT Act, Mr. Benson. Says on this complaint here you gave 'expert advice or assistance derived from scientific, technical, or other specialized knowledge,' according to the official language right here—and your expert assistance later appeared on other websites linked to your so-called client's websites. When we clicked through enough of those links, we found sites with violent, anti-American remarks. Because those websites advocate extremism, you broke the PATRIOT Act's 18 USC §2339A, Providing Material Support to Terrorists."

Benson stared at him.

"Are you nuts? My job is to provide 'expert assistance.' That's why the bank employs me, fool. I don't have to say anything to you. I have the right to see the evidence for myself."

Lieutenant Millstone shook his head. It was clear that Benson still didn't get it.

"You don't got a right to see squat. Providing 'material support' to organizations on this secret list here is illegal."

"When this gets to court, my little friend, the jury will throw it out. My lawyer will eat your lunch. You'll face a civil rights violation for this."

Benson grabbed the secret list from Millstone and crumpled it, tossing it on the floor.

"The rules governing military tribunals are different, Mr. Benson," Commander Clancy said. "We can detain you indefinitely, in secret, away from the media. We can even use certain, ah, debriefing techniques if we have any plausible reason to believe it could save the lives of possibly thousands of people."

Millstone paced the room, getting all worked up.

"Civilian law is a circus. Ignorant juries let criminals go free every day. If you're one of those celebrities or a rich guy with a fancy lawyer, you get off."

"That's absolutely right," Clancy said. "The stakes are much higher today. New enemies, new tactics, Mr. Benson. We can't afford to have these lawyers getting people off when we already know they're guilty—that's why we don't try these cases in civilian courts. There will be no lawyers." He said *lawyers* with utter contempt.

"The people need to feel safe."

Benson picked up his foam coffee cup. He hadn't touched the vile liquid within. With a backhand toss, he splashed the coffee in the officer's faces. He crunched the empty cup and threw it at Clancy. The officers backed up in their chairs and looked down at their stained suits, their faces dripping.

"How does that make *you* feel?" Benson taunted. "Next time it will be hot."

Millstone was livid at this assault and mockery. His face instantly turned red; his body stiffened with outrage.

"You son of a bitch!"

Millstone lunged across the desk, trying to grab Benson, who neatly sidestepped out of the way. Benson looked down upon the sprawled Millstone with a smirk. The lieutenant became even more furious, shaking with anger. Commander Clancy held Millstone down on the desk until he regained control of himself. Millstone picked himself up and sat down with a defeated thump, glaring at Benson.

"Here's the deal," Clancy said, pointing at Benson. "You help us, you help the Homeland, we help *you*. Win-win."

"You still have to answer for my dog."

"We have discretion in these matters but you have to cooperate. We pull a few strings and you can walk."

"We can do this the easy way or the hard way," Millstone said, pushing some papers across the desk at Benson. "You choose. Sign this and we can move forward."

"What the hell is this?"

"It's a statement, you know, kind of like a confession."

Benson read the first paragraph. Standing up, he ripped the statement into little pieces and gathered them in his fist. He threw them in the air; the confetti fluttered down upon Millstone's head.

"I'm not signing anything. I want my lawyer."

"Mr. Benson," Commander Clancy said, in a patronizing tone, "why do you need a lawyer if you're not guilty?"

He leaned in to read Benson's face. Benson stared right back at him. With a sigh, he handed Benson a photograph.

"Okay, let's just go through a few simple questions and we'll call it a day, all right?"

It was a blurry picture shot from a surveillance camera. The subject appeared to be of average build with a graying mustache. He wore a gray suit. His face was partly in shadow.

"You know this man?"

"No."

"You work for him?"

"I said I don't know him."

"Where'd you meet? Company business or on your own time?"

Benson balled up the photo and threw it at Clancy's face. Startled, Clancy jumped back in his rickety folding chair and fell over.

"I don't know this creep."

Lieutenant Millstone helped Clancy off the floor. They looked at each other, mortified.

"Look, Mr. Benson," Clancy said, "if you don't cooperate we'll take that as strong evidence you're holding out. And so far, it looks like you're hiding something, concealing or falsifying critical evidence. That's a serious felony right there. So is making what might turn out later to be false statements to a federal officer or refusing to *fully* cooperate in a federal investigation—18 USC §1510, Obstruction of Justice. Your silence in this investigation is highly suspicious. You were arrested for a reason, right? So don't waste everyone's time—there's no sense trying to prove you're innocent."

"I don't have to prove a damn thing to anyone."

"Now that's not cooperation, is it?" Millstone said. "I said we could do this the easy way or the hard way. Looks like you made your choice."

"Okay, it's already 1300 on a Friday," Clancy said, studying his wristwatch, "and we're all tired. Let's start over on Monday, say, 0930?"

"See you Monday then—with my lawyer and reporters. I won't stand for this."

Benson immediately made his way to the door, but Clancy moved surprisingly fast to block the exit, holding his arms up.

"Oh, I get it," Clancy said. "Oops, we made a mistake!"

He looked at Millstone, suddenly bursting into laughter so intense that he started coughing uncontrollably, his eyes tearing.

"We got the wrong man!" he said, wiping his eyes with his hands. "You just walk outta here, tell your story to the *New York Times*, is that it?"

Commander Clancy shook his head in mock sadness, a mean smile on his face.

"No, I don't think so, no can do. You'll be our guest this weekend. Corporal!" he shouted outside the door. "Show him his room."

11

Tear Down Those Walls

THOUSANDS PACKED THE STANDS and crowded onto the college stadium field. Banners of red, white, and blue were draped across the top of the stage, emblazoned with "Reclaim the Dream National Tour™" and its website, ReclaimTheDream.us. Security agents in dark suits placed themselves conspicuously around the stage, standing ramrod straight with their hands clasped in front of them, eyeing the audience and speaking into wireless headsets. The throng had waited several hours already, and President King was starting 15 minutes late as well, as was his custom. He believed that anticipation made the party faithful even more eager and receptive.

At last, he strode confidently onto the stage, a wide and friendly smile on his face, waving and pointing to onlookers as he made his entrance. Gigantic, multifaceted movie screens on either side of the stage magnified his image a hundred times larger than life. The cameras followed him as he made his way.

He gripped the sides of the lectern and gazed leftward, then panned across to the right, taking in the whole of the crowd, who were made to feel as if he were looking at each of them personally. The band died down. He straightened up, a grave expression on his face, and paused, as if thinking how best to begin an address of the utmost importance. He removed the microphone from its holder and stepped out from the lectern to the edge of the stage. He looked down upon the people in the front row. He peered up into the bleachers.

"Thank you. Thank you."

His voice was greatly amplified, filling the stadium.

"Thank you, ah, North Dakota. The Flickertail State, right? You gotta love that."

He stepped back to receive applause and cheers.

"Our new administration is working hard to protect Americans from harm," he said, reading from the tele-prompters that had been carefully concealed at both ends of the stage. "Safety and security; that's our tag line. We're going to be the most focused in history on this, like a laser beam. We're hiring up in the national security industry and that'll boost the economy and put our young people back to work so they can start contributing to this country and pay their taxes."

The audience clapped enthusiastically.

"You know, there are those who would destroy our way of life and enslave us. They would have us suffer perpetual war. One of the terrorists believed to have carried out the Capitol attack was said to have hoped that that would be the beginning of the end of America as we know it. Now that's just plain crazy. But let's be clear—if we're going to defeat the enemy within, we'll need a new strategy. It's no good chasing the terrorists around *after* the crime's done; it's too late. See, you find where they're hiding and arrest them *before* they attack. If we don't act, the terrorists will go, 'Hey, you know, they're weak.' That would mean the terrorists have won—and no one wants that."

"King! King! King!" the crowd erupted.

"Listen, you have nothing to hide? Then you have nothing to worry about. The Constitution does not specifically say citizens have a right to privacy. Can't find it in there. You can't have 100 percent security and then have 100 percent privacy and zero inconvenience. There are some tradeoffs involved. And the Bill of Rights does not protect vicious killers; can't find that in there, either. So we have to get tough with those who would take down the Homeland. That's right, my friends, I'm not afraid to talk sedition. They're on the Internet talkin' defiance."

The crowd was getting whipped up.

"Trash talkin' our government, exposing us and our families to attack, promoting hatred and violence, recruiting radicals to their cause. Well, ideas have consequences, my friends, and bad ideas have bad consequences. In the ongoing battle for mindshare from an audience with a short attention span, our side has to come up with the best ideas, and we've got 'em; we're rockin' an' rollin'. National security, you know, we've gotta balance that with individual rights."

Spontaneous cheers broke out, leading to a standing ovation.

"And I'll tell you somethin' else. We can't have the police fussin' around, wasting time with approvals and warrants and arguing about who's in charge while the terrorists are runnin' around loose. We can't fight 'em with 1,300 separate intelligence agencies in 10,000 separate locations, each workin' their own territory—and that's a fact."

The teleprompters froze. Some people in the audience shouted, "Amen!" and "Hallelujah" during the pause. For a few tense seconds, King froze in place. He walked back to the center of the stage. By the time he got there, the teleprompters had begun scrolling again.

"That's not sharing. That's not workin' together. That's not cooperation. Listen up: we got the National Guard. We got the NSA. We got the CIA."

King looked out at the audience with an incredulous expression.

"We got the ATF, the FBI, the DEA, and the DIA."

He shook his head in disbelief, a wry smile on his face.

"We got the DHS, TSA, JTTF, ICE, state police, county and city police, and so many others we literally can't keep track of 'em all, much less control. Who's responsible for this mess?"

King paused dramatically. Someone in the front shouted, "We are!" but not loud enough for the microphones to pick it up.

"No one, that's who. No one's in charge, it's all fragmented, so we gotta merge 'em all into a unified Homeland National Security Administration."

King shook both fists in the air.

"Tear down those walls!" he cried out, in ringing tones.

The crowd rose to its feet as one.

"King! King! King!" they chanted.

King glowed, in this, his magic moment. He beamed at the officials and local dignitaries seated on the stage with him. He waved to the audience with supreme confidence, a faraway look in his eyes. At last the audience stopped chanting his name. As they began to seat themselves he removed his suit jacket and rolled up his sleeves. He loosened his tie.

Looking out at a sea of nodding heads and smiling faces, King leaned over the stage to touch hands with those in the first row. People got out of their seats and made their way over so that they might also shake the president's hand. Frantically shouting into their headsets at each other to do something, his security detail watched with deep suspicion anyone touching their man. This rally had been drawn together hurriedly, without the time required to properly interview "persons of interest." Too much movement in the stands would definitely increase the threat danger. Even though everyone had passed through full-body scanners and received a thorough patdown on the way in, it would be easy enough to smuggle in weapons anyway. They would have to warn him, in the bluntest terms, about never wading into a crowd of ordinary people again.

"Thank you, thank you for your support!"

King held up a hand, nodding slowly as he panned across the stadium, waiting patiently for the audience to quiet.

"And I'll tell you something else, my friends. We've got to secure our borders. History shows a country that can't control its borders can't last long. Under our new Secure Our Borders initiative, the border walls with Canada and Mexico will be built up and hardened. We'll hire 35,000 more Homeland Security guards to man the southern border as part of our Southern Border Fencing Strategy. Maybe 5,000 more for the Northern Border Fencing Strategy. That's 40,000 new jobs right there, protecting the Homeland."

The audience roared their approval.

"Radar, infrared, ground sensors, motion detectors, mines, electrified razor wire, armored personnel carriers, fortified guard towers, weaponized drones—you name it, it's in there, all these enhanced security measures that'll operate inside the 100-mile border security zone surrounding the Homeland. The terrorists won't be able to penetrate all this and attack us again. Log on to MySOB.gov for the whole deal. So maybe you'll need to allow an extra few hours to cross the border, but hey, it'll be worth it. Saving lives is worth a little inconvenience. We owe this to our children."

"King, King, King, King!"

"With your support, we will write the next great chapter of America's history. Hey, thanks North Dakota, you've been great. Thank you!"

12

You're with Us or You're with the Terrorists

THE CORPORAL LED BENSON down a short hallway into a stark holding area with lockers and a group shower. The soldier wore a uniform with a distinctive fractal camouflage pattern Benson hadn't seen before; not the usual tan, gray, and green; but tan, various shades of gray, and black. He was made to strip and enter the shower, where he was disinfected and subjected to an extremely thorough inspection. He was forced to open his mouth while his cheeks were scraped for DNA samples. Upon redressing, he was presented with a "fish kit" of basic toiletries and supplies.

They walked down a long ground floor corridor lined with scores of cells. Each cell had a metal door with a number and a steel mesh observation porthole. The second story of the building, also lined with cells, was open to the peaked glass ceiling, the sole source of light in the daytime. Hazy sunlight filtered through from above, casting long shadows. Everything was freshly painted in the same glossy, medium gray.

They stopped at a cell. With some effort, the scrawny corporal, who looked to be maybe 20, pushed the heavy, creaking steel door open. Benson stood at the entrance to the bleak cell. It was perhaps three yards deep and two wide, barely enough to hold a small cot. A wash basin with paper cups and a toilet were in the corner. A strong odor of disinfectant permeated the air. There were no windows, the only illumination coming from a powerful floodlight mounted in the low ceiling. Everything appeared fairly new. With a sinking feeling, Benson realized that this was where he would be spending his weekend.

"Move it!" the corporal said, nudging the muzzle of his rifle into Benson's back. "Get in there, I ain' got all day."

Several hours passed. Benson sat on the edge of the cot, his weary head in his hands. There was nothing to occupy him; no reading material, no video. Except for the odd door slamming, echoing from somewhere down the corridor, there were no sounds. His fine suit had become wrinkled and musky from grime and perspiration. A guard peered in on him through the porthole every so often.

He tried to doze away the time and keep up his strength. The bed was too small, and he curled up uncomfortably on it. The mattress was hard and thin and faintly stank of sweat and urine. The metal bars of the bed frame pressed into his back through the mattress. He slept fitfully, trying to find a tolerably comfortable position. He lay on his back, his forearm shielding his eyes from the dazzling light.

And then the music came; a strong, pulsing beat ringing off the cement floors and pounding through the open atrium. The thumping bass vibrated right through his exhausted body. He could feel it rattling his teeth.

♪♪ *"Yeah-h, you!"* ♪♫
♪♪ *"Shook me al-l-l-l-l night long ... "* ♪♫
♪♪ *"You! Shook me al-l-l-l-l night long ... "* ♪♫

Save for brief intermissions, the wretched song repeated throughout the night.

♪♪ *"The walls start shakin'!"* ♪♫
♪♪ *"Earth was quakin'!"* ♪♫
♪♪ *"My mind was achin'!"* ♪♫
♪♪ *"We were makin' it!"* ♪♫
♪♪ *"You! Shook me al-l-l-l-l night long ... "* ♪♫

During the respites he immediately fell asleep, only to be harshly roused when the music resumed.

Every few hours a guard noiselessly passed a plastic meal tray through a slot at the bottom of the cell door. It was invariably some kind of cold convenience food wrapped in cellophane; perhaps a small, plain sandwich of cold cuts, a snack cake, and a Kool-Aid® juice box. Time wore on.

"Rise and shine, sweetheart!"

Benson had been trying to sleep, the powerful light shining as always, when a guard threw open the steel door and barked at him. The guard's presence was welcome; it meant that the weekend had finally passed. Benson opened his crusted, bleary eyes. He tried to get up but tumbled wearily back on the cot. His body was stiff and achy; his head, groggy.

"Wake up, cherry, we ain't got all day."

Benson heaved himself to a sitting position on the cot and pushed himself onto his feet, shaking off his lightheadedness. The guard following, Benson was marched through the sea of identical cells. He tried to see behind the gray steel doors as they walked past. He thought he could detect some faint activity through some of the portholes, but it might well have been his imagination. The walk helped to invigorate him to some extent, easing the ache in his knees and back.

With Benson in front, they stood before a closed, windowless door. Benson looked behind; the guard motioned with his rifle for Benson to open the door. Benson turned the knob and forcefully pushed the door, causing it to slam into the wall behind. The two young men who had been lounging at the table within were jolted to their feet by the jarring crash.

These two appeared to be just a few years out of high school. They wore loosely fitting, aviator-style olive-drab jumpsuits with a small, stylized bear paw print embroidered on an oval badge on the left chest. Below their name tags was printed "Team HVT."

Benson entered the room and took a seat. One of the young men stared at him while regaining his composure, his flushed face returning to its normal pallor. His short blond hair was combed forward and teased into a stiff, upward-spiked wave at the front.

"How was your weekend, Tom?"

"Who the hell are *you*? And you will address me as *Mr. Benson*, sonny."

Hungry, dirty, and irritable, Benson examined this "Valdez, Juan." No stripes or other insignia identified his rank or affiliation.

"Los alojamientos están faltando," he said to Valdez. "Música ruidosa. Las luces no apagarán. Tu madre es puta."

"What? What'd you say?"

"The accommodations are lacking. Loud music, the light won't shut off. I'm afraid I won't be able to award five houses in the *Michelin Guide*."

"Yeah, I guess."

Valdez took a seat opposite Benson.

"Mr. Benson, have you thought about your, uh … your *situation*?"

Before Benson could respond, the second man jumped in. He had wavy hair and closely cropped sideburns down to his earlobes, which looked like they held earrings in the off-hours.

"People need to wake up to the reality of the terrorist next door. Ordinary people with jobs and normal families, people just like them."

Benson didn't like what this "Jefferson, George" seemed to be insinuating.

"You're new at this, aren't you, kid? Are you stupid? Do I look like a terrorist?"

"You know what?" Valdez said, leaning across the table. "You can't tell just by looking. The New Terrorist isn't a brown guy with a bomb in a backpack. He's educated, middle class, technology-savvy. Someone just like you, you know what I'm sayin'?"

"*You* don't know what you're saying. You're an imbecile, a trained parrot."

Benson shook his head, looking down.

Without warning, Valdez smacked Benson in the face. Glaring with cold hatred, Benson fought his natural instincts to kill this Juan Valdez right there. He could have done so rather easily, and with pleasure.

Valdez got up and paced behind the table.

"The State has invested a lot of time and money to find terrorists *before* they strike."

Benson was further inflamed at being lectured to by this punk with a badge.

"We're at war with radicals, Mr. Benson. We think they're recruiting from outside their own group. We're told they hate our clothes, our music, our movies, our books. They hate our sports, our food, our religion, our freedom. They hate everything and everyone and they've sworn jihad."

Benson tilted his head, looking straight into the young man's blue eyes, smirking.

"We need results!" Valdez said, suddenly raising his voice. "Conspiracies must be uncovered," he said, looking Benson in the eye, "and we have one right in front of us."

Benson smiled meanly.

"Mr. Benson, are you willing to serve your country in its time of need? For the greater good? Are you a patriot, sir?"

"You're with us or you're with the terrorists," added Jefferson, George. "Time to choose sides. Just sign the statement; we have plenty to convict you, anyway. We'll go easy on you and wrap this up, maybe do some kinda plea bargain, even. So wha' do you say?"

Benson sat back in his chair. He folded his arms across his chest. He leaned forward, his elbows on the table, and clasped his hands together. He looked at George Jefferson for a long moment and frowned. He sat back in his chair again. He looked down at the table and pursed his lips. Valdez and Jefferson watched him anxiously, evidently hoping for a quick break in the case. As Valdez had mentioned, they needed results.

"I say you're snot-nosed, goofy punks. I say you don't know what *patriot* even means."

Marched back to his cell, he passed another prisoner in the corridor, his guard shoving the haggard man forward whenever he slowed. The prisoner briefly made eye contact with Benson before turning his head down. Gaunt and frail, there were dark circles under his hollow, sunken eyes. A bad bruise marked his left cheek.

Benson's guard pushed him along. Arriving at his cell, the steel door clanged shut behind him. It was nearly frigid inside. As the hours passed, it felt even cooler. He began to shiver uncontrollably.

"Guards! Turn up the heat!" he shouted repeatedly through the little steel mesh porthole in the door until he was hoarse. He could see straight ahead, but the view to either side was severely limited.

"I'm freezing, do you hear me? Guards!"

His voice echoed through the corridors. From far off, he thought he heard someone laughing, but then all was silent.

He lay on his cot, curled up tightly to preserve body heat. The blanket and pillow were gone. Laying on his side, he clasped his hands together for a makeshift pillow. Extreme exhaustion finally overtook him, and he dozed, shivering, his feet and hands becoming numb.

♪♪ *"That's me in the corner ... "* ♪♪
♪♪ *"That's me in the spot—light,"* ♪♪
♪♪ *"Losing my religion."* ♪♪
♪♪ *"Trying to keep up with you ... "* ♪♪

The music blared. The song cycled on and off at random intervals, never letting him doze for longer than 30 minutes at a stretch, keeping him in a state that was neither fully asleep nor awake.

♪♪ *"And I don't know if I can do it ... "*♪♪
♪♪ *"Oh no, I've said too much ... "*♪♪
♪♪ *"I haven't said enough."*♪♪
♪♪ *"I thought that I heard you laughing ... "*♪♪

"So, what can you tell me about Thomas Benson?"

Taking notes on his pad, Lieutenant Millstone interviewed Benson's employees and coworkers. They met in the same conference room that Benson had used to hold his meeting some months before.

"Ooh, has he been charged with a serious crime or something?" Kay said, bubbling with excitement. "Is that it?"

"I didn't say he's been formally charged with anything."

"Well, I just thought you're a cop and—I mean, he was acting, you know, *suspicious*. He never asked for my input even though I'm professionally certified with 16 years' experience at the same job, well, not at the same job exactly, I've been promoted a couple times, of course, but I've seen them all come and go, and this one was different."

"He never listened to anyone," Stacy said. "Like, he always wanted everything his own way. He thought he was such a know-it-all, like he knows everything. He looked at you in a way that, you know, made you feel really dumb. It was kind of humiliating, in a way."

Lieutenant Millstone nodded sagely to Stacy.

"Yes, I think I see what you mean. What can you tell me about his overseas activities? Foreign business transactions? Related meetings? His calendar is vague."

"Even though I supported him, he, um, he didn't really support me back, you know?" a junior staffer said. "It's a question of trust, you know? He wasn't really a team player."

Millstone was visibly annoyed. This session was severely testing his patience. He made no attempt to hide his displeasure, shaking his head at their comments, and yet they continued whining.

"Totally not a team player," Stacy said.

Millstone abruptly folded up his notebook and strode to the door, leaving them at the table.

"Yeah, he wasn't a team player at all, you know?" Kay said to his back. "Hey, Lieutenant Millstone, when will we hear back from you? I mean, will we get updates? I could help with your investigation—how about *that*?"

Millstone was already halfway out the door. He looked back at her over his shoulder.

"No."

Ragged, his clothes shabby, sporting several day's beard, his hair dirty and unkempt, Benson was marched to the interrogation room. Wearing the same uniforms and embroidered badges, of about the same tender ages as the last ones, two new agents awaited. They examined some documents spread out on the table, drinking coffee from foam cups. "Williams, Gart" was the more studious-looking of the two. Dark brown hair spilled over his forehead to the top of his glasses. Reading something of apparently consuming interest, he ignored Benson's presence. "Bookman, Lew" slouched in his chair, one arm draped over the back. Benson took a seat.

Bookman took a long drag on his cigarette, letting the smoke lazily drift out of his mouth and nose without blowing. He regarded Benson without expression and took another drag.

"You look like hell," he said.

"What day is this?" Benson shouted. "How long have I been here?"

He banged the flimsy metal table hard with his fist. One of the cups fell over, spilling the contents onto the documents and into Williams' lap. Bookman watched his colleague hastily back up from the table. Williams stood up, staring at his soiled pants and papers. Taking a deep drag from his cigarette, Bookman exhaled slowly through his nose.

"What difference does it make?" Bookman said, flicking the ashes into his coffee cup.

"My wife! She must be worried sick."

Williams looked up from the table to observe Benson directly for the first time.

"The neighbors saw your arrest."

It seemed to give Williams pleasure to say it to Benson's face.

"My job?"

"Your employment authorization's been revoked," Bookman said, wiping off one of the stained documents with a napkin. "Maybe we could get it reinstated. Maybe you could go home today. All we're asking is a small sacrifice for your country."

He turned the document around and pushed it across the table.

"What the fuck's wrong with you, Benson? Sign the statement and we could wrap this up. That's not so hard, is it?"

"You mean, if I just sign this paper, I can walk out of here, free as a bird?"

"Sure, pretty much."

"I can return home as if nothing had happened? Nothing on my permanent record?"

"Yeah, that sounds about right."

"That seems like a pretty good deal, wouldn't you say?"

"*We* think so."

"A small sacrifice for my country."

"You got it."

"Blow it out your ass."

Bookman smiled condescendingly and looked over at Williams.

"Oh well."

He slouched in his chair and inhaled deeply on his cigarette, blowing the smoke at Benson. Hungry and desperately tired, the smell nearly made Benson retch.

"Look, Benson, we can still make a deal, it's not too late. Why don't you sleep on it? Let's keep dialoging, keep the lines of communication open. I'm sure reasonable people can come to an understanding."

13

Welcome to Camp 6

T HERE WERE JUST A FEW OTHER PRISONERS in the expansive exercise yard. Haggard, feeble figures in bright orange jumpsuits wandered about, grateful to be free of their tiny cells for even a little while. The unseasonably cold spring rain soaked their clothes through to the skin, providing the only shower they would have that week. Sentries toting Remington Modular Sniper Rifles patrolled the catwalks over the yard. Whenever an inmate attempted any sort of communication with the others, a guard would react swiftly with a sharp thrust of his rifle butt into the prisoner's ribs.

Dressed in an oversized orange jumpsuit, the sleeves and pant legs rolled up to keep his hands and feet free, Benson had been forced to run around a gravel track several times already. He dropped to his knees, panting, although he wasn't out of breath. He did not want to give them the impression that he could do this all day.

A furious guard stormed over, driving a rifle butt into his side. He fell over onto the gravel, the sharp, stabbing pain paralyzing him.

"Keep runnin', maggot." The guard stood over him, threatening to jab Benson with his rifle again. "Move your ass!"

"I'm begging you," Benson said between labored breaths, "let me rest a minute."

"Ya need your exercise! Move and don' stop till I say! Are we clear?"

Benson struggled to his feet, rubbing the pain away from his ribs.

So these are the rules of engagement. I am at war, again. Survival is all that matters now.

After exercise, Benson lied down on his bed and closed his eyes. All was silent for a long time, and then screeching music blared across the compound.

♪♪ *"You could say I lost my faith in science and progress,"* ♪♫
♪♪ *"You could say I lost my belief in the holy church,"* ♪♫
♪♪ *"You could say I lost my sense of direction ... "* ♪♫

Benson lay on his cot, wrapping the pillow around his ears to muffle the noise.

♪♪ *"But if I ever lose my faith in you-u-u,"* ♪♫
♪♪ *"There'd be nothing left for me to do-o-o ... "* ♪♫

Like all soldiers, he'd been through SERE training—Survival, Evasion, Resistance, and Escape—but he was a younger man then. With enough discipline—and some luck —he could stay alive in extreme wilderness or hostile urban environments.

For a time.

Wearing a black hood shrouding his upper body, Benson balanced precariously on a stool. Attached to his hands and torso were electric cables. His arms were to be raised away from his body and held virtually motionless. They forced him to stand erect like this for what seemed like hours. In his military days, standing stiffly at attention was a drill he'd endured for long stretches. Some recruits would faint and crumple from the strain, especially in hot weather. The idea was to instill mental and physical discipline. He had heard that they no longer did this in the service.

Losing his balance in the darkness, he triggered a vicious jolt, causing him to fall blindly off the stool and smack the cement floor with his shoulder. With each round on the stool his anxiety increased, making it ever more difficult for him to maintain his balance.

Returned to his cell, Benson lied down gently on his bed. Beyond the physical pain and constant discomfort was the mental anguish. He was miserable in this wretched place and wracked with guilt.

Even I didn't know it was this bad. They brought it all home—and I helped make it happen.

He rubbed his aching shoulder and winced.

Politics makes you stupid.

He heard screaming and crying from somewhere outside. He went to the door and put his ear to the mesh porthole.

"Please—please, no-o-o-o!" a woman wailed, and then more howling and yelling. Sometimes it was frantic; some unimaginable punishment being dealt out, brutally administered, merciless. At other times, the crying from the corridor was more of a plaintive sobbing. There being nothing at all that he could do about it, it was highly distressing. The shrieking and bawling and whimpering seemed to be coming from somewhere to his right, then to his left, and then back again. It suddenly dawned on him that he must be listening to a recording.

Faint sounds came from the corridor. Benson leapt off his cot and peered out the porthole. A guard was coming down the hall, his keys rattling on a large metal ring on his belt. The guard stopped in front of Benson's cell and peered inside the porthole, taken aback to see Benson gaping back at him just inches away with an insane, raving expression. The guard snorted and bent down, grunting with the effort, and pushed a meal tray through the slot in the door.

Benson paced in his cell. He regarded the dry, gray meat slice on stale white bread with disgust. Next to it sat a small bag of potato chips. Still, he forced himself to eat all of it, every last crumb; there wouldn't be any more until the next meal—whenever that might be—and he wished to preserve his strength for as long as he could. He drifted off to sleep on his back with his knees bent, leaning them against the wall to help relieve the pressure on his lower back from the thin mattress and hard bed frame.

And then the music blasted again.

♪♪ *"We'll be fighting in the streets,"* ♪♪
♪♪ *"With our children at our feet,"* ♪♪
♪♪ *"And the morals that they worship will be gone."* ♪♪

He put his fingers in his ears to hush the racket.

♪♪ *"Pick up my guitar and play-y-y,"* ♪♪
♪♪ *"Just like yesterday-y-y,"* ♪♪
♪♪ *"Then I'll get on my knees and pray-y-y ... "* ♪♪
♪♪ *"We don't get fooled again! No, no! Don't get fooled again!"* ♪♪

At length, the piercing music stopped and he napped restlessly.

A guard entered his cell and banged his rifle butt against the steel door, the loud clang jolting Benson from his torpor. They marched to the interrogation room and waited outside. The door burst open and a man emerged, pushed by a brute of a guard, causing the prisoner to nearly fall on his face. He looked to be in his late 50s. His sweaty prison uniform was torn at the chest. Except for his left eye, bruised and swollen shut, his face was drained of all color. He glanced fleetingly at Benson with his one good eye and disappeared down the corridor, his guard shoving him ahead.

Benson entered the room. He faced new interrogators, wearing the same emblems and uniforms as the others.

"How are you today, Mr. Benson?" said a slight female sporting short, strawberry-blond hair.

She spoke in a high, adolescent voice. Her pleasant, girlish face oozed congeniality. Benson was reminded of the psychology students he had known in his college days. He pictured this wisp in a lab coat proudly playing the role of a serious researcher, perhaps dangling some cheese on a string for hungry rats running through mazes, carefully jotting down her scientific-sounding observations in neat handwriting for extra credit.

"It's strange, but I'm feeling tired and a little hard of hearing, Miss—"

He leaned over to look at her name tag. He continued looking at her chest long after reading the tag. She shifted uneasily in her seat amid the strained silence and offensive gawking.

"Miss Betty Bradley," Benson said at length, still staring at her bosom. "Yes, of course. How charming."

"Well then, Mr. Benson," broke in the other agent, "Elliott, Steve," with a winning smile. "Feeling more cooperative today?"

Benson cupped a hand to his ear.

"My ears are ringing," he said in a loud voice. "What did you say?"

"I said," the young man responded in an equally loud voice, "are you gonna cooperate?"

"What's that?" Benson shook his head. "What'd you say?"

Agent Bradley cupped her hands around her mouth trying to amplify her normally whispery voice to something just beyond ordinary speaking volume.

"Can—you—hear—me?" she said.

"No, I don't think orange is my best color." Benson glanced down at his uniform. "It gives my complexion an unhealthy, sallow look, don't you think?"

The smile fading from her face, Betty Bradley was quickly losing her composure.

"I said, can—you—hear—me?"

Benson shook his head.

"Write down your question."

Steve Elliott fished out a pen bearing the bear paw print logo, loudly tore paper off a pad with an exaggerated, peeved gesture—all the while giving Benson a dirty look—and hastily scribbled something on the sheet. He pushed the note at Benson across the table and sat back, moody and petulant. The subject was not responding to multiple environmental and social stimuli in carefully controlled settings as documented in the official field guide, *Tactical PSYOP, Doctrine for Joint Psychological Operations 13.26*. The guide described the unequivocal success of similar experiments, regardless of ethnicity, gender, or socioeconomic status. After an unsettling period of deprivation and radical disorientation, subjects were so desperate for human interaction that they would naturally bond with the "interviewer."

A classified section of the *Army Field Manual* stated that coercive techniques would "induce psychological regression in the subject by bringing a superior outside force to bear on his will to resist." Compared to the benchmarks of normal subjects in the database, they should have built a relationship with Benson by now, generated some trust. But maybe this particular subject wasn't normal; he certainly wasn't responding in the normal way. Oppositional Defiant Disorder? Antisocial Personality Disorder?

Agent Elliott perspired and clenched his jaw. He had a spotless High Value Target interview record to this point, and eligible for further promotion if he passed the next exam.

Benson had sat stock-still, examining Elliott with a cold, appraising eye. Churning inside, Elliott looked away. Benson picked up the note.

Although it was just one line, Benson took his time reading Elliott's message. Suddenly lunging over the table for the agent's pen, he forced the startled Elliott to scramble back, his folding metal chair nearly collapsing beneath him. Elliott kept his balance only by gripping the table's edge with both hands.

In the ensuing silence, Benson inspected Steve Elliott as though he were an insect. He wrote his reply underneath Elliott's question, pushing the note back at the agent and reclining in his chair, not taking his eyes off Elliott's.

Elliott broke away from Benson's intense gaze to pick up the note. At the top of the page was his own question: "RUR to coperate?" Benson's reply appeared just below.

"PO UR SOL," Benson had written.

"What's all this?" Elliott said, slamming the paper down on the table.

"If my texting lingo is up to date," explained Benson, "it means piss off, you are shit out of luck."

Hands clasped on top of his head, Benson was marched from the interrogation room, a guard with a rifle trained on him close behind. The guard pushed him along to a new block in a different wing located far from the one in which he had been housed. They stopped in front of an open door. With a jab of his rifle, the guard hustled him into his new cell. He stood inside the entrance and let his hands drop to his sides. This cell was pristine, almost sterile. Except for the toilet and wash basin, everything from floor to ceiling was freshly painted in dark gray. A heavy steel bed was bolted to the cement floor.

"Welcome to Camp 6," the guard said. "Enjoy your stay."

The guard booted the hefty door closed. Benson spun around to face him as the door clanged shut.

He sat on his bed, listlessly watching a meal tray pass through the door slot. Except for a disembodied hand occasionally pushing a tray through the opening, he hadn't seen or even heard another human being for weeks. The guards wore silent rubber shoes. White noise was constantly pumped into his cell. He heard nothing except the sound of his own voice. He had no sense at all of day or night, one hour being the same as the last.

The meals here came in a pink foil bag adorned with an American flag, labeled "Humanitarian Daily Ration—Food Gift from the People of the United States of America." They were always exceptionally bland, delivered at random times, but just once per day. Inside the bag were other foil bags, usually containing beans and rice, some kind of stew, an Oreo™ cookie, a Pop-Tart®, and perhaps a few crackers and Skippy® peanut butter. The portions were just small enough to keep him slightly hungry and lethargic. He took a bite of cracker and tossed the rest on the bed.

He dropped to the floor and did a few rounds of pushups. In extreme conditions, he knew, only the mentally tough and physically fit pulled through. Prisoners of war, forced labor camp inmates, and concentration camp victims who survived such harsh conditions had extra reserves of inner strength upon which to draw. It was embedded in their constitutions, a mark of extraordinary character. The weak and the hopeless lost their will to live and slowly died.

He hooked his feet under the bed and cranked out some situps, each repetition coming increasingly slower and tougher. *My body may be a prisoner*, he told himself, grinding out the repetitions, *but not my spirit. I will not be controlled. I will not be ruled, commanded, dominated, or led. I am not afraid.*

He collapsed to the floor, utterly spent, his pulse throbbing in his temples, but nonetheless pleased that he could still do 50 situps without stopping. He knew that this would not last. Lying on the floor, he gazed at the tiny fisheye lens in the ceiling.

In every vessel there is a leak.

He panted, sweat pouring off his forehead.

I will find it.

He sang popular songs out loud and invented new lyrics to fit the melodies. Hearing something, anything, even his own voice, was somehow satisfying in the unchanging, hushed silence. He practiced over and over, trying to improve upon the original lines. Sometimes he would burst out laughing, giggling foolishly at outlandish songs he had dreamed up. He worried over this; perhaps it was a sign of impending insanity, but he dismissed these thoughts, just as he shrugged off periods of utter despair and abject depression. Man is a social animal, he reasoned—or so he hoped—with a full range of native, complex emotions. If he was removed from the social settings in which he could express those emotions, his brain would play tricks to get the stimulation it needed.

Playing elaborate chess games using bits of toilet paper for the pieces, he worked out the moves with imaginary opponents, to whom he gave names to make it seem more real. He was able to stay engaged for hours at a stretch at this, there being nothing else to occupy his attention.

He put his hands on the floor, kicked his legs up against the wall, and pressed himself up and down, grinding out a grueling set of handstand pushups. His strength was definitely fading. Crawling to the bed, he ate the remains of a stale shortbread cookie and lay back, exhausted.

Closing his eyes, he dozed in the foggy languor between drowsiness and sleep, letting go of the anger and shame, his mind free and drifting. Dreamy classical music played gently in the background, the rhythms lush and stimulating. The soft scent of lavender and sandalwood candles perfumed the air. Jane reclined on the bed, her head turned away from him, her silky lingerie riding up and exposing her gorgeous long legs. A shoulder strap of her red satin slip was pulled down, baring her breast. He moved closer to the bed.

At his approach, she turned to face him. She smelled of roses and warm vanilla. He looked down upon her, enthralled, his heart skipping. Looking into his eyes, she dipped a succulent, ripe strawberry in whipped cream and took a bite. The sweet red juice ran past her lips, down her chin, to her breast. She offered him the strawberry and licked her fingers, watching with heavy eyes while he ate the rest.

She scooped some whipped cream with a finger and put it to his lips. He licked and nibbled her finger, then kissed his way down her throat, down the trail of strawberry juice.

They kissed passionately, hungrily. His hands cradled her face, her warm breath panting in his ears, her tender lips wetly caressing his. The ceiling fan slowly circled round and round in a hypnotic rhythm, gently cooling their flushed skin. Her scent, her softness and warmth, her sheer beauty flooded over him. Moaning with pleasure, her legs and arms tightly enfolded him, drawing him deeper, the raw intimacy fierce and consuming. He told her that he loved her beyond words and meant it with his very soul.

A powerful hand clamped onto his shoulder, digging in painfully, ripping him away.

The loneliness was crushing.

His face buried in his pillow, he clawed it savagely with his fingers and dropped clumsily to the cell floor. Lying in pain, he massaged his temples and chewed his lower lip.

A rat scurried by along the wall's edge, stopping nearby. It stood up on its hind legs, twitching and sniffing the air.

"Jane, is that you?"

He stared at it, not believing his eyes.

"How'd you get in here? No, I don't know why I'm here, but it's good of you to come and visit. Do you want to play Scrabble? You always win, but I want to try again. You will? Great!"

He laid his head sideways on the floor.

"C'mon honey, how 'bout a kiss first?"

He closed his eyes, puckered his lips and waited. He opened his eyes, disappointed. The rat scurried off a few steps, sniffing the floor.

"It's been so long. Sure, it's okay, we're married. You're a lovely girl, c'mon sweets, be romantic. Here's some food."

He flung a piece of cracker on the floor near the rat, who eagerly snatched it and ran off.

Benson curled up on the bed, pulling the blanket over him but for his face. Massaging his temples with clenched fists, his body trembled in spasms of pain.

"My head! It hurts so bad, Jane, make it stop! O-o-ow."

He pulled the blanket completely over him and rolled over on his side.

Hours passed. Benson hadn't stirred. Soiling his clothes, an evil stench permeated the small cell. A meal tray was passed through the door slot. It sat on the floor, untouched.

A guard opened the porthole on the cell door and peered inside. Eaten through in spots, the last meal tray remained on the floor, "Jane's" droppings scattered on top. The guard retched when he caught the wicked smell, hastily withdrawing his face from the opening.

"Hey Frank, come here real quick. The stupid fish has croaked! Damn it, Frank, we're gonna get in real trouble for this, are you kiddin' me? Holy shit."

The two guards cautiously entered the cell, goggling at the body on the bed. Holding their noses, they searched around for clues.

"What the fuck happened here?" Frank was absolutely furious. "Damn it, Hasan, you fucker, we weren't supposed to fuckin' kill him, you fuckin' idiot. You were supposed to be fuckin' watchin' him," he said, jabbing his finger into Hasan's chest.

"Don't you blame *me*, Frank, you were supposed to be watchin' too, not chillin' in the break room all the time."

Frank's features clouded with a fresh realization that imparted even more anxiety.

"Oh, my God, OMG. My fuckin' review's comin' up next month."

Frank looked squarely into his comrade's panicky eyes.

"Okay, now—now you look here, all right? We didn't do fuckin' nothin', you fuckin' got that, nothin'! We're not fuckin' responsible, all right? I'll file this under 'Self-Injurious

Behavior Incident' and that'll be fuckin' that, I'll back you up and you back—"

"Yaaa!"

Throwing off the sheet, Benson suddenly rose from the bed. In the same motion he kicked Hasan in the head, who jolted back, tottering and dazed. Another kick and Hasan's skull struck the concrete wall. He slithered slowly to the floor, leaving a trail of blood on his descent. Benson immediately struck Frank in the throat with the outer edge of his palm, causing the guard to stoop and clutch his windpipe, gasping for breath. Clasping both hands on the back of Frank's head, he twice brought his knee up hard into the guard's ribs. He heard a soft crack and let Frank fall away to stagger sideways and collapse under his own weight.

Wheezing and panting, fighting the immense fatigue washing over him, Benson hurriedly changed into Frank's uniform. He strapped on a holstered gun and pulled his hat brim low. Hasan lay motionless, bleeding onto the floor.

Silently closing the cell door behind him, Benson cautiously entered the hall. Before him stretched a long corridor of identical cells. He searched in both directions, but no exit signs were posted. Walking quickly down the corridor in the direction he guessed might be the way out, all was empty. Machinery quietly hummed in the distance. He continued swiftly, looking behind for any sign of trouble.

He turned a corner. Two guards stood directly in front of him, gripping their guns with both hands, the barrels aimed at his face.

"Freeze!"

14

Any Last Requests?

His hands shackled to heavy iron rings mounted on the cinder blocks of the inner yard, Benson kicked wildly at the two guards trying to control him. His own guard uniform was torn and ripped off his body from behind, the shirt collar choking him with the force. It took several hard yanks until the buttons popped off and the shirt shredded around his waist, leaving his torso bare.

He waited an interminable time, sweating in the stifling summer heat and humidity.

Crack! The whip strafed across his back with a shocking sting; his face welled up and twisted with animal rage from the searing pain. The few other prisoners in the yard stood around watching the spectacle. Crack! Each cruel stroke inflicted an electrifying jolt that struck him to his core.

He turned his head for a glimpse of his tormentor, nearly catching the whip on his face. An athletic woman stridently wielded the lash, her pretty face displaying neither pleasure nor remorse. She wore a flight-style jumpsuit similar to that of the other agents, but in a cream color; formfitting and open to the neck. Winding up like a baseball pitcher, she grunted with the effort of each savage stroke.

He ducked his head beneath his shoulders and waited for the strikes, delivered at unpredictable intervals, aimed precisely at different areas of his back, legs, buttocks, and

119

shoulders. The sharp whipping sound of the lash streaking through the air sent him into convulsions even before the vicious crack wracked his entire body with excruciating agony. With each unrelenting stroke he became increasingly numb; he cried out in sheer torment less and less. He slid limply down the wall until his knees hit the ground, his head slumping forward, his arms stretched taut in the shackles, silent and still.

The woman broke off her attack, gathering up and coiling the long, tapered whip in exact, even loops, meticulously fitting it inside its carrying case. She slung the handle over her shoulder and walked away.

Shuddering, naked and face down on top of the bed, his back and legs scarred and crusted with dark, dried blood, Benson awoke in his cell completely disoriented. He turned his head to each side, suddenly realizing where he was. The motion instantly produced a splitting headache. He laid still until it subsided. Gingerly struggling to rise, he pushed himself up with his arms. The slight movement sent shooting pains from his oozing wounds down his back to his buttocks and legs, and he collapsed on the bed.

It took much persistence to force open the meal-tray slot at the bottom of the door. On his hands and knees, Benson turned his head sideways, trying to get his mouth closer to the opening.

"Guard! Guard! I don't have any clothes or blanket. It's crazy c-c-cold!"

The thick, deadening fog of white noise pumped into the corridor muffled his voice. He was naked; clothes rubbing on his raw wounds would probably be too painful to wear, anyway. He could only bear to lie face down on his bed or stand up, but now it was freezing inside.

Entreaties like this had never produced any reaction before, but he figured it was worth a try from sheer desperation.

Through the blanket of white noise he thought that he could hear faint footsteps approaching. Maybe they were finally showing some small measure of mercy. Perhaps they saw that this was a simple, reasonable request. His hopes soared.

He retreated from the door just in time as it flew open and smashed into the wall. One of the two guards held a heavy bucket. Recoiling like a discus thrower, he hurled the contents onto Benson. Icy water splashed off his naked body, freezing and burning his wounds at the same time. He stood there speechless, rigid with shock as the bone-chilling water dripped off him.

Both guards enjoyed a spirited laugh. The other guard threw some clothes on the floor. They landed in a puddle of ice and water. In that moment, Benson forgot his discomfort. He seethed, glaring at his captors with a passionate hatred, the intensity of which was unlike anything he had ever felt before. His fury only added to their amusement.

He picked up the soaked clothes and held them close, bundling them tightly into a heavy, dense ball.

"I don't like the cut of these," he hissed.

One of the guards sneered at this bravado, turning to his comrade.

"You believe this?" he said. "You believe this guy?"

Benson hurled the ball of wet clothes with all his strength, striking the guard squarely in the groin with the hefty wad. The man turned to face Benson, his eyes wide with shock and pain. Groaning, he doubled over and fell onto his side, seizing his crotch with both hands and softly crying.

"They're just not me."

Benson stood naked over the guard, dripping water on him, the better to humiliate him.

"*You* put them on—over your panties, you pus-sucking weasel."

• • •

His head covered by an orange hood, hands in thick orange mittens, his feet in bulky orange socks, Benson knelt on the floor, stooped over. His mouth was gagged and bound with duct tape. Industrial-grade noise suppressors covered his ears. Someone tied his hands together behind his back. The room was filled with prisoners in the same attire kneeling in the same position on the cement floor. Watchful guards stood over them, rifles at the ready. A psychiatrist in a white coat moved among the stooped prisoners, stopping from time to time, carefully recording her observations of the captives in various stress positions.

Benson was forced to kneel like this for a long time at each session. After only a few minutes his knees and back would ache terribly. Before long, the weight of his head bearing down in the stooped position would cause excruciating, dull pain in his upper shoulders and neck. He would raise and lower his head to relieve the gnawing soreness, but there was never much relief. His muscles would begin cramping, then tingling, and he would feel numbness come on. His hands and feet would grow cold. His knees pressing on the unforgiving floor would hurt badly; he would shift around to move the pain points to other spots, and then shift back again when that position, too, became unbearable.

In the first of these sessions, unable to endure any more, he had stood up, slowly and stiffly. Before he could reach his full height he was kicked in the back of his knees and fell over, sprawling on the floor. The doctor had hurried over, shuffling through her notes to make an entry of the exact time and pressure points that gave out—valuable data to populate tolerance threshold charts that might prove useful one day to soldiers in combat.

The sensory deprivation was so extreme that he couldn't hear himself breathe. His only physical sensation was of the slight movement he could make—undetected or perhaps tolerated by the guards—and the acute discomfort. His back throbbed with pain; the blood pounded in his temples. He stretched his fingers and moved his head back and forth for mental and physical stimulation. A guard came over and silently placed his boot on the back of Benson's head, pinning his forehead to the floor until the message was understood.

Time stood still without the senses. He thought that he could hear voices, but of course that was impossible. The more that he tried to resist, the more that he lost control, until there was no sensation at all left in his body. He floated upward, slowly at first, and then faster. The guards and the doctor frantically clawed at him as he drifted higher, but their hands just went right through him. Soaring above the compound, he left it behind until it was only a speck over the lush landscape. He wafted over a lake. It was warm and sunny; he floated effortlessly with the light breeze, happy to be carried away to wherever it might take him. He did a somersault, turning end over end, and then tried a barrel roll, reversing after several rolls to spin in the opposite direction. He was joined in his aerobatics by pigeons, sparrows, and other small birds, up to red-tailed hawks and golden eagles of enormous wingspan, all of them matching his graceful movements in unison, a carefree dance in the heavens. He was at peace with the world.

The sun sparkled off the lake far below, the ripples glittering in the water. Families in rowboats looked up in the sky to see him swooping and gliding with the birds. They smiled at him, the children waving and laughing. He laughed and waved back.

One of the birds hovered in the air next to him, an oversized hummingbird with a red throat. It seemed to be staring right through him with its glowing eyes. Alarmed, he realized that it was a machine, a miniature drone. He felt himself growing heavy and falling rapidly. In terror, he hurtled to Earth, crashing through the roof of the compound. They poked him with a knife, cruelly laughing as he jerked wildly on the floor with each brutal stick, the doctor recording the subject's clinical reactions on her clipboard. Psychiatrists hovered over him, their murky voices plotting, dropping heavy weights on him, kicking him, stomping mercilessly on his head. Bound and defenseless, they heaved him over a cliff into the ocean far below. He spun end over end, out of control, dazed and disoriented, nausea rising, heart pounding wildly, dashed to pieces on the sharp rocks, writhing and suffocating in the surf, his lungs filling with icy salt water, eight-year old Daniel grasping his hand in his own, their bodies pitching helplessly together in the crashing underwater current. Help me, Daniel cried, his stricken, innocent child's face bleating, help me Dad, crying so frantically that he lost his breath, gasping for air, gurgling and turning color. Battered and tossed by the waves, they floated higher, breaking free to the surface, desperately inhaling life.

"Please, have a seat," the new agent said.

He tapped on his computer and then looked at Benson with a satisfied expression. This one was a little older and seemed more experienced than the others, with a self-assured air about him. He leaned forward earnestly, lacing his fingers together on the table.

"Mr. Benson, my name is Steven Austin. You've sure been through a lot, we do understand. Sometimes we might be a bit overzealous, but we're tryin' our best, really. We're workin' to make our enhanced interview programs fit the law, and—well, you know, let's just say we're workin' on it. A lot of this is pretty new. It's not easy, these are not your routine criminal cases, no. Your regular civilian courts aren't really—well, they're not really equipped for this kinda thing, I mean, they're fine when it comes to drug crimes and firearms possession and gambling and tax evasion and seatbelt and helmet laws and prostitution, sure, but they've also let dangerous suspects go free who might've turned up later on the battlefield, and we can't risk letting even one guilty suspect go free. There's just, you know, there's too much at stake. We call it the Precautionary Principle. Normal juries can't really handle this, uh, this *situation*, either; too specialized. The Homeland's in danger and we just wanna get to the truth, that's—"

"You talk too much."

Benson massaged his throat and swallowed with difficulty.

"And don't use that creepy word 'Homeland' around me."

"Just give us what we need and it'll all end. No more rough treatment, you have my word."

Benson responded with an icy stare.

"Here, I wanna show you something."

Austin nodded discreetly to his colleague, who spun the monitor around so that Benson could see it directly. It was a video of two men hotly arguing outside a coffee shop on a busy street. The men made threatening gestures and shouted at each other before stomping away in opposite directions. It appeared to be shot at a high vantage point from the other side of the street. Wearing a business suit, one of the men resembled Benson, at least from that distance. Sirens, honking, and other traffic noise dominated the video. At certain points, the camera quivered erratically or randomly zoomed in and out of focus. The man in the suit climbed into a car that looked like the kind Benson drove, screeching away into the traffic.

"That's 'Wally' al-Watanabe, and the other guy," Austin leaned in, lowering his voice to a conspiratorial whisper, "is *you*."

He sat back in his chair, looking at Benson in eager anticipation.

"Well, what do ya think about that?"

Benson stared at the screen, his brow furrowed. He pursed his lips and turned his face down, saying nothing for a while. He looked at Austin with great concern.

"My throat," he whispered hoarsely, "my throat is sore. Can't talk." He massaged his throat. "Get me some coffee first. Make it really hot. Please."

Oscar Goldman, the other agent at the table, brightened immediately.

"That's more like it," said Agent Goldman. "You're finally smartening up."

In a sweeping, dismissive motion, he waved both his hands at the guard standing in front of the door.

"Quick, you—get the coffee."

Goldman snapped his fingers and waved again to get the guard moving, but he just stood there. The guard pointed at his chest, silently mouthing, "Me?"

"Don't just stand there, you rumhead, move it! You heard Mr. Benson, very hot. And make it snappy."

The two agents flashed an expressive glance at each other.

After some minutes, the guard shuffled back sullenly into the room with a white foam cup, two pink packets of artificial sweetener, and a stir stick, setting them on the table. The coffee was exceedingly hot.

Benson held the cup to his face and sniffed, wrinkling his nose. Looking directly at Austin, he tore open one of the packets and dumped the white powder in the cup. He stirred it with the plastic stick and looked doubtfully at the steaming contents. An oily film swirled on the surface. He set down the stick and examined the coffee. He raised the cup to his nose, inhaled the burned scent, and shook his head. He set the cup down on the table and stared at it.

Austin was fidgeting in his seat.

"C'mon, Mr. Benson, we have important matters to discuss, you know? A lot of time has gone by and we'd like to wrap this thing up real quick, okay?"

Benson took the tiniest sip with a pronounced, noisy slurp, twisting his face in disgust. He put the cup down gently. It was burning hot.

"You insult me," he said in a loud voice. "This tastes like shit."

"So it ain't Starbucks—so what?" said Agent Austin.

"You try it."

Benson leaned forward and splashed the burning coffee in the agents' faces. They held their hands to their scalded faces in horror. The searing liquid dripped down their necks and inside their mock flight uniforms.

"The brightness is exceptionally low," Benson said, settling back in his chair. "The back flavor is burned and bitter. Musty, gamey notes on the front end. An exceptionally lackluster effort."

Benson struggled to complete his daily self-imposed exercise regimen. The exertion of completing even a few pushups left him collapsed in a winded heap. Tired and hungry, he had begun hallucinating in random fits, his mind drifting off on its own. It took all of his determination to stay balanced and lucid. He couldn't seem to concentrate on anything, not even the chess games with his imaginary toilet-paper opponents.

I feel myself fading away.

The thought filled him with worry. It was the beginning of the end, a downward death spiral until his mind and body were destroyed forever.

He lay in bed and massaged his forehead in a vain attempt to relieve a sudden headache. The controlled environment was starting to achieve its purpose. He had known it would, eventually; no one could hold out forever. Prisoners are reduced to a state of learned helplessness wherein nothing is under their control. Noise and quiet, cold and heat, food and drink, light and darkness, confinement and space; all are manipulated randomly to disorient the senses and distort reality. Nothing makes any sense. Actions have no logical or predictable outcomes. Isolation, capricious cruelty mingled with acts of kindness, utter dependency for nourishment and the exercise of basic bodily functions—these are their tools.

It was in one of these acts of kindness that Benson found himself out in the yard, one of their random, special privileges. It was unbearably hot and muggy outside. A warm rain poured down intermittently. Under the watchful eyes of soldiers manning the gun towers looming over the yard, the prisoners milled around, shuffling aimlessly, not daring to talk or even to look at one another. Benson was miserable, his mind wandering darkly. He had long imagined that he would leave this world from old age, of natural causes. Not like this.

I'm no hero. They're wearing me down. I'm losing control, wasting away into nothingness. It would be so blissful to just let go and end the struggle. It would be so easy to just give up.

There would be no words of wisdom he would pass on, no profound truths to share with loved ones gathered around his deathbed, no statue erected to his memory. The world would continue on just the same without him, as if he had never been born. No drama, just quietly disappeared and forgotten. He had always wanted his life to count for something, to have some meaning or ultimate purpose, and yet his path had taken him here. A dead end.

He tried to summon up a prayer from the liturgy. There had to be one for the hopeless and the downtrodden, for the dregs and the ostracized of the world. A prayer for those who would be raised from the dust, casting off the yoke of oppression; a prayer for deliverance from tyranny.

A prayer for those with nothing left to believe in.

Despondent and listless, his mind in a fog, he drew a blank, and so he made up his own prayer.

"Dear God," he said out loud, looking toward heaven, "please forgive my feeble words. I've never asked anything for myself. Now I'm asking. Save me. Get me the hell out of this."

A guard ran over and jabbed him in the ribs with his rifle. Returned roughly to his cell, he collapsed on the bed. No sooner had he shut his eyes than a baby's crying was broadcast throughout the compound. Whimpering softly at first, it turned into the frantic, hysterical squalling of an infant in extreme distress. His own son had cried like that with occasional bouts of colic; crying jags so acute that he had literally lost his breath, gasping as if he was drowning, crying with no air and no sound coming out, gurgling and suffocating and turning color. More than once, they almost thought they would lose him. It was a terrifying time.

He used his pillow to block the noise, to no real effect.

Benson had been dozing in a groggy haze when two guards burst into his cell. He awoke with a violent start. One guard stood watch next to the door, both hands on a submachine gun strapped around his neck; the other tied Benson's hands behind his back and jerked him to his feet. With Benson in the middle, the three trooped single file down the corridor and exited the building into a yard Benson hadn't seen before. They stopped in front of a concrete wall pocked with bullet holes. A line of soldiers facing the wall stood at attention, their rifles pointing skyward. They wore the same uniforms as all the other soldiers here, a special camouflage pattern in tan, light gray, medium gray, and black, with a matching beret bearing a distinctive unit insignia Benson didn't recognize. None of them would make eye contact with him, studiously staring straight ahead, looking at nothing.

The guard to his rear bent over to make some adjustments in the rope that bound Benson's hands behind him. In that moment, Benson spun around, dragging the guard off balance. Leaning back, he brought his left shin up hard into the man's groin. The guard doubled up, paralyzed with pain. Benson punched his right knee into the man's face, sending him crashing to the gravel on his back.

The other guard rushed Benson from the side. His hands still tied, Benson sidekicked the guard's leading leg at the knee, breaking it with a crunch. The line of soldiers dropped their weapons and came running. A bear of a man lunged at him, wrapping his arms around Benson's waist from behind and squeezing hard. Benson stomped on the man's foot with his heel and smashed the back of his head into the man's face, breaking his nose and teeth. The soldier collapsed in agony, clutching his bloody face in his hands.

His chest heaving, gulping air, Benson faced several soldiers forming a tightening circle around him. He rushed one of them, kicking him squarely in the ribs with all his effort. The man fell, but the others tackled Benson, pinning him face down on the ground, piling on and crushing him with their weight until he could hardly breathe.

A uniformed officer sauntered over, his shoes crunching on the gravel. Benson saw the dark brown pant legs with blue stripes approach. The colors were unknown to him. He struggled to raise his head to look up from under the pile of soldiers. The bars and nameplate identified this officer as one "Captain Kelly." Benson dropped his head to the gravel again.

His arms still securely bound, the soldiers yanked him to his feet. A blindfold was tied around his eyes. He was shoved in front of the concrete wall.

"Any last requests, Mr. Benson?" Captain Kelly said.

"A one-way ticket to Canada," Benson replied between strained breaths. "Coach will be fine."

"Ready! Aim!"

Benson turned around.

"Shoot me in the back, cowards!"

Captain Kelly moved in close, pointing his gun at Benson's head.

"Fire!" he yelled.

Benson fell down in a heap.

15

Team VIPR

BENSON HAD FREQUENTLY BEEN UP LATE the past year putting together a complicated banking deal for a Middle Eastern client. It wasn't his usual line of work, but he'd volunteered for the assignment anyway, thinking that it might help broaden his horizons and provide a much needed challenge. Almost immediately, he regretted it. It was far more laborious and protracted than he had thought possible. The time zone difference meant some long nights in his upstairs home office. Although she knew it would probably be temporary, Jane was unhappy, feeling neglected. It seemed to her that there was always something "temporary" coming up between them.

"Tom's been so distant," Jane confided to her friend one day while they were out shopping, poring over the racks at a clothing store. "He's always on the computer, always working—even when he's home. We never talk anymore."

"I had the same problem."

"Really?"

"You better believe it," her friend said. "So he's working late—again—which he *says* is for me and the kids, so I go, 'Hey, what about *us*? We need some alone-time, like when we were dating, you know, before kids. Hello, we need to communicate,' I tell him. 'It's the foundation of a healthy relationship, everyone knows that.' So he goes, 'You know, when I *am* home, it's like you're always making plans to go out shopping or something.' He gives me this look, and he goes, 'You're guilty, too.' So I had to admit he was right—at least this time."

"What did you do?"

She dragged Jane over to the Intimate Apparel department. Jane held aloft a skimpy garment on its hanger. It was all strings and red satin and lace. She held it up to her face. She could see her friend right through it.

"You want me to wear *this*?"

Jane felt that she was still in good shape, but it didn't seem quite appropriate for a woman of her age—not that she looked or felt old. It's just that mature woman don't wear these little items, she figured. At some point, a woman gives up things like bikinis and short skirts. This certainly seemed like one of those things. Sexy lingerie would seem ridiculous after having been married such a long time. Tom would think it was stupid, too, she was sure.

"I know it sounds crazy, but Tom will take a whole new interest in you—and you'll love it, too. Trust me on this one. Works every time."

"But I'm still the same woman whether I'm wearing sweats or a teddy, right?"

"Wrong."

They had just finished dinner when Daniel announced that he would be spending the night at a friend's. Benson drove him over there. Upon returning, he went straight up to his home office and logged onto his chat group, reading for a while to catch up on the conversation. Someone had written, "We shoud bomb there jihad taliban ass's to smitherens." A reply read, "Id nuke those terrorist aholes myself, mass asasination or like poison there narcotics with anthrax LOL." Benson sighed. Another day of thoughtful, civilized discussion. He wondered why he bothered with this stuff. He hardly ever posted anything anymore. The chats and social network sites had been mildly interesting at first, but it was getting stale and consuming precious time he didn't have.

He leaned back in his chair, rubbing his eyes. It was getting late. He was only halfway through a business proposal due first-thing the next day and he needed to stop procrastinating. He'd brought work home with the idea that he might be able to better concentrate away from the office and the meetings and the ringing phones. It wasn't working out as planned.

He heard soft music playing from down the hall in the direction of their bedroom. He recognized the lush harmonies of Ravel's *Daphnis et Chloé Suite No. 2.* Jane used to play classical music when she was in a romantic mood. It seemed like it had been a long time since he'd heard that suite. He put his feet up on the desk and closed his eyes, savoring the gorgeous melodies.

Jane appeared in the doorway, wearing sultry, arresting lingerie. She leaned her shoulder against the doorframe, lounging provocatively.

"Honey, are you coming to bed?"

He opened his eyes, astounded. She hadn't worn seductive lingerie since their early years. Jane smiled warmly. Her sheer red slip, only partly covered by a long black satin gown left untied, exposed a deeply plunging neckline and long, bare legs.

Rising from his chair, he put his hands on the small of her back and buried his face in her throat, her soft hair caressing his cheek. She wrapped her arms around his neck, standing up on her toes, pressing her body tightly to his. She draped one leg around him and rubbed herself against him. The subtle scent of roses and vanilla and the warmth of her delicious body was intoxicating. Looking into his eyes with smoky lust, she held his face in her hands, kissing him wetly and deeply. He picked her up off the floor. She clung to his shoulders, her legs gripped around his waist. They kissed hungrily, their passion building.

Jane hopped off, flushed and breathing heavily. She took his hand in hers. He could feel her pulse beating through her hand.

"I'm ready for bed, baby," she said.

"Give me five minutes." Immediately, he regretted saying something so amazingly stupid.

"Five minutes," he croaked, his mouth suddenly having gone bone-dry.

Jane stood so close that he could feel the heat radiate from her body. She let the slinky black gown slither off her shoulders to drop softly at her feet. Looking at him with heavy eyes, she slowly pulled down a red satin shoulder strap, baring herself. His heart raced.

"Five minutes," Jane whispered in his ear.

She grazed her lips against his, her eyes wide open.

"I'll be waiting."

His eyes followed her as she sashayed to the bedroom. He should have dropped everything. What could possibly be more urgent? Still, he had to finish a proposal for lending to these Muslim countries or his head would be on the line. And yet, this wasn't a final agreement. Maybe he could save time by leaving some items open for discussion at the meeting tomorrow and wrap it up later.

It being against their religion to pay interest, no one would lend them money. They were getting around it by selling their assets to the bank and then leasing them back at a premium. When the lease ended they would own everything again, just as before. It was just like borrowing with interest, without actually calling it interest. The more he thought about it, though, the more complex it would be to make it function properly, especially to have it pass muster with the various taxing authorities. He sketched out the proposal, at last satisfied that it would work. The details could wait.

It was almost two hours later that he looked in on Jane. The bedroom was dimly lit. The music still played gently and sweetly. The faint scent of lavender and sandalwood candles, long burned out, lingered in the air. Rose petals were scattered on top of the blanket. An open bottle of champagne, two crystal flutes, and a silver bucket filled with melted ice were on the nightstand. A silver platter held ripe strawberries and a bowl of whipped cream.

He stood at the side of the bed, gazing down at her with a heavy heart. On her side, facing away from him, she slept softly, her arms embracing her pillow. The silky red lingerie rode all the way up her bare legs, exposing her lovely figure. He watched her bosom rise and fall gently with each breath. He sighed, filled with regret.

I'll take her out to dinner tomorrow, he promised himself. *Just the two of us.*

An elderly woman held a phone closely to her mouth, looking over her shoulder. Although alone in her darkened house, she used one hand to surround her mouth, speaking in hushed tones. A light was on in an upstairs room in the house next door.

Benson's house.

She waited anxiously for the operator to come on. Annoying music played through the phone while she peered up at the room next door. A slick mechanical voice came on the line.

"Please wait. All operators are busy serving other customers. Your call is important to us and will be answered in the order received." The irritating music returned. After several more iterations of recorded message and music, she heard a click.

"Hello?"

"Thank you for calling 1-800-TIPS," said a friendly voice. "My name is Kimberly, ID 977-88-A521. For quality purposes this call is being recorded. How may I help you today?"

"This is Mrs. Rosy Parker at 1169 Morning Glory Circle? A man next door is acting real strange? I swear he never goes to sleep, the lights are on all night. Maybe—maybe he takes drugs!"

She became agitated over her breaking insight. It explained everything. She should have seen this earlier; how obvious it all seemed now. Her heart started racing; she breathed heavily into the phone trembling in her hand.

"Okay, please calm down, ma'am. Ma'am? Now could you please spell your name for me? And I'll need your REAL ID number, too."

"Oh my, maybe he's on crack? I'll bet he has weapons, too, I think I saw them one time in his garage. Shit! Can you check, I'd feel *so* much safer. And I understand there might be a little ... um, reward?"

Benson and Jane drove down the road mostly silent, looking straight ahead. Their conversation was somewhat strained after the events of the previous night. They were headed to a charming, romantic restaurant where they could relax and talk, a place where Benson could be forgiven for the night before and they could start over. The image of Jane in her sheer red lace and satin slip had been burning in his mind all day long. Red and blue lights flashed in the distance.

"I've been preoccupied with work. It's temporary, I promise."

Jane was usually talkative, but not tonight. She had put herself out and had been snubbed, feeling deeply wounded.

"Uh huh."

"Uh oh."

Benson slowed the car to a crawl. The pulsing lights of squad cars and police vans blocking the street created a hypnotic strobe effect in the dark, the sight of which always aroused in him an inexplicable anxiety. "Team VIPR" read the sandwich board signs placed along the curb. With a broad movement of his flashlight, a cop directed Benson into a vacant parking lot cordoned off by barricades. Drivers were exiting their cars, interrogated by police working in teams roving from car to car.

Benson pulled into the lot and lowered his window. A meaty cop leaned over and stuck his head partway inside the car, uncomfortably close to Benson.

"Problem, officer?"

The cop held a rifle in his right hand, resting his left forearm on the door sill. Checking out Jane, he then peered into the backseat. He eyed Benson for a few seconds before speaking.

"Good evening, folks, I'm Officer Russler. Where you headed tonight?"

"Out," Benson said.

"We're going out to dinner," said Jane.

"Well, we don't wanna keep you too long, you should be on your way in a couple minutes with a little cooperation. You both U.S. citizens?"

"Are we being detained or are we free to go?" demanded Benson.

"I asked you a simple question—now you both U.S. citizens, or what?"

"I don't have to answer any questions. Are we being detained or are we free to go?"

"Identification, please."

Seething inside, Benson reached for his wallet and displayed his REAL ID.

"Take it outta the wallet."

Officer Russler examined the card, frowning at it for a long time, inspecting both sides. Benson stared at the dazzling strobe lights surrounding them, his anxiety rising by the second.

The cop passed the card back to him.

"Know why I pulled you over?"

"Why don't *you* tell *me*?"

Russler abruptly stood up and opened Benson's door.

"Step outta the car, please."

"You don't have any right—"

"So now you're gonna tell me *my* rights? Get outta the car, *now*."

Russler barely gave him enough room to exit. The instant Benson managed to struggle upright, the cop clamped a powerful hand on his shoulder from behind, digging in painfully. He grabbed Benson's opposite wrist, holding it tightly behind his back, and then pushed him over to the front of the car, slamming Benson down until his chest hit the car's hood.

"Spread your legs," Russler commanded.

He muttered some police code into his shoulder radio. Another cop ambled on over, snapping on blue latex gloves as he went. Russler kicked Benson's feet apart some more. Jane stayed inside the car, aghast.

"What the hell's going on?" Benson yelled.

"You have drugs or cash? Firearms? Anything illegal?"

The other cop moved in behind Benson, feeling down his chest, then under his arms and down his back. The cop squatted down and ran his hands up Benson's legs, starting at the ankles, then up his thighs. The cop rose to his feet, groaning with the effort. He ran his hands over Benson's buttocks and in between, making Benson flinch through gritted teeth.

"Please remain there, sir."

Another cop wandered over with a German shepherd pulling vigorously on the leash.

"Bismarck, sit! Sitzen sie! Good evening, folks," the new cop said. "I'm Deputy Officer Fox. Thanks for your full cooperation tonight."

Fox handed Bismarck's leash to the blue-gloved officer, then went around to the car's rear and spread out a tarpaulin on the ground. When he was done, he returned to the front.

"Okay, Bismarck, check *this* out," he said, pointing to the driver's door.

Bismarck jumped onto the door and began vigorously scratching at it with his paws.

"Looks like we got an alert," Fox said.

Russler and Fox ransacked the trunk, throwing everything on the tarpaulin, while Benson remained spread-eagled over his car's hood. They examined the trunk's contents with some curiosity, holding up a camouflage jacket, outdoor boots, flares, rope, bottled water, dried food, knives, fishing tackle, and other articles before tossing them each on the growing pile. Bismarck was very interested in the dried rations on the ground, sniffing energetically.

Fox went over to the open driver's door and waved an electronic scanning wand around the car's interior. He shoved it into all the nooks and creases in the seats and pockets. From behind, the dog sniffed Benson's legs and then his crotch, and began growling.

Fox inserted his wand into a leather holder on his utility belt. He peered inside the car at Jane.

"Ma'am, can I see your purse?"

"No," she said, firmness in her voice. "I do not consent to a search."

"It's mandatory, ma'am. For your own protection."

Deputy Officer Fox dumped the contents of Jane's purse on the car's hood right in front of Benson, rifling through the contents. He found a lipstick case, twisting the metal cylinder until the lipstick popped up, examined it closely, and then put it down. He found two condoms and placed them together on the hood. He picked up a tampon and held it to his ear, rolling it in his fingers like a cigar. He sniffed it and then showed it to Bismarck, who took no interest in it. He found a few store receipts from Jane's lingerie purchase, inspecting them with his flashlight, and then he looked Jane over inside the car. He handed Jane her empty purse and walked away without a word, Bismarck pulling hard at the leash.

Officer Russler finally let Benson get up. Benson had never been so angry; he could hardly contain himself. He considered the different ways that he might kill Russler and watch him die.

"Just a random checkpoint for weapons and drugs," Russler said, walking away. "For your own protection," he said from over his shoulder. "You have a nice evening."

Benson had originally picked a different restaurant, one he knew to be Jane's favorite, but it was full until 9:00, and so he settled on another that appeared suitably romantic, judging from its website and favorable reviews. The pictures showed linen on the tables, candlelit dining, and price fixe menus. No decisions to make; intimate, private booths. They could have a long, leisurely dinner, without distraction.

"Bonsoir, Monsieur et Madame Benson. You are a little delayed tonight, yes? But no matter, I believe we can fit you in. Welcome to La Grande Maison."

Their waiter appeared to be in his mid-30s and smoothly professional. Clad all in black, including a black tie and a small black apron around his waist, he spoke with the very lightest of Parisian accents. He led them to their table, where they sat side by side, and handed them elaborate menus written in a fancy calligraphy that made it challenging to read in the subdued light.

"My name is Swanson. While you look over our selections tonight, may I start you off with some drinks? Apéritifs, oui?"

"Oui," Jane said. "Apple martini, s'il vous plaît."

"Très bien. And for Monsieur?"

"Je voudrais un grand Aviation gin tonic. Avec de l'eau tonique Fever-Tree, si vous en avez. Et citron vert, pas citron."

"Excuse me?"

"A large Aviation Gin and Fever-Tree tonic. Lime, not lemon."

Their drinks arrived swiftly. Swanson set them down with a promise to return for their orders. Benson took a deep, satisfying draft and settled back into the plush, high-backed seat. Jane swallowed a mouthful and closed her eyes, sighing. Benson studied her face, not saying anything. Dark brown hair fell in curly wisps across her forehead. Freckles still dotted her smooth cheeks. The cute girl he'd married had matured into a lovely woman. She opened her eyes, took another long gulp, and gave him a naughty smile, looking at his lips and then his eyes.

Swanson came walking over. Before he reached their table, Benson said, "Deux plus, s'il vous plaît." He held up two fingers, whereupon Swanson retreated.

Jane played with her martini glass, twirling it around slowly and running her fingers along the stem, absorbed in thought.

"Tom, listen—you'll never guess, I'm so excited. I was offered a position with Senator Dixon."

Dining alone at a nearby booth, a man turned his head in their direction. Benson caught his gaze and the man quickly turned away.

"My new job might mean travel for a week or two every month."

Benson stared at her for a moment.

"I didn't even know you were interviewing. You made some great connections; I guess they've paid off for you. We hosted a lot of those fundraisers, didn't we? I'm glad that's all over. Never again. I can't stand those people."

He took a sip of his drink.

"Dixon, Dixon ... isn't she the one in the news trying to broker another peace process in the Middle East or something? Well, good luck to her. That's great, congratulations, but what am I supposed to do—"

Just then, Swanson returned with their drinks, setting them silently on the table. Jane raised her glass and sipped.

She winked at him, flashing a sexy smile that made his pulse beat faster. She moved in closer until they were touching. Benson put his arm around her and caressed her neck. Jane relaxed against him and put her hand on his thigh. He could almost hear Ravel playing.

Benson was glad he'd made time for this. Work could go to hell. The bank could go to hell. And if they didn't like it, they could fire him. The hell with everything. Jane could work for the two of them in her new high-powered job.

"We are featuring tonight for you the cuisine of Aquitaine," Swanson started off. "We begin with pan-fried duck foie gras with caramelized onion, served with a chicory and fresh black truffle salad, accompanied by a glass of fine Muscat noir, a most distinguished appellation. This is followed by Jambon Bayonne. This is a Bayonne ham prepared in the traditional style, or, if you prefer, poissons de moine avec des champignons et le coulis; this is monkfish medallions with mushrooms and coulis sauce ... "

Swanson went on to describe all the courses in exquisite detail. Finally, he departed with their order.

"As I was saying," Benson said, "what am I supposed to do without you when you're gone?"

"Well, it's a great opportunity. It's not like you'll really miss me."

He softly kissed her neck.

"I'm already missing you."

16

No Deal

"YOU ALMOST HAD ME THERE," Benson marveled, banging his fist on the table with such force that it startled Captain Kelly.

"Next time, you have me dig my own grave first," he said, in a high-spirited mood. "Then you stand me up in front of the hole, see? And then—bang!" Benson clapped his hands. "I fall into the pit. It's so much more dramatic. I saw that in a movie once."

Benson's insolence, his mockery and defiance, absolutely astonished Captain Kelly, leaving him gaping like a fish. The "execution" had not only failed to break Benson, it seemed to have had the opposite effect. He'd never come across anything like it.

"I assure you we will next time, Mr. Benson—with *real* bullets."

Benson slapped the table and laughed heartily, enraging Captain Kelly further.

"You give us what we need," Kelly shouted, his face red, spittle flying, "and we could let you go! Let's make a deal!"

Benson leaned back in his chair, folding his arms. How pathetic was this? Unworthy to wear the uniform, whatever uniform this was. In all his time in the service, he hadn't come across such a contemptible misfit. A cretin like this would never have made it into the officer ranks. Even if by some chance he had, some incident would have exposed his degenerate character; he would have disgraced himself and the corps and been dishonorably discharged in short order. Perhaps the new military had been stripped of its former honor to become a political tool staffed by political appointees and corruptible functionaries willing to obey any orders, no matter how unlawful.

Benson sighed.

"You're no Monty Hall." He shook his head in mock sadness. "There will be no deals."

Benson lay on his back, hands clasped behind his head, straining to perform a few situps. Drained, he gazed up at the ceiling and had hardly shut his eyes when the cell door banged open. Barely tethered to a strapping guard, a ferocious German shepherd lunged for Benson. He shielded his face from the rearing, barking dog, almost as tall as himself on its hind legs. Physically painful in its relentless assault, the constant barking provoked an instinctive reaction of fear at such close range, in such tight quarters. He recoiled from the animal's hot, foul breath. The dog snapped its jaws near his face, grazing his cheek with its jagged teeth, drawing blood.

"Down on the floor!" the guard commanded, yelling at Benson over the barking. "Down! On your stomach! Hands behind you!"

The guard slapped tight metal cuffs on Benson's wrists, all the while ordering the dog to stop its incessant barking, repeatedly shouting, "Kaiser, stoppen es!" and "Kaiser, halt die schnauze!" to no effect. When he was finished with Benson, he kicked the dog with an angry curse. Whimpering, Kaiser backed up into a corner.

Benson was marched to an area of the prison compound he had never seen. They passed an inmate in the hall going in the opposite direction, roughly prodded by a guard. The prisoner was dripping wet and short of breath, looking like she'd seen a ghost. The water trail on the floor led to a room filled with instruments and a stainless steel water tank. Another burly guard like the one who accompanied Benson waited inside for them, and one of those agents with a small, stylized bear paw print on his outfit. Absorbed with computer terminals on a stainless steel counter running the room's length, a skinny doctor in a lab coat busily typed commands on each one in turn.

His dirty orange jumpsuit roughly yanked off, Benson was stripped to his ragged underwear. Kicking and screaming, he struggled against the two guards as they fought to lay him down on a long, wide board. One held Benson down by the throat while the other went to work. His arms were straightened out by brute force, held away from his body, and bound with straps mounted to the board. As one of the guards moved to bind Benson's ankles together, he kicked his leg free, striking the guard's chin with a powerful snap. The guard's face was bloody and Benson was sure he'd broken some bones or teeth. The other guard stomped on Benson's chest with his knee, crushing him with the force and knocking the wind out of him.

A new guard promptly arrived to replace the injured one. The doctor walked over, recording some observations on a clipboard as he went. He snapped a monitoring device on Benson's finger. The two guards heaved the board up with Benson strapped on it, placing him in the tank face up in the chilly water.

"Okay, Benson," Agent Scott Tracy leaned in closely with sour breath, "no more foolin' around, the fun an' games are over. Wha' do you know about financing terrorism? How'd you do it? Who were your contacts? Let's go, give it up."

"Are you talking? Did I give you permission to talk?"

"Let's see how he likes a little dunk."

The guards draped clear cellophane loosely over Benson's face, tucking it in around his head to keep it approximately in place. A guard dipped a bucket in the tank and poured a steady cascade of water over his head. Holding his breath, struggling to break free, Benson jerked back and forth, as if in a seizure. The cellophane let in water. He battled to hold his breath as the streaming continued onto his face. Enveloped and overwhelmed, he felt that he was really drowning; he was surely going to suffocate and die. Panic overtook him. Finally forced to succumb, he breathed, inhaling water.

The torrent ceased. The doctor recorded the subject's elapsed time, heart rate, and blood oxygen saturation. Benson hacked uncontrollably, but his lungs wouldn't clear. They removed the cellophane from his face.

"Ready to talk?"

"Kiss my ass, you sweaty porker," Benson coughed out. "Go defile a goat, you degenerate, evil little muppet."

Tracy was floored.

"Let's see how he likes a little swim."

The guards replaced the cellophane and lowered the board until only the very top of Benson's face was above water. Tracy snapped his fingers and the water began pouring. This time, Benson closed his eyes and breathed slowly through his mouth, minimizing the intake of water, gulping it down when it became too much, and trying to calm his mind by imagining that he was just floating in a pool.

For a time it worked, and then the inescapable feeling of drowning and panic suddenly returned.

"Stop! I can't—I can't b-breathe," he gasped.

"Ready to talk now? I thought so. Excellent."

The guards hoisted the board out of the water, propping Benson up against the tank and removing the cellophane. Water streamed down his face. Gagging, he glared at his captors, clenching his fists tightly bound to the board on either side of him.

"You tell me how you financed the Saudi operation!" Tracy screamed at him. "Who'd you deal with? Tell me now!"

Benson thrust his head forward off the board. His chest was heaving. He seemed about to say something, unable to get the words out. Tracy eagerly leaned in closer. Benson spat a mouthful of water in his face.

"Got turned on, didn't you?" Benson sneered. "You got excited, you twisted pervert. Go ahead, do it again! You want to. Admit it, you depraved slimeball, you worthless hack—you're aroused."

At a loss, Agent Tracy looked at the guards. The technique had always worked so well before. Prisoners would always confess. "I—"

Tracy looked at the guards again, but they only returned blank stares. "I—"

He stared at the floor.

"Just take him to his room," he sputtered.

Confined in his cell, cold and hungry, Benson heard foot-steps approaching at a fast clip, the heavy boots stomping ever closer. The guard slammed the steel door open and marched him quickly down the corridor. He was shoved into the interrogation room with such force that he fell to the floor. Two agents dressed in flight-style, olive-drab jump-suits had been talking excitedly to each other. They abruptly interrupted their chatter at his arrival, staring at him as he crawled to the nearest chair.

"Mr. Benson, let's be straight up, we wanna believe your story, we've seen all the interview notes," one of the agents said, gesturing at the piles scattered across the table. "We wanna help, but you have to help us, too. Fair is fair, right?"

"Don West." Benson laughed in his face, shaking his head. "Hey kid, why don't you get a real job?"

"Look, Mr. Benson," said Zachary Smith, the second agent. "The public needs to feel we're doing our jobs. They're scared. Another attack *must* be prevented. That's our mission and we take it serious."

He seemed almost apologetic.

"Look, we can't just sit around while the Homeland is under attack. You're not the kinda man who puts his selfish personal needs ahead of his country, are you? We can't be only thinking about ourselves and forget about everybody else, can we? Let's put this, uh, *inconvenience* behind us?"

"Inconvenience."

Benson stood and flung his chair at the wall. The ever-present guard slouching by the door suddenly straightened up, but Smith held up his hand for the guard to back off.

"Inconvenience—is that what you call it?" Benson said. "How about *torture*? How could you do this? Americans, for God's sake."

"Okay, so lemme tell *you* something, Mr. Benson," Smith replied. "You think we're just a bunch a' whacko sadists? You think we don't know anything about due process? You think we *like* doing this? We don't like it one bit, but we have no choice. These terrorists are after nuclear and chemical weapons and they'll destroy the Homeland when they get their hands on 'em. It's the greater good here versus evil. My own sister was killed in a—" Smith choked up, "in a suicide bombing. She was at the mall with her friends … " he drifted off, struggling to regain his composure, "but at least we don't torture."

"So we don't have the best heating and lighting," Agent West added, shrugging. "Maybe the music's a bit too loud. You call that torture? Electrocution, mutilation—that's *real* torture."

"Yes," said Agent Smith, "that's absolutely right. Hooking your balls up to a car battery, now *that* would be real torture. Or cutting your dick off. Or shoving a hot probe up your ass. No, we don't do any of that."

He nodded to West, who wholeheartedly agreed.

"We abide by a professional code."

"A professional code," Benson said. "You have shit on the oath that every soldier swears."

"Well, we aren't um—we aren't really soldiers."

West plunked a photograph down on the desk.

"You know this man, right?"

"No. So who the hell *are* you people?"

"The truth, now. You know this man?"

"Same question, same answer."

"But our informant—let's call her 'K'—says you know him. You went to the same mosque on the same day as our asset. We got K's testimony right here."

"Mosque? You bungling little stooge." Benson leaned over the table until his face was close to West's. "Your paid informant is a mindless toady."

The guard in the corner gripped his rifle a little tighter, ready for some action.

"Okay, I'll prove it to you," West said. "We set up surveillance in mosques to see what they were doing in there—and now we know. Freedom of religion is one thing, okay, but insurrection? That's crossing the line."

West played a murky black-and-white surveillance video from a laptop. A middle-aged white woman wearing ridiculously oversized black robes—more like a big black blanket—took a seat in the back of a mosque. It was fairly dim in there. A service seemed to be in progress. She peered around uneasily, apparently trying to blend in. The camera panned out to take in the congregation, most of whom appeared to be of Mideastern ethnicity. The men wore normal Western suits, shirts, and slacks. The women wore long dresses and headscarves, sitting mainly in the roped-off sections by themselves in the back. The camera zoomed in to focus on several men seated in front, but it was too dark to clearly identify them.

Was one of those men supposed to be *him*?

"This is your proof? You poor, confused little dumb-ass, you chowderhead. Here's what I think of your proof."

Benson grabbed the laptop. Spreading it apart, he raised it over his head with both hands and hurled it to the floor. It fractured into pieces, making a satisfying cracking sound.

West backed up from the table and jumped to his feet.

"What did you know and when did you know it? Cooperate, dammit!"

"I will *not* cooperate in my own destruction.

"I will *not* back down."

Benson cleared the table of the documents with a sweep of his forearm. They all fluttered to the floor.

"I will *not* go along or get along.

"I will *not* give in, ever.

"I will *not* give up. You will get *nothing* from me."

West suddenly slapped Benson. Feeling his face for blood, Benson massaged the sting from his jaw, his eye on the guard at the door, who remained on high alert. Benson's eyes glittered with hatred.

"The man in this photo has been designated a Politically Exposed Person," said Agent West, pushing the same snapshot as before across the table. "This PEP has been accused of marketing narcotics. The Terrorist Financing Operations Section believes the alleged proceeds may be financing terror ops."

"Narcoterrorism," broke in Agent Smith.

"Yes, very good. As I was saying," West gave his colleague a dirty look, "TFOS found corporate layering, transfers between bank accounts of related entities and charities for no apparent reason we could figure. That's suspicious. The Bank Secrecy Act requires five reports to be filed that shoulda been filed—FinCEN Form 104, Form 105, Form 110, Treasury Form 90-22.1 and 90-22.47—and they weren't. That's suspicious, too. But maybe the biggest problem is OCC Form 8010-9, 8010-1 Suspicious Activity Report. Banks must file a SAR for any suspicious transaction potentially relevant to any possible violation of any law, regulation, or pending law or regulation. Failure to do so is enough right there," West eyed Benson, leaning in, "to get you a $100,000 fine and five years in prison. *Personally.*"

Impressive, thought Benson. The thicket of new financial regulations was virtually incomprehensible even for bankers and their teams of seasoned lawyers. Established legal terms were continually being redefined, the rules were constantly changing, and the number of such dictates and their complexity ever growing. And yet this young guy seemed to know all the regulatory claptrap off the top of his head.

"Well, how about this, Don West. Listen closely now, boy genius—maybe we didn't suspect anything."

"Okay, look," said Agent Smith. "It takes big money to fund global terrorism. Starting to get the big picture now? You arranged and bundled the financing and then you laundered the money through your bank."

"And why would I do that?"

"You tell *us*, Mr. Benson."

17

Phantoms of Lost Liberty

"I N A DRAMATIC MOVE, THE PRESIDENT reshuffled his top advisors. Also up next—five people die in a horrifying freeway accident. You won't want to miss this."

Benson and Jane were watching television, lounging in bed.

"Tom, can we please turn this idiocy off?"

"In a minute."

"If you spent one-tenth the time on *me* as you spend working ... we just don't talk anymore."

Upon their return home from La Grande Maison, Benson was more than a bit miffed when Jane slipped into her cozy old sweatpants and fraying top—not that ultra-sexy, little red number from the night before—tied her hair back, and hopped into bed with some sort of instruction manual on her lap. There would be no perfume and rose petals tonight; no champagne and scented candles. No strawberries and whipped cream.

Benson didn't understand her. They had just spent two hours eating, talking, and reminiscing, had they not? He changed the channel.

"Hey look, the Leneau show is on."

The talk-show host rubbed his hands together and cocked his head, an impish smile on his face.

"Please welcome Defense Czar Donnell Trumble."

The audience clapped politely, but Jane was hardly in a mood to join in the celebration.

"You know, there's so much going on in the world, Mr. Secretary, especially the Middle East. It's a hornet's nest of trouble and age-old animosities."

Leneau leaned in for a response, but none was forthcoming. He was about to try a less subtle question when the defense secretary suddenly sprang to life, flashing a smirk for a split second. He narrowed his eyes.

"The entire world is our battlefield," Trumble said softly, in smooth, evenly spaced words, "and the Homeland is, of course, part of that battlefield. We are in the process of building extensible infrastructure in order to encapsulate unlawful enemy combatants who may pose a threat to national security."

The audience clapped. Trumble squinted to see beyond the bright stage lights into the theater. He leaned forward in his seat, his brow furrowed. He seemed to be in his own little world, completely self-absorbed, as though speaking only to himself, reading from some internal script.

"There are certain, uh, let us say, *mission-critical facilities* across the Homeland that we are repurposing for the Global War on Terror."

The lights reflected off his elaborately coiffed, lustrous sheet of golden hair.

"There are those who say that gathering certain intelligence may impose on traditional civil liberties, but we don't really have a choice. We're at war now."

"Here comes Trumble!" Leneau said, in a feeble effort to lighten up the tone. This was, after all, supposed to be an entertainment show. This Trumble was proving to be a tough character.

Secretary Trumble stared at the host. His enigmatic expression did not change.

"If you knew what we know you'd *comprendo*," he said, tapping his temple with a forefinger, "but of course we can't really tell you anything. State secrets, you know. Too sensitive."

He smoothed his hair into place, emerging from his trance-like state, becoming more animated.

"Like it or not, we *are* the world's superpower. We have a moral duty to intervene around the world—if we don't, we'll allow evil to flourish. So it's time to mobilize the Homeland and prepare."

Trumble squinted out at the audience and then eyed Leneau.

"You do believe in duty, don't you, Jay?"

"Sure, I guess so, but—"

"You do believe in being prepared, don't you?"

"Well, sure, I was a boy scout and everything, but—"

"Then you would know we must foster morality in places where death and destruction are the way of life. Now, I don't know about *you*," Trumble said, poking Leneau's chest with his finger, "but I'd rather be photographed by hidden cameras than get on a train with men carrying bombs in backpacks. Getting blown to bits is more an intrusion of privacy than carrying an identity card."

He leaned back in his seat.

"Am I right or wrong?" he asked the audience.

Scattered applause rippled through the theater.

"I ask you," Trumble leaned forward at the edge of his seat, gazing directly at the audience, "would it be better to give foreign terrorists the right to formal due process and then have millions die in a raging inferno? Better to give rights to terrorists and then have your city incinerated in a nuclear holocaust? You think I'm kidding? Then think again. They've been raised to hate us; that's their mindset. If you're sitting on a ticking time bomb you have to defuse it now, not later. Do the rights of terrorists come before the rights of the community? We have to make some reasonable tradeoffs here. 'Balance' is the word we're using—a *balanced* approach, if you will. Now, the fanatics who attacked us will keep attacking until we're destroyed or submit. That's how they're getting to heaven with the virgins, you know. Am I right or wrong?"

There followed an uncomfortable silence.

"Mr. Defense Czar, we keep hearing these war rumors, you know, where it might cost the lives of 500,000 foreign people, among them women and children and the sick and elderly. Do you think the price is worth it?"

"I think this is a very hard choice, but the price ..." Trumble drifted off in deep contemplation. "We think the price point is absolutely worth it. Sometimes you have to take a few liberties to get where you want to go. It's all about balancing—"

Leneau thumped his desk.

"We need to take a break. Unusual Mother's Day gifts coming up next!"

"Tom, can we please turn this off? I want to show you something."

"Hang on, I just want to watch this one little segment," Benson said, changing the channel. "Five minutes."

"Please give a warm welcome to my next guest, ladies and gentlemen. You know him as the Big Man with the Master Plan, the Sire of Surveillance, the Sovereign of Security— our own Department of Homeland Security chief Mikhail 'Mickey' Cherkov!"

The secretary peeped out from behind a curtain, waving at the audience as he made his way. Leatherman, the show's host, leaned into Cherkov's shoulder as they shook hands, whispering something. They both smiled and took their seats.

"Thanks for coming, Mr. Homeland Czar. So what's the deal with—"

"To those who scare peace-loving people with phantoms of lost liberty, our message is this: your tactics only aid terrorists, for they erode our national unity and diminish our resolve. They give ammunition to America's enemies and pause to America's friends. They encourage people of good will to remain silent in the face of evil."

Secretary Cherkov was deeply gratified by the vigorous clapping. The speech lessons were working. His coaches had told him to act assertively and with confidence even if he felt a little nervous inside. He wasn't coming across as a little milquetoast anymore. They had even advised him to gain a little weight so he wouldn't appear so drawn and hollow-eyed. A little sun wouldn't hurt either, they said, but he didn't have much time for that.

Leatherman fidgeted with a pencil.

"So, how do you fight a War on Terror, anyway?"

He watched the pencil roll off his desk.

"Well, Dave, we are in the process of transitioning to a real game-changing paradigm, leveraging internal functionalities in terms of our brand new Safety First Initiative, or SFI."

Cherkov could have kicked himself for retreating into corporate-speak banality. His "phantoms of lost liberty" opener had come off perfectly, just as rehearsed, but then he had blanked out.

Except for a puzzled expression, Leatherman had nothing substantive to offer to this last comment, so Cherkov continued on.

"There are no absolutes; no right, no wrong—" Secretary Cherkov interrupted himself, not sure if he really agreed with what he'd just said—but no matter. They had told him that communication was 95 percent body language anyway, and here he was, sitting up straight, chest puffed out, the very picture of sincerity and conviction.

"It's really about what needs to be done and the uh, the will to do it," Cherkov said. "When push comes to shove, at the critical moment, we as a nation may have to defend our freedoms with our lives if necessary, just like the founding fathers pledged their lives, their fortunes, and their sacred honor. I believe we'll rise to the challenge."

He was beginning to find his voice again.

"And we finally have a strong leader to advance our democracy and remoralize our nation."

Leatherman scooped his pencil off the floor and flung it at the cameraman, followed by a phony sound effect of breaking glass. He mugged for the cameras, twisting his elastic face sideways into a bizarre expression. The audience was highly amused.

"Don't go away. Stupid pet tricks coming up next, ladies and gentlemen!"

"Tom—we need to work on our relationship."

The vacuous talk shows having consumed the better part of an hour, Benson was now greatly fatigued. He'd nearly fallen asleep watching them. Mindless entertainment helped him forget about a difficult day, and this was about as difficult as they came.

Jane handed him a booklet, holding a copy of the same in her lap, pencil in hand.

"Oh, no," he muttered.

It was some sort of relationship kit. He viewed the forms and the stubby little pencils with apprehension. Nothing good could possibly come from this.

"This is *Dr. Filbert's Relationship Inventory Survey.* You complete the detailed questionnaire and then it goes into a database where you find out how you compare with thousands of other couples. I saw it on his show."

"Dr. Filbert? Is he still on?"

"It graphs the results against a range of benchmarks and gives you a relationship analysis score. That tells you what you need to work on. There's even an 800 number to get in touch and learn more."

"No, no, come on. No. Not now. We should have done this an hour ago. I'm tired. Maybe tomorrow."

He turned over and buried his face in his pillow.

"Okay, first question: name the 12 things you appreciate most about me."

"I am weary, I say. Be gone with you, woman. Take your leave, or I shall call the guards."

"Tom!"

Resigned to his fate, he sighed and sat up, looking with despair at the long list of questions spanning several pages. He would have no choice but to go along for the ride.

"Well, let's see. Your hair is nice." He checked that off.

"Good sense of humor—check. Likes to fill out surveys—check."

Jane looked at him with deep disapproval.

"What? What'd I do?"

Her withering look reminded him of his mother's expression, when, as a boy, she had scolded him for something bad he'd done. He didn't have the foggiest recollection of what that was now, but he could picture her scowling face as clearly as if it were yesterday. She would go on and on, during which time he had to sit quietly and be respectful, not letting his attention wander too much.

"You're being passive-aggressive again," Jane said. "I'm sure that's what Dr. Filbert would say, like when you say you'll do something and then 'forget' to follow through."

His father was a man of fewer words. He would lean in and stare down the boy with his piercing eyes. "You know what you did wrong?" The young Benson would nod yes, casting his eyes downward, contrite. Of course he knew. He didn't enjoy admitting his guilt, and his father wouldn't subject him to the indignity of a lengthy inquisition or force him to sign a formal confession. The lesson learned, the matter would be over forthwith.

Benson had tried this method, so oddly effective in his youth, on his own son, without success. Daniel would argue for the defense from different angles, exploiting technical loopholes and logical contradictions in the prosecution's case.

Benson would sit back, astonished. Sometimes he had to stifle his laughter, marveling at the boy's audacity. Still, a fiercely independent spirit was something to be encouraged in today's more ordered society, with its conformists, company tools, and bureaucrats dominating the landscape.

"Tom! Are you listening?"

"Yes, of course. What'd you say?"

18

Dear Blank

Presidedent King sat comfortably in a large, winged-back chair. The congressional leaders surrounding him stood stiffly, clasping their hands in front and staring into the bright camera lights, blinking and wearing frozen grins.

"My friends, civilization's at stake," King said. "American interests are being threatened anew by another rogue regime. Our new enemy teaches that innocent individuals can be sacrificed to serve a political vision. This probably explains their cold-blooded contempt for human life. We believe they may have inherited nuclear weapons prototypes from the last rogue regime or that they're in the process of building them and they may be getting pretty close. Either way, we're not gonna wait for proof that could come in the form of a big, smoking mushroom cloud."

The distinguished congressional leaders shuffled on their feet. Their stiff grins began sagging.

"Let's be real clear: we must defeat them over there so they don't come over here. We call it the Flypaper Strategy. You draw your enemies to a single area away from everything and then you just finish them off. You wipe them out on *their* turf. So it follows that we're gonna need a pretty big flytrap. I now call upon the distinguished senior representative of the People's House."

Representative Rankle stepped forward. He cleared his throat, followed by an uncontrollable cough. He hacked into a tissue, examined the foul discharge, and stuffed it into his pocket.

"Those who love this country have a patriotic obligation to defend this country," Rankle said, holding the microphone so near to his mouth that his croaking voice reverberated with shrill feedback and loud echoes, rendering him barely intelligible.

"So we're calling on all our young men and women to join hands and defend the Homeland. Draftees must reflect America. All must participate—whites and minorities, the educated and the uneducated, the privileged and the under-privileged, the disenfranchised and the disadvantaged."

He fished the tissue out of his pocket and hacked loudly into it, wiping off his mouth.

"For those who say the poor fight better, I say give the rich a chance."

He waited, but the reporters had no questions.

"And also, some economists, they're saying this'll help reduce youth unemployment and give the economy a big shot in the arm while they're serving their country."

At a separate press conference, Defense Secretary Trumble held court. He leaned forward in his chair until his lips brushed the array of microphones in front of him, jabbing his finger in the air for emphasis as he spoke. He wore his signature navy-blue suit and red power tie. Standing behind him were aides wearing similar suits and ties.

"Since 1980," he told the assembled conference, "the Selective Service has required—under penalty of a five-year prison sentence—those who are 18 to 26 to register in order to furnish us with a pool of fresh, young resources for a national emergency. Now is the opportune time to empower those national resources."

Trumble narrowed his eyes, looking around at everyone without blinking. It unnerved people and helped close big deals.

"According to the SS, 25.8 million young men and women are eligible to assist the 1.5 million active service members and 900,000 currently in the reserves. Those unsuitable for military service will be inducted into the Citizen National Service Corps under the provisions of the Universal National Service Act."

The mail carrier had Benson sign a receipt, and then he rummaged through his bag, pulling out a manila envelope addressed to Daniel.

"Thank you, sir. You have a real nice day."

The only markings on the envelope were Daniel's name and address, the lasts four digits of his REAL ID, and "For Official Use Only—Unauthorized Opening Subject to Severe Criminal Penalties." With a warning like that, Daniel was scared to touch it. Except for the occasional birthday and holiday card, it was most unusual for him to get any kind of letter in the paper mail; rarer still to have it hand-delivered. He sometimes received credit card solicitations offering low introductory interest rates. They often came in phony, official-looking envelopes like this one so that they wouldn't be thrown away, unread. On the other hand, he had been waiting anxiously for an acceptance letter from the University of Virginia. The whole family had gone on a tour of several universities. Daniel had finally settled on his father's alma mater. Perhaps this was the letter.

"For me? What is it?"

"Open it and find out."

Benson didn't like the look of this. It reminded him of Internal Revenue Service notices, none of which ever bore glad tidings.

Daniel tore apart the envelope. He read the letter silently, his expression transforming from mild curiosity to wild-eyed horror.

"Dear _____," it began. "Congratulations. You have won a special lottery and been given the opportunity to defend the Homeland in its time of need. You are hereby directed to present yourself for Armed Forces Physical Examination (AFPE) to the Military Entrance Processing Station (MEPS) named above by reporting at 6:58 a.m. on the indicated date to your Local Office." It was stamped, dated, and auto-signed by some petty local official with an obscure title.

Shocked, Daniel held the notice from the Selective Service, *Order to Report for Armed Forces Physical Examination*, loosely in his hand. He watched it flutter to the floor, staring after it in silence. Benson picked up the letter and read it for himself, hiding his alarm.

He put his arm around the boy's shoulder.

"I know you'll serve your country with distinction."

"They didn't fill in my name. It's a mistake, I don't have to go."

"Your name is on the envelope. They know who you are."

"*You* don't even know me! You don't know ..." Daniel looked away, his eyes beginning to tear. "You don't know who I am, you have no idea. I'm not brave and tough like you. I'm not a black belt like you. I'm no fighter."

He stared off into space.

"I'm no war hero."

Jane was out of town, doing her monthly stint in Senator Dixon's home district office, a place the Honorable Senator herself hardly ever visited. Jane's new job was not exactly what was promised, mainly involving the recording of constituent's opinions of pending bills and handling angry complaints and even threats. They came in by the hundreds every day, by email, letter, and telephone. Benson was on his own.

Although Daniel said he wasn't hungry, Benson persuaded him to go with him to Daniel's favorite restaurant anyway. He thought it would aid conversation, but Benson had to prod Daniel to say anything. They placed their orders and Daniel fell to brooding. They sat in silence for a while.

"War won't settle anything, it'll just make new enemies," Daniel said at last. "Meanwhile, I have to sacrifice my life to the State."

He put his head down on the table.

"Cannon fodder. I'll be a war slave."

"Daniel, don't look at it that way, you're being too dramatic. It'll all be over quickly enough. You'll come out of this a new man."

Daniel suddenly sprang to life. He looked at his father with new hope.

"Dad, what if I go to Canada and sit this out? I could go to college there and return when it's all over."

"I'm afraid you wouldn't get past the border wall. Once you're on draft notice your REAL ID status automatically changes. The security checkpoints are heavily fortified. They're inspecting everyone trying to leave—you need a valid reason on the exit form. They wouldn't let you out."

"Then I'll get a fake Canadian passport. I'll walk and talk like a Canadian and say I was just visiting the U.S. for a few days and now I'm returning home—you know, to Canada."

"It doesn't work like that," Benson said. "Others have tried."

"So I'll just borrow someone's ID, someone who looks like me. They never really check those things anyway."

"No, I don't think so. It can't be done, not anymore."

"Then I'll be a conscientious objector—for religious reasons."

"They don't allow that anymore. What you'd really need is a personal waiver from the president or secretary of defense or someone like that."

Daniel brightened.

"Hey, you have connections to powerful people in D.C., right? You had that picture of you shaking hands with the president. That must count for something. You could get me a deferment or reprieve or whatever they call it, right?"

"That snapshot was just a photo-op thing. There were probably thousands like me. After the election, they wanted nothing to do with me. I didn't raise enough money or maybe they didn't like my attitude, I don't know."

"Let's call Mom tonight at her hotel," Daniel said. "She works for one of those senators, maybe she can work out a deal."

19

Welcome to National Airport

Jane was preparing one of her elaborate Italian omelets for their Sunday breakfast. As she whipped the eggs and sautéed the vegetables, Benson relaxed at the kitchen table with the Sunday news. Once they sat down to eat, though, he put it away. The results of *Dr. Filbert's Relationship Inventory Survey* clearly showed that he needed to work on "communication skill sets" and "supportive engagement strategies."

"Jane, you outdid yourself. This frittata—sensazionale. The eggs are fluffy and the peppers are crisp and delicious. That's goat cheese inside, isn't it? Il caffè espresso è la perfezione. Congratulazioni—tre stelle. Sono in fiamme per te. Ti desidero ora."

"Thanks—I think. You know, you don't have to do this."

"No, no, I want to. The news can wait. So how's your new job going with what's her name, the senator?"

"Well, I did want to tell you about something strange that happened on Friday. A man walks into the office, maybe 20 or so I guess, a skinny foreign guy. He's wearing a black suit—a bit too small—with dirty running shoes. Something just looks *wrong* about him. He goes to the front desk and says he wants to *see* Senator Dixon right away. 'You can't just see her,' I say to him, 'you have to make an appointment, she's very busy, but you can fill out the form and put it in the basket over there and they'll get back to you in 10 to 14 working days.' He leans

166

across the front desk to see down the hallway, and I tell him she's not in. He's really creeping me out now. I ask him his name, and he says, 'Barber,' or something like that. So I ask him what's his business here, and he gets in my face and starts telling me all about the peace process in rapid-fire, broken English."

"Yikes. You really should be able to defend yourself at work. There're a lot of suspicious characters running around. A little gun would do the trick. I'm thinking maybe a Beretta Nano."

"You know we can't defend ourselves—weapons aren't allowed—but they say not to worry, they have really tight security. So anyway, this goes on for a few minutes. He starts to get really worked up, something about his parents killed in some war with America when he was little, I couldn't really tell what he was saying. I picked up the phone to call security and he ran like a shot. I don't know how he got past—"

Just then the phone rang. Benson answered it, holding the phone to his ear, saying hardly anything to the caller. He grew increasingly agitated and paced the room, speaking in hushed tones.

"I'm so sorry," he said, quietly. He put the phone down.

"What is it? What happened?"

"Jared Morris, our old friend from college. He went out for a run in the park and dropped dead. His wife is in shock."

"That's terrible—how awful."

Although they hadn't seen much of each other in the last few years, they were still good friends with the couple. Benson had roomed with Jared at the University of Virginia.

"He was our age," Benson said.

He looked sadly at Jane.

"No warning. The funeral is Tuesday."

"Welcome to National Airport—You Are Entering a Federal Security Zone," warned the sign. "All Persons and Property Subject to Seizure." Guided into inspection lanes similar to those at the borders, drivers presented their REAL IDs for scrutiny. Armed Transportation Security Administration officers patrolled up and down the lanes and between the cars, walking tightly leashed Dobermans. As the cars crawled through the checkpoint, signs exhorted them to support their country in its time of need: "Buy Stimulus War Bonds— Support Our Troops *and* the Economy—Major Credit Cards Accepted."

A TSA security officer came over and rapped on the taxi window with his knuckles. The driver rolled down his window.

"Who are these people here?" the officer asked the driver.

"These people are my passenger, yes? Very fine people, no trouble. Okay, so I take to airport, yes?"

"Roll down the rear windows, please."

The officer peered into the backseat. He examined the footwells and the seatback pockets. His dog stood up on its hind legs and eyed the passengers within.

"Open the trunk, please."

Moving to the rear of the taxi, the officer rummaged through the luggage, flipping the cases and bags over, inspecting everything with an electronic scanning wand. He examined the spare time compartment with a flashlight, then slammed the trunk lid closed and returned to the passengers in the back seat.

"What's the purpose of your travel today, folks?"

"That's private," Benson said.

"We're going to a funeral," said Jane, giving Benson a scathing look.

"What's the final destination on your ticket?"

"That's private, too," Benson said.

"Providence," said Jane.

"Tom!" she whispered, "you're not going to change the geopolitical situation today. This hired goon can arrest us for noncompliance."

"You got your tickets? Let's see 'em."

"No," Benson said. The Doberman gave a low growl. "I didn't print them."

"So you got 'em on your phone, or what?"

"No."

"A'right, let's see your identification."

"You don't have any r—" began Benson, but Jane stopped him mid-sentence with a sharp jab in the ribs.

The officer swiped their cards through a reader on his utility belt. He stood up and mumbled something into his shoulder radio, out of their line of sight.

He bent over and eyed Benson and Jane for a few seconds, looking at their faces in silence.

"You need to show some proof a' where you goin', a'right? I'm gonna let you travel today, but jus' so you know next time. You have a nice trip, folks."

He tapped the taxi roof twice and they were off.

They stepped out of the taxi to the curb, where they were greeted by yellow-and-black striped barricades manned by soldiers in fatigues and sunglasses, rifles looped over their shoulders. Attack dogs jumped up and down with excitement, intently staring at all the travelers.

They made their way through the airport to the extensive screening line. Every 10 minutes, a blaring loudspeaker broadcast in a flat tone, *"Attention, citizens. Your attention, please. Today's threat level is Brown—or moderately serious risk of terrorist attack—for all domestic and international flights."*

An attractive woman at the head of their security lane hesitated before entering the body scanners.

"Okay, c'mon, let's go, into the scanner," a TSA security guard on the other side of it said to her. "You're holdin' up the line, darlin'. Stand with your bare feet on the yellow shoe outlines and make sure there's nothin' in your pockets."

"I don't think I should go through the scanner."

"And why's that, honey?"

"Well, I—I think I might be pregnant," she said, quietly.

"Baby Shower Opt-Out, Lane 2!" the guard yelled in a booming voice. "Fanny Pack, Lane 2! Okay, darlin', why don't you stand over to the side, right over here."

The woman was ordered to spread her legs and stand with her hands over her head. A female security guard donned some flimsy latex gloves and frisked her up and down, putting her hands on the woman's breasts and squeezing at different spots. Another guard came over and waved an electronic wand over the woman's crotch and wherever weapons or drugs might be concealed on her body.

"This yours?" the guard at the x-ray asked her, pointing to her suitcase, whereupon it was flung open, exhibiting some rather intimate garments to the subtle amusement of bystanders. Finding nothing further of interest, the woman was allowed to repack her belongings in embarrassed silence.

An elderly gentleman with shoes in hand was next in line. He wore a charcoal pinstripe suit and burgundy tie, standing out from the more casually attired people waiting placidly, most of them dressed in jeans, sweats, running shoes, T-shirts, and even a few in pajamas and slippers. Benson and Jane stood barefoot right behind the gentleman, their keys, shoes, belts, coats, wallet, handbag, computers, watches, and phones having already been deposited in gray plastic bins. They removed the toiletries from their luggage, placing them in clear bags and then into separate gray bins. Overhead signs displayed illustrations of shoes, underwire brassieres, and bombs with a red X drawn through each.

"I remember a time," the elderly man blurted out, "when you just went onto the airplane with your ticket, simple as that. And your family meeting you, they'd be right at the gate, soon as you stepped off the plane."

He spoke to a muscular security guard cradling an Uzi submachine gun.

"You can find all this stuff, whatever you're looking for here, in all the jails, you know that? Jails, you know, and they have all the best security there, too."

The security guard stared at him blankly and then glanced at the wall clock. He checked his wristwatch.

"Now, we could have just allowed the pilots to carry guns, see, and I wouldn't have to stand here waving my arms around like a flaming jackass. Those fellows know how to shoot, too. They're ex-military, same as me. We fought to preserve our freedom, and now look at this. Are you guys ex-military, too?"

The guard now expressed a sudden interest. The vast majority of passengers went through the lines without making so much as a peep, not even a "hello." They kept their heads down and studiously avoided eye contact. It was never a good thing to be conspicuous at a security checkpoint.

"Did I hear right?" The guard spoke in a harsh voice. "Did you just say, 'pilots and guns?'"

"No, I just meant that—"

"You makin' threats? 'Cause that's what I think I just heard. Okay, step outta the line, gramps."

The guard led him to a separate area, snapping on blue rubber gloves as he went.

"Stand over here." He pointed to an outline of shoes printed on a rubber mat.

"Behavior Detection Officer, Area 3, please," he called out.

BDO Bob had been busy watching the travelers a few lanes away. When things were slow, he would sometimes engage them in a little light banter, secretly looking for unreasonable anxiety or irritableness, or perhaps atypical facial expressions or body language. The kids would often ask him about his gun, club, handcuffs, pepper spray, and taser, but the adults knew better. In his three years on duty, the only travelers he'd pulled out of the lines for suspicious behavior turned out to be upset about running late and possibly missing their flights.

He walked over to Area 3 and watched the gentleman disrobe and get frisked in front of gawking onlookers, themselves in various stages of disrobing for the scanners. No one said anything.

"The world has changed, Grandpa," said BDO Bob.

To his burning shame, Benson said nothing either, and yet what could he really do? Defend the honor of an old man and expose himself to enhanced security procedures? Would he be led off, too, escorted somewhere for questioning by entry-level operatives whose big thrill for the day would otherwise be discovering a forgotten penknife or a hidden flask of whiskey? Benson was reminded of those old World War II movies in which a line of passengers would be waiting to board their train. A State security agent would walk up and down the line, giving everyone a cursory examination, his very presence making them skittish. The agent would pull out of the line a particular traveler for no apparent reason, escorting him away. The rest of the sheep would immediately pretend to put the incident out of their minds and board the train, properly subdued and put in their place. The real saboteur, a trained professional, would, of course, escape detection, knowing exactly how to get past security.

Still, Benson had the feeling that he should have acted. He should have done *something*. He was just like the train passengers in those old movies. Once-proud Americans were learning to be submissive, deferential to any character in a uniform.

Old folks staggered out of their wheelchairs and their walkers, hobbling through the scanners as the Blueshirts motioned for them to come through. An old woman with a vacant expression sat in a wheelchair with oxygen tubes in her nostrils. The guards searched her thoroughly while she sat there, running electronic scanning wands over the oxygen tank, into the wheelchair compartments, and over and under her body before pushing her through.

Jane was boiling.

"Maybe we should've just driven to the funeral."

Benson was about to respond, but was rudely interrupted by a jarring announcement bellowing throughout the terminal: *"Attention, citizens. Note your surroundings and report suspicious items or activities to the Authorities."*

The latest generation one-view, full-body scanners had just been installed at National Airport. Producing a precise, lifelike rendering, some studies found them to have somewhat better accuracy in certain cases than images blurred by "privacy software" when it came to identifying smuggled items hidden in body cavities. As the airport nearest to the nation's capital, security had to be the very best.

Jane entered the scanning booth. She put her hands up as directed, rotating around, first in one direction and then the other, closely watched by a guard issuing instructions throughout.

"Okay, honey, spread your legs some more for me," the guard said. "Okay, that looks real good, now just hold that position."

A few feet away, guards hovered around the concealed screening monitor as Jane was scanned. Benson saw them pointing at something. He took a guess and was outraged.

And again, he said nothing, burdened with a terrible feeling of guilt and shame. Speaking up, he told himself, would be a foolish gesture serving only to bring unwanted attention to himself and Jane. They *both* could be singled out for enhanced screening. But his self-rationalizing wasn't at all convincing; he was a warrior, supposed to be made of sterner stuff than this—and now it was too late to do anything.

Inside the scanning booth, the screen flashed a message, narrated by a robotic male voice.

"Welcome to F.A.S.T., the Future Attribute Screening Technology demonstration laboratory. Press 1 for English, 8 for other languages."

Jane pressed 1 and waited.

"Benson, Jane Lynne, you will be asked a series of questions. Please remain calm and absolutely still. Look straight into the screen with your eyes wide open. Do not worry. You will not be harmed."

The booth became bathed in blue light. Lasers in the four corners of the screen flashed on her face and in her eyes, recording skin temperature, iris movement, pupil dilation, heart rate, galvanic skin response, and so on.

"One moment, please."

An hourglass symbol spun in the middle of the screen.

"Benson, Jane Lynne, baseline physiological data successfully recorded," announced the robotic voice. "Let's proceed. Benson, Jane Lynne, did you show your personal ID to an authorized transportation security professional?"

"Yes."

The system froze for a few seconds while it evaluated Jane's response.

"Will you be smuggling an explosive device onboard today?"

"No."

"Are you from the local geographic area?"

"Yes."

"Do you have illegal narcotics with you today?"

"No."

"Are you carrying $10,000 or more in cash or negotiable instruments?"

"No."

"Do you plan to detonate an explosive device today?"

"No."

The system froze while the results were compiled. Jane waited, fidgeting and biting her lip, eager to avoid the dreaded secondary screening area.

"Benson, Jane Lynne, congratulations. Please continue through. Enjoy your flight."

In the next lane, a security guard knelt before a small child.

"Hi kid, what's your name?"

The little girl remained silent and wary, looking intently at the guard's face.

"That's okay," he said. "Gimme your shoes, okay? And I'll take your teddy bear and your doll, too. Stand over there in the body scanner where that nice woman just went, okay?"

The girl looked back at her parents standing in line just behind her. Reluctantly, they timidly signaled their guilty approval. The girl went through the same routine as Jane, holding her hands in the air and having her naked image processed, except that the scanning booth robot asked if she was in the custody of her legitimate parents and if they might have explosives or illegal drugs with them today.

A plump, middle-aged woman glided through security, her nose in the air. She wore a business suit and gave the air of being someone important.

"Hey, stop, you!" shouted a security agent. "Put all your stuff on the conveyor belt and remove your shoes and coat and anything in your pockets."

Filled with sudden wrath, the woman turned on him.

"You blind, you freakin' moron? You see this goddamn badge, you know who you dealin' with? I'm a member of Congress, scumbag! I don't got to line up at no goddamn security! Understand?" she said, holding up her badge.

The guard held up his arms to block her entry. He was having none of it.

"Hold it right there, gran—security!"

Two Blueshirts promptly ran over. Taking a firm grip of the woman's arms, they walked her away as she fought them, cursing them out with every halting step. Everyone in the long lines turned to watch the spectacle. The woman sagged down and the guards propped her up under her arms, dragging her backward across the floor.

A supervisor rushed over, breathless.

"Hold on, she's right! Let 'er go."

The honorable U.S. Representative dusted herself off in exaggerated, theatrical fashion.

"I'll have your freakin' jobs, assholes."

"But I thought he was in great shape," Jane said.

"He was—on the outside," Benson said. "Things are not always as they seem."

The long funeral procession made slow progress down the boulevard. Jared Morris must have made many friends in his relatively short life. They passed a sign at the side of the road. "See Something, Say Something™," it read, with an illustration of a frightened woman on the telephone looking over her shoulder.

They stood by the gravesite amid the mourners. Jane put her arm around the grieving widow. Benson, however, had no comforting gestures or words to offer. His mood was black; his old friend was being lowered into the ground before his time. Permanent, he reflected sadly. Game over.

"The Lord is my shepherd, I shall not want," read the clergyman, in somber, even tones. "He causes me to lie down in green pastures."

Benson's thoughts wandered off. All of our little plans seem so urgent, and then we get a shocking lesson on what's really important, brutally reminded of our own mortality. Nothing is forever. Life is short and the clock ticks on. He would preserve his youth and vigor for as long as he could— not with surgery or hair dye, but with sweat.

"Vanity of vanities, all is vanity. I saw all the deeds that are done under the sun; all is vanity and a chasing after wind. All go to one place, all are from the dust, and all turn to dust again."

Watching his wife console Morris' widow, he admired her ability to reach out to others with genuine empathy. She offered comfort, something it would be difficult for him to even attempt, fearing that it would come off as contrived. One didn't look into the face of death, as he'd done numerous times, without losing something preciously human. The battle trance that all soldiers know has a numbing effect that allows them to survive and function in the moment, but leaves them to deal with the psychological toll later—or never.

"There is nothing better than to eat and to drink and to be merry. The race does not belong to the swift, nor the war to the mighty, neither do the wise have bread, nor do the understanding have riches, nor the knowledgeable, favor; for time and fate will overtake them all. That is the end of the matter, all has been heard. Fear God and keep His commandments, for that is the whole duty of everyone."

And with that, the clergyman folded up his Bible and all was silent, a time for private reflection.

Benson hated funerals; he'd had enough of death. If even the noblest of pursuits were like chasing after the wind, what was he supposed to do with his remaining years? Eat, drink, and be merry? There had to be more to life than that. Benson wished that he, too, could have the same conviction that he saw in the clergyman and written on the faces of so many of the mourners; the conviction of absolute certainty, where the universe was divinely ordered and made perfect sense, whether we could understand it or not. A place without lingering doubt, without suffering. A place without fear.

The soldier learns to hide his fears. Anything could be a mine or a bomb that could blow him away if he barely touches it, and if it doesn't kill him on the spot in a violent explosion, it could blow his limbs off and turn his organs to mush. Years had passed since he was in battle, and while the anxieties had receded to the background, they had never wholly vanished. He was always and everywhere on his guard.

The only people in his life with whom he could open up were Jane, and to a lesser extent, Daniel. But perhaps he was being unduly charitable to himself with this self-assessment. Jane—to say nothing of Dr. Filbert—might well disagree. As for Daniel, he seldom spoke about his military experiences with his son, preferring that he choose a different path in life. He didn't want to romanticize war or make it seem attractive as some sort of career option.

He went over and gave his old friend's wife a brief hug, concealing his distress at the sight of her hollow, red eyes.

"I'm so sorry," he said, quietly.

20

Preemptive War

Guards led Benson down the hall to a room jammed with electronics. His wrists and ankles were manacled to an oversized, black metal chair by two brawny agents sporting the same pseudo-military outfits as the others had before them. A white-coated doctor carefully attached an elaborate device of delicate metal cables to Benson's head, hovering around him, fussily adjusting and calibrating the apparatus just so. The articulated silver cables reached like tentacles around the top of his head, anchored to electrodes on his forehead and below each ear. The general effect was that of an electronic octopus clinging to his scalp.

Dr. Gannon finished his adjustments and began checking off the items on his list, noting the instrument's specific settings and the subject's baseline physiological measures. Benson jerked his head sharply. The apparatus came away, falling onto the floor.

"Damn it all!" Dr. Gannon said.

Angrily ripping the sheets from his clipboard and crunching them up, he threw them at the floor, cursing.

"That took 23 minutes! I shall be forced to start all over!"

"What's this *gizmo*?" asked Benson, airily.

"This gizmo, as you call it," Dr. Gannon's voice dripped with disdain, "works along somewhat the same general principles as the fMRI. The very latest evolution, a most advanced design."

179

He spoke slowly, as though trying, with some difficulty, to converse with a small child.

"Your brain will be electrically scanned by this device, you see. It maps neural activity by imaging hemodynamic response. I don't expect you will know what that means. No, of course not."

He thought for a moment.

"If you are lying, you see, areas of your brain will light up on the screen. We'll *know*." The doctor tapped his forehead with a finger. "No escaping the truth, you see?"

"Well, I'll be damned."

Benson turned to face Gannon behind him as best he could, given the restraints on his limbs.

"You a *real* doctor?"

"I earned my Ph.D. *cum laude* in experimental biochemistry," Gannon replied, curtly. "I am a *research scientist*."

"That's not a *real* doctor." Benson turned around in his chair to face forward again. "You're not an M.D., you obviously weren't good enough for medical school. You're a fake, a wannabe, an also-ran. And now they've got you doing experiments on helpless prisoners with your silly gadget."

Dr. Gannon's fists shook in anger. He seemed about to strangle Benson, who paid him no mind.

"I don't expect it was a top-tier school, either," Benson said. "I don't expect you were nearly smart enough. No, of course not."

With a menacing look, one of the agents came over to calm Dr. Gannon down. Gannon excused himself to go to the restroom. He returned after some minutes, still testy, but resumed hooking Benson up to his brain scanner, grumbling all the while.

The agents gathered around Benson.

"Okay, Mr. Benson, I'm Special Agent Malloy."

Dr. Gannon retreated to the back, monitoring the dials and controls. Malloy tapped something on a keyboard, reading a screen mounted just behind Benson.

"And this is my partner, Agent Reed."

"Delighted to meet you both. We must get together for coffee one of these days and trade stories. Maybe you'll join our prison book group? We're reading *Rights of Man* by Thomas Paine this week."

"Okay, I'm just gonna read the questions and you just go yes or no. Got it? Okay, here we go. Is your name Thomas David Benson?"

"Yes."

"All right, coming up now ... just a minute ... and that's ... that's real good."

"Do I get a cookie?"

Malloy squinted at the screen as he tapped some more commands.

"Okay, Mr. Benson, next question. Have you had financial or other transactions or dealings with Cuba, Iran, North Korea, Sudan, Libya, Iraq, Afghanistan, Yemen, Pakistan, Somalia, Myanmar, Lebanon, Zimbabwe, Saudi Arabia, Columbia, Algeria, Venezuela, Syria, Uzbekistan, or any other country to which the United States has prohibited transactions?"

He waited for a response.

"Uh, Mr. Benson?"

"I'm thinking. Can you repeat the question?"

Malloy repeated the question with considerable petulance, waiting again for an answer.

"Mr. Benson?"

"I thought Saudi Arabia was supposed to be our good friend and ally. No longer?"

"I wouldn't know anything about that. Just a yes or a no."

"What's the big problem with Cuba? They make some pretty good cigars."

"I wouldn't know anything about that, either. Yes or no."

"Venezuela and Columbia grow some really great coffee."

"I don't know anything about that. Just a yes or a no."

"Well, I don't believe I've had *dealings* with those places, in the strictest sense of the word, but the way that transactions are linked and routed around the world today makes your question a bit ambiguous. It's just not that cut and dried anymore. Anybody could be said to have had *dealings* with someone who had dealings, and so on, if you go back far enough. We are all connected in the great circle of life, are we not?"

"Yes or no," Malloy said with rising annoyance, "I just need a simple yes or no."

"All things considered, I think I will go with a qualified 'no.'"

There was a long silence while the system evaluated Benson's response. An hourglass symbol spun in the middle of the screen.

"Okay, next question. This time, only yes or no, all right? Okay. Are you acting on behalf of any person or entity listed on the U.S. Treasury Department classified list of Specially Designated Nationals and Blocked Persons or the U.S. Commerce Department Denied Persons List or Entity List?"

"I don't have any of those asinine secret lists, and I would guess you don't either. All right? Okay? Are we done here? My time is valuable."

"Let's just skip that question."

"No, no, no!" Dr. Gannon said, vigorously shaking his head. "I do not approve waiving the established test protocol. I'm afraid I must insist. You *must* go down the list in order, precisely as prepared."

Agent Malloy held up a photograph for Benson.

"So you know this guy?"

"Nope."

"Where did you meet?"

The doctor fussed with some dials in the back, muttering to himself.

"We didn't meet."

"Are you guilty?"

"Everybody's guilty of something."

"Just answer the question, Benson, yes or no. Are you guilty?"

"Do you mean guilt in a literal or a figurative sense? There is the guilt we feel over things we've done or left undone—but that would require a conscience. You wouldn't know anything about that. There is the guilt about violating common moral standards—but that would presume not being a psychopath. There's guilt by association, but that's only circumstantial. Then there's guilt in a legal sense—but that requires a proper judge and jury, the presumption of innocence, and the rules of evidence. You wouldn't know anything about that, either."

Agent Reed, silent to this point, motioned Malloy to the rear of the room with a slight nod of his head. They spoke in hushed tones.

"I dunno," Reed whispered, putting his hand on Malloy's shoulder and leaning in close. "Not convinced, you know?"

"I told you it doesn't work," Malloy agreed, shaking his head. "Let's conference with Dr.—"

"Excuse me over there! Sorry to interrupt your heart-to-heart," yelled Benson, "but does it bother you that there's no proof of your goofy plot? Does the truth count for anything anymore?"

Dr. Gannon stomped over to the agents, fuming.

"You stupid, stupid knuckledraggers!" he hissed in a low voice. "Birdbrains! You are ruining the examination. The interview process is most delicate, you muscleheads. You must let *me* run the interview! I must insist."

The agents returned to Benson. Malloy still held the photograph, studying it for a moment.

"Well, Mr. Benson, you were in a *position* to cause harm. We're not working with formal guilt *after* the fact. That's too late."

"That's right," Reed said. "We find dangerous fanatics and flush out their sleeper cells *before* they act. That's *preemptive* war."

There was a pregnant pause in the room, and then Benson burst out laughing. The agent's demeanors went from serious to steamed in an instant.

"You couldn't preempt *dick*, you pathetic losers. The only thing you're flushing is the toilet."

21

I'll Prove You're Wrong

"No shoving, please! Move along quietly!" barked the military police.

The long line crawled. The young men came in all sizes and shapes, from the athletic to the ungainly, and from every social, economic, and ethnic demographic. The female conscripts ranged from the fashionably clad to the frizzy and the frumpy. Once inside the doors of the Military Entrance Processing Station they submitted their forms and supporting documentation and were checked off, one by one.

They lined up for their fish kits of camouflage pants, jackets, shirts, boots, toiletries, and other items of clothing and supplies, all stacked neatly in gray plastic bins. The men passed through a team of barbers, given identical buzz cuts, and shorn of any mustaches and beards. The women had their hair cut to a uniform length and pulled back into small ponytails. The floor was piled with clumps of hair of every color and texture. Earrings, tongue studs, nipple and genital piercings, eyebrow clamps, nose and lip rings, navel jewelry, and other such adornments were removed and placed in clear plastic bags with their names and numbers on preprinted labels for retrieval at some later date.

The recruits changed into their uniforms and assembled in the adjoining gymnasium. With its wood floors and high ceilings, the room greatly amplified all the nervous chatter.

Master sergeants went through the groups, checking off their lists. Once it was all done, the women went off to another gymnasium, led by female sergeants. The men were ordered to line up. Some stood stiffly at attention, much as they had seen it done in the movies, while others slouched. The noise died down.

A drill sergeant moved up and down the lines, coming to stop in front of Daniel, staring up and down at this boy with oversized fatigues hanging off his skinny frame. The sergeant slowly circled Daniel and came back to face him, looking directly into his eyes, just inches from his face, scowling.

"What's your name, soldier?"

The sergeant yelled loud enough so that everyone could easily hear.

"Benson," Daniel said, staring straight ahead, scared to death of this badass. "Dan Benson."

The sergeant looked this Dan Benson over with deep disapproval. He glowered, his dark eyes boring into Daniel, who struggled against his instincts not to look back.

"Benson, sir!" the sergeant screamed into Daniel's ear, giving him a start. "Gimme 50, you pussy!"

With extreme effort, Daniel struggled to perform a few feeble pushups.

The sergeant stepped lightly on his back with one boot.

"Listen up, you dumb rocks!" he yelled at the assembly, paying no mind to the exhausted weakling below him. "You're gonna be killin' ragheads 'n a few months, you worthless bunch a' cherries. And this," he stared them down, hands on his hips, "is Day Zero!"

The sergeant glanced down as Daniel continued without success to overcome the minor weight on his back. His arms trembled, his hips sank to the floor, and his face flushed a deep red. Finally, he collapsed in a heap, intensely humiliated, his head pressed sideways on the hardwood floor, puffing hard.

Distaste written on his face, the sergeant looked at the recruits, his boot planted squarely on Daniel's back.

"I sure ain' got much to work with, but you're gonna be tough sumbitches or die tryin'."

The sergeant looked around the gym.

"YOU HEAR ME?" he bellowed, in a sudden rage. "I—will—not—tolerate—shitbaggers!" he said slowly, each word emphasized, at the top of his voice.

"AM I CLEAR?"

"Wake up, cherries," the drill sergeant sang out with exaggerated sweetness.

He had quietly entered the barracks where the men were still sleeping. It was just before dawn. Standing in the middle of the room, feet widely planted, he surveyed the slumbering recruits from beneath the broad brim of his hat.

"Rise an' shine, sweethearts!"

The men stirred lightly on their beds.

"Move!" he screamed. "When I give a comman' you will hustle! Now line up!"

Daniel picked his head up off the pillow, groggy. His neck and back ached from the hard, thin mattress. It was only 0545 hours and they'd hardly gotten any sleep.

"Welcome to Hell Week."

The sergeant said it as a threat, in a low growl. The recruits didn't know what it meant, but they struggled off their beds and stood in formation in their T-shirts and briefs.

"I am Sergeant Shultz."

He walked slowly down the line. The men stood rigidly, staring straight ahead.

"Did I hear me a snicker?"

Schultz came to an abrupt stop.

"Someone find that funny?"

All was silent. Schultz stared down a poor recruit, yelling an inch from his face.

"Was that you, shithead?"

"N-no-no sir!"

He went over to Daniel.

"Now how 'bout you?" His hot breath assaulted Daniel's face. "You already made trouble for everyone here an' we hardly got goin'. I don' like you."

He circled around Daniel, glaring at him.

"No, I don' like you at *all*. You find my name funny?"

"No sir!"

"I don' like liars. The truth must count for somethin'. Liars do not belong in my corps," he shouted at the men.

"Am I clear?"

"Sir, yes, sir!" the men shouted back.

"You will become motivated, disciplined, physically an' mentally fit."

"Sir, yes, sir!"

Shultz moved up and down the line as he spoke, staring down each recruit in turn.

"You will learn to take pride in yourself, in the corps, an' in your country, but right now you got *nothin'* to be proud of. You're dirt—you're even lower 'n dirt. Am I right?"

"Sir, yes, sir!"

"Get down on the floor! Kiss it! That's where you belong. You ain' accomplished nothin' in your short, miserable lives, you're all a bunch a' soft pansies, afraid to get your little hands all dirty. You ain' never worked hard a day in your goddamn life. Am I right?"

"Sir, yes, sir!"

"You're spoiled little brats, you been coddled your whole life. You don' even know the meanin' a' hard work. You don' belong here with *real* soldiers; you ain' fit to be in their presence. You ain' fit to lick their boots, you ain' earned the privilege. Am I right?"

"Sir, yes, sir!" they yelled from the floor.

"I didn' tell you to stop, now did I? Keep kissin' the floor."

Schultz was silent for a few minutes.

"Stan' at attention. Move it!"

The men stood ramrod straight, puffing their chests out.

"You will become American soldiers, sworn to defend the Constitution of the United States against all enemies, foreign 'n' domestic. You will defend your country's freedom. You will be capable of defeatin' any enemy on any battlefield. Am I clear?"

"Sir, yes, sir."

"I said, am I clear?" he bellowed.

"SIR, YES, SIR!"

Minutes later, the soldiers were jogging slowly down a dusty road. Shultz led the company, trotting along easily. He pulled back to let them run past.

"Tighten up over there! Nuts to butts!"

He began singing, in time with his steps.

♪♪ *"A yellow bird with a yellow bill,"* ♪♪
  ♪♪ *"A yellow bird with a yellow bill,"* ♪♪ the men repeated.
♪♪ *"Was sittin' on my window sill."* ♪♪
  ♪♪ *"Was sittin' on my window sill."* ♪♪
♪♪ *"I lured him with a piece a' bread,"* ♪♪
  ♪♪ *"I lured him with a piece a' bread,"* ♪♪
♪♪ *"Then I smashed his fuckin' head."* ♪♪
  ♪♪ *"Then I smashed his fuckin' head."* ♪♪

They arrived at a clearing dominated by a wooden tower topped by a small cabin high above the ground. Thick, knotted ropes hung from beams secured to the cabin. The recruits climbed the ropes and then shimmied down clumsily, standing in formation when done, their chests heaving, sweat running down their backs. Not a few had enormous difficulty making it up and down, reducing the movement of men to a near standstill.

"Too goddamn slow!" Shultz yelled, pacing back and forth with a grim look on his face, his assistant following closely at his heels. "I coulda shot your flabby asses on that

rope like fish 'n a barrel. You're so goddamn slow you couldn'
get outta your own way. My old *grandma* could kick your fat,
swollen asses on this little bitty course."

He spat on the ground.

"No, I ain' got much to work with, that's for dang sure."

Sergeant Schultz led the men to an open field studded
with old tractor-trailer tires. Daniel spent the next half hour
pushing one of the huge truck tires end over end, dropping
it on the ground, picking it up, and repeating the exercise. It
took every last ounce of his willpower to hoist the massive
tire and heave it over. All around him, the men grunted and
strained, pushed to their limits. Schultz blew the whistle; the
men stopped instantly with intense relief. They drank from a
water fountain and rested in the shade of some trees.

Daniel perspired freely, taxed physically and mentally to
the hilt. He'd never worked so relentlessly hard in his life, but
now, at rest, he felt a strange feeling of satisfaction at having
pushed himself more than he ever knew that he could. He had
overcome a challenge that he would have thought impossible
a few hours ago. He wiped his forehead with his sleeve.

"Sir," Daniel said, instantly arousing the wrath of the
sergeant with his impudence. "When's breakfast?"

"Breakfas'! How do Belgian waffles an' apple crepes with
whip cream sound? Maybe some fancy *expresso* to go with
it. One sugar or two? You shitbagger! This ain' no summer
camp, college boy. You gotta learn to run on empty."

He shook his head at Daniel's audacity.

"Nap time's over!" he barked to the whole company, in a
foul mood. "Get up, keep movin'!"

Daniel labored with all his might to lift a big sandbag.
Sergeant Schultz watched impassively as Daniel quivered
and shook under the load. He had gotten much stronger
since he had arrived at boot camp, but he couldn't quite heave

the bag higher than his head, no matter how dogged his determination.

Without warning, Schultz wheeled around and punched him in the stomach.

"Drop that bag an' you jus' bought 50 a' those lifts, you hear me, boy?"

Daniel keeled over and fell to his hands and knees, vomiting.

Schultz watched him with outright contempt.

"You don' got what it takes, college boy," he said, looking away. "You thought you were better 'n everyone. Got some news for ya."

He squatted down. Daniel was still retching in the dirt.

"You ain' no man. You ain' no part a' no man."

Daniel hacked at the ground on his hands and knees.

"You're wrong! Sir." Daniel turned to face the sergeant, his face bright red and wet with cold sweat. "I'll prove you're wrong."

Schultz stood and surveyed the surroundings.

"You do that, boy. You jus' do that."

"Double time, march!"

The heavy packs bounced off their backs as they ran under the hot sun. Each step felt like a mile. Daniel was utterly wretched; his sweat-soaked fatigues clung to his body, chafing his skin with every stride. He desperately yearned to stop the suffering but wouldn't permit himself to let go and give up.

Sergeant Schultz jogged at the front of the pack, dropping back to the middle to inspect his recruits.

♪♪ *"The moral of the story is,"* ♪♫ he sang, in time with the even rhythm of his steps.

♪♪ *"The moral ... of the story ... is,"* ♪♫ the men sang between strained breaths.

♪♪ *"To get some head you need some bread."* ♪♫

♪♪ *"To get some ... head ... you need ... some bread,"* ♪♫ the recruits sang out, puffing furiously.

♪♪ *"Sound off! One, two."* ♪♫
  ♪♪ *"Sound off … one … two."* ♪♫

Daniel grew lightheaded. Spots danced before his eyes and the tips of his fingers tingled. His field of vision closed in, his breathing became shallow, and his ears clogged up.

"Company, halt! At ease."

Daniel crumpled where he stood, resting on top of the pack strapped to his back, fighting the almost irresistible urge flooding over him to roll over and black out. His ears rang with a shrill buzz; nausea rose in his throat. He broke out in a cold sweat, feeling chilled despite the heat. The sergeant was saying something to the men but he couldn't make any sense of it in his misery and confusion.

He breathed deeply, willing himself to remain conscious, focusing on a nearby tree. In a few minutes, he started to come out of it. The spots in his vision went away and his ears began clearing.

"An' now, you dumb cherries, you know the meanin' a' hard work," Schultz was saying. "Intensity a' effort in trainin' will keep your sorry asses alive in battle. But your own sorry ass ain' important, it ain' worth shit. Only the company's important. You are individuals no more; you are a team. You will think as *one*, you will act as *one*, you will stay together as *one*. You will leave no one behind, no matter what."

Sergeant Schultz moved over to Daniel, squatting down to evaluate his condition. His stern face, for once, betrayed no hint of anger, but of concern.

"I expect this level a' effort ever time. Am I clear?"

The men nodded, understanding all too well.

"I said! Am I clear?"

"Sir, yes, sir!"

22

Building a Shared Vision

THE SIDEWALKS WERE FILLED WITH PEDESTRIANS, mainly office
workers out for lunch or just breaking free for a stroll on a
pleasant day. A man struggled to park his ancient station
wagon on the tree-lined street of outdoor cafes. The car's
rear sagged from the heavy load in back. There being no
other suitable spots on this block, he shoehorned his car in
between the others parked on the curb. Backing up, he looked
in the rearview mirror and noticed that he hadn't shaved in
a few days. A patchy gray growth covered his lined face. He
reversed slowly until he bumped the car behind.

He pushed against his door to get out but it was battered
and sagging and wouldn't easily yield. He threw his weight
against it until the door creaked open on its rusty hinges.
Exiting the car, he shuffled as fast as he could down the
sidewalk, looking behind every few steps and bumping into
people. He had almost reached the end of the block when he
was forced to stop and catch his breath. Wheezing, he looked
back at his car, confused. His mind was whirling.

Months earlier, he had met two men. They had approached
him just as he was most down on his luck, utterly without
hope or purpose. He had no money, no job, and no friends.
His English was bad. Yet, they had encouraged him, bought
him things, kept his company, and slowly won his trust. They
provided training and sophisticated military-grade equipment.

They even paid him handsomely. These strangers, his new best friends, had given him a reason to live. He must now, they strongly urged, serve a cause greater than just himself. He would finally have "some skin in the game," as they had put it.

It had seemed almost too good to be true; the fulfillment of his deepest prayers. Now he wondered if they knew what the hell they were doing. After all, he didn't really know them too well, only a few months. They weren't of his people, either. And where were they now? What skin did *they* have in the game? Perhaps he had foolishly trusted them.

Sauntering back cautiously, cursing them under his breath, he circled his car and peered inside. He couldn't see much through the filthy glass. He went around to the rear, trying to open the station wagon's tailgate, but his car had locked bumpers with the one behind and he had great difficulty reaching the latch. He put a foot on the other car's bumper for balance, and, struggling for leverage, pulled open the tailgate.

The blast was deafening, a hurricane of force, destroying the shops and restaurants down the whole block and most of those on the opposite side of the street. People in the immediate vicinity were blown to pieces, scattered about in the street and sidewalk. Those further away from the explosion lay at crazy angles on the ground, coming to rest at whichever way they were thrown, their limbs twitching amid sparkling glass shards. The horrified and paralyzed survivors stared dully at the charred carcass of the burning wagon.

"Attention, citizens," blared loudspeakers on the LAV-300 armored personnel carriers patrolling the streets. *"You are hereby directed to remain in your homes until informed otherwise. You will be notified when you are free to leave and resume your normal activities."*

The LAVs parked and discharged the troops and SWAT police riding within. Clad in black assault uniforms, body armor, and helmets with dark face shields, they patrolled the deserted neighborhoods, their M4A1 carbines at the ready.

Surrounding a large, historic house, they went to work. The battering ram pounding the front door cracked the transom windows. The wooden doorframe tore off in places. Inside, a small dog yapped away. A policewoman booted the door open and the team burst into the house. It was expensively furnished, tastefully decorated with valuable works of art.

Pointing shotguns in their faces, the team cornered the parents and their two children, repeatedly yelling, "Don't move! Down! Down on the floor! On your stomach. Arms out!"

The father of the clan got down on his knees. His wife and kids lay face down on the floor, as ordered, cringing and crying.

"What's going on?" the father yelled. "What right do you have to barge in here like criminals?"

"Get down on the floor, asshole!" Commander Clancy ordered.

The yapping little dog latched onto one of his pant legs and wouldn't let go, snarling and biting.

"Tiger, leave it!" the father cried out. "No, Tiger, leave it. Tiger, come! Leave it! Tiger, sit!"

Clancy shot Tiger and went about his business.

The police ransacked the house, going through each room and carefully carting the evidence outside, some of it quite fragile. The process took almost two hours. The whole time, Clancy stood over the suspects, keeping them prone on the floor. His police and military colleagues came over every so often to confer.

"Okay, folks, you can get up now," Commander Clancy said. "Mr. Seth North, you are a person of interest in connection with the station-wagon bombing."

"But—but I don't have a station wagon anymore."

"That's not what our records say. You will please come with us. We can discuss it on the way."

• • •

"My friends, we have succeeded in building a shared vision."

President King spoke to the nation from the Oval Office. He wore a well-tailored black suit with American flag pins on the lapels. His desk was clear but for a small desk flag and a statuette of the destroyed Twin Towers in New York City.

"It's a vision of keeping America safe and secure, a vision where ordinary people can stroll the sidewalks without getting cut down in cold blood. Where young mothers pushing their babies in strollers can stop for an ice cream and say hello to their neighbors without getting massacred. Where our senior citizens can amble along and not be accosted by the enemies of freedom. Where our young people can grow up to become responsible adults who work hard and pay their taxes and not die a horrible death to satisfy some antigovernment maniac's version of paradise. Where outraged communities can come together and say, 'We're not gonna take this anymore.'"

King shifted to face the cameras on his right.

"This terrible station wagon tragedy, where scores, maybe even hundreds, of decent, law-abiding citizens met a violent death, among them friends and neighbors, small children out on school field trips enjoying the nice spring weather—that's not part of the shared vision. We don't yet know how many innocent victims laid down their lives; they're still trying to identify the gruesome remains. Our hearts go out in prayer to all the dead and the dying and their grieving families."

He turned in his chair to face the cameras on his left.

"While the nation mourns this dreadful slaughter of its loved ones, you can take heart knowing that your federal government is doing something. Legislation is now making its way through Congress. It is called the Enemy Expatriation Act and it represents a significant step forward in the Global War on Terror. Enemies of freedom will be stripped of their citizenship to face swift military justice under Section 412 of the USA PATRIOT Act. The terrorists will no longer be able to use our freedoms against us. I will sign the EEA into law as soon as it crosses this desk. That is my solemn pledge to you this day.

"Meanwhile, by the authority you have vested in me as your commander-in-chief, I have invoked Executive Order 16058. The neighborhood and surrounding areas where the alleged criminal or criminals are thought to have lived or worked is in total lockdown—'shelter in place' is the term we're using. Citizens are asked not to leave their homes while our police and military conduct house-to-house searches. The arrests have already begun."

The black BearCat, with its high road clearance and mammoth tires, drove right onto the front lawn. Paramilitary troopers hung off the side running boards of the massive 16,000-pound armored personnel carrier. An unmarked car screeched to the curb. Pulling down their face shields, the troopers scrambled to take up their positions. It was just after midnight.

The lieutenant exited the car and squatted down behind the open driver's door.

"Location's QOA," he said into his radio. "We're checkin' the reg."

He spotted the aging station wagon parked in the driveway.

"Yeah, maybe the owner's not a frequent flier, but we got enough to move. What's that? C'mon, are you freakin' serious? No way, you're shittin' me. C'mon, I got an operation goin' here! We're ready to move."

Lieutenant Millstone threw the radio handset on the car seat. The huddled team waited for his signal.

"Hold off a minute, boys, we gotta wait for the TV guys. I'll give 'em five minutes and that's it."

The *COPS* crew arrived seconds later.

"Okay boys, cuff and stuff."

One of the troopers kicked the front door. It cracked but remained stubbornly closed. Shrieks and wails emerged from the house. A man yelled from inside. Another trooper turned the doorknob, throwing open the door and tossing a flashbang grenade into the hall. The ferocious explosion lit up the front of the house. The troopers stormed in through the thick black fumes and charged up the stairs.

Minutes later, a young man and woman exited their house, dazed, their ears ringing, hands raised over their heads. A phalanx of troopers surrounded them with rifles drawn. The hall carpet was on fire.

"Amber Wong and Wayne Wong!" Millstone shouted at them through a bullhorn, crouching from behind his car. "We need to ask you a few questions. You will please come with us."

23

Dad Would Be So Proud of Me

"To be a real soldier, you must possess four things."

Sergeant Schultz reviewed his men standing at attention, walking up and down the line, yelling in their faces.

"One! The warrior mentality. Two! Extreme endurance."

He briefly stopped in front of each man and looked him in the eye before moving on.

"Three! Outstanding combat skills. Four! Supreme discipline—full control a' your mind an' body."

No one dared return his fierce gaze.

"Now who here thinks he's a damn warrior, who's got some big goddamn balls, move one step in front."

The men hesitated among themselves, looking at each other.

"American soldiers ain' automatons. They don' blindly follow, they lead. All it takes is one courageous sumbitch to take a stand, do the right thing an' change the world. Now who's a damn warrior?"

Daniel screwed up his courage and took a step forward.

Schultz circled Daniel, scowling.

"So you think you're a goddamn warrior, that right, puddin' head?"

A few of the recruits couldn't suppress a smirk. The sergeant immediately caught it, glaring at them.

"Sir, yes, sir!"

"A warrior is prepared to engage the enemy at all costs without regard to his own welfare. A warrior's prepared to fight an' conquer his fears. He does this without hesitatin' so his company'll survive. He don' care how big, how strong, how well-equipped the enemy might be. A warrior has a high sense a' personal honor an' integrity. He's determined and strong-willed like a bull. He don' care what's in front a' him, he don' yield. *That*'s what makes a real warrior."

Schultz looked at the men with narrowed eyes.

"Now I hoped *everyone* here woulda answered 'yes' to my question. I see now that I was wrong. I see now that you are *not* prepared. I see now that you are weak-willed an' soft. Get on the floor! 'Cept you, puddin' head. You remain standin'. All the rest a' you shitbaggers, you will gimme a hundred pushups. At the end a' each pushup, you cherries will yell at the top a' your lungs, 'I am a warrior!' You will stay on the floor until your hundred are done. When you're done you will stand at attention. Do not try to fool me—I *will* be countin'. Am I clear?"

"Sir, yes, sir!"

"Begin!"

The recruits began yelling, "I am a warrior," at different times, each according to his strength and stamina, so that the barracks soon became filled with men shouting continuously.

"Louder, I can' hear you!" bellowed the sergeant.

"I am a warrior! I am a warrior! I am a warrior! I am a warrior!"

After several minutes, the first of them to complete the hundred stood at attention, and then the others, one by one. The last few fought with all their might to finish, collapsing on the floor after each partial pushup completed, furiously sucking air. At last the men all stood at attention.

"Now *that* was a real sorry spectacle, absolutely pathetic. My old *grandma* coulda done it in half the time and she wouldn' be breathin' hard, neither. You ain' no warriors, that's for dang sure."

The barracks were filled with the sound of men wheezing and coughing.

"Now over here, we have just one goddamn warrior among you."

Schultz looked at Daniel as he addressed the puffing recruits, for the first time, Daniel imagined, with a faint modicum of respect. He felt proud and scared at the same time.

"This here warrior's prepared to fight an' conquer his fears —an' his fear today is drownin'. Today, he's gonna conquer his fear a' drownin' with his supreme discipline an' his warrior mentality."

Daniel was not encouraged by all this talk of drowning, but it was too late; he was already committed.

"Soldier, are you a goddamn warrior?"

"Yes, sir!"

"Everyone follow me outside."

Daniel felt dread building in the pit of his stomach. "I am a warrior," he quietly chanted on the way out. He would fight at all costs. He stepped outside, alarmed at the sight of a large barrel suspended overhead. He was directed to stand beneath it and steeled himself for the worst.

"This ain' no play time; a soldier could be captured and tortured. If he gives up, if he gives in, if he quits, he dies."

The rush of water streamed onto Daniel's head, slowly at first and then with gathering force. The torrent was terrifying. He moved his head back and forth, but there was no escaping the deluge.

"Aack!" he blubbered through the waterfall. "S-stop! Can't—I can't breathe!" he sputtered through the streaming water, his eyes clenched tight.

"Gimme 10 goddamn seconds!" Schultz roared. "You can do it, Benson, you're a goddamn warrior! Do not move from that spot!"

And he didn't.

After rest and rations, the men ran with their gear through rough terrain, up and down small hills. The choppy ground demanded their utmost concentration to avoid a serious tumble. Daniel really felt that he was now a warrior, his feet moving in a steady, coordinated beat over the broken ground. He felt energized, his mind and body now united through mental and physical discipline. If he could conquer his inner fears like that, he could conquer anything.

"Keep movin'!" Schultz yelled out, running in the middle of the pack.

Daniel marveled at his seemingly unlimited stamina, his toughness, his strength of character.

"Don' give up, don' ever quit!"

They headed for camp. It was 1600 hours, time to hit the showers and then prepare for inspection. Peeling off their sweaty uniforms, the men ran for the cool water. The feeling of relief was immense. Daniel luxuriated in the invigorating spray until he was the last one left.

A couple of recruits were lying in wait as he stepped out of the showers and toweled off. Sneaking up, they each emptied a bucket of freezing water on him. Daniel stood there speechless, rigid with shock, the icy water splashing off his body.

"You bastards!"

"Man-up, Benson! You can do it—you're a goddamn warrior!"

They ran away, laughing.

But for BearCat armored personnel carriers and huge Bulldog X SWAT trucks rumbling by, kicking up dust on the unpaved road, all was quiet. Troops hung off the side running boards of the BearCats, on the lookout for an ambush. Tucked inside the Bulldog armored trucks, troops manned the gun ports. Brilliant red, white, and blue lights flashed as a warning. It all made for an impressive show of force in an urban operations zone, intimidating whatever enemy combatants remained here.

The rest of the company patrolled the battered urban street on foot. They were told that this sector had not been swept recently by armored bulldozers, and so they were to exercise extreme caution. Insurgents might be in the area, traveling undetected through underground tunnels from which they could emerge to spring an ambush. The rubble-filled streets would be ideal for planting booby traps. The buildings could provide cover for hidden sniping posts.

Daniel huddled against a dilapidated house by the front door, holding his M4A1 carbine with M320 grenade launcher mounted under the barrel. His heart pounded fiercely. Two other soldiers covered the entrance. Taking a deep breath, Daniel burst into the house, firing away into the shadows, followed by his comrades. They were met with a hail of gunfire from somewhere inside. Falling hard on his back, Daniel's rifle went off into the ceiling. A shower of plaster rained down on him. His face was caked with white dust. Yelling and turmoil filled the murky building.

Daniel peered up from the floor at one of the senior instructors, mortified.

"You're lucky this was a simulation," the instructor said, sadly. "You'd be dead, son."

Drill Sergeant Schultz counted them off. After 30 pushups Daniel was still going strong, his dog tags clanging on the floor with each repetition. No longer a skinny kid, he was muscled and tough. His arms filled the sleeves of his T-shirt and his back flared as he moved up and down. Balancing himself against a post, Schultz stood on Daniel's shoulders with both feet. With great effort, Daniel was able to knock out yet more pushups, and the two of them went slowly up and down. Schultz looked out at the company, absolutely glowing. He almost smiled. No one had ever spotted him in any state of happiness, or even—as far as they could tell—remotely proud of anything his recruits had ever accomplished. Nevertheless, Schultz was undeniably impressed now, riding up and down on Daniel's back.

"Listen up, you worthless cherries!" he bellowed. "*This* is how you do pushups!"

The marching band played a number of stirring military standards, including "Stars and Stripes Forever," "Anchors Aweigh," and "Seventy-six Trombones." The reviewing stands were packed with spectators; parents, aunts and uncles, siblings, cousins, and grandparents. Some wore formal attire— jackets and ties, dresses and heels—while others wore outfits more at home on the beach, including halter and tank tops, souvenir T-shirts and hats from the gift shop, flip-flop sandals, and oversized basketball shorts.

The soldiers lined up in eight square blocks of 20 by 20 on the field, the men and women separated. The spacing between each block of soldiers, altogether four blocks long and two blocks deep, was precisely equal.

The commanding general ceremoniously made his way to the podium. He gathered his notes and contemplated the scene. Assembled before him were 3,200 of the best and brightest. It had taken these young men and women some seven or eight months to negotiate their way through Basic Combat Training and Advanced Individual Training, depending on their specialty.

"Ten-hut! Spectators and honored guests," said the adjutant general, "you will please remove your hats and stand for the playing of our national anthem."

Most of the audience covered their hearts with their right hands, the others dutifully following suit. After the moving performance the crowd erupted in cheers.

"Ladies and gentlemen, honored guests, it is my privilege to introduce to you today our CG, Major General Arthur K. Pippin, Jr."

"At ease," Pippin said. "Ladies and gentlemen, honored guests, please be seated."

This was one of many such speeches that General Pippin had delivered that autumn. A slideshow began playing on the giant screens arrayed around the stadium. In his high, thin voice, Pippin narrated a long history of the corps and its triumphs in perfect time with the unfolding scenes on the slides, which often featured archived video of battles savagely fought to a narrow win.

"I have felt the call to serve," narrated a recorded male voiceover from a current television spot trying to gin up recruitment, "and I will commit to carry that feeling close to my heart until my country feels safe and the cry of those less fortunate has been silenced."

The parents in the audience squirmed, the show evoking images of possibly harrowing prospects in store for their sons and daughters.

"I will go wherever there is tyranny, injustice, and despair, anywhere in the world, with courage and resolve to end all conflict, instill order, and help those who can't help themselves."

With that, marching bands began parading on the field, forming elaborate, intersecting patterns.

"Cadets," General Pippin said, "congratulations. You have been given the opportunity to defend the Homeland in its time of need. We will now recite the oath of enlistment. Raise your right hand and repeat after me:

"I—state your name ...

"Do solemnly swear or affirm ...

"That I will support and defend ...

"The Constitution of the United States ...

"Against all enemies, foreign and domestic ...

"That I will bear true faith and allegiance ...

"To the same ... "

Pippin completed the oath, the cadets threw their hats in the air, and the bleachers broke out with cheers and an extended standing ovation.

"You are truly the tip of the spear," said General Pippin, beaming. "In the proudest traditions of the United States Armed Forces you will defend with honor the freedoms and liberties that made America great. And I just wanna say, congratulations."

A few soldiers began chanting "hooah!" and all the others joined in.

Daniel found his mother on the field. He looked striking; most impressive in his full dress uniform. Jane's heart swelled with emotion as her eyes took in her handsome young man. He stood straight and tall, muscular and fit. The training and discipline had obviously been good for him. His upright military bearing and arresting appearance reminded her strongly of Benson some 20 years before.

She wiped her eyes.

"Daniel, we are so proud of you."

Daniel gave his mother a long hug, reluctant to let go.

"Hey," he said, looking around, puzzled. "Where's Dad?"

"He's, uh, well, he couldn't make it today, but I know he'd be *very* pleased."

"Couldn't make it? What?"

Before he could inquire further, Sergeant Schultz came over. Daniel saluted him smartly. Schultz returned the salute, slowly and deliberately, looking Daniel straight in the eye. Daniel had never been shown this kind of respect by his nemesis. He was extremely moved.

"You made it, college boy." Schultz shook his hand and slapped him on the back with undisguised pride. "Welcome to the service."

"Thank you, sir."

Dad would be so proud of me.

24

Unsuitable for Release

AGENT GAGE GLANCED AT SOME REPORTS, waiting impatiently for Special Agent DeSoto to begin the session. Benson took Gage for a fresh recruit, learning the ropes, as it were, still in orientation. DeSoto was older than his colleague and his hair was cut very close, indistinguishable from Benson's regulation prison cut.

Benson had ample experience in this hellhole to observe that after a long stretch here, but for their uniforms, it could be difficult to distinguish captor from captive. The harsh prison environment, with its daily savagery and bullying, its physical and psychological torture, would brutalize the guards and agents almost as much as their prisoners. The routine, State-sanctioned exercise of absolute power and control would desensitize them to the torment of others. The cruelty and suffering they inflicted on the prisoners would corrupt them, too. In time, they would inevitably become damaged human beings.

Nor were Gage and DeSoto much freer than the prisoners they interrogated. They couldn't simply walk out of a top-secret facility as if they were ordinary citizens. Their movements and actions would be tracked and recorded especially closely for any hint of breeching sensitive State secrets. One slip of the pen or tongue and they might easily find themselves on the wrong side of the cell doors. Whatever they might have thought they were signing up for, the reality was surely different. They were inmates of a sort themselves.

Benson wondered how such people, reasonably intelligent and even patriotic—in their own way—could be turned so easily. Perhaps they were so captivated with the idea of changing the world, their egos so stoked by the prospect of personally making a difference, that they jumped at the opportunity to sign up. These young people wouldn't have had the life experience to know any better, making them easy prey for any grandiose cause that cynically promised to remake the world. The more ambitious and idealistic the cause, the more attractive it would prove to impressionable young minds.

A doctor in a white lab coat held a hypodermic needle in the air, flicking it with her finger. The finger-tapping distracted Special Agent DeSoto's attention. He had seemed to be in a kind of trance, deep in thought.

DeSoto tore his gaze away and turned to Benson.

"Mr. Benson, let's just get down to business. You're gonna be classified as 'Unsuitable for Release.' I'm like, well, I'm real disappointed. I promised my boss early on, you know ... "

DeSoto sighed, apparently referring to an unpleasant recollection.

"I mean, unless something comes out of this last-chance interview, this is it, the end of the road. After this, you won't remember anything. You won't even remember your own existence."

Special Agent DeSoto stared quietly at the floor and then at Gage. Judging from the silence and gloom, Benson surmised that Team HVT had lost precious "reputation capital," its standing taken down a notch by its wretched failure on his case. The only sound was that of the guard in the corner shifting his weight onto the other foot, causing the ring of keys on his belt to jingle.

"This is all a joke, isn't it?" Benson said with all the derision he could muster. "I've had enough of this. Your boss was absolutely right, DeSoto; no doubt he's ashamed of you and your incompetence. You're a total failure, a real turkey. You wouldn't know a *real* terrorist if he bit you on the ass. What a loser, what a write-off you turned out to be, what a washout and a dud. What an embarrassment."

Benson smirked and shook his head.

"You'll be fired and disgraced within days. You'll never work again. Your career is over."

"You!" DeSoto stirred with sudden vehemence, shaking his finger at Benson. "You caused us a whole lotta trouble. We tried everything with you, we did it the easy way and the hard way. Good agents were ruined 'cause a' you and all we got was diddly-squat."

Benson laughed at him, meanly.

"So you think this is all a big, fat joke, do you?" DeSoto lost his composure, spitting as he yelled. "This is no gag, Mr. Benson—we're at war!"

Benson smacked DeSoto's face with the back of his hand, catching him hard near the eye with his knuckles. The man staggered back, piling clumsily into the doctor, still holding her syringe in the air. Falling backward to the floor, she stabbed herself with the needle, shrieking as the syringe flopped up and down, stuck fast in her neck. Horrified and gurgling, she was unable to bring herself to pull it out.

Benson instantly grabbed his folding chair and dashed to the guard at the door, holding the chair like a bat, and smashed him in the face with it. Bending to retrieve the guard's gun from the floor, he felt a hard object on the back of his head.

"Freeze! Get up real slow. Now turn around."

DeSoto pressed his gun against Benson's forehead. The agent's right eye was swollen a dark purple and nearly shut. He gingerly rubbed it with his free hand.

"We been at this for months and we hardly got anywhere!"

"Correction," Benson said. "You got *nowhere*. You have *nothing*. You're a disaster."

DeSoto tensed with rage.

"Oh yeah? Well, if cold and sleep deprivation don't work, maybe this will."

DeSoto leered, holding the gun with his right arm stiff and straight.

"Whaddya say now, tough guy? How 'bout some more a' those wisecracks? You ready for this, bitch? I could blow you away!"

"Roy, what're you doing—stop it!" Agent Gage said, frantic. "Knock it off!"

As a young combat soldier, Benson had been ambushed by a lone grunt appearing from nowhere. The enemy wore dirty, torn clothes; a bandana with some kind of insignia being the only thing distinguishing him from anyone else. He had motioned Benson to drop his rifle, moving behind and pressing his gun to the back of Benson's head, execution-style. Spinning around and stepping into his attacker, Benson trapped the gun and the man's arm against his body, striking repeatedly with his free elbow into the man's neck and nose and eyes. Reaching around with his free hand, he yanked the gun away, pistol whipped the man in the face and fired two quick rounds to the head. It was gruesome, but he did what he had to do.

Special Agent DeSoto's breathing was rapid and shallow, his forehead beaded with perspiration. His closed eye was smarting, causing him to screw up his face into a grimace. Suddenly scared and overwhelmed, DeSoto hesitated now that he'd taken it this far.

In a flash, Benson moved his head to the left, bringing his right hand under the barrel and his left hand behind DeSoto's wrist, violently twisting the gun backward into the agent's gut. Snapping DeSoto's trigger finger, the gun broke free and clattered onto the floor.

Being caged for months, the constant interrogations, the wanton cruelty and deprivation, had reduced Benson to the level of a desperate, wild animal. In a blind rage, his instincts took over. He felt nothing and thought of nothing except attack, flying at DeSoto with an uppercut to the stomach, knocking the wind out of the agent. Holding the back of DeSoto's neck with one hand, he repeatedly struck the agent's face with his elbow. Staggering, DeSoto took a sluggish swing before falling to the floor, fighting for breath through a crushed nose and broken teeth.

Benson immediately turned to Agent Gage, who had observed the brawl with fright, not moving from his spot except to stand. Throwing his whole body into it, Gage threw a big right hook. Benson blocked it and moved in, stunning Gage with a right cross, then gripping Gage's shoulders tightly and punching his knee into the agent's stomach. Gage doubled over, but Benson was too weakened to finish him off. Both men fought to recover.

Gage pulled out a club from somewhere, swishing it in the air, leering and threatening. He moved closer until he'd backed Benson into a corner, raising the club behind him to strike a deadly blow. Summoning all of his strength, Benson kicked his head, sending him flying back. Gage's skull smacked the concrete and he slithered down the wall to sit on the floor.

Benson grabbed the guard's gun from the floor and pulled him farther away from the entrance. The guard stirred with the movement. Benson struck him sharply in the forehead to keep him still. He concealed himself behind the door.

After several minutes, two guards entered the room, astonished by the sight before them. One of their comrades lay sideways on the floor. A syringe jammed in her throat, the doctor lay on the floor face up, semiconscious and babbling incoherently, her eyes glazed over. One of the agents lay sprawled on the floor, coughing and spitting blood. The other agent was in the corner, open-eyed, a bloody trail down the wall against which he slumped.

Benson slammed the door behind the guards. He side-kicked the one closest to him in the knee, cracking it. The guard collapsed to the floor, crying in extreme pain. The second guard drew his gun, but Benson was on him first, pummeling his face and kidneys. Rendered senseless, he dropped to the floor, curled up on his side.

Benson bent over, panting, holding his legs for support. Already in a weakened state, he had nearly exhausted what little stamina he still possessed.

The guard with the shattered knee lay on the floor, crying. When Benson came to stand over him he ceased his moaning, looking up silently in a growing panic. His gun holstered beneath him, the guard snaked his hand under his arched back to get at it. Benson, breathing hard, watched him attempt to unfasten the snap, but the guard's own weight and the paralyzing pain were too much to overcome. Benson stomped his heel on the guard's hand, crushing the delicate bones.

Getting down on his knees, he pressed his forearm into the man's throat. He felt no sympathy for this bastard. The guard panicked in wild, extreme distress, fighting for air, thrashing back and forth, kicking his legs up and down. The veins in his neck and forehead swelled; his eyes bulged. Even in combat, Benson had never killed with his bare hands. He felt sickened. The guard blacked out and Benson instantly released his choke.

Peeling off his orange jumpsuit, Benson suited up in the guard's uniform and hat. Reaching into DeSoto's outfit, he pulled out his identity card and yanked off the clip-on badge attached to the collar. He dragged the bodies to the front of the room underneath the door's high observation window to a spot where they wouldn't easily be seen from the hall. Rummaging through their clothes, he pulled out identification wallets and money. He tucked a gun into his waistband.

Wiping the sweat off his forehead, he shut the door quietly behind him, walking in what he hoped was a casual manner down the corridor, searching for the way out. His heart thumped madly.

The building seemed to be arranged like a maze, and although he had spent interminable months captive inside it, he knew almost nothing of its layout. He passed rooms that all appeared the same except for small black plates on the wall marking their locations. Moving from B-82 to B-81 and on down, he guessed that continuing to B-1 could end in a central foyer or main corridor from which he might spot the exit.

Agents and guards down the hall walked quickly toward him. His heart racing, he walked purposefully, as if he knew his destination by rote. He passed several men and women, some of whom were dressed identically to himself and some who wore suits; others sported the olive-drab jumpsuits of the interrogators. Benson pulled his hat down low. The few who paid him any fleeting attention did not have their gazes returned. He walked on, looking straight ahead, adopting a slightly bored expression to better fit in.

The corridor emptied into a central hall. Signs mounted on the painted cement block walls indicated the exit, and he continued on. He passed a portrait of the president on the wall. It was one of his campaign posters, the one in which he was staring off into the horizon, a confident, slightly crooked smile on his face, looking every bit the intrepid leader. Near the exit was a large glass window with a sliding partition set into it. Behind it sat a receptionist and other office staff in small cubicles, but they paid him no attention.

Benson swiped DeSoto's identity card in the reader next to the exit door. A red light flashed on the reader. Covering the blinking light with his hand, he tried again, flipping the card around. To his considerable relief, the lock released with a soft click. He casually walked out as if he were going for a smoke. He found himself in the same bleak and imposing courtyard from which he had first encountered this depraved, criminal institution from the backseat of a squad car months before.

Walking to the outer gate, he spotted a metal door with a card reader mounted near the handle and made for it.

"Hey buddy!"

The rough voice shook him deeply. He swiped his card in the reader, but nothing happened.

"Hey you! Yeah, you! Wha' do you think ya doin'?"

He froze. A guard in a glass booth at the gate's entrance was speaking to him through a microphone mounted in the window. Benson again swiped his card and pulled the handle down, the same way he had done it inside the building. It wouldn't budge. Alarmed, he tried yet again, with the same result.

"You must be new aroun' here," the guard said. "Turn the card aroun' an' pull *up* on the handle," indicating the correct motion with his hand.

"Hey buddy, your shift already over?"

Benson nodded but didn't look at the man.

"You're probably tired, aren't ya? Well, I'm sure as hell tired a' sittin' aroun' all day, I'll tell ya that. I can hardly wait till break. What a time I'm havin' here."

Benson said nothing, not wanting to engage. He did as the guard had instructed, and the gate opened.

"You all set? You goin' home?" the guard inquired. He would not be ignored.

"Home, sweet home," Benson said.

He hustled away from the guard's booth until he was out of sight. The street was deserted. He threw his hat, tie, and jacket behind some bushes, disrobing as he went. He ripped off the epaulets and badges on his prison guard's shirt, taking care not to tear the thin fabric, then rolled up the sleeves and untucked his shirt for a more casual look. He came to a major intersection where he quickly blended in with the pedestrians and bustling traffic.

His senses were assaulted by the cool autumn breeze, by the trees shedding their brilliant red and gold leaves, by the sounds of people and cars and buses. The sun shone weakly, gently warming his face. He felt exhilarated and free.

He passed a metal utility pole studded with loudspeakers and Biometric Optical Surveillance System cameras pointed in different directions. One of the cameras had been shot up, the wreckage still mounted to the pole. Moving independently, the four remaining cameras were distinct in size and appearance, two of them equipped with high-intensity lamps for night vision. Benson kept his head down. The other pedestrians appeared to go about their business as if the things weren't there.

"You there in the gray shirt!"

The loudspeakers on the pole started blaring, startling people on the sidewalk, freezing them in their tracks. Benson's heart skipped a beat.

His shirt was a light gray.

He picked up his pace, looking for an alley or some other means of quick escape.

"Yes, you over there!"

Benson ran for it, even if meant attracting attention. He would not be taken prisoner again. He was armed and would fight to the death if cornered. He had run only a few steps when the loudspeakers blared again.

"Pick up your trash and deposit it in the receptacle on your left. Thank you for your compliance."

A woman had tossed a cigarette butt on the road. She looked around and located the source of the broadcast, staring with disbelief at the pole while doing as she was told. Benson slowed his gait to a relaxed stride.

After walking for another quarter-hour, he figured he had covered at least a mile. Tired and hungry, he ducked into a busy delicatessen, making his way to a booth in the back. The place was crowded with patrons and waiters moving in the narrow spaces between the tables. The smell of real food was irresistible. Not aware of feeling hungry before he stepped inside, he became ravenous while waiting for service.

A television mounted on the wall near where he was sitting played a current affairs show. No one in the bustling restaurant was watching. A raving lunatic in military-style costume and Arab headdress was on a rant addressing a boisterous crowd, protected by rifle-toting bodyguards right there on the stage with him. He raised his hands in victory, a mean smile on his gnarled face. It seemed that this new dictator was threatening vengeance for years of trade sanctions and wars. He stabbed his finger in the air for emphasis with each of his talking points, pausing now and then to allow the crowd to cheer. He bore a striking resemblance to the dictator he had replaced the year before, whose name Benson had forgotten. The noise in the restaurant made it too loud to hear the show, and he had to settle for reading the transcript scrolling across the bottom of the screen.

An expert on Middle Eastern affairs from the King administration came on the show to explain that American interests abroad could be in jeopardy. The show's host then switched to footage of the highlights of President King's recent speech on the matter to a special joint session of Congress.

"This modern-day Hitler must be removed," King had declared, flanked by the seven generals and admirals of the Joint Chiefs of Staff. "Experts believe they may have the yellow cake and terrorist training camps. Weapons of mass destruction and mobile labs to make killer biological and chemical weapons. Drones that can fly—"

Congress interrupted his speech with immense applause. King raised a hand and waited until they had calmed down.

"Weaponized drones that could reach our cities with the Hellfire missiles. Facing clear evidence of peril, we cannot wait for proof that could come as a big, smoking mushroom cloud."

The camera panned out to the audience. Leading congress-people and chairs of farm and business welfare subcommittees, military-industrial directorates, climate-change sustainability panels, economic fairness boards, human rights panels, regulatory and licensing commissions, price and wage control councils, fair trade committees, equal opportunity tribunals, and prominent corporate-union cooperatives nodded sagely in agreement.

Benson looked around for a waiter to come to his table, but they all seemed to be occupied.

"The international community has nearly reached a virtual consensus. We may be facing a threat that could be imminent. The Department of Intelligence just came out with a report that says some of their more senior officials, probably even including their Supreme Leader, may now be more willing to attack the Homeland as a possible response to the real or perceived actions threatening their rogue regime.

"Experience shows the doctrine of appeasement has failed. They've ignored all the United Nations' resolutions and mandates and motions and commissions and special sessions and emergency sessions. We've tried years of trade sanctions and kinetic military actions in our ongoing Overseas Contingency Operations. They have no medicines and hardly any food and still they're goin' forward with their plans anyway. It's time to put all our cards on the table. Our coalition forces—"

Wild applause broke out. King pursed his lips and waited patiently to resume.

"Our armed forces in the region—the coalition of the willing—they're not gonna sit around waiting to be attacked. Our new enemy teaches that innocent people can be sacrificed to serve a political vision. That vision is to impose their kind of law on all of us. We don't share that vision, it's not democratic. They can't vote; they don't have any freedom. The freedom of speech. The freedom of worship. The freedom from want. The freedom from fear. And they make their women—"

He was interrupted again with thunderous applause.

"And they make their women wear those long, black clothes that cover their faces and they don't let them drive cars, either."

He looked down upon the packed House, moving his eyes over the hundreds of representatives and senators. He gazed up at the spectator galleries. The momentary silence was dramatic.

"It's time for a change."

A few members of Congress stood and clapped feverishly. As they did so, the others joined in until everyone was on their feet, even those from the other party. King bowed his head modestly, waiting for the applause to draw down.

"Hi, I'm Kevin, welcome to Sunny Jim's Deli. I'll be taking care of you today."

Kevin the waiter retrieved a marker from a front pack he wore around his waist, whose pockets bulged with napkins, games, crayons, and balloons. His little blue vest was dotted with promotional buttons. He wrote his name upside down in thick letters on the white paper tablecloth, with a circle over the *i*.

"You look like you're gonna collapse. Can I start you off with some nacho chili cheese fries or maybe our signature jalapeño mozzarella sticks? They are so-o-o good."

"Give me the biggest pastrami you can make and a large coffee."

Kevin tapped out the order on his tablet.

"Okay, chief, your order's in," he said, and left as quickly as he had come.

Benson observed with fascination the customers eating and talking, the cooks and waiters chatting, the toddlers in their high chairs banging their cups and throwing food off their trays. Real life. No one watching, no one controlling, everything perfectly normal. For everyone but him, things were probably much as they had always been. Their lives hadn't been turned upside down. Only a short time ago and another world away he had escaped from a wretched prison.

He resumed watching the news show, now on an extended commercial break. A slick announcer offered precious metals for sale; all one had to do was call a toll-free number to learn more about "why gold and other precious metals could be right for you." A fake newscast-style presentation featured a fake anchorman-woman team vigorously promoting non–genetically modified plant seeds as part of a strategy for something they ominously referred to as a "food security plan."

The commercial break finally concluded and the new dictator resumed his speech, denouncing rumors of an impending invasion. The crowds roared their support.

"Fine, will you let 'em come!" he said, his fist pumping the air. "Gang of international villains find ferocious tiger devour for glorious motherland. I am promise mother of all battles. Americans be surrender or burn in their tanks! Oh yes, my friends, they surrender, it is they who surrender!"

Kevin returned with a gigantic sandwich and coffee. Benson tucked into it with exquisite satisfaction. He consumed most of it and drank down real coffee in between bites. Had food ever tasted this delicious? It restored him almost to his old self. He sat back, closing his eyes for a moment.

He opened his eyes to discover Kevin standing over him.

"My, that was quick," Kevin said. "Can I interest you in our Molten Chocolate Volcano Lavacake or our signature Rock 'n' Roller Coaster Coconut Cream Cobbler? They are so-o-o good."

"Give it a rest, Kevin. How about some foil to wrap up my leftovers?"

Benson returned to the show. Mideast mobs marched in the streets, their fists punching the air as they chanted, AK-47s raised high. A waiter switched the channel to a gameshow in which contestants dressed in outlandish costumes could win cars, refrigerators, televisions, and various household appliances if they correctly guessed the retail prices of the items on display, helped along with boisterous encouragement from the studio audience. Even some of Sunny Jim's customers played along, shouting out the prices.

Benson paid his bill and stepped out onto the sidewalk. Fishing the REAL ID cards and other identification from his pocket, he wrapped them all in the tinfoil.

25

Home, Sweet Home

H₁ₑ HAD ANTICIPATED THIS MOMENT for months. The sight filled him with longing for what had been. The fantasies had turned over and over in his head, an endless movie in which the hero somehow pulls through, reclaiming his former life and his rightful place, complete with the triumphant homecoming, the tearful, joyous reunion, and all the requisite hugging and kissing. At last, through the long months of anguish following his abduction, through the endless, sleepless nights consumed with gnawing worry and fear, Jane would be overjoyed that he was safe in her arms again. These scenes, so real to him playing in his mind day after day, had kept him alive, filling his miserable existence, its hardship and brutality, with hope and purpose.

This had been their home for nearly a decade, the place where he had raised his only child with his beloved Jane. This was where they had built their lives together. It was filled with precious memories, both happy and sad. He had planted that maple himself in the front yard when they moved in; it now towered over the roof. The garage door still had the dent where Daniel had bumped the car into it while learning to drive. The yard had fallen into disrepair; weeds and moss had taken a foothold and the bushes were overgrown, but no matter; the pleasure he felt was overpowering.

He was home again.

Jane arrived. She turned the key in the lock and removed it, pushing open the door. Footsteps approached from behind. She froze, inhaling sharply and dropping her keys. They clattered to the brick porch with a jarring sound that made her jump.

"Mrs. Benson!"

"You scared me to death," Jane said, her heart racing.

"Sorry to startle you, ma'am," said a policeman looming over her. "We are sorry to inform you, ma'am, your husband escaped detention at approximately 1042 hours Tuesday. We don't know exactly where he is but we'll stay close by. Just in case."

He tipped his hat.

"For your own protection, ma'am."

"For my own protection." Jane took a deep breath to calm herself. "Sure. All—all right."

The cop peered inside the dark house for a minute in silence before lumbering back to his car. Jane shut the door behind her and leaned against it, closing her eyes for a moment. She locked the door and flipped the hall light on.

"It's good to be home," Benson said.

After the initial shock of seeing him, he had imagined that she would run into his arms and they would embrace. He would hold her tight and bury his face in her soft neck, a feeling of intense relief flooding over both of them. Tears would run freely down her freckled cheeks. He would be alive; nothing else would matter. Against insurmountable odds, he'd returned from the missing and the dead.

Indeed, she stared, wide-eyed, struggling to get the words out, overcome by raw emotion. After all these months, her long-lost husband now appeared before her like an apparition.

"But he said ... how did—"

"It doesn't matter; I'm back, Jane, I'm back!"

Benson took her hand. She pulled it away.

"I missed you so much," he said.

After she fell into his arms, she might well find his monstrous ordeal too difficult to comprehend. If it hadn't happened to him, even he would have found it incredible.

Jane eyed him suspiciously.

He stood there, stunned.

"That's—that's not exactly a hero's welcome," he stammered.

Jane coldly appraised him, looking him up and down.

"You're not exactly a hero. Just what do you think you're doing, do you have any idea of what *I've* been through? The shame and humiliation, while you went and got yourself arrested—"

"Got *myself* arrested?"

"I have connections, I worked for Senator Dixon, remember? After your arrest I got a job with her replacement."

"But I didn't—"

"You were laundering money and drug running. They seized our bank accounts, our brokerage accounts, everything, under the asset forfeiture laws. They impounded our cars and auctioned them off. They ransacked all the rooms and stole jewelry and things. They confiscated your power tools. They hauled off your gun safe and the motorbikes and your fishing and camping gear. They found the hidden safe with the emergency cash and our passports and drilled it open. They stole your boat and trailer. They were like kids in a candy store; they grabbed everything but the house. I had no money left to contest it and now it's all gone, all our savings, everything."

She began crying, the tears running freely.

"Daniel … they sent him overseas. And Petey—they just left him there for me to find him like—like *that*. I'm all alone."

She wiped her eyes.

"You look like hell."

"You wouldn't believe what I've been through. The torture, the interrogations every—"

"And to think I trusted you. I never would have believed a man like you—never! Mixed up with terrorists. A man with your record of service."

"Mixed up with terrorists?" he choked out. "No. No! Lies. What can I do to convince you?"

"You can turn yourself in and face the consequences," she said, bowling him over with her matter-of-fact manner. "Go to trial. If by some crazy miracle—"

He couldn't believe any of this. He grabbed Jane and kissed her. She pushed him away, disgust in her eyes. He was devastated.

"No," she said through tears. "You can't do this to me again. You have no right to come here and endanger me."

"But honey—"

"Just go. Do what you need to do, I don't even want to know. Damn you, Tom," she said, with a loathing he had never seen in their long marriage. "Just be gone in the morning."

She ran upstairs, slamming the door behind her. Left alone in the dim light, he stared dumbly at the closed bedroom door. *His* bedroom door.

Heading downtown early the next morning, he entered a large, old building. Formerly a library, it was now the State Educational and Cultural Center, and practically empty.

The clerks staffing the information desk ignored him as he walked past and entered the PetroChina Educational Wing. Lines of cubicles extended down the aisles. Open reading spaces with comfortable seating and adjustable monitors surrounded the cubicles. Benson took a seat. "Identification Required to Access this Workstation" said a small sign on the monitor. He swiped Agent DeSoto's REAL ID through the reader. After a delay, an exploding pink bomb icon appeared on the screen. *Today's threat level is Pink. Be aware of your surroundings and report suspicious activities to the Authorities. Please press Enter to continue.*

The next screen required him to check off each statement before continuing:

- ☑ You are not, and are not acting on behalf of, any person who is a citizen, national, or resident of, or who is controlled by, the government of Cuba, Iran, North Korea, Sudan, Libya, Iraq, Afghanistan, Yemen, Pakistan, Somalia, Myanmar, Lebanon, Zimbabwe, Saudi Arabia, Columbia, Algeria, Venezuela, Syria, Uzbekistan, or any other country to which the United States has prohibited transactions.

- ☑ You are not, and are not acting on behalf of, any person or entity listed on the U.S. Treasury Department classified list of Specially Designated Nationals and Blocked Persons, or the U.S. Commerce Department Denied Persons List or Entity List.

- ☑ You will not use this computer for, and will not permit this computer to be used for, any purposes prohibited by law, knowingly or unknowingly, including, without limitation, for the development, design, manufacture or production of missiles or nuclear, chemical or biological weapons.

"Siri: find George Franklin."

Photographs of Franklin in various settings and poses populated the screen, some of them embarrassingly private. Benson swiped through, noting present and previous addresses, friends, employers, and memberships in social networks and professional societies. It seemed that Franklin had pursued graduate degrees and earned a doctorate from the School of International Graduate Studies at the Naval Postgraduate School. Benson selected a satellite view of office buildings, zooming in to identify the location, then switched to a street-level view, examining the entrance to Franklin's building and its immediate surroundings.

•   •   •

Mounted on the top floor, the giant, illuminated blue eagle logo could be readily seen across the city. White police cars were parked end to end around the entire building. Striped barricades blocked the entrance, on which the sign informed visitors that they were "Now Entering a Federal Security Zone." Soldiers with rifles slung over their shoulders passed the time talking among themselves, their German shepherds resting next to them. Benson strode past them with the air of an important man on official business. The dogs sat up on high alert.

He put his few belongings, belt, and shoes in a gray plastic bucket. The conveyor took it silently through the x-ray. The Homeland Security guard on duty rubbed his eyes, paying a cursory glance at the monitor and then at his watch. Benson went into the scanning booth, held his hands up, and spread his legs. The guard stroked him all over with a big electronic baton, rubbing it over his crotch, it seemed to Benson, a bit too keenly. Without the belt, his pants began falling down.

"Okay, you can drop your hands now," the guard said.

Benson pulled up his pants and threaded the belt through the loops while the guard watched him dress. A computer screen displayed a thumbnail image from Agent DeSoto's REAL ID.

"Destination?"

"Franklin. George Franklin."

The guard handed him a visitor's badge. On the way to the elevators he passed a portrait mounted on the wall of President King pointing off-camera to the metaphorical future, rendered in simple primary colors, the same one that had been used in the campaign. He got off the elevator, walking past a sea of identical cubicles to the outer offices with expansive views of the city ringing the perimeter. The carpets and furnishings were quite plush for a State office building. It was all very quiet. Some people momentarily looked up from their terminals as he walked past and then returned to whatever it was that they were doing.

He stopped in front of an office door, marked with Franklin's name and "4GW Special Activities Directorate" underneath. He knocked lightly on the door.

"Enter."

Benson opened the door. They stared at each other.

"Dr. Franklin, I presume?"

"You are?"

"Colonel Thomas Benson, at your service."

"Tom?" Franklin seemed not to understand what he'd just heard. "Is that really you? My God, it's been, what, 12, 15 years? Your hair—"

He eyed Benson up and down.

"You look like you've been beat up."

Benson entered Franklin's office and unbuttoned his shirt. He tossed it to the floor and turned around. Ugly scars, still not fully healed, crisscrossed his back like tire tracks.

"Whipped."

"Who did this?" Franklin demanded.

"Your Department of Homeland Security."

Franklin was speechless. He hurried past Benson to close the door.

"Looks like you've done well for yourself," Benson said, buttoning his shirt. "Scandinavian Contemporary in quilted maple. Very nice."

"We meet again after all these years." Franklin paused to take in his old friend and brother in arms. "Yes, I have done rather well. But by all rights, I shouldn't be here, I shouldn't even be alive. On our first tour together, you shot a sniper about to kill me. I didn't even see him. You were watching out for me."

"I was just doing my job."

"If your *job* was to be my guardian angel. On our last tour, I was knocked out. You carried me away from hell; I didn't even know what happened. Others told me the whole story, years later. They told me," Franklin leaned in, "that you carried me, barely alive, on your shoulders, away from the blast. I take it that's all true?"

"More or less."

"Hardly anyone survived. I still don't know how you did it. I'm in your lifelong debt, of course."

"You don't owe me anything."

"No, I owe you *everything*."

Franklin grew quiet, lost in thought, staring off into space.

"I woke up in the hospital. My vision was blurred, my ears bled, some broken bones. I eventually healed from the blast—physically. Mentally, I needed time, a long time. I felt tremendous guilt for surviving. So many of my brothers died. Why should I have pulled through when they didn't? Stupid, isn't it?"

"It's not stupid. We've all been there."

"I woke up night after night, locked in the same battle, reliving the nightmare, soaked in sweat. I dreaded sleep. I tried drinking, sleeping pills, and much worse. I wound up an addict. I'm still struggling with smoking, but that's the least of it. I've never told this to anyone."

Franklin was silent awhile, twirling a pen in his hand and looking at the floor.

"I was married for a few years, Tom, did you know that? My wife didn't understand. I didn't understand, either. I finally admitted I needed help. I never remarried."

He sat up straight and faced Benson.

"But *you* never needed help, did you? Always confident, always fearless."

"Everyone has fear," Benson said. "Not everyone shows it."

"You gave us leadership. It gave me the strength to carry on."

"You already had the strength. I only helped you find it."

"Speaking of which, how *did* you find me?"

"I have my ways."

"It's not safe to talk here." Franklin scribbled on a scrap of paper. "Meet me at my house tonight, 7:00. Here's the address. But you probably already know it, don't you? And here I haven't asked you anything about yourself."

"We'll catch up later. I'm driving a small brown four-door. See you tonight."

Benson pushed the heavy glass door to exit the building. The instant he did so, a raging klaxon went off. Flashing red lights pulsed and the door closed automatically in front of him, trapping him inside the building. His heart thumping in his chest, he repeatedly tried to force the door open and escape, desperately throwing his weight against it, but it was immovable. Just outside, the guard dogs howled, jumping up and down. He turned around to see a guard rushing over, almost upon him. He braced for a fight.

"Hold it right there!" the guard said, struggling to shout over the alarm. "You forgot to return your badge to the recycling bin."

"To the airport, Jagdeep," Benson said to the cab driver.

They turned off the road just before the snarled inspection lanes began. He got out and made his way to the first car rental agency.

"Hello, and welcome. Have you rented with us before? What kinda car would you like?"

The rental agent seemed almost too sincere. He wore a white shirt and green tie around a collar too large for his neck. His green company blazer appeared barely worn.

"Sporty, two-door, flashy."

"Excellent, I have just the thing, you'll just love it," the rental man said, typing on his terminal while he spoke, "and will you be taking advantage of our collision damage waiver? It's only $24.95 per day and covers you as primary insured. Accidents happen, you know. Better safe than sorry."

"No."

"And will you be taking advantage of our prepaid fuel option today?"

"No."

• • •

Benson parked within viewing distance of Franklin's house in a yellow Mustang. Elegant townhouses framed each side of the street. He looked at his watch. It was 4:30 p.m. The sun was beginning to set.

The time passed. He kept checking his watch. It was now 5:30; the occasional car went by and a few pedestrians strolled the quiet, treed sidewalks. It was already dark.

At 6:15, black sedans parked near Franklin's house. Men exited the cars and dashed into the house without knocking. At 7:30, some of the men left the house and drove away in the opposite directions from which they had come. Benson waited and counted them off. By 8:00, the remaining men had left Franklin's house.

Franklin opened the door, startled.

"T-Tom? But I thought—you can't blame me for being careful. Look, I'm sorry but you just walked in from nowhere with stolen ID."

Benson said nothing.

"I might've known you wouldn't meet at a time and place of my choosing," Franklin said. "You would stake out the place to be sure. Yes, I might've expected that."

Franklin opened the door and motioned Benson inside. He looked up and down the street before closing the door. Franklin led him to his study, filled with books and artifacts from his travels. Benson perused the titles before taking a seat. Franklin's library included *The Road to Serfdom*, *The Cult of the Presidency*, *Democracy: The God that Failed*, *The Ethics of Liberty*, *Crisis and Leviathan*, *The Law*, *The Politics of Obedience*, *For a New Liberty*, *Why Government Doesn't Work*, *A Nation of Sheep*, *Omnipotent Government*, *Common Sense*, *The Interrogator*, *Top Secret America*, and numerous biographies of great historical leaders and works on the American Revolution.

"I spent the afternoon researching," Franklin said. "There may be tens of thousands like you in State detention centers.

The official records aren't too clear on this; they use fake names or case numbers for the prisoners. It makes the disappearances complete. Even if someone knew you were inside, he still couldn't find you without tremendous difficulty."

"You're well-connected. I need a new identity. I want to strike back somehow."

"And how am I supposed to help you 'strike back?'"

"I have nothing left to lose."

Franklin appeared to be wrestling with conflicting thoughts, as though unsure how he should proceed.

"Have you been in contact with family?"

"My wife blames *me*. I can't go home. My son is gone, too; drafted. I don't know what's become of him."

Franklin thought some more, evidently weighing his options. He wrote an address on notepaper.

"Meet me here tomorrow, 5:30 p.m. There are some people you should meet. No tricks this time."

Benson closed the door quietly behind him. From the front window, Franklin watched him leave and picked up his phone.

The streets were fairly empty in this part of town at night. Benson drove at a leisurely pace, not wanting to attract attention. His eyes scanned the rearview mirror every few seconds. He became curious about a car following at a cautious distance. He could see it only in silhouette, its headlights obscuring any detail. Was it deliberately following or just happening to be going in the same direction?

He reached a side street and accelerated into the corner, the car skidding out of the turn as he pressed the pedal down. The other car was indeed pursuing. Benson floored it; the Mustang's tires chirped as the car leapt forward. The dry leaves on the street whipped up as he increased his lead.

He pulled up hard on the parking brake and turned the wheel sharply; the tires squealed and the car spun around to face his pursuer. He gunned the Mustang, smoking the back tires, and barreled straight for it. The cabin filled with the scent of burning rubber; the engine roared. In a state of total focus, a strange sense of complete calm overtook him. Time slowed down. His mind quieted and the rest of the world was totally shut out.

He bore dead on, just seconds from impact. The other car continued to race ahead, rapidly closing the distance between them. At the very last instant, the driver swerved to avoid a certain fatal collision, smashing into a bank of parked cars, showers of sparks glittering off its side. The careening automobile slammed into another car, vaulting over part of it, and turned over onto its side, smoldering. The top wheels spun freely. Trapped inside, its occupants fought to shake off the stupefying effects of the collision and escape, yelling weakly and kicking feebly at the doors over their heads. The smoking vehicle caught fire from the leaking gasoline. The flames grew until the car erupted.

From his rearview mirror, Benson saw the flames and then heard the bang. The effect of the adrenaline coursing through him suddenly made itself felt. Wheeling directly into an empty parking lot, he inhaled deeply and blew out, four seconds in and four seconds out; the "tactical breathing" technique he'd learned long ago in the military. Trembling, his pulse throbbing in his forehead, he shut the car off, placed his head on the steering wheel, and closed his eyes. When the shaking subsided, he drove off.

26

This Is Why We Fight

"Do you have a reservation with us, Mr. . . . ?"

A pianist played Broadway show tunes in the hotel lobby next to an ornate, wood-paneled lounge.

"No."

"Very well, not a problem, I assure you. You'll be staying with us for one night then, Mr. . . . ?"

"Flint." Benson gazed up at the chandeliers and the vaulted ceilings studded with plaster reliefs. "Derek Flint."

"We have a very nice room on the first floor, Mr. Flint; a lovely junior suite, convenient to the garage. The bellman will bring your luggage, yes?"

"No. I'll get my own luggage—and I'll take a room on the fourth floor near a fire exit."

"Certainly, Mr. Flint. Will you please excuse me for just a minute?"

The clerk went over to a computer at the opposite end of the reservation desk and retrieved a document entitled *FBI Communities Against Terrorism: Potential Indicators of Terrorist Activities Related to Hotels and Motels*. "Guests who request specific room assignments or locations" was one of the indicators listed. "Arrive with unusual amounts of luggage" was another suspicious sign.

"Okay, I think we're all set," she said, walking back over to Benson.

He looked closely at this "Ambrosia" from Escondido, California, according to her name tag. She fussed with the rings on her fingers and pushed her hair behind her ears. With a forced smile, she handed him a room key inside a little packet of promotional materials and then turned away. He looked at her for another moment and then made for the elevator.

Hanging the "Do Not Disturb" sign on the doorknob, he stripped down to his briefs, switched off the lights, and fell into bed, bone-tired.

Half an hour passed. The door handle turned slowly, a thin tool having been inserted to release the latch. Light from the corridor threw the intruder's shadow into the dark room. He silently closed the door. His eyes were not yet accustomed to the darkness and he could see almost nothing. He stood still, on edge. Turning around, he froze in place, stunned.

Benson landed a kick to the man's groin, causing him to double over, and then struck him sharply in the face with his knee. The man staggered in pain and shock. Lunging forward, still half blind in the shadows, the man took a wild, arcing swing, throwing all of his weight behind it. With a lightning jab, Benson struck him in the ear and then punched his face at eye level with a right hook. The intruder groaned and toppled to the floor.

Benson turned him over, pulling out a slim leather case containing a badge and other identification. Donning the intruder's black baseball-style cap, he ducked his head out the door.

"Sensitive area secured," he whispered in a husky voice. "Target neutralized."

Benson stood behind the door, holding it open. Dressed in the same dark clothes and cap as his partner, the second agent hurried in. Once he got partway through the door, Benson slammed it closed on the agent's leg and banged the agent's head back against the doorframe. Opening the door wide,

Benson grabbed the man and pulled hard, but he didn't fall to the floor. He spun around unsteadily and reached inside his jacket. Benson delivered a vicious kick to the hand gripping the gun. He moved in, sending a back kick into his gut. The agent careened onto his back, hitting his head on the floor.

Dragging them both into his bed, he removed their clothes and threw them out the window. After being found naked in bed together the next morning, nothing they said would be given the slightest credence.

He dressed quickly, tucking their identity documents into his pockets, watching the two agents for movement. He grabbed their guns and tucked them both in his waistband, pulling his shirt over. Glock 27s, subcompact 40 caliber; FBI or CIA issue, he guessed.

They stirred lightly. He went over and hit both of them on the forehead to induce a mild concussion. They wouldn't be awakening anytime soon.

Closing the hotel door quietly from the outside, he went out into the night.

They walked past the pond and the merry-go-round until they came to a picnic table. Benson pulled out the agents' identification wallets from the night before and tossed them on the table, scanning the open expanse of park uneasily.

"Why did you send your goons to my hotel?"

"That wasn't me." Franklin seemed genuinely puzzled.

Nearby, kids romped on the elaborate wooden play complex, climbing across bridges and scaling rope ladders, scampering in the forts and taking the slides down to their mother's waiting arms. A father pushed his delighted toddler on the swing. Some boys flung sand at each other, alternately laughing and crying, their frantic parents yelling at them to stop. It brought back bittersweet memories of a time long gone.

Franklin examined the wallets.

"So what happened?"

"Let's just say they're getting in touch with their feelings."

"I'll bet they are. Come with me. I want you to meet some people."

They walked to the far end of the parking lot where Franklin's Jaguar waited. The back and side windows were darkened, which, except for official vehicles, was strictly illegal in the District. The sight of those dark windows stirred up Benson's ugly memory of his arrest and subsequent ride in the squad car.

"You'll need to put this on," Franklin said, handing Benson a blindfold.

The last time he'd worn a blindfold was in front of a firing squad. He was anxious enough as it was; he'd be even more vulnerable sightless.

"You understand, of course. Just a precaution."

Franklin opened the rear door and Benson settled in. Franklin headed out of the park, making frequent, sudden turns through side streets.

"After the war, I drifted, without any meaning to my life," Franklin said. "Following a string of terrorist attacks, I still wanted to serve my country somehow, but my war days were definitely over. I discovered that I could contribute without actually going to war. I joined the Department. I dedicated myself to my new mission, all fired up, believing I was doing something really worthy, protecting my country from attack and all that. Here was a clean line between good and evil, and I was on the side of good. Those were some great days. I built a new life around my work."

Franklin watched Benson through the rearview mirror.

"But I started to question what we were doing. There was—and is—no real oversight. We just tell the congressional committees what we want them to hear and they have to take our word for it. And on top of that, they're sworn to absolute secrecy, so there's no media to stir up any trouble."

"No, we wouldn't want any trouble," Benson said.

"We violated every principle of Western law. The few terrorist cases that went before juries collapsed on flimsy, coerced evidence. So we moved the difficult cases out of the country where the laws were a little more ... *forgiving*, if you know what I mean."

"I know exactly what you mean."

Ahead was an overpass. "Today's Threat Level Is Silver," read the sign overhead. "Report Suspicious Persons to the Proper Authorities." Cameras at either end of the sign scanned license plates as the cars zipped by. Franklin pressed a button on the dashboard and the Jaguar's plates flipped over with new numbers.

"We gave up our freedoms to catch the 'bad guys,'" Franklin said, "but we don't know who's bad and who's good, so *everyone* must be monitored, *everyone* a suspect. We put together a network of paid informants, internal passports, and random checkpoints. Special laws were passed to arrest terrorists—but how do we even know who's really a terrorist if not by a fair and open trial? Because the president says so? Because a secret tribunal, appointed by, and reporting to, the president, says so?"

"Back to the Dark Ages."

"We were told these things are necessary in a time of war. It would apply only to foreigners and radicals; to *them*, not us. It would be temporary."

Darting the car down a side street, Franklin accelerated rapidly.

"In the beginning we had a few minor, if questionable, successes. We found unhinged psychotics, trained and funded them, and then arrested them just before they were supposed to blow something up. But as these and other secret programs grew, as their missions broadened to collect all public and private data on every citizen, they've been turned against the people. What begins as simple data collection and invasion of privacy, as bad as that it is, inevitably turns into something much worse—secret arrest, 'enhanced' interrogation, indefinite detention. I've seen this unfold with my own eyes."

"I've seen it unfold as well," Benson said.

"The new powers we were handed haven't prevented any attacks. Criminals make it their business to evade detection; they know where the weaknesses exist. You can't inspect and spy upon everything and everyone. Any collection of facts and figures, even if it's a massive collection, is fairly useless. Motivation and evil intent can't be put into a database. It's the average person who thinks he has nothing to hide, who naively expects his innocence to protect him, who is caught up in the snare. His innocence will be no protection. The State doesn't need to prove his guilt and he won't get a chance to defend himself in court."

"If you're arrested then you must be guilty."

"But still I told myself it couldn't happen here, not in the Land of the Free and the Home of the Brave. We'd learned from the horrors of the twentieth century; we wouldn't follow that path. We'd seen the terror, the torture, the starvation. We knew of the midnight knocks on the door, the mass deportations by cattle car to parts unknown, the Gulags, the camps. We were too jealous of our hard-won freedoms to follow the old authoritarian playbook. We were much smarter than that. I was wrong."

Descending a steep ramp, the car entered a garage beneath a narrow four-story townhouse.

"Americans wanted to sacrifice for the cause, to contribute whatever was asked of them. They believed—and I was one of them. I helped make it happen. I thought of going public but no important media outlet would take it. They were afraid of getting caught up in sedition or treason charges, both punishable by execution. My own life wouldn't have been worth a nickel, either."

They exited the car. Franklin removed the blindfold. Entering a security code, they took an elevator to an unmarked floor. Franklin led them into a conference room filled with people. Upon seeing him enter, everyone took their seats around a large, polished wood conference table. Franklin stood at the head with Benson sitting off to the side. Behind them loomed an enormous Betsy Ross flag, the symbol of the American Revolution, with its 13 red and white stripes and ring of 13 white stars on a blue field—except for a "II" situated in the center of the stars.

Franklin looked down the table. Silence came over the room.

"Sitting next to me is someone I want you to meet. If he looks a little beat up—excuse me Tom—it's because he just escaped from a Homeland National Security Administration black-site prison. These super-maximum security facilities were recently added to the existing stock of 'supermax' prisons throughout the country. Some 600 of these prisons are standing by in the event martial law is declared."

A slideshow of the facilities began playing on a screen behind Franklin. The exteriors featured extensive guard towers and razor wire. The interiors were all painted the same glossy, medium gray on the inside, with two floors of exposed interior corridors visible from open-air atriums extending to the roof, each corridor having long rows of identical steel doors fitted with observation portholes.

"National Security Presidential Directive 20/51 gives the president vast powers once he declares a national emergency. It gives him effective control of Congress, the courts, the Internet, and private industry. The president alone decides what qualifies as an emergency and determines when it's over—if ever. The National Defense Authorization Act authorizes arrest and indefinite detention without charge or trial. HNSA prisons are currently being used as secret interrogation centers by authority of the Military Commissions Act. They are staffed with Civilian National Security Force personnel and contractors, in cooperation with DHS and other intelligence and law enforcement agencies. Prisoners are called Unlawful Enemy Combatants. No one has ever escaped—until now.

"Tom Benson was a senior executive, the chief information officer for a major bank. He was my commanding officer in two tours of duty."

Franklin looked at Benson with genuine admiration.

"He twice saved my life at great risk to his own. He needs our help and we need his. Tom?"

Benson rose. He took a moment to compose his thoughts while everyone stared at him in silent curiosity.

"What I have to say would shock any true American; anyone who loves the founding ideals that America represents. I am guilty of no crime. The State did not have to prove its case in any court. I was not allowed to contest the accusations against me. There was no judge, no jury, no legal counsel. Until a few days ago, I was held captive for seven months."

The horrifying memories came flooding back; the sleep deprivation, the water torture, the freezing cold, the mock execution. He cleared his throat, fighting back the emotions.

"I was whipped, sleep-deprived, and slowly starved. I was drowned and frozen. I was locked in total isolation and put in stress positions to drive me mad."

He took a deep breath before continuing.

"I was arrested at my house. The street was filled with cop vans and SWAT police. It was even filmed for the evening news and a TV show. They said I laundered drug money to finance terrorism—a hopelessly stupid case, relying on hearsay from paid informants. I was to be their poster boy for the Terrorist Next Door, the idea being that if an average person like me could be a terrorist, then so could anyone—your neighbors, the grocery clerk, your kid's teacher. The first time I tried to escape I was nearly whipped to death."

The cruel lashing flashed into his mind, its electrifying pain paralyzing his body, destroying his will. The recollection of the unspeakable physical and mental suffering darkened his features. He looked at each person down the long table in the silence, seeing their absorbed, serious expressions, except for an attractive brunette in her 30s, on whose face was a faint smile. She looked directly into his eyes and tilted her head slightly.

"The second time I was successful. I—"

"Excuse me," said a man, raising his hand. "Are we really supposed to just swallow all this? How did you get out of there with all that security?"

"Gilbert!" said Franklin, but Benson put his hand up.

"No, I don't blame you," Benson said. "I was in the interrogation room. An agent pressed a gun to my forehead. I struck back in a rage; I smashed his face in. I kicked the second agent in the head, sending the bastard flying into the wall. His skull smacked the concrete. Two guards came in to investigate but I attacked them first. I made sure they were knocked out or—well, I don't need to go into the details. I took their guns, IDs and badges; I put on their uniform and hat. As calmly as I could, I walked out of prison as if I were just another guard going on break."

Gilbert was incredulous.

"Yes, but even if you—"

"Once free, I ditched the hat, tie, and jacket. I tore off the epaulets and badges and rolled up my sleeves. I untucked my shirt and kept my head down."

"Come on—how do we know any of this is true?"

Franklin nodded to Benson. Gilbert looked around the room for support but everyone's attention was on Benson. Staring at Gilbert, Benson slowly removed his shirt. He had recovered much of his vigor and strength in the last few days. The incarceration had left him lean but hard. He turned his back to the meeting. The marks the lash had left across his back were still vivid.

Franklin stood to take control, but he too couldn't help but stare at Benson's scars.

"This," Franklin said, "is why we fight."

"This doesn't feel right," Gilbert said, as he sat down, deflated. "He comes along at just the right time. I don't believe in coincidences."

"Sometimes," Franklin said slowly, his anger rising, "fortune smiles upon you. Anna? Do you have something to say?"

It was the woman Benson had noticed before. She was looking his way.

"Later."

"Well, then—do I have a motion to admit Tom Benson into our ranks?"

He scanned the conference room.

"All in favor—"

"Police! Open up!"

The relentless pounding of battering rams shook the house. The Patriots watched the outside surveillance monitors in horror. After many tries and much effort, battle-clad police kicked through the front entrance, scrambling over the smashed remains. The Patriots bolted for a concealed exit in the conference room.

Letting the others run past, Benson stayed with Franklin, who was standing stiffly and sweating, his eyes closed.

"I'll be all right in a minute," Franklin said between rapid breaths.

"We don't have a minute."

Benson hustled him out the exit. They ran down a dimly lit underground passage. After covering some distance, Franklin stopped to catch his breath. They listened to the Patriots' footsteps as they disappeared ahead down the tunnel.

"How did they find us?"

"Not *us*, my friend." Franklin panted. "It's *you*. You're still wearing a few of those guard clothes. They must be chipped. Take them off. Yes, everything."

Franklin felt along the seams to the label on Benson's shirt. "Levi's 24601®," it read. "Proudly Made in the USA." He crunched the label between his fingers.

"There's an RFID tag in this label. There must be more in here."

He threw the shirt onto the rest of Benson's clothes and tossed a lit match on the pile. The fire built briskly, flaring up the corridor before dying down just as quickly.

"It's the only way to kill those buggers. I'll go fetch some new duds—now don't go anywhere."

He vanished down the passage in the same direction in which the others had traveled. His footsteps grew increasingly faint until it was deathly quiet.

Alone in the dim light and the silence, Benson waited. He had been naked like this before, confined in his cell, cold and hungry, until they had come to get him. He felt exposed and defenseless. It seemed as if Franklin had departed a long time ago. He thought that he could hear far-off voices shouting and arguing fiercely, echoing off the cement walls of the tunnel.

Multiple footsteps approached at a fast clip. They sounded just like those he'd heard so often before, the heavy boots stomping ever closer, slamming the steel door open with a ferocious, ringing clang like a giant gong, the uncontrolled ferocity careening into him, vicious attack dogs knocking him to the floor and tearing at his flesh, ripping his skin off in bloody strips, devouring him alive, fighting over the scraps.

He fought to control his thumping heart and the wild anxiety welling up in the pit of his gut. Finding a corner away from the weak light, he pressed his sweating body up against the cool wall. "It's all right," he repeatedly said out loud, breathing deeply.

The footsteps grew louder and turned the corner.

Franklin dropped a large shopping bag on the floor. The sudden noise made Benson jump, but relief immediately flooded through him that it was only Franklin. He closed his eyes and his heart stopped racing so fast.

"Boss, Armani, Zegna?" Benson asked. "You know I'm particular."

"None of the above. No one will charge you with being a slave to fashion."

Minutes later, Benson held his hands out to his sides, looking down at his new outfit with a deep frown. He was dressed in ill-fitting, dirty rags.

"Excellent," Franklin said, nodding with approval.

They went quickly down the tunnel.

"We didn't really have much time to prepare for your arrival; besides, this will be useful for a small job I have for you. No one bothers Undocumented Resident Nationals— what we used to call homeless, vagrants, drifters, transients. They don't have bank accounts, healthcare authorizations, credit cards, or driver's licenses. No identity cards, housing permits, or employment authorizations. The State doesn't know where they are or how to find them and it doesn't really care, anyway. They can go anywhere without arousing suspicion."

Judging from the zigzag route they traveled, Benson figured that they were moving beneath several connected buildings.

"You will go undercover. I have a mission for you."

"What if I don't accept?"

Franklin cracked open the door to the street, had a quick look, then closed it again.

"Not having second thoughts, are we? You're already in a little too deep for that—a hunted fugitive, an enemy of the State. You won't escape capture a second time."

He put a wad of money in Benson's hand.

"You will use cash, nothing larger than fifties. Larger bills are chipped. This is $5,000."

They stepped out onto the dark street. A patrolman passed by on the sidewalk, glancing at them from the corner of his eye. After a little while, he moved on.

"This is a microchip scanner," Franklin said, handing Benson a small black item. "It can read REAL IDs to a range of 30 feet. Good luck, Tom."

"Wait—what do I do now? How do I find you?"

"You don't find *me*. I'll find *you*."

With that, he disappeared into the night.

27

George Has a Job for You

Benson sat on a bench in his bum's outfit early the next morning, holding a hand-scrawled sign. "pleas help Gd bless," it said. He tried to engage passersby but hardly anyone would even acknowledge his presence. Maybe the startling difference between his station in life and theirs aroused a vague sense of guilt in those with whom he crossed paths. Some registered just the briefest of glances in his direction before averting their eyes, perhaps trying to avoid what could become an unpleasant encounter.

He mulled over his fundraising strategy to this point. He had earned only $10 so far. Maybe the highway off-ramp would be a better venue in which to ply his trade.

"Five dollars for your troubles."

Someone put a folded $5 bill in Benson's hand and continued down the sidewalk without pausing. Beneath the money was a crumpled note. "Be at Fourteenth and Pennsylvania by Freedom Plaza in one hour," it read.

Waiting at the intersection at the appointed time, Benson wore casual clothes that he'd just bought with Franklin's cash. A BMW pulled over to the curb directly in front of him. The passenger-side window rolled down.

"Looking for a date, sailor?"

It was Anna from the Patriots. He got in. Anna pulled out into traffic.

"I already made 15 bucks, and the day is still young. Where are we going?"

"George has a job for you."

They drove at a rapid clip, switching lanes frequently.

"If any of the thousands of access points into REAL ID were penetrated," she said, "you'd have the Social Security numbers, birth certificates, driver's licenses, and more, of 350 million people."

Glancing at the rearview mirror, Anna floored the car to get through an intersection before the light turned red. The engine howled; Benson was pushed back in his seat.

"It would be identity theft on a colossal scale," she said, looking through the rearview mirror again. "Untold riches await the one who cracks it. Someone will find a way. We have to get there first."

Benson looked through his side mirror to view the road behind, but he didn't see anything unusual.

"Why? To get rich?"

"No, to restore what America used to be—when we had a Bill of Rights. Before people disappeared, before secret military tribunals and checkpoints. Before surveillance and torture."

Anna made an abrupt turn at an intersection, cutting off another car, and sped down the thoroughfare.

"Money is the lifeblood of the welfare-warfare State," she said. "People must be paid, weapons bought, computer systems installed, buildings constructed. What if the State couldn't pay its police and military, its security agents, spies, and informers?"

"They'd probably quit instantly. 'System disruption,' I think it's called."

"*Grand* system disruption. We won't have to fire a shot."

Anna pulled up in front of a large, fancy hotel, parking in the circular driveway. Bellmen in white quasi-military uniforms with gold braid on the shoulders, white gloves, and navy blue hats ringed the entrance, loading and unloading cars and escorting guests.

"I've already registered us," she said. "You'll check in as my husband."

"You're staying?"

"You don't want me to stay?"

She turned to face Benson, obviously hurt. Soft chestnut hair fell in waves around her lovely face.

"Oh, I see," she said. "You have your principles, yes, of course—but then, your loyalty has been betrayed, hasn't it. And after all you've been through."

Benson was amazed.

"There are no secrets," she said, quietly.

She looked at him for a moment, and then handed him a photograph.

"We will follow a key person in an upcoming operation. He could be, let's say, untrustworthy. We will need to confirm before he's activated."

Benson studied a picture of a handsome man in his late 30s. He wore a tailored, expensive suit.

Anna handed Benson a small paper bag.

"We call this 'fairy dust.'"

Inside the bag was a pouch of tiny metallic particles.

"You will wait in the lobby for him. When our man exits the building, get some fairy dust on him. It'll stay in his clothes."

"What is it?"

"RFID active smart tags, each smaller than a grain of sand. Collectively, they pack the punch of dozens of conventional tags."

Taking him by surprise, Anna suddenly kissed him. She pulled her face back from his and kissed him again, this time on his cheek. It was the first time a woman had lovingly touched him in more than seven months.

"I think you're wonderful," Anna whispered. "This is the easy part, my dear. We'll cover the rest in our hotel room tonight."

"Spare some change? Yeah, right, thanks a lot."

Benson positioned himself where he could see directly into the lobby. Business people hustled in and out of the building through the revolving glass doors. Dressed as a beggar, he held a cardboard sign at chest height on which he had scrawled "pleas help sick cat Gd bless."

Spotting his man inside the lobby, Benson slipped inside the doors and checked his scanner. The display glowed, "Olson, Bernard," with his likeness.

Benson went directly up to Olson, who seemed to be distracted and impatient, as if he might be waiting for someone.

"Hello, kind sir, can you possibly help me out?" Benson said, uncomfortably close to Olson and coughing. "I used to be an SVP. Help a man down on his luck?"

"No!" Olson said with disgust on his face. "Go away!"

Benson coughed into his partly open palm. A cloud of the RFID powder sprayed Olson. He reeled back in revulsion. An elderly private security guard came running over as fast as he could, his bulky walkie-talkie, ring of keys, and the other tools of his trade bobbing and jangling with each step.

He fumed at this outrage in his lobby.

"Get the hell outta here!" He pointed his finger at the door, pumping his arm. "You get the hell outta here right now!"

"Hack! Sorry, sir."

"Look at what you've done, you horrible bum, you," said Olson, wiping his face with the back of his hand and swiping at his suit jacket. "Do you know who I am? I should have you arrested."

At that moment, an analyst working in a dimly lit work gallery peered at a monitor casting a green glow onto his face.

Banks of monitors with analysts seated before them filled the hall. Blinking, colorful icons dotted an overhead video map. The analyst zoomed in until the satellite view of buildings became sharper and clearer. The smallest details of cars on the street and pedestrians on the sidewalks became identifiable. The analyst could even pick up normal conversation if there were no buses or trucks close by.

"Roger that, we have a lock. Maintain scan."

Olson hailed a taxi to a sex therapist's office. The recorded conversation revolved around issues of personal insecurity and self control that he had apparently been wrestling with for a long time. With a keystroke, certain lingering medical conditions embedded on Olson's REAL ID instantly popped up on the analyst's terminal. Surveillance drones then tracked him to a lively bar. He became friendly with a few men he met, where, perhaps drinking a bit too much, he revealed compromising details of his position at the National Security Agency.

"Help a man down on his luck?"

Benson banged a cup against his leg, rattling the coins inside. Franklin laughed and sat down next to him on the park bench.

"'There are a thousand hacking at the branches of evil to one who is striking at the root,'" Franklin said.

"Thoreau."

Franklin dropped a coin in Benson's cup.

"We are striking at the root, Tom. That's where you come in. We need access to the source database. We're developing a cloning algorithm that will link personal identifiers from REAL ID with all financial and tax records. This card," he said, fishing around in his briefcase and handing a slim metal case to Benson, "has high-security clearance. We altered the chip's programming, our very first clone. How do you like your picture?"

Benson opened the case and examined the card's front and back. It was flawless.

"We need to keep moving," Franklin said, standing.

"George, I'm concerned about Gilbert. He could be a risk."

"Gilbert Ward is one of the top data experts in the world. I would trust him with my life—as much as I'd trust you."

"What happened to Olson?" Benson said.

"He didn't work out. We cloned his ID for your alias—you're holding the result. As it happens, he called in sick for a few days. We trust that gives you enough time."

"What about my son, Daniel? Did you find out anything?"

"He was deployed—that's all I've found so far. You'll have to excuse me now, I'm running late for one of our 'touchpoint' meetings. We're discussing the president's initiative for the military, intelligence, and technology sectors to collaborate somehow. It's codenamed 'PRISM.' Look, we even have buttons."

He handed Benson a small plastic button with the initiative's logo, a beam of white light emerging from a prism in a rainbow of colors. Benson slipped it into his pocket.

Sprawled on a bench, Benson watched the pedestrians go by. His hand-scrawled cardboard sign read "alms for the por." A familiar figure approached.

"Gilbert! Help a man down on his luck?"

They strolled down the street until they were halfway down the block.

"The usual ID theft is that some punk steals personal data, opens a credit account and buys fancy TVs, jewelry, and designer clothes until he's caught," Ward said. "This is very different."

"If you think you're going to charm the pants off me with those lines, think again."

"I'm still not buying the whole thing, Benson, just so you know. Keep walking and don't look at me."

Benson's anger flared.

"At a deep level, REAL ID is linked to all financial trans-actions and tax returns. We'll crack it and reveal everyone's identity and cloning details on the Web. We'll make it all public—brokerage and bank accounts, credit cards, birth cer-tificates, social security numbers, all of it. When anyone can assume anyone's identity, a financial system built on secure transactions will crash. Boom!"

Benson wanted to smack him.

"The NSA's Stellar Wind program houses everything," Ward went on. "The annual American Community Survey census of your income, health, family, travel, lodging, and personal habits; it's in there, too. Even your passwords are in there. The current network of fusion centers will probably link up to it at some point. Aggregating and centralizing data like this is a real treasure trove for identity thieves."

"Tell me more."

"Security is still very basic. They are not exactly concerned about *protecting* your privacy; the whole point is to *invade* your privacy. They've built a massive database that captures financial records, phone calls, emails, blog entries, website browsing—*everything* known about you, public or private, accurate or not. Citizen risk profiles are run through an algorithm that calculates a threat analysis score based on how closely you match typical terrorist profiles. One little problem: there's no such thing as a typical terrorist. Despite the headlines, there haven't been enough attacks to construct anything statistically valid."

"Lies, damned lies, and statistics."

"The idea is to find potential criminals and disloyal subjects hiding in plain sight. The higher the threat score, the more you become one of their 'persons of interest'—and then the surveillance intensifies. In fact, that's how you were picked up, Benson. You tripped all the wires, didn't you?"

Benson didn't like the way Ward was looking at him.

"The standard terrorist target profile is nearly worthless. By now, most of your terrorists know not to buy one-way plane tickets with cash; they know they should check some luggage and rent a hotel room like normal people. They don't try to buy 10,000 pounds of fertilizer at once; they don't deposit $20,000 in cash at the local bank. This makes them just about impossible to find through predictive data mining. Knowing an individual terrorist's history and quirks tells you almost nothing about who will be a future terrorist. It's worse than trying to find a needle in a haystack—it's like trying to find a needle in a haystack of needles. But none of that deters NSA. They are in love with the concept."

"Stupid is a boundless concept."

"Stellar Wind runs threat profiles against semiannual sweeps of the entire population, but even assuming a 99 percent accuracy rate, at 350 million a sweep times two sweeps a year, that comes to seven million false positives a year, a little less if you exclude children. Maybe up to 1 percent would move on to the next round, the 'interviews.' You know all about that. That's 70,000 citizens arrested every year, based on an improbably low error rate. Owing to the nature of Stellar Wind's design, we believe visitors and most non-citizen residents are missed."

"Then it probably misses all the terrorists. Ironic, isn't it."

"You might say that, Benson. And then there are the citizens who are *not* false positives. They may not fit the profiles but they're anomalous in other ways—unusual interests, hobbies, beliefs—and therefore suspicious to the authorities. Or they might just want to shut up their critics and blackmail political rivals and control judges. Even if such people aren't detained they could still find their bank accounts frozen and employment authorizations attached to their REAL IDs quietly turned off, banished to a virtual internal exile as Undocumented Resident Nationals."

"So how are you planning to break in?" Benson asked.

"In data security, it's the human factor that's often over-looked. The weak link could be the lowly paid, frustrated clerk who wants to live the high life and impress his girlfriend; it could even be a certain highly paid software engineering consultant gone rogue. The system ultimately operates on simple trust and the fear of getting caught—but everyone has his price. Isn't that true, Benson? That's certainly one way to break in. The cloned REAL ID you were given also functions as a Common Access Card using two-factor authentication. It'll gain you access to NSA networks. That's another way in—*your* way in, Benson."

"For a second there, I thought I heard you saying something about penetrating Stellar Wind. Crazy."

"Crazy, but not stupid. The main operations hub is a massive server complex in Utah fed by a network of listening posts, geostationary satellites, and secret monitoring rooms in telecom facilities all over the world. All the data is fed into the Multiprogram Research Facility in Tennessee and then to NSA headquarters in Fort Meade just a few miles from here. Shouldn't be a problem for a tough guy like you, right? That's why you're on the team. You'll receive further instructions at the hotel."

"You're supposed to be a big IT expert," Benson said.

A shadow of a smile crossed Ward's face.

"So why don't you go in yourself, Ward? Why do you need me?"

"I don't have your particular background," Ward replied, stiffly. "You're fairly well-known in certain circles, I have to give you that. COMSEC and network security are definitely not my fields. And you can tell I'm not in the best shape. That may come in handy."

They walked on in silence.

"So Benson, I have to ask *you* something. Why didn't you encrypt? Why didn't you use Tor or another anonymizing service? How is it that a person with your background—"

"If they can watch the entire Internet all at once, then they can watch all the traffic entry and exit relays, too. Some of them are actually operated by the State. Proxies are not invulnerable, either. No one is really anonymous. Besides, I didn't think I had anything to hide."

"That's the stupidest thing I ever heard."

"And now *I* have something to ask *you*," responded Benson, simmering. "How do you know so much about Stellar Wind? What makes *you* such an authority?"

Ward looked at Benson with the tiniest hint of pride.

"I helped build it."

28

Get Me the Hell Outta This

THE BOOMING ENGINES DRONED LOUDLY inside the cavernous transport aircraft. Hard bench seats were bolted to the floor throughout the cargo hold. There were no windows, call buttons, reading lamps, or any of the conveniences of passenger jets. The airplane pitched and rocked as it bore through the night. After 13 hours of rough flight the gigantic rear hatch was thrown open to the blinding sun.

The newly minted soldiers straggled out, weary and dirty. It was easily 100 degrees. Waves of heat shimmered off the tarmac in the distance. A strong, steady wind blew stinging sand and dust in their faces. The few scraggly palm trees in the desolate landscape bent over in the wind, barely alive, the fronds rustling in the scorching breeze. Beyond the low terminal building and the hangar loomed an endless expanse of beige sand and rock.

Daniel shielded his burning, tearing eyes from the intense light with his forearm. Hungry, thirsty, and greatly fatigued, he was groggy and nauseous, feeling a terrible headache coming on. High gusts stirred up the dirt into whirlwinds. The recruits were coughing, covering their noses and mouths with their hands.

"Welcome, everyone. I'm Major Lamb."

Daniel lined up with the rest of the company in front of the military compound. Weak and dizzy, he struggled just to

remain upright, the vibration and noise of the last 13 hours
and now the blazing heat and light severely taxing what little
vigor remained.

"And congratulations." Lamb's soft voice was barely audible
against the wind. "You have been given the opportunity
to defend the Homeland in its time of need and preserve
American freedom. On the front lines over here, your fellow
soldiers are your brothers. You'll eat, shit, and shave with
them. They'll look out for your sorry ass and you'll look out
for theirs."

The draftees grumbled at this inhospitable reception,
especially considering the arduous journey to get here, but
Major Lamb took no notice.

"Okay, that's about it. This'll be your home for the next 18
months, grunts. Unpack and be ready for inspection at 1230
hours. Dismissed."

Daniel's bunk was a small, thin mattress on a bare metal
frame. Identical rows of stacked bunks lined the long walls
of the sparse, cheerless barracks. The bed frames, walls, floor,
and ceiling were all painted the same glossy, medium gray.
He unpacked his bag and plopped himself down on the bed,
dispirited, looking up at the underside of the top bunk before
closing his eyes to catch what little rest and relief that he might.

A thunderous explosion hit the barracks, flinging him
off his bed. Dust and debris showered the air; bare light
bulbs suspended from the ceiling danced on the ends of their
cords. Huddling on the floor face down, he protected his head
between his arms.

"What the f—"

"Stay down."

Major Lamb stood nearby, examining the damage to the
ceiling.

"It's just rainin' a little iron. You get used to it."

Another explosion rocked the barracks. The lights flickered and then burned steadily.

• • •

"I'm shot!" a pathetic, mournful voice cried from inside a building. "Help me!"

The street was deserted. Scattered fires in the houses and apartment blocks belched dense, billowing smoke, their crumbling facades scarred with bullet holes. Broken pieces of concrete littered the ground. The acrid smell of phosphorus hung in the air. Daniel and the other soldiers pressed up against the entrance of the bombed-out building. It was dark inside.

"Where are they?" Daniel yelled into the building, his heart thumping.

"Dunno! Can't see nothin'!" came the reply from deep within.

Something fell, clattering onto the floor. Daniel looked at his comrades.

"Could be an ambush," whispered one.

"No way," Daniel said, "he's one of ours—we leave no one behind."

He entered the building with the other soldiers hugging the walls. All was quiet. There was no furniture in the room, just bare cement and exposed foundation blocks. Shot in the neck, a soldier reclined in a corner. Another lay on the floor, blood oozing from his chest.

Daniel crept to the soldier in the corner.

"Where are they?" he said, in a low voice.

"The courtyard," the soldier groaned. "Shoot the fuckers."

Crouching against a cement wall, Daniel sprayed bullets in the courtyard's direction. A barrage came back his way, blasting the wall above, filling the air with smoke. Flying cement chips stung him through his uniform.

"We need support! Get fuckin' support!" Daniel shouted into his shoulder radio.

He tore around a corner, his carbine blazing. Through the smoke he took down one of the enemy and watched him shout in pain as he fell.

Another insurgent fired on Daniel and a soldier from the opposite direction. Bullets ricocheted off the wall; sharp fragments zipped through the air. They returned fire, taking cover behind a cement partition. Bursts exploded around Daniel and the other soldiers, pinning them down.

Dear God, Daniel mouthed silently, *get me the hell outta this.*

He peeked out to see the enemy, who wore dirty jeans, a black T-shirt, and a manic expression on his face. "Allahu Akbar! Allahu Akbar!" he yelled crazily between bursts.

Daniel launched a grenade and hit the ground. The blast was earsplitting in the cement block room. Stinging fragments shot back at him. A section of the ceiling cracked and caved in onto the cement floor, sending up clouds of choking dust. Daniel's face was plastered with white soot caked around his goggles and inside his nose. He felt as if he'd been punched hard in the gut. A loud whine rang in his ears.

He shook his head and got up slowly, balancing unsteadily. He stood over the two terrorists, their bodies twisted and torn up. Pieces of their flesh and organs stuck to the walls. Daniel instantly felt sick, fighting to keep down the rising nausea. He retched and vomited on the floor in a corner where he hoped no one would see.

The support soldiers rushed in. The soldier whom Daniel had just spoken with had been killed in the firefight. The other wounded American on the floor bled profusely inside his uniform. Dark red wet spots on the fabric spread. Daniel dropped to one knee by his side and averted his eyes. He didn't want the soldier to see what he was looking at.

"Medevac's on the way, kid."

He looked to be about the same young age as Daniel. The wounded soldier stared at him with blank, glazed eyes, and dilated pupils. Daniel took the soldier's hand in his. The skin was cool and clammy. The soldier's heart beat rapidly; his breathing came shallow and fast. Dazed, he was going into shock.

Daniel spat on the floor, failing to clear the dust coating the inside of his mouth and the phlegm in his throat. The spit bomb stirred up a pile of fine powder from the floor, curling lazily up in the air against the backdrop of the blinding sun outside.

"You'll be okay, kid. Just hang on."

Soldiers surrounded a cluster of damaged buildings. They were told that terrorists were holed up inside. Daniel aimed his rifle at the buildings, moving the sight from window to window. Helicopter gunships thundered ever closer, their blades beating the hot air, rustling the sparse clusters of palms and stirring up choking clouds of dust and sand. Once they came into range their autocannon fire blasted the compound.

CIA Deputy Officer Boyd "Dirty Bull" Beecham stood immediately behind the soldiers, dashing in a black leather jacket and matching short-brimmed cap, looking like a World War II flying ace.

"Come outta there with your fuckin' hands up!" Beecham yelled through a bullhorn. "I repeat, surrender! Come out now! Corporal!"

He turned to a young man standing next to him who knew some of the language.

"What're the right fuckin' words?"

The corporal wrote down what to say and Beecham again raised his bullhorn.

"Okay, listen up, freaks! Ba man biaid! Man alkol nemi-nousham, you little bastards!"

He repeated it several times, but there was no reaction from the terrorists hiding within.

"Corporal! Are you shittin' me? You sure those're the right fuckin' words?"

Sporadic bursts erupted from inside the buildings. Daniel couldn't see any movement but he fired into the empty windows anyway. The ricochets and blasts went on and on. Finally, Beecham held up his hand to cease fire.

An army officer came over, surveying the scene with binoculars. They discussed strategy.

"Damn ragheads been holed up for hours," Beecham said. He threw his bullhorn on the ground. "Let's step it up! Shock and awe, baby."

In short order, huge, eight-wheeled Stryker MGS armored fighting vehicles moved into position. Laser-guided missiles found their targets, rocking and shattering the structures. Daniel and the other soldiers emptied rounds into the windows and doors and then ceased on orders. Small fires burned throughout the compound, the black smoke curling into the sky. All was relatively quiet.

Deputy Officer Beecham reached for his binoculars.

"So where the hell are they? Must be a fuckin' underground bunker in there."

He spat on the ground.

"Let's try some a' that CS gas. That'll flush 'em out."

Soldiers launched missiles from shoulder-mounted rocket launchers, their courses traced by white smoke trails arcing through the air. Blinding explosions lit up the interior of the compound. Fire burst through the windows and door openings. The compound's roofs collapsed and burned in the inferno.

Transfixed, the company watched as the buildings were consumed in fire, marveling at the stunning pyrotechnics, better even than the fireworks displays on Independence Day back home. Before long, all that was left were the ruins of the cement walls that had stood against the onslaught.

His binoculars trained on the action, "Dirty Bull" Beecham shouted into his handset against the background noise.

"Mission accomplished, sir."

Loaded with insurgents shackled to their seats, a convoy of military transport vehicles rumbled down a ravaged urban street. The sides of the matte gray converted school buses were caked with dirt, their windows locked shut and barred with steel rods. The convoy meandered slowly down the street, bumping and lurching in the ruts and potholes, accompanied by troops marching alongside. The few residents to be seen peered fearfully out of their squalid homes, silently watching the procession march past in the rubble. The putrid stench of human waste and rotting garbage fouled the still, hot air.

Not far away, rioting mobs were busy smashing shop windows and setting cars on fire, unaware of a forbidding column of tanks fast approaching. Warnings blared through the tank's loudspeakers as they came within range.

"Turn back! Disperse immediately! Salam dooet e man. Moazeb bash! Rooze khoobi dashteh bashid."

Caught up in their mad frenzy, the stern warnings went unheeded.

Nearly invisible from the ground, Predator drones flew soundlessly far overhead, the small windowless craft whirring in the thin, clear air. Trailed by dense white exhaust plumes, laser-guided Hellfire missiles accelerated to supersonic speed, striking a building thought to harbor insurgents. The building exploded in flame. After a minute, the top floor collapsed to the street below. Overcome by wild panic, the raging crowds scattered.

29

Rock 'n' Roll Time

"Y_OU'LL BE OUR GUEST for one night then, Mr....?

"Helm. Matt Helm."

"Oh yes, of course, welcome, Mr. Helm."

Benson got the distinct feeling that the front desk clerk was looking him over, but why? He was wearing perfectly normal, stylishly casual clothes and even carrying a small traveling bag to better blend into the surroundings.

"It looks like everything has already been taken care of, Mr. Helm. Would you like to sign up for our frequent guest program? Twelve stays earns you one free night redeemable during most weekends and you can also earn one complimentary adult beverage credit during your stay in the lounge."

"No."

"That's fine, sir. Please enjoy your stay, and if you need anything, just call down and ask for Richard."

Benson opened the door to his room. Anna lounged on the bed, reclining against the headboard, exquisite in a clingy, little black dress. He closed the door and went over to the bed. Long legs and slender, bare shoulders. She looked up at him, her soft fragrance of cinnamon and orange perfuming the air.

"Beat it," Benson said. "Scram. Get lost before I call the cops."

"Oh, please. Don't be so dramatic. You need me, it's part of the plan."

"I don't need any plans."

Anna propped herself up on an elbow, her legs splayed sideways across the bed.

"I have our instructions. We'll be working very closely together." She kicked off her heels. "George thought I would provide a needed distraction."

"I don't need any distractions."

"Not for you, tough guy; for all those red-blooded men at NSA. I'll help you get inside."

They sat on the bed, studying the maps, drawings, and other documents spread out before them. Benson was impressed with their depth and meticulousness. Only a well-placed insider could have developed all this.

"Isn't it fantastic?" Anna said, moving closer to him. "Every detail has been worked out."

"That's what worries me." He stared off into space. "Something feels wrong."

"You just need to relax, you're all tense. Why don't we have a drink and unwind a little? I make a mean martini."

She rose from the bed.

"Anna, why are you in this? Why are you risking everything?"

Anna sat down on the bed next to him.

"I had no interest in politics; both parties always arguing about nothing. They're the same, really. But my brother was very involved. He was an antiwar activist—a Registered Political Lobbyist. We were involved in a few 'kinetic military actions' at the time, and who knows how many other secret wars and special ops deployments were in the works. My brother organized protests and rallies, really good at it, too, building huge numbers across the country, generating positive headlines."

She was silent for a moment.

"And one day he disappeared. Months went by. The police were absolutely no help, but I knew George—he's a good friend—and we tracked him down. George knows just about everyone and everything; the smartest person I ever met, a true mastermind."

Anna laid down on the bed, staring up at the ceiling as she spoke.

"We discovered my brother was arrested for 'Domestic Terrorism.' That was two years ago. He was moved some-where, but we don't know where, or if he's still alive or—or dead." She was in tears.

Benson laid down next to her. Here was a beautiful, sensitive woman with a depth he hadn't suspected.

"I'm sorry," he said, softly.

Anna took a breath to calm herself. She said nothing for a while.

"Your story is like my brother's. I imagine he's trapped down there, too; I'm almost sure of it. We're still searching."

She stared at the ceiling again and wiped her eyes.

"I have a unique position with a certain amount of influence, if I do say so myself. George thought I would be useful to the Patriots, and of course he could trust me. Trust is so critical."

She turned to him again, looking into his eyes.

"I—I work for the Internal Revenue Service. Programming Control and Technology Security Branch."

"I need that drink now."

Anna went over to the bar, putting ice in martini glasses and pouring out gin and vermouth. Benson watched her from behind preparing the cocktails. He came over to her.

"Anna, do you have a cell phone?"

She looked at him curiously but went to her purse and retrieved it. He turned the phone over in his hands.

Anna handed him his drink.

"Cheers," she said, clinking glasses. "To our mission. To liberty."

Downstairs, paramilitary police rushed by the front desk and took up their positions to secure the lobby. The senior officer in the party barked orders to his subordinates and then turned his attention to the clerk.

"You there!" Vice Commander Chauncey Peters, DHS Special Investigations Directorate, shouted to a frightened Richard, flashing his badge to the clerk. "You remain where you are."

People in the lobby instantly stopped what they were doing and backed away until they bumped into the walls.

Benson dropped Anna's phone on the floor and stomped on it with the heel of his shoe. Anna watched helplessly as he tossed the smashed phone out the window.

"My phone! What're you doing?"

"No distractions," Benson replied.

"Where's the register?" demanded Vice Commander Peters. "You there, what's your name? Richard? All right, Richard, you will show me everyone who registered in the last two days."

IT Specialists attached to the Department of Applied Digital Forensics, Business Data Security Command, set up a remote data center in the lobby, streaming everything to NSA for analysis. They went through thousands of accounts, poring over names, home and work addresses, REAL ID biometrics, detailed travel itineraries, credit card data, and bank records. Computer screens displayed the present locations of current and former hotel guests on a global map. DHS police in camouflage assault uniforms prevented anyone from entering or leaving the lobby. Several hours passed until they found what they were looking for.

"Homeland Security! Open up!"

DHS police banged on Benson and Anna's hotel room door and rattled the handle, trying to force it.

"Open up!"

They pounded the door some more.

"You there, what's your name?" Peters shouted at the terrified clerk standing at the edge of the group. "Richard? All right, Richard, open it."

Richard promptly unlocked the door and ran away at a gallop down the hall. Silently, the police entered, cautiously spreading out. One of them found the bedroom, its door closed, and motioned for the others to come over. Quietly opening the door, they snuck into the dark room and surrounded the bed, their weapons drawn. They saw a spooning couple covered by a blanket.

"Freeze! Get up real slow," Vice Commander Peters said. "Hands in the air."

Nothing happened. He repeated his command, but the couple didn't stir. He grabbed a corner of the blanket and tore it away. The pillows had been arranged to look like two people sleeping.

Benson and Anna stared up at their hotel room from the street, now ablaze with light against the mostly dark building. It was quite late and the street was nearly empty.

"How did you know?" Anna said.

"At least no one will bug us now."

Benson walked over to an unmarked squad car parked nearby. He peered inside before opening the unlocked door. Anna nervously scanned the street for trouble while Benson squirmed over on his side to get under the dashboard.

"Tom, what are you doing?"

"And now for a little distraction of my own."

After a few minutes, the car abruptly roared to life. He rolled down the driver's window. Shifting the car into neutral, he wedged a rolled-up floor mat against the gas pedal. The engine revved to redline, shattering the calm night.

"Get back!" he yelled over the din.

Standing outside the car, he gingerly reached through the open window and bumped the transmission into gear with a quick snap of his hand. The car tore off, its tires screeching, sending clouds of burning rubber into the air. The empty car accelerated madly but stayed roughly on course.

Directly ahead was a compound of historic buildings crowned with gabled roofs of hammered copper. Walls of hand-wrought red brick partly covered with ivy lent a stately atmosphere. A pyramid logo with light shining from a human eye onto a globe of the world appeared discreetly over a command post guarding the entrance.

"Nice place they have there," Benson said. "A shame if anything happened to it."

The squad car crashed through the front gate and spun wildly in the small inner courtyard, careening into the main building. Plowing into the front wall, it erupted in a fiery blast, orange flames and black smoke reaching into the night sky. Panicked guards ran out into the courtyard, darting back and forth in the chaos. The old brick wall slowly gave way, collapsing on the burning hulk of the police car.

Spellbound, Benson and Anna watched the explosion from the sidewalk. The sight of the improbably elegant prison compound on fire brought back a flood of bitter memories. What suffering and cruelty lay just beyond those walls? Benson watched the fire with a grim satisfaction.

A gathering wail of sirens broke his reverie.

"That should keep them busy for a while. It'll be dawn soon. Rock 'n' roll time."

"I didn't know you were capable of something like that," Anna said.

"You don't know what I'm capable of."

Benson pulled the plain, dark car into a vast surface parking lot populated by thousands of vehicles. In front of them loomed two tall buildings covered in black mirrored windows. He turned off the engine and rubbed his eyes. It was midmorning. Physically fatigued but mentally energized nonetheless, he steeled himself for the task at hand.

"Anna, I—"

He stopped himself in mid-sentence and turned to look at her for a moment, silent. He took her hand. She squeezed his hand in her own.

"I think you're wonderful, too," he said.

He kissed her cheek, then got out of the car and opened her door.

Two cameras mounted over the entrance followed them as they went up the walk. Just inside the front doors was an elaborate security checkpoint, none of it visible from the outside. "Entering Federal Security Zone," read the sign. "All Persons and Property Subject to Search and Seizure." Soldiers with rifles slung over their shoulders observed Benson and Anna without expression.

They put their slim briefcases on the conveyor belt and undressed before walking through the body scanners. Anna attracted the attention of the soldiers as she stooped over to slip on her shoes. She put on her blazer and tossed her long brown hair over the collar.

Upon presenting their identification, a soldier peered intently at their cards, squinting at them and shining a small purple light on each, meanwhile sneaking furtive glances at Anna's shapely legs set off by a short, fitted skirt. The usual female functionaries in their plain institutional attire and cropped hair passing through here didn't look anything like this striking woman before him.

The monitor displayed their pictures, fingerprints, retinal images, and voice prints, finding an exact match.

"Enter your PINs, please."

"Identity Confirmed," flashed the monitor.

"Destination?" the soldier asked.

"Stellar Wind."

The soldier gave them badges to clip on their breast pockets.

"Go ahead, Mr. Olson."

He gazed at Anna with a smile, tipping his hat.

"Miss Lane."

Walking down a carpeted corridor, they came to a pair of heavy glass doors featuring the NSA logo of an eagle grasping an antique, prison-type skeleton key in its talons. "Stellar Wind" appeared beneath the logo. A portly military policeman slouched on a stool just outside the doors. He silently took their identity cards, swiping them through the reader and staring at the monitor, waiting for the system to respond. An hourglass symbol slowly rotated on the screen.

"Please enter your PINs."

Anna leaned over, a sexy smile on her face.

"Thanks, Officer," she said.

The MP brightened up at this, returning the smile. He handed them their cards and straightened up on his stool.

"Thank you, Miss, but to be honest, I'm not really an officer, you know. The thing is, is I joined up to serve my country and all that kinda thing, and this is where they stick me. I'm in a prime a' my life, ready for action, you know what I'm sayin'?"

"You're *still* serving, in your own way," Anna said. "'They also serve who only stand and wait.' Now if you'll excuse us—"

She turned, preparing to go through the doors, but he wouldn't release the lock.

"Mind you, I'm makin' the best of it, I got me into some debt trouble a while back you know, and the pay isn' so great, but I'm comin' along, I'm doin' okay."

She responded with silence.

"So anyhow, you have a nice day," the MP said, finally.

Inside the data center they were met by a junior officer in shirtsleeves. Anna greeted him with a fetching smile.

"We're from Accelerated Computer Machine Engineering Corporation," she said. "Checking ISO 9340 compliance. Here's my business card."

"Contractors, ha! Get tons of 'em every day. Okay, I'll need to check your IDs."

They signed their names in a log and were led to a large room. Banks of terminals lined the walls. But for two programmers in uniform hunched over a desk, the room was empty.

"Okay, here you are, ma'am."

The officer grasped his nameplate, lifting it a bit off his shirt.

"The name's McCarthy. You need me for anything, you just ask. Anything at all."

Lieutenant McCarthy walked away, looking back at Anna over his shoulder as he went.

They sat a few chairs away from the other programmers and got to work.

"IBM Blue Gene/Q massively parallel supercomputer," Benson whispered.

Lines of code scrolled down the screen.

"Tens of thousands of nodes working simultaneously. There's the link—take a picture. Each node contains its own memory and copy of the operating system and application. Each subsystem communicates with the others. A high-speed data exchange protocol ties them together."

Benson and Anna continued to work, eventually attracting the notice of the two programmers a few stations away. One of them came over and peered at the screen from behind Anna's shoulder.

"Hey, where you folks from? You're not allowed to take photographs, you should know that."

"Time for your *distraction*," Benson said to Anna, speaking through his teeth.

Anna walked over to the programmer's partner, taking the next chair, the other one following her.

"We're from Accelerated Computer Machine Engineering. You don't mind me being here, do you Colonel Foster?"

"Well, heck no, Miss, but I'm just a captain, see, and this here's a second lieutenant."

"Excuse me, *Captain* Foster. I just assumed you were senior."

Anna turned to the lieutenant, looking him up and down approvingly.

"Hi, Lieutenant Parks. You're both so fit."

"Well, ma'am," Parks said, "I can't say we've seen much action, I mean, *yet*—but we could be deployed overseas any day now, though, it's true, so we have to stay fit. It's all the exercise, ma'am, comes with the job."

"I wish everyone would take their oath to defend our country seriously. It makes me feel so much safer. How do you relax with all that pressure?"

"Well, you know, pool and video games and stuff," Captain Foster cut in. "There's lots of things to do around here. You'd be surprised."

"I'll bet you have girlfriends to ease the load, if you know what I mean."

"We're sort of in-between girls—if you know what *I* mean," Parks said.

"Look, I have to supervise our new trainee guy over there," Anna said, hooking her thumb over in Benson's direction, "but I'm going out with my girlfriend tonight for drinks. Why don't we all get together after work? Give me your card, and I'll call you later?"

Captain Foster and Lieutenant Parks were delighted.

Anna got up and sat next to Benson, peering at the monitor with him.

"From the looks of it," Anna whispered, "we should be able to write remote client access and fly through the intrusion detection system."

Benson stared at her.

"I happen to know a little something about technology security myself," Anna said.

"Then we're almost there," Benson whispered back. "Mainly off-the-shelf security and commercial operating systems here. There are at least 70 separate databases. It looks like none of them are well-connected. Unbelievable. This shouldn't give me too much trouble. Here he comes again. Keep him occupied."

"Ma'am, excuse me for the interruption again, but what did you say you're working on?"

"It has to do with national security. I can't say more without official clearance. Procedures, you know."

"Yes, ma'am, I fully respect that. I'll just call our commanding officer."

Benson could hardly contain his alarm. Anna stood up and yawned, stretching her arms overhead. Her blazer fell open, revealing a tiny camisole underneath.

"There's no hurry," Anna said. "We'll be here awhile. Can we get some coffee first? My lips are parched." She licked her lips. "I have something personal I would like to talk to you about."

"Sure, let's walk over to the canteen."

They ambled out the door and were gone a half hour. When they returned, deep in conversation, Benson was already standing, eager to depart.

"Yeah, sounds great, Miss Lane," Captain Foster said, "but you know what? I still should make that call."

"Don't bother," Benson said, "we're done here. Thanks for all your hospitality. We'll be going now."

Lieutenant Parks rushed over.

"Wait just a minute, sir. I'm just gonna call our CO—"

Benson kicked Parks in the stomach, then kicked out to the side to catch Foster. The programmers doubled over, dumbstruck, the wind knocked out of them. Benson kicked Foster in the throat, then sent his knee into Parks' chest. Parks sank to the floor. Foster lunged slowly for Benson but collapsed on his knees and went down, gasping.

Benson knelt over them with an anxious eye on the exit. The two men were fighting for breath.

"The LSD—let's have it," Benson said.

He dropped a small sugar cube in each of their mouths. It dissolved almost instantly.

"You have a nice trip, boys."

He stood and straightened his suit. They strolled out past the MP at the outer door, still slouched on his stool facing the corridor. He looked at Benson as if he were expecting something.

"You have a nice day," Benson said.

Quickening their pace, they headed swiftly for the exit.

"Hey, you!" a soldier called out. "Stop right there!" The soldier came running, a hand on his shouldered rifle. "I said, 'Stop!'"

Benson reflexively moved into a fight stance, pivoting around, his fists up, the adrenaline pumping.

"You need to put your badges in the recycling bin on your way out. Sir."

Scrambling into the car, they sped down the highway in silence. An overhead sign flashed a message: "See Something, Say Something™—Report Suspicious Activity—Call 1-800-TIPS."

"They'll discover a security breach and shut the whole system down," Anna said.

"I don't know about that—those two clowns will be out of it for a few days, at least."

Benson took the next exit.

"By the time they schedule a meeting to discuss what happened," he said, checking his rearview mirror, "and another meeting to decide what to do and another to get approval for someone to authorize something, it'll be too late."

30

You'll Be All Right, Kid

THE PONDEROUS GEAR and searing heat made for an almost intolerable burden, draining the life out of a young soldier. Daniel carried over 100 pounds of weapons, ammunition, armor, food, water, and other equipment. Inside his combat uniform, boots, helmet, goggles, and gloves, the temperature was probably 115 degrees, but he was in superb shape, acclimated as well as anyone could be to such grueling conditions after more than a month spent on tour. He would prepare for these expeditions by putting himself in the proper frame of mind with the warrior's discipline he had developed. He felt tough and equal to the challenge, which he regarded as a test of his personal worth.

He remembered the dare that Sergeant Schultz had issued, the look on Schultz's face, the words coming back to him in Schultz's voice. "*Now who here thinks he's a damn warrior, who's got some big goddamn balls, move one step in front.*" He had stepped out in front.

Sweat trickled down his spine as he patrolled with his company on the dirt road.

I am a soldier.

He took a sip of water from his hydration tube.

Dad would be so proud of me.

The company marched slowly past empty buildings, most of them in some stage of decay or destruction, interspersed

274

with the occasional occupied, but dark, apartment block. Electricity was sporadic here.

Without warning, insurgents appeared from around the corners of buildings on both sides of the road, firing M16 assault rifles, weapons that had been issued in vast quantities to the new civilian security force, the Department of Public Safety. They wore the same outer tactical vests and Enhanced Combat Helmets as the coalition soldiers they were attacking.

Retreating for cover while returning fire, the soldiers in the rear tripped a roadside bomb, setting off a massive explosion next to Daniel. He dropped to the ground, unable to move. Clutching his lower left abdomen, he looked down. Under his hand a spreading patch of blood darkened the bottom of his jacket. He took his hand away and pulled up his shirt. In pure horror, he saw his own guts protruding, his blood seeping copiously from the wound onto the dirt.

"I'm hit! I'm fuckin' hit!"

The words came out as though he were yelling through a mouthful of cotton from far away.

"Help me!"

His speech was slurred, as if he were intoxicated.

Lying on his right side, he was surprised to find that he was not feeling intense pain, but numbness. The cacophony of the battle drowned out his cries. A feeling of tightness gripped his lower body, compounding the rising dread overtaking him. His heart racing, he strived to remain calm, concentrating on keeping his breathing steady. He pressed down on the wound with his left hand to stanch the flow and contain his organs. The battle raged around him while he lay helplessly in the dirt.

The fighting subsided. He couldn't breathe properly. He felt something on his face and wiggled his jaw. It felt strangely loose. He touched his right hand to his mouth, and then to his nose, but he couldn't feel anything. He drew his hand away. It was wet with blood. A severed leg and arm lay on the ground next to him, the rest of the soldier a short distance

away, wailing in agony. Daniel suddenly realized that he had
been struck in the face by flying body parts. He desperately
tried to wiggle away but stuck fast to the ground. Wounded
soldiers lay on the ground writhing in pain, while others lay
dead, their bodies broken and twisted, their faces planted in
the dirt.

A corporal came running over to Daniel, squatting down
beside him.

"Medevac's coming!" the corporal shouted. "You'll be all
right, kid. We'll get you out, just hold on!"

He examined the wounds, trying to be encouraging, but
his alarm was unmistakable. He applied a bulky dressing
and then a pressure bandage to secure it. Daniel groaned and
vomited. He felt chilled.

The company took up defensive positions, on guard for
another ambush.

A Medevac helicopter flew in at treetop level, darting and
zigzagging, dodging snipers and rocket-propelled grenades
launched from the ground. It came in quickly, bouncing hard
upon landing. Poised for a hasty retreat, the blades kept
beating briskly. Medics sprang out of the open doors in a mad
dash to load the survivors and get airborne while precious
time ticked away.

Strapped and buckled into a litter, Daniel's limp body was
hoisted into the Medevac.

"Don't let me die!" Fighting to stay conscious, he grabbed
the medic's hand with a crushing grip. "Don't let me die." He
spat out some bloody teeth.

The twin engines boomed; the blades kicked up a swirling
storm of dirt. On the ground, soldiers secured the perimeter,
squinting down the sights of their rifles, alert for any movement. Running well past time when they should be in the air,
the last litter was heaved onboard, each additional second on
the ground rendering them increasingly vulnerable to attack.

The last medic scrambled into the helicopter.

"Go! Go!" he yelled.

The door still open, the pilot gunned the helicopter and it jolted skyward. The sharp, rocking motion made Daniel groan.

A terrorist jumped out of his hiding place behind the bushes, a little hole he'd dug and covered with branches. With a camouflaged grenade launcher already perched on his shoulder, he took hasty aim and fired. It narrowly missed the Medevac, exploding nearby. The craft rocked back and forth, hovering precariously, pitching and yawing as the pilot fought to regain control.

The terrorist laughed with joy. In giddy excitement, he fell to the ground to prepare another volley. Opening the box of grenades, he grabbed one and was immediately torn up in a hail of bullets. Bursts continued to riddle his lifeless body, making it jump and dance on the ground.

The Medevac flew in jerky patterns over the treetops on its tortured path to the nearest Combat Support Hospital. Daniel groaned, shifting in and out of consciousness. Lurching to its destination, his helicopter was one of several Medevacs hovering over the landing pad awaiting their turn.

A long procession of wheeled litters streamed into the Emergency Medical Treatment tent. An explosion rocked the EMT, overturning supply carts and knocking medics and doctors to the floor. The lights flickered and then extinguished. But for a few voices in the dark, all was silent, the constant hum of the air conditioners having cut out. The emergency generators took over and the lights became bright and then dimmed, reaching full strength again after several minutes.

Daniel was finally wheeled into the EMT. Two litters ahead of him was a young soldier, his left arm gone, his torso and legs punctured by shrapnel. A burly soldier, his right leg hanging by sinews, was next.

"X-rays over here, move it!" a doctor yelled over the commotion.

Leaning over a litter, another doctor examined a soldier pierced with glass and nails. The slightest movement gave him unbearable agony. He flinched with excruciating pain as the doctor delicately cut off his T-shirt.

"Just frags and soft-tissue damage. Sorry son—we'll get you to the OR soon as we can. Wheel him aside," he yelled, making his way through the waiting litters, performing triage as he went.

A medic charged through the line of litters.

"Out of the way, move, move, move, bodies coming through!"

"Internal blood pooling! Sonar scan, stat."

Daniel's chin was peppered with shrapnel. Most of his front teeth were missing. His lips were gashed open and swollen purple and black. A medic stood over him, tenderly cradling Daniel's head in his hands.

"Benson—it'll be okay."

Though well accustomed to such sights, the medic fought to choke back the tears welling up inside.

"You're gonna be all right!"

Daniel stared with glazed, unblinking eyes.

"Benson! You hear me, Benson?"

He clutched Daniel's hand tightly.

"You're—gonna—be—all—right!"

Daniel's face was an empty mask. The medic felt his wrist for a pulse as his insides spilled out onto the floor.

Against a blaring siren, a mechanical voice boomed through a loudspeaker, "*Incoming! Incoming! Incoming!*"

31

Live Free or Die

THE CONFERENCE ROOM WAS PACKED with many more people than Benson remembered from the last meeting. He spotted Anna near the end of the table. She locked her eyes with his.

Franklin rose to address the Patriots. Behind him loomed a giant Betsy Ross flag with the "II" in the middle of the circle of stars. The room hushed.

"Like sheep, the people are easily panicked. Throughout history, rulers have understood this well. Had we not panicked, had we not surrendered to mass hysteria and submitted to fear, we would still be free. But we, the people, eagerly sold our precious liberty for phantom promises of safety and security. We struck a very poor bargain. We got neither liberty nor security.

"Freedom of speech was the first casualty in the War on Terror. Paid informants spied in our workplaces and in our stores, in our restaurants and bars, at sporting events and in houses of worship. State functionaries searched through our mail and listened in on our private conversations. They read our email and online communications and monitored the websites we visited. Any speech or writing that could be taken the wrong way, say the wrong thing, or offend the authorities could be labeled 'hate speech' or sedition. 'If the freedom of speech is taken away,' said Washington, 'then dumb and silent we may be led, like sheep to the slaughter.'

"The desire for economic security—the 'freedom from want' —found expression in a multitude of ruinous entitlements dividing the people into warring factions battling each other for the spoils. As Bastiat put it: 'The State is that great fiction by which everyone tries to live at the expense of everyone else.' Tax-funded intellectuals laid the necessary groundwork, preaching that a personal surplus of anything beyond mere subsistence was intolerably selfish, morally wrong, unneeded, and undeserved—the outcome of pure chance and not enterprise. Life being nothing more than a cruel lottery, the majority were thereby persuaded to view themselves as victims, one of the many have-nots, entitled by that reason alone to the labors of their fellow citizens.

"The political elite happily obliged in the theft, redistributing the wealth of the people like so much free candy to spoiled children, the State accumulating ever more power all the while. When, at last, the wealth of the nation itself proved insufficient for the majority to live off the State—its production capacity ravaged through inflation, taxes, and strangling regulations—the State simply borrowed more to keep it all going, burdening the people with crippling debt.

"State control of the economy—what the people may produce, who they are permitted to employ, in what occupations they are licensed to work, what goods and services they are allowed to buy, what housing they may occupy, what the schools may teach their children, what foods they may eat, what medical care is allowed, what vehicles are permitted, how much they may earn and how much they may keep —meant regulation of life itself. A command-and-control economy delivered command and control of the people. A planned economy meant the people's lives would be planned to conform to the social engineering of society. They would be directed, pushed, and pulled by the planners, rewarded or punished for their actions or inactions.

"The growing numbers of those dependent upon the State for their daily sustenance in one way or another made control of the people all the easier. A dependent people learn to be helpless; they come to believe that work and initiative amount to nothing. They seek short-term pleasure and entertainment above all; they want someone or something to provide for them. A dependent people are a submissive people.

"Mirroring its rise to dominance in social and economic affairs, the State became aggressively international in its ambitions, eager to flex its muscles to fix a world in need, driven to find great new challenges to take on outside its own territory. Not content with merely policing its own citizens, it would now police the world. Through its unchallenged military might it would conquer the enemies of freedom, bestowing peace and democracy upon hostile lands whose grateful citizenry would welcome the marching troops with garlands of flowers strewn at their feet. So it was that a country blessed by the protection of two oceans and two friendly neighbors on its borders nevertheless went 'abroad in search of monsters to destroy.'

"And yet the security of even the most formidable State in world history could be crippled easily enough by crazed malcontents armed with box cutters and underwear bombs. More would have to be done to fight this insidious menace—a total War on Terror; a war unrestricted in its weapons, combatants, or territory. With the War on Terror now a global conflict, the distinction between the war front and the home front inevitably became blurred. The fight would not, after all, be waged only over *there*, as we had been assured, but over *here*; and not just against the terrorists—petty criminals, lunatics, and smalltime saboteurs all—but against *us*, employing the same strategies, tactics, and firepower so well field-tested abroad. As Madison had warned, 'The means of defense against foreign danger historically have become the instruments of tyranny at home.'

"'Freedom from fear,' the natural longing for safety and security, was cynically exploited through endless wars against enemies whose identities were ambiguous and ever-changing, in pursuit of unachievable objectives that were ever shifting. The people united around the State to protect them from enemies the State itself had created. Yet, evil, shadowy foreign enemies weren't enough to keep the requisite level of fear at a fever pitch. They were too distant, the danger too remote. Agents provocateurs were therefore dispatched to incite acts of domestic terrorism. For those plots which it instigated and then halted at the last second, the State could arouse deep-seated fear and yet claim credit as the protector of the people. How easily the people were duped to accept any intrusion, inconvenience, or demand in the name of security.

"By their own vote, by the people's own endorsement, our Republic has became an elected tyranny. To win election, these demagogues steal the people's wealth and redistribute it to their supporters. They enact laws favoring the few at the expense of the many. They bail out and prop up the unscrupulous and the unprincipled. Cunning and shrewd, they dress their campaigns in vaguely utopian language, relying upon crude emotion and widespread ignorance. They would transform America and change the world, eliminating poverty and deprivation from the land. There would be food for the hungry, clothing for the naked, shelter for the homeless. The people would be fully employed and own nice homes, enjoy good health and secure retirements, and live in harmony with nature. In the new *Pax Americana*, our needs would be few and our desires limited; we would be content with our lot.

"But these false messiahs also spoke stirringly of national honor, national unity, and the Greater Good with ominous invocations to citizen obligation, sacrifice of life and liberty, and mandatory national service. Their noble-sounding fantasies were to be achieved through compulsion, putting the people to the service of the State. Individuals striving to better their own lives and that of their families, wishing to be left in peace to pursue life, liberty, and happiness, were deemed small and selfish, unworthy of a great country. In the pursuit of 'national greatness' we would sacrifice our blood and treasure building vainglorious monuments to an expanding State whose appetite could never be satisfied. A society built upon such force and compulsion always ends badly.

"As the State's power and reach swelled, 'special opportunities' emerged for those who craved power and control over others. The worst elements of society, the ruthless and the corrupt, the parasites, the manipulating and the scheming; all now had a fitting place in which to exercise their ambitions. The greatest of these special opportunities would be concentrated in the figure of the president. He would pose as our deliverer and protector, our supreme leader, our savior and redeemer. He would be a godlike figure. Corrupted by the grandeur and authority of the office, his soul poisoned by the 'will to power,' he might even come to believe it himself. Great power is a heady liquor. Those who consume it are soon overtaken by its exhilarating effects.

"The two dominant political parties shrewdly split the people into warring tribes, while State power, which they took turns exercising between them, grew unchecked. The parties were only superficially different, more a matter of style than of substance. The slogans and the actors may have differed, but on matters of any importance, Team Red and Team Blue were essentially the same team advancing much the same agenda. Universal surveillance, a command economy, and a state of perpetual war were only their means to an end. The real end was always power and control.

"Once the 'Supreme Law of the Land,' the Constitution has become a dead letter, the plain meaning of its elegant language tortured and twisted into an instrument by which the State controls the people—instead of the means by which the people control the State. When the Supreme Law of the Land is willfully violated, then the land is lawless. Congress has become a criminal organization, itself unrestrained by the laws, rules, and regulations it so zealously enforces on the people. And yet, the people have willingly tolerated, even approved, of this lawlessness. Indifferent to outdated notions of limited government, individual autonomy, respect for privacy, and the rule of law, the people have come to welcome the new, unrestrained State as its magnanimous benefactor, not its oppressor."

The room was deathly silent.

"The logical culmination of all that has come before is now upon us. We are tracked and recorded. Our movements, finances, medical histories, reading materials, friends, associates, and social clubs are indexed, profiled, and scored. They told us it was to find the terrorists, but they don't know who they are—so they must track everyone. Tagged like cattle, we carry our identity cards everywhere under severe penalty of law, seeking permission to work and even to travel about in our own country. Even then, we are subject to abusive checkpoints, strip searches, and intimidation. We are no longer free human beings born with the natural right to life and liberty as enshrined in the Declaration of Independence. We are, instead, potential threats to national security."

A soft, muffled thud came from above.

"Internal passports. Secret arrests, civilian military tribunals, a shadow justice system. Spying by drone and satellite. Warrantless search and seizure. 'Extraordinary rendition' to 'black-site' prisons. 'Enhanced' interrogation. 'Ghost' detainees. This is what we have come to. The State can 'disappear' you in a modern reprise of *Nacht und Nebel*. The president claims the authority to murder you or anyone else, whether at home or abroad, meting out death by armed drones stalking the skies or by any other means, drawing up a biweekly 'kill list' in secret meetings with intelligence and military operatives for the purpose. Elite Special Operations Forces now numbering some 100,000 personnel conduct secret wars across the globe, answerable to him alone.

"As at the time of the Revolution, the State is again making war on the people, calling them enemy combatants and stripping them of their citizenship and their liberties. The executive, this time in the person of the president, again recognizes no limits on its power. There is nothing it cannot do, no area of life that it cannot intrude upon. Where once everything not expressly forbidden by law was allowed to the people as their prerogative, now everything not expressly allowed is, in effect, forbidden. The courts and Congress, designed as checks on each other's power, have shamefully abdicated their responsibilities and today serve mainly to enforce the will of the executive. Like the kings of old, the president enacts his own laws through executive orders, presidential directives, signing statements, and executive agency regulations. He has become a Caesar.

"Within a generation the people will be living in an open prison of their own making. The living memory of what it meant to be free will have disappeared. The people will have become accustomed to subjection, losing the right to live, work, and travel as they once pleased. A formerly free people will be restricted by papers, permits, registrations, authorizations, approvals, and licenses, removing their capacity to act in accord with their natural talents and inclinations. For those who refuse to obey the orders, laws, mandates, acts, regulations, codes, and statutes, there is the punishing force of the State lying in wait, its fines, prisons, and brutality lurking just beneath the surface. 'Government is not reason, it is not eloquence, it is force. Like fire, it is a dangerous servant and a fearful master.'"

A faint sound of music came from above, detected by only a few people around the table. They looked at one another with curiosity.

"Americans could have extinguished the fire; it was always in their power, yet they have chosen not only to wear their chains and shackles, but to make them heavier and tighter. Dropping their eternal vigilance, naively trusting, they have voted for their own destruction. They have acted stupidly. They do not yet see troops patrolling the streets with machine guns. They do not yet see tanks on every corner. The new order in the New America is still in its infancy, hidden away, but gathering its strength. The people are still allowed to vote and so they believe they must still be free. 'None are more hopelessly enslaved than those who falsely believe they are free,' said Goethe. Even so, we will give the people back their liberty, whether they want it or not. They will be free again, whether they deserve it or not."

Benson sat back in his seat, his hands on his temples, deep in contemplation. The scars on his back prickled. He straightened up, feeling the wounds tug. He reflected on his own tacit endorsement of the New America, of his capture and monstrous imprisonment. He thought about his honor and mission. He could be no "summer soldier," no "sunshine patriot." He would do his duty to his country. There could be no other choice.

"The National Security State has emerged not to keep the people secure, nor to safeguard their liberty, but to protect and strengthen its own existence. But in the process of amassing great power and control, it breeds conflict and creates enemies. It becomes a victim of the same fear it has so carefully nurtured. Gone are the days when presidents could mix freely among the people. With their heavily armed contingents and fortified vehicles, with the elaborate security measures they must take everywhere they go, their own freedom is severely curtailed. Desperately and tragically craving admiration and even adoration, they become, instead, obliged to fear the people as threats. The people become the enemy. The servants of the people become their masters.

"Following a long train of abuses, whenever any form of government becomes destructive of liberty, it is the right of the people to alter or to abolish it—so says the Declaration. Governments must serve, not rule. The second American Revolution will starve the State until it is again 'bound by the chains of the Constitution.'"

The flag behind Franklin billowed ever so slightly, as if by a passing breeze.

"The clock is running out. If we fail to act it will be too late to prevent a catastrophe. We may be just one or two terrorist attacks away—whether real or manufactured—from a full-on police State. We will not sit idly while the foundations of our Republic are shattered forever. We will not suffer perpetual war. We will not be enslaved. We will again be a fiercely independent, peaceful, and industrious people. Not warriors. Not sheep. Not serfs. Americans will not be ruled. We will live free—"

Franklin gazed at each person at the table.

"Or die."

There was a muted, distant rumbling overhead. The table trembled almost imperceptibly.

"When injustice becomes law, resistance becomes duty. Those State officials and military officers among us swore a sacred oath to defend the Constitution. Let us now honor the pledge that we freely took. And may God bless you all."

Benson remained seated, brooding, as everyone filed out. Anna lingered at the door, watching him, until she, too, exited the room. Benson and Franklin were left alone.

"You must understand that this would have been impossible without you," Franklin said. "You were the missing link necessary for our success."

The rumbling and music from above was getting louder.

"You have a unique combination of skills," Franklin said, but Benson's thoughts were elsewhere.

Franklin put a hand on Benson's shoulder.

"I know it's tough. We've all paid a heavy price, you more than anyone. You deserve the Medal of Freedom for your valor."

The Black Hawks thundered overhead. Stryker MGS armored vehicles arrayed in formation. Loudspeakers set up around the office building blasted music so tremendously loud that it physically hurt.

♪♪ *"You know the day destroys the night ..."* ♪♫
♪♪ *"Night divides the day."* ♪♫
♪♪ *"Tried to run ... Tried to hide ..."* ♪♫

Led by CIA and DHS agents, soldiers on the ground awaited their orders. Helicopter machine guns sprayed a series of staccato bursts into the building. The mirrored windows cracked and smashed to the ground.

♪♪ *"Break on through to the other side!"* ♪♫
♪♪ *"Break on through to the other side!"* ♪♫

CIA Paramilitary Operations Officer Casey "Stalker" Adams, Special Activities Division, in black leather jacket and matching cap, leaned out of one of the Black Hawks. His amplified voice could barely be heard over the beating blades and the shrieking music. The building already had several fires raging inside.

"Surrender now!" Adams yelled, severely straining his voice. He swallowed hard and coughed. "I repeat, surrender now! Come out now to impact minimal collateral damage," he grunted, his face flushed with the effort.

"Damn DHS getting in the way again!" he protested to his colleague piloting the craft. "I hate those guys."

DHS Officer Claude "Butch" Browner, Special Operations Group, surveyed the siege from the ground through his binoculars. He wore a shiny black jacket emblazoned with the reflective yellow letters of his agency.

"So where's the rest of 'em? I just can't figure it," Browner said to the soldier next to him.

"Maybe they're underground—yeah, I bet that's it," he said, all excited. "Well, this should take care of it. Major Bernham! Deploy five canisters of CS—and make it quick now."

"Sir, this is a *Homeland mission*—a Homeland mission, sir!" Major Bernham shook his head in disbelief. There had to be a mistake. "Civilians, beyond the rules of engagement. Sorry, sir, I'll need special orders."

"Civilians, my ass!" Browner barked in a flash of anger. "I don't give a flying fuck where they're from. They're terrorists, sonny. Extremists. Nutcakes. The world is different now, understand? You just go do as you're told and there won't be any trouble, you hear?"

"But there're fires burning! You know damn well what would happen, I mean, sir, if CS gas hits it—"

"Shake 'n' bake," Browner growled. "You got your 'special' orders, Major—or should I say, *Captain*. I'm beginning to not like your attitude."

Browner took up his binoculars again. The major turned and walked away, glancing back at Browner several times.

Minutes later, soldiers launched rocket propelled grenades loaded with CS. White corkscrew smoke trails followed each missile into the building. A series of explosions erupted; fire burst through the windows. The building was quickly engulfed in flames, throwing off dense plumes of gray smoke and soot. The occupants fled for their lives, scrambling over the wreckage and escaping through the blown-out windows. Soldiers fired rounds into the building.

CIA Officer "Stalker" Adams was aghast as he observed the developing scene. He saw, and even felt, the explosions. Helplessly watching the building's unarmed occupants flee into machine gun fire, he became enraged.

"Goddamn DHS! This is an atrocity, look at what they've done!" he screamed in frustration to his colleague in the helicopter. "They'll take all the credit for this, those backstabbers, you just know they will. I hate those guys."

DHS Officer "Butch" Browner dropped the binoculars from his eyes.

"Bought the farm!" he said into his handset. "Yes, sir, I'm pretty sure we got 'em all. DHS did a great job here, sir, very professional. Mission accomplished, sir."

The soldiers streamed over the grounds, picking through the ruins. Benson and Franklin had watched the unfolding drama on monitors fed by closed-circuit television cameras.

"Looks like they had the right street address," Franklin said, staring coldly at Benson, "but they didn't know about a certain underground command post built to survive a nuclear blast, did they?"

Benson did not remove his gaze from the monitors.

"It would seem that they did not."

The soldiers swarmed directly overhead. They would find nothing but typical offices and a basement level reduced to smoking rubble, and the incinerated, gruesome remains of whatever unfortunates had occupied the building.

"We have survived a couple of close calls recently, have we not?" Franklin said, airily.

"We have indeed."

"Extraordinarily lucky, wouldn't you say?"

Benson broke his gaze from the monitors. The silence hung in the air.

"Sometimes fortune smiles upon you," Benson said, and abruptly left the room.

Franklin caught up with him in the command center. The underground retreat was a beehive of activity. Video walls loomed overhead to the high ceilings; scores of operatives staffed the various command stations arrayed in pods.

Benson whirled around, marveling at the colossal scale.

"Amazing. Sophisticated communications, defensive systems, a gym and restaurant. It's a fortress. What else do you have here?"

"Gold, of course, and an extensive food supply. This bunker was designed for the Continuity of Government program in case of attack or insurrection. It has the best technology and fortifications to ensure that high State officials survive the worst. We removed it from the classified facilities database and it 'disappeared.' We'll be safe here."

Jane unlocked the front door. It had been a difficult day at the office and she was beat. She dropped her keys and purse on the hallway desk and removed her coat. She walked into the kitchen and turned the light on.

The shock floored her; she leaned against the wall for support. Benson sat calmly on a chair, silently watching her. He hadn't forgotten the uncharitable reception he'd received from their previous meeting, but that was in the past; he had to let it go. The authorities had lied to her. He realized now that his adventure would be too fantastic to digest all at once. She would naturally have trouble accepting it.

The events she'd experienced firsthand—the checkpoints, inspections, and virtual molestation at the airport, the frightening VIPR roadblock on their way to La Grande Maison, the ransacking of their house and the seizure of their property— were only the most visible parts of something much uglier brewing. Whether traveling by bus, car, train, or plane, checkpoints and inspections were a normal part of most everyone's day. The general public might be vaguely aware that some new security measures had been enacted, but they were surely applied only to deserving suspects, and in just a few, select cases at that.

"You're not safe here. Jane, we have to leave. Everything will change tomorrow, there'll be chaos everywhere. Your life will be in danger. Jane, please, honey, we have to go—right now."

She just stared at him and picked up her phone.

"Jane, you have to trust me on this."

"I'm calling the police."

He made no attempt to intervene.

"Nothing. No service," she said, dumbfounded, dropping the phone on the counter.

"It's already happening. Let's leave right away, we'll go to a secure place. Please listen to me—we have no time to waste."

"I—I have to think ... "

More in sadness than frustration, he departed alone.

32

A Significant Step Forward

Everyone stopped what they were doing to watch the giant, multifaceted overhead screens in the cavernous main gallery of the Patriot's command center. A handsome middle-aged man and an attractive young woman peered gravely into the cameras.

"We are getting unconfirmed reports," the man's pleasing, rich voice boomed throughout the bunker, "of potentially serious security breaches at some of our major banks." He had a full head of dark hair with just a touch of gray at the temples. "Spokespersons have no comment. Let's go now to our financial correspondent, Alan Greenbach. Hi, Alan, how're you doing?"

"In terms of your specific question, Keith, I can offer a qualified 'affirmative' at this time."

"Alan, we're hearing rumors of financial security, um— issues," said the show's female host. She had long, shiny dark hair and beautiful, big brown eyes. "Rumors are swirling that the Chinese are concerned about holding on to U.S. debt in the present atmosphere of uncertainty."

"Marcela, I just interfaced with our banking czar and top Federal Reserve and Treasury officials," Greenbach said, speaking slowly. "According to some experts, who, we are given to understand, are highly placed in the administration, it seems that there is not, in fact, a viral situation at this time juncture. Nevertheless, there are certain rumors swirling in important circles in reference to the desirability of capital controls, along with new documentation and reporting requirements in order to help deal with this presumed crisis of confidence—"

"Alan, sorry to interrupt, but we are now getting unconfirmed reports that some major banks have halted all transactions. Other reports are coming in that the Chinese may be trying to dump all their dollar reserves. No word yet from the banking czar. Alan?"

Greenbach held a finger to his earbud, listening to breaking reports. He nodded his head.

"Well, Keith and Marcela, here is the approximate situation on the ground as we are currently understanding it. According to informed sources at this point in time, with the information we have available to us—excuse me."

Greenbach sneezed a few times.

"As I was saying, it is, without an appreciable amount of doubt, probable that the dollar will be vertically challenged as the debt infrastructure will have to be monetized."

The show's hosts looked at each other, at a total loss.

"So what happens next?" Keith said. "What can we expect?"

"Yes," said Marcela, "for the benefit of our viewers, can you tell us what it all means?"

They waited for Greenbach to collect his thoughts.

"Well, you know what, Keith and Marcela? When you have a cascading financial system failure on your hands—and I would hasten to add that we lack sufficient econometric models upon which to draw for clarification and insight—you have, let's say, and I'll make a rough calculation here, oh, I would estimate … maybe eight days to economic collapse. More or less."

•   •   •

"Attention, citizens," blared the loudspeakers. *"Today's threat level is Gold—acute risk of terrorist attack. Report suspicious activities and socially dangerous persons to the Authorities."*

Black BearCat armored personnel carriers and Bulldog X SWAT trucks cruised slowly down the capital's streets, troops marching alongside. Brilliant red, white, and blue lights flashed, accompanied by piercing siren bursts. Continuous Threat Level Gold announcements issued from loudspeakers mounted on the vehicles. With their black helmets, black face visors, flak vests, ballistic shields, and body armor, the troops hanging off the BearCat's sideboards and marching on foot resembled a robot army.

The troops aimed their rifles into building entrances and packed alleys as they went past. Crowds wandered in front of the patrols, parting before them and trailing in their wake. Signs on striped barricades warned people to stay off the streets. Stacked piles of tires burned here and there, the dense, black clouds of acrid smoke fouling the air.

A crowd swarmed outside a Wells Fargo Citibank branch.

"Where's our money? What'd you do with our money?"

The terrified employees and customers trapped inside were desperate to escape, but all exits were blocked. They dared not try forcing their way through the mob.

"We're occupying this bank until they give us back our money," said the leader of a band of hooligans, his voice screeching through an electronic megaphone, earning applause and whistles of appreciation from the ranks.

"Come outta there, you candy-ass cowards, we know you're in there. Open up, show your ugly faces!"

Punks uprooted metal recycling receptacles from the sidewalk and heaved them through the bank's windows. The great panes of glass shattered, cascading to the ground in a river of jagged splinters gleaming in the afternoon sun, mesmerizing the crowd. People inside the bank huddled against the far walls and dived under desks and counters.

Soldiers fired rounds into the air and the mob dispersed in panic. Small arms gunfire could be heard throughout D.C. Fires raged around the city, the smoke plumes soaring into the sky. Despite their sirens and horns blasting, fire trucks and ambulances could not get through the blocked traffic. Desperate families fleeing by car found themselves unable to move, angrily honking their horns in a rising crescendo of noise. Gridlock snarled the city.

Frantic hordes overran supermarkets and convenience stores that had suddenly closed when electronic payments stopped going through. Realizing that they would be hungry and thirsty within a day or two, looters snatched doughnuts, cake, frozen pizza, ice cream, potato chips, soda pop, candy, and anything else that they could get their hands on. Thieves broke into electronics stores, struggling to carry off televisions and audio equipment, fighting each other for the booty in the store's dark interiors. Whole families ransacked undefended appliance superstores, using hand trucks to wheel away the washing machines and refrigerators. Mobs descended on car dealerships, trying to break in and drive away. Usually unable to find the keys, they left the cars' alarms honking and their lights blinking; the more resourceful among them drove off to become ensnarled in the gridlock.

Rampaging youths torched businesses and vehicles, smashing shop windows as they advanced, while BearCats massed at the end of the street in their path. The more they destroyed, the more frenzied and emboldened the youths became. Joined by other mobs, they faced down the BearCats, daring them to attack.

"You wanna piece a' this?" screamed one of their leaders.

"We're occupying the streets!" yelled another through an electronic megaphone.

"Hell—no! We won't go! Hell—no! We won't go! Hell—no! We won't go!" they chanted.

"We demand our elected officials do something and real quick. We're taking back America, reclaiming the dream. Hear us roar!"

The lead BearCat commander opened the roof hatch and stared at the crowd. He went below and stuck his head out of the hatch again, looking around with binoculars. He switched on his microphone.

"Attention, citizens," he said in a low monotone through the tank's loudspeakers. "Unlawful behavior will not be tolerated at this time. This is a Code Purple. Noncombatant evacuees must leave the bridgehead line at once."

He radioed their position to NORTHCOM and awaited further instructions.

Invisible to the surging throngs below, a squadron of Reaper drones flew silently at 20,000 feet through the clear skies. Their cameras converged on the historic Chase Bank of America building nearby. Hellfire missiles surged to their targets. The top floor of the bank turned into a fireball, showering the streets below with burning fragments. The drones swooped in, buzzing the mobs with tear gas and pepper spray. The shrieking crowds fled for cover.

"Wardrobe! Fix that suit and tie, will ya? He can't wear it like that."

The president sat in his custom-made leather chair, practicing his lines while the film crew bustled about.

"Makeup! Nose and forehead—too shiny. Could use a quick touchup shave, too. Chop chop. We don't have all day, let's move it!"

The glare created by the clusters of camera lights made King squint and look away.

"Okay people, cue the teleprompter. All right, Mr. President, ready? Let's go then. Five, four, three, two, one, and—action."

A one-note tune like that of a telephone dial tone was simultaneously broadcast to all media outlets. At 20 seconds, a recording came on.

"Ladies and gentlemen," the announcer said, in a deeply melodious voice, "we sincerely regret interrupting your regularly scheduled radio and television programming for a special message from your president."

The director pointed at President King and silently mouthed, "Go."

King shuffled some papers—a random collection of inter-office memos the film crew had assembled the day before—laying them down carefully so that the corners met precisely. He folded his hands on his desk and leaned forward, appearing thoughtful and earnest.

"My friends, we are pleased today to announce a significant step forward in the Global War on Terror. We have certain evidence of an alleged terrorist conspiracy to harm our financial system, posing a serious threat to our national security. It is believed that this secret conspiracy was possibly launched through sleeper cells in the Homeland, presumably foreign in terms of their nationality, who have laid dormant until this point in time."

The monitor from which he was reading began to flicker slightly.

"The terrorist threat that led to the declaration of a national emergency on September 14, 2001, has continued to the present time in full effect. Therefore, by authority of National Security Presidential Directive 20/51, the USA PATRIOT Enabling Act, and by authority of the National Defense Authorization Act, as amended, I hereby exercise their provisions delegated to me as your commander-in-chief. As I speak, our United States Armed Forces and National Guard are attempting to restore order by any means necessary, in order to encapsulate unlawful enemy combatants who have reportedly attacked the Homeland with cold-blooded contempt."

Franklin quietly watched the address with a serene look on his face, but Benson felt a growing unease at this latest development.

"Is this part of the plan?" Benson said, more an accusation than a question.

Franklin tore his gaze away from the monitors.

"I have my ways, too."

"We are not happy, Colonel Benson."

General Jerrick paced around the room. His attention was captured by the colorful, animated electronic displays of active Overseas Contingency Operations around the world. They covered an entire wall. Constantly changing, they were almost hypnotic.

"Not really happy at all."

Benson sat still, facing the desk at which he sat as the general spoke from behind him. Benson's uniform bore the red and blue insignia of the Distinguished Service Cross and the Army Achievement Medal in stripes of blue and green.

Jerrick returned to his desk and sat down heavily.

"You went off the reservation, under the wire and all that sort of thing."

Leaning over, he opened a drawer and pulled out a cigar from an elaborate mahogany case with Cuban inscriptions. He offered one to Benson, who declined with a curt nod. The general clipped the end and lit it, vigorously puffing away to get it started, and sat back with a look of deep satisfaction.

"I failed to take them out, sir."

"Well ... " General Jerrick said, watching the cigar burn, "we won't hold that against you. At least you tried, and that's what really counts today, isn't it?"

He sat back in his chair and slowly exhaled toward the ceiling, watching a perfectly formed smoke ring float up in the air.

"Gutsy, Benson, I'll give you that."

Jerrick inhaled, holding the smoke in his mouth.

"I couldn't have pulled you out, Colonel, not even if I'd wanted to."

"I was given to wonder about that, sir. This was to be more of an intelligence mission, if I recall correctly. I was to be promptly rescued if I got into trouble. I was not supposed to spend seven months in the Gulag; that wasn't the plan. Sir."

"Plans have a way of changing, Benson. We all have to be flexible. The fact is, we couldn't really find you. Apparently the records are altered; the identities are randomly changed so no one can find anyone. You disappear without a trace. It's as if you ceased to exist."

"As if," Benson said. "I take it, sir, that you don't really know what's going on down there—with all due respect."

"It's a different branch, Benson, that Civilian National Security Force. It gets kind of complicated."

He took a long puff.

"It's still in the very early stages, you know. These things take some time to mature, to find their way, as it were. But they tell me everything is run by the book."

"By the book," Benson said.

"Your military record is no longer classified. This operation has been expunged from all records. We thank you for your service to your country. You are free to return to civilian life—or maybe to active duty."

Jerrick sat up in his chair, tapping the cigar ashes into a tray.

"We do like your initiative, Benson, your *pluck*. Maybe we could offer you something in a Homeland mission post—a command appointment, say, Special Assistant to the Vice Commander of NORTHCOM, C2 Section?"

George Franklin stood and tightly crossed his arms as he observed Benson and General Jerrick through one-way glass in the adjoining room.

"Well, what say you, Colonel? How about it?"

"They believed they were true patriots, sir, launching a second American Revolution. They aimed to stop what I went through as an Unlawful Enemy Combatant."

"Interesting. And what do you think, Colonel?"

The murmur of people talking and typing documents from outside drifted into the room.

"My wife is missing."

Jerrick took a long drag on his cigar, holding the smoke. He exhaled and chomped lightly on the end, then held it at arm's length. It was burning evenly all the way down, the ash holding tight to the cigar. The color of the cigars in the box was very consistent, too. He wrote a note to order more through his special contact.

"My only son—killed in action." Benson choked up. "He was barely 18."

Daniel's face rushed into Benson's head. Daniel as a toddler, Daniel as a young boy. The last time he laid eyes on his only son. The horrible way he must have died.

"That's tough, I'm very sorry. It's the nature of our, ah, business, Benson, but he did his duty. Turns out, we spent American lives and money freeing those people to vote and what do they do? They go and elect another dictator—and not a particularly friendly dictator, either; can't do business with this one. That's just how it goes sometimes. Well, we'll fix that. Anyway, your country is proud of you. You've earned the Medal of Freedom for your valor, you know. The president himself would normally decorate you personally, but he's not free."

General Jerrick walked over to a metal bureau, pulling out a case from the top drawer.

"Speaking of medals," Jerrick said, presenting a small wood and leather box, "this is posthumously awarded to your son, Private Daniel Steven Benson."

In embossed gold letters, the lid was inscribed "GWOTEM."

"From field reports, Colonel, we believe he must have served his country with distinction. You should be so very proud of him."

"What is it, sir?"

"Go ahead, open it and find out."

His stomach churning, Benson slowly opened the lid. Inside was a gold-colored medallion of an eagle clutching a snake, set on top of a shield and two crossed swords. The satin ribbon attached to it was boldly striped against a pale blue background.

The *Global War on Terrorism Expeditionary Medal.*

Benson closed his eyes in silence, his pulse pounding. He snapped the lid shut, looking at General Jerrick, his eyes tearing. He rose and abruptly left the room.

"Colonel Benson!" General Jerrick shouted after him. "You are *not* dismissed!"

The free-for-all had taken a more violent turn. The packs of rioters turned their unfocused rage on random objects, shooting their weapons, smashing shop windows, and torching and overturning small cars as they went. Reflected in the sparkling shards on the pavement, the fires lit up the street in the late afternoon sun.

The rioters didn't notice the advancing columns of military police in black battle gear peeking over their ballistic shields, creeping forward in a flying wedge formation. A cluster of Stryker MGS armored vehicles came from the opposite direction, boxing the rioters in, one of many Stryker brigade combat teams hastily deployed across the District. Undeterred, the rioters hurled Molotov cocktails at the vehicles. The explosions lit up around the Strykers, rocking them. Their gun turrets spun around slowly to face the rioters. The big guns fired, jolting the vehicles back. Coordinated rounds of explosive phosphorus charges instantly destroyed a cluster of looted stores, turning them into white-hot firebombs. The flames quickly consumed the apartment building above, the occupants within desperately trying to escape the intense blaze.

The rioters dispersed, screaming and rushing right into the advancing police. In alarm, the police fired away. As the front lines of rioters were cut down, the rest of the screaming mob confronted a unit of LAV-300 personnel carriers waiting for them, shooting at the armored vehicles with handguns. The bullets made pinging sounds off the armor. The LAVs switched on their acoustic sound cannon. Rioters within three city blocks were crippled with excruciating pain in their eardrums, scattering frantically from the source of the piercing noise.

"Turn back," boomed the loudspeakers on the street poles, the deafening warnings coming from all directions. *"Your attention, please. Turn back now. All noncombatants are hereby directed to disperse immediately."* Tear gas canisters concealed within the poles popped open, spewing clouds of toxic gas into the fleeing crowds.

Hoods pulled over their heads, a gang of rioting youths threw rocks into the massive windows of a magnificent old building. Once housing a powerhouse financial institution founded in the 1800s, it had been merged out of existence years before. It was now office space and a discount furniture emporium. The jagged holes in the plate glass let the gang see into the building. The occupants cringed in fright.

"Come on out, you cowards!"

One of the youths hurled a burning Molotov cocktail inside.

"You stole our money and now you're gonna pay!"

The fireball blew furiously out of the building and back into the gang, cutting them down with razor-sharp glass and thick, flaming gasoline. Inside, choking smoke wafted through the ground floor. Interspersed among the dead were the screaming survivors.

"Attention, citizens," blared the street loudspeakers. *"Today's threat level is Purple. Curfew is 2200 hours. All non-uniformed persons must be off the streets by 2200 hours. That is all."*

33

We Cannot Afford to Wait

T︎HE BLACK HAWKS HOVERED OVER THE WHITE HOUSE in a dia-
mond formation, their blades kicking up fierce winds, rustling
the magnolias, maples, and elms dotting the estate. President
King heard all the commotion from his office. Sitting from
his desk, he peered out the windows, but he couldn't see
anything unusual from that vantage. He shot a quizzical
glance at an aide, who responded with a shrug. Helicopters,
after all, were a common sight on the grounds.

Stryker armored vehicles moved to surround the White
House in a defensive formation, their big guns aimed outward.
Gripping machine guns, paramilitary police and troops streamed out of scores of Bulldog X SWAT trucks. Wearing bulky
bulletproof uniforms and helmets with full face shields, they
took up their positions to secure the perimeter.

King continued his speech from the Oval Office. His eyes
had become accustomed to the bright camera lights. He no
longer squinted, appearing natural and at ease.

"And so, my friends, we are in a transnational war against
an enemy who intends to wipe out Western civilization, no
doubt motivated by poverty, inequality, and social injustice.
These zealots—who, I am given to understand, represent
only a tiny fringe element of their religion—have been raised
from birth to hate us and everything we stand for, and they
hope to go to their heaven or whatever it is through our

complete annihilation. Intelligence sources say more of them may already be here awaiting orders from abroad. Make no mistake, the enemy doesn't wear a uniform. You can't tell by—just by—looking."

The glaring lights had suddenly gone dark, leaving the office lit in its normal warm, soft glow. King looked around; seeing nothing otherwise out of place, he gamely continued on.

"Our responsibility to history is already clear—to answer these attacks and rid the world of evil. Freedom and fear are at war, and there will be no quick or easy end to this conflict. It will be fought on many fronts against a particularly elusive enemy over an extended period of time. The struggle begins now. We cannot afford to wait until millions of our citizens die in a big, smoking mushroom—"

Paramilitary police burst into his office, positioning themselves on either side of the door. Startled, King fumbled with the loose papers he was holding, scattering them all over the floor. An officer in a black overcoat sauntered in from the hallway, stopping just inside the entrance. All power shut off. The soft hum of air conditioning died; the sudden quiet interrupted only by scuffling somewhere outside in the corridor and the muted roar of helicopters overhead. Soft daylight filtered in through the partly curtained windows, casting long shadows across the darkened office.

"What the fuck is this?" King said.

He slammed his heavy chair aside, coming out from behind the desk.

"I didn't send for anyone. I'm in the middle of my goddamn speech."

Seeming to realize the implications, he suddenly quieted. He moved a step closer to the windows and cautiously peered out, seeing the helicopters and a flurry of activity on the grounds.

"Are we under attack? Terrorists?"

The officer strode further into King's office, taking in the ornate furnishings, the artifacts and expensive gifts from world leaders. The film crew was furiously tearing apart their equipment and jamming it into bags and boxes, avoiding eye contact. The officer picked up the Twin Towers statuette on King's desk, examining it from different angles. He gently placed it back on the desk.

"Uh, yes. Yes, sir, that's it exactly, Operation Northwoods, sir. We're at REDCON-1. The vice president is already waiting for you in the Naval Observatory bunker. For your own protection, sir."

"Operation Northwoods?"

Nothing remotely like this had ever happened before. King looked around at these silent, intimidating paramilitary police standing at the ready in their black battle gear with weapons drawn.

"Never heard a' that one."

King looked doubtfully at the officer, who stared back at him in silence. There was more scuffling outside the office, and then a shot was fired.

"I—I was just on my way to Mount Weather."

"Mr. President, you will please come with us. We'll explain on the way."

Packed with rioters and protesters, convoys of retrofitted school buses made the short drive over to RFK Stadium. The rolling stadium doors were flung open and the processions drove inside to park in tight, end-to-end formation on the field. Other buses streamed in from opposite directions in long lines. As they passed the gates, National Guard Internment/ Resettlement Specialists checked them off, radioing directions to the teams shepherding the multiple streams of traffic. The passengers were catalogued, relieved of any possessions, unshackled, and herded into makeshift, cramped quarters located throughout the complex. The buses then drove off to pick up more internees.

A column of M1 Abrams battle tanks equipped with the latest Tank Urban Survival Kits rumbled through the center of town. Meeting with abandoned cars, the tanks rolled right over them, the windows cracking and bursting, the cars crushed and flattened under the heavy metal treads. The roar of engines thundered through the streets as the tanks advanced. Sporadic fires amid roiling clouds of thick black smoke lit up the darkening sky.

Turning a corner, the column came within sight of the main mass of rioters.

"*Your attention, please,*" broadcast a warning from the tank's loudspeakers at earsplitting volume as the column rumbled forward. "*Disperse immediately. This is a Code Purple. Noncombatant evacuees must leave the bridgehead line at once.*"

Benson ran in front of the column. The tanks slowed their advance at the astonishing sight of a senior officer in dress uniform blocking their way. Waves of exhaust heat and noxious diesel fumes washed over him. The booming growl of unmuffled gas turbine engines thundered in his ears. His heart thumped in his chest as the huge tanks loomed over. He held up his hand for the tanks to halt.

The mobs stopped dead in their tracks, astounded by this unthinkable confrontation between a lone man and fearsome military power.

The column lurched and halted; the engines switched off and the racket died down. The lead tank commander opened the hatch and climbed out partway. Leaning over, he stared down at Benson from his high perch, thunderstruck.

Benson stared back, his eyes steely, his face set hard and resolute.

"I am Colonel Thomas Benson."

He spoke through a special bullhorn that broadcast wirelessly through the network of street loudspeakers. Tremendously amplified, his voice rang throughout Capitol Hill and beyond.

"We soldiers swore a sacred oath to support and defend the Constitution against all enemies—foreign *and* domestic.

"We are the guardians of the Republic. We do not fight for the vanity of politicians. We do not fight for State glory. We fight to defend the lives and liberties of the people.

"We will *not* obey unlawful orders to impose martial law.

"We will *not* seize Americans and imprison them as enemy combatants in their own country.

"We will *not* lay siege to our own cities.

"These are acts of war against the people whose lives and liberties we have sworn to defend with our own. Our fellow countrymen and women are *not* the enemy."

The bullhorn signal was somehow interrupted.

"*Attention, citizens,*" the street loudspeakers announced, in a flat, metallic voice, "*Today's threat level has been upgraded to Red—serious risk of terrorist attack. Please report suspicious activities to the Authorities.*"

The other tank commanders opened their hatches to gape at Benson. Those in the column's rear raised their binoculars to see what was going on up front.

"We will *not* obey unlawful orders for summary arrest.

"We will *not* subject Americans to secret trials or military tribunals.

"We will *not* commit treason against our country."

Benson dropped the bullhorn to his side. He searched for understanding on the commander's faces. All soldiers were to live by their sworn oath. It had been drummed into them from the beginning.

"Remember your sacred pledge to defend the Republic from attack—within and without. We soldiers have the right and the duty to refuse unconstitutional orders violating the rights of the people.

"Do *not* make war on our own people.

"Do *not* obey criminal orders."

The tank commanders remained silent and passive.

"We are soldiers!" The passion in Benson's voice rose to a veritable battle cry. "We are the last stand against tyranny. Americans do *not* fire on Americans. Men, obey your conscience!"

The hatch of the lead tank closed, the commander disappearing within. The engine started and rumbled, idling for a moment. The tank shuddered, suddenly jumping forward. The other tanks sprang to life, the massive engines roaring. Iron determination written on his face, Benson stayed rooted to his spot. The exhaust heat and fumes washed over him again. They would have to kill one of their own to advance. The lead tank jolted closer, so close that it was almost on top of him. The roar was deafening.

And still Benson did not move.

The lead tank engine switched off. The other tanks shut down.

Soldiers streamed out of the hatches. All down the column, they jumped out, congregating on the torn-up street. They came to gather in front of Benson, milling around, uncertain of what to do next.

Out of the corner of his eye, Benson saw a lovely woman running toward him. He was stunned. Her curly, dark brown hair bounced with her steps, the wind pushing it back from her face. She ran into his arms, nearly knocking him over. He buried his face in her neck in a long, tight embrace, a feeling of intense relief flooding over him. Tears ran down her freckled cheeks.

"Tom, I—"

"Don't say anything."

He kissed Jane and hugged her even tighter. He held her at arm's length, not quite believing his own eyes, and then embraced her again.

A soldier came over and saluted smartly, looking Benson in the eye with deep admiration.

"Sir," he said, "what happens now?"

It was an innocent and heartfelt question.

Benson returned the salute.

"We lost our way," Benson said. "Life was not meant to be lived on a leash."

He looked at the earnest, youthful face in front of him. All was quiet here, for now. In the distance, the early evening sky lit up with explosions. A smoky haze colored the horizon. Thunderous booms and bursts of machine-gun fire were heard from far off. Rolling blackouts darkened the capital city.

"We will start over."

Afterword

*S*TATE OF *T*ERROR explores the wisdom of Benjamin Franklin's timeless warning: "Those who would give up essential liberty to purchase a little temporary safety, deserve neither liberty nor safety." It focuses not on terrorist acts, horrific as they are, but on the dire consequences to civil society of exchanging liberty for supposed safety. If history serves as a guide to understanding the present and anticipating the future, then the society depicted herein may well portray the logical outcome of events unfolding today. *State of Terror* is not so much a prediction as it is a warning, extrapolating from long-running trends pointing in the same direction.

"No nation could preserve its freedom in the midst of continual warfare," wrote James Madison. Whether called the Long War, World War IV, Overseas Contingency Operation, or the War on Terror, civil society—based upon free expression and free association, the right to due process, secure property rights, protection from arbitrary search and seizure, the rule of law, and public trial by a jury of one's peers, among others—would be torn apart by continual warfare, to be replaced by something very different.

In past wars, emergency measures suspending civil liberties were mostly reversed upon cessation of hostilities. A peace treaty would be concluded and life could return to normal. In a war without end, without well-defined enemies and territories

—or even coherent objectives—there can be no cessation of hostilities, no peace treaties, and no return to normal life. In preemptive war, the distinction between potential terrorist and peaceful citizen is blurred. Anyone could be a potential terrorist.

Some of the dialogue in this novel comes from actual statements made by U.S. public officials. Taken in isolation, such statements may seem benign. Counterterrorism laws and secret programs can appear to have a noble purpose. Yet, when the rhetoric and events are connected, a disturbing progression unfolds. Over time, bad ideas have bad consequences.

Here, in rough chronological order, are the most important laws and programs framing *State of Terror*:

1. **The USA PATRIOT Act** of 2001, as amended, discards independent judicial warrants and other Fourth Amendment constitutional protections in the Bill of Rights prohibiting arbitrary searches and seizures. Activists and protesters can be charged with "Domestic Terrorism." Section 505 of the Act greatly expands the use of "National Security Letters," essentially self-written search warrants lacking probable cause requirements and judicial oversight. Those served with National Security Letters are forbidden to tell anyone about them, itself a violation of First Amendment guarantees of freedom of speech. In widespread use by the FBI, they are also reportedly used by Homeland Security, the Pentagon, and the CIA.

2. **Total Information Awareness** (TIA), a program of the Defense Advanced Research Projects Agency, was launched in 2002. It attempted to combine financial transactions, medical histories, travel and telephone records, reading materials, emails, and Web browsing into a comprehensive database. The idea was to discover hidden terrorist patterns and then look for similar patterns in the general population. Officially cancelled after media leaks, TIA went underground, changing its name to ADVISE (Analysis, Dissemination, Visualization, Insight, and Semantic Enhancement), a program of the Department of Homeland Security's Threat and Vulner-

ability Testing and Assessment section. It was reported to be developing a massive data mining system to calculate a threat analysis score for everyone in the United States. This program, too, was officially cancelled. The National Security Agency's mass surveillance data mining program, PRISM, reportedly operating since 2007, has a purpose similar to TIA.

3. **Stellar Wind**, the codename for another surveillance program of the National Security Agency, will operate in conjunction with the Utah Data Center (formally known as the Intelligence Community Comprehensive National Cybersecurity Initiative Data Center). Originally scheduled to be operational in late 2013, construction has been plagued by electrical surges causing equipment "meltdowns," postponing completion by a year. The largest in a network of "data farms," the Utah Data Center will reportedly intercept, store, and analyze all communications, including the complete contents of emails, telephone calls, Web searches, text messages, and blog entries, and gather data on parking receipts, travel itineraries, financial records, and book purchases. Other data farm sites include Colorado, Georgia, and a large facility under construction at NSA headquarters in Fort Meade, Maryland.

4. **The Terrorism Information and Prevention System** (Operation TIPS) of 2002 was an administration proposal to encourage neighbors, utility technicians, and home meter readers to become informants and report anything "suspicious." TIPS was subsequently cancelled after the media published articles raising concerns of civil liberties violations.

5. **The Homeland Security Act** of 2002 consolidated certain intelligence units and police functions in a new, cabinet-level department.

6. **The REAL ID Act** of 2005 established a de facto national identification card—in effect, an internal passport. REAL ID would incorporate various biomarkers in the card's microchip, and contain proposed radio-frequency identification (RFID), not unlike current U.S. passports. The implementation deadline has been regularly extended due to concerns about its cost.

7. **The Military Commissions Act** of 2006 contained the power to kidnap and "disappear" people, declaring them "unlawful

enemy combatants" without formal charge or public trial. It eliminated the ancient right of habeas corpus; the right to challenge one's imprisonment before an impartial judge. The habeas corpus provision was struck down by the U.S. Supreme Court in 2008, but the rest remains.

8. **National Security and Homeland Security Presidential Directive 20/51** of 2007 allows the president to take control of all State functions, including the Congress and the federal courts, and to direct the private sector in a "catastrophic emergency," self-defined by the president.

9. **The National Defense Authorization Act** for fiscal 2012 and 2013 established the president's authority to designate, capture, and imprison suspects in military prisons indefinitely without charge or trial, including U.S. citizens on U.S. territory, and to ship them to any "foreign country or entity," a power already claimed to be inherent in the 2001 Authorization for Use of Military Force Against Terrorists Congressional joint resolution. The AUMF, being open-ended and not a formal declaration of war, is itself problematic.

Today, the political left and right are melding together so that both can achieve their ends. The Left generally promotes State intervention domestically, while the Right generally favors State intervention abroad—but intervention is intervention. In a grand compromise produced by blurring the distinction between domestic and foreign, we get domestic intervention and foreign intervention—the worst of both worlds; an ever-growing, increasingly dangerous welfare-warfare State.

The War on Terror is being fought domestically through destruction of "essential liberty" at home and by open and covert war abroad. The technology and weaponry in *State of Terror* is already in use or has been demonstrated on the battlefield. The enabling laws are already in place. The building blocks of a future police State are gradually being constructed. By themselves, these building blocks may not constitute the existence of such a State any more than a pile of bricks constitute a house, but they provide the means to create and administer it, which is temptation enough. As James Madison said in a speech to the Virginia Convention in 1788: "I believe there are more instances of the abridgment of the freedom of the people by gradual and silent encroachments of those in power than by violent and sudden usurpations."

Whether the society portrayed herein becomes reality will ultimately be determined by the voters, the courts, and other sectors of society.

John Brown
October 2013

Join the conversation at State-of-Terror.com.